Hannah Robinson's Carrot and Fig Cupcakes

5 ¼ tablespoons softened butter

5 ¼ tablespoons brown sugar

2 small eggs

9 tablespoons self-rising flour

1/2 teaspoon baking powder

5 ¼ tablespoons grated carrots

1/2 teaspoon mixed spices (ie. nutmeg, cinnamon, clove)

1 ¾ tablespoons figs, chopped into raisin-sized pieces

Line a bun tray with 12 paper cases. Preheat oven to 375F. Put butter, sugar, eggs, flour, and baking powder into a bowl and beat until creamy. Stir in the grated carrots, spice, and figs and mix thoroughly. Divide evenly between the paper cases and bake for about 15–20 minutes, until well risen. Cool on a wire tray.

For the frosting, sift ½ cup icing sugar into a bowl and add enough freshly squeezed orange, lemon, or lime juice to make a soft paste. Spread onto the cooled cupcakes.

SEMI-SWEET

A Novel of Love and Cupcakes

ROISIN MEANEY

five
spot

Copyright © 2010 by Roisin Meaney

All rights reserved. Except as permitted under the U.S. Copyright Act of 1976, no part of this publication may be reproduced, distributed, or transmitted in any form or by any means, or stored in a database or retrieval system, without the prior written permission of the publisher.

5 Spot
Hachette Book Group
237 Park Avenue
New York, NY 10017
www.5-spot.com

5 Spot is an imprint of Grand Central Publishing.
The 5 Spot name and logo are trademarks of Hachette Book Group, Inc.

The publisher is not responsible for websites (or their content) that are not owned by the publisher.

Printed in the United States of America

First U.S. Edition: April 2011
10 9 8 7 6 5 4 3 2 1

Meaney, Roisin.
  [Love in the making]
  Semi-sweet : a novel of love and cupcakes / Roisin Meaney.
    p. cm.
  Originally published as: Love in the making. Dublin : Hachette Books Ireland, 2010.
  ISBN 978-0-446-57011-4
  1. Businesswomen—Fiction. 2. Bakeries—Fiction. 3. Female friendship—Fiction. I. Title.
  PR6113.E175L68 2011
  823'.92—dc22

2010028948

For the monsignor, who'll know why

Semi-Sweet

January

H ang on," he said. "Just…hold on a minute, would you?"
They were already late, Hannah struggling into the
hastily bought black dress that was beginning to look horribly
like a mistake. Too stiff to flatter her curves, too long to feel
sexy in, too short to hide her knees. Too young, damn it, for a
thirty-two-year-old to get away with.

Why had she listened to a shop assistant who was paid to
tell people how great they looked, no matter what inappropri-
ate thing they put on? But Hannah had listened, because the
shop was about to close and she had to buy something. And
now she was 140 euro poorer, and she hated the dress.

And they were going to be late, and it was her party. And
she'd cut the damn tags off.

"I hate this dress," she said, doing up the three oversize
buttons that for some reason had seemed charming in the
shop. At least Patrick would tell her she looked lovely, and
she'd pretend he wasn't lying. How could a dress that cost 140
euro not be lovely? At least it had to be well cut, didn't it, at
that price? And the fabric must be halfway decent.

"Isn't it awful?" she asked. "Don't know what possessed
me—I could easily have worn my blue." She waited for him
to say all the right things.

But he didn't.

"Hannah, there's something I need to tell you."

She began to rummage through the biscuit tin that held her jewelry. "Great—now I've gone and lost one of my good earrings." Cross with him for not reassuring her, but where was the point in starting a row when they were practically out the door? The last thing she needed was for him to be in a sulk for the night.

"Patrick, come on," she said, still poking through the tin. "The taxi will be here any minute. Where's your clean shirt?"

He took the three steps that were needed to reach her, and put a hand on her bare forearm. "Hannah, will you please stop doing that a minute," he said evenly, "and listen to me? Will you, please?"

She stepped sideways, leaving his hand behind. At least she loved the deep red shoes with the shiny silver heels that Geraldine, knowing her daughter's taste so well, had set aside for her the minute they'd come into the shop.

"Patrick, we haven't *time*—it's nearly ten to." She slid her feet into the soft leather, admiring how much thinner her ankles immediately became—how did a high heel manage that? "*Please* will you get changed?"

"I'm not going." So softly that she nearly missed it.

"You're what? What?" Turning too quickly, her hand catching the edge of the biscuit tin, knocking it off the dressing table, sending it flying, tumbling onto the wooden floor with a clang, earrings and bangles and necklaces rolling and clattering everywhere as she turned back to him, ignoring the mess.

"What do you mean, you're not going?" She searched his face. "Patrick, what's up? Are you sick?"

He shook his head, but she saw now that he did look a

bit pale. He must be coming down with something, and she'd been in too much of a hurry to notice it.

"I've met someone," he said rapidly, his eyes skidding away from hers. "I'm really sorry, Han—honest to God, I never meant it to happen, I swear."

Hannah's head felt as if it were emptying, everything inside it draining out as fast as it could. The sudden feeling of lightness made her sway; she grabbed the edge of the dressing table and held on. "You've...what? You've *met* someone?"

A year and three months they'd been together. He'd taken her to Paris; he'd said "I love you" in all kinds of weather. You didn't take someone to Paris and then meet someone else. It just wasn't done. It was plain bad manners, if nothing else.

"I'm so sorry."

His face was terribly pale, she realized now. A little lilac vein thudded gently in his temple. Two deep grooves ran the width of his forehead. A faint gray circular stain the size of a two-euro piece sat on the shoulder of the white shirt he'd been wearing all day. She wondered what could possibly have caused a stain like that, in that particular place.

"Han, say something."

His voice brought her back. She noticed that breathing was becoming something of an issue. She moved toward the bed and slumped onto it. She leaned forward, resting her head on her black nylon knees and inhaled deeply, feeling the air shuddering into her.

"Are you okay? Han?"

His voice sounded thick. Maybe he was crying. She hoped he was crying. Her knees smelled of lavender.

A horn sounded outside. She lifted her head carefully. "There's the taxi," she said. "Come on, you need to get ready."

Her words sounded breathless, as well they might. Patrick was standing in the same position, not crying but looking as if he might be thinking about it. Her head felt so light, with nothing left inside.

"I'm sorry," he said again. "I can't go. I can't...pretend anymore."

Pretend? She clutched handfuls of the duvet. Her palms were damp. "Don't be silly," she said. "Of course you're coming—it's all arranged." She squeezed the cotton-covered feathers as she curled her toes inside the red shoes.

"Hannah," Patrick said, "I feel terrible about this, honestly. It wasn't planned. I never meant to hurt you."

The horn sounded again, a short, polite bark. Hannah let go of the duvet and stood up. "Come on," she said. "You still haven't changed your shirt."

He shook his head. "Han, I'm leaving. I'm moving out tonight."

"No you're not," she said. She picked her way across the floor, avoiding the spilled jewelry, and took her bag from the chair by the wardrobe. "I'll wait for you in the taxi," she told him. "Don't be too long."

She lifted her coat from its hanger, pulled her blue scarf from the shelf. "You've got five minutes." There was a tiny buzzing in her ears. Something was lodged in her throat. She pushed her arms into her coat sleeves. "Don't bother picking up that stuff; I'll do it when we get home."

She walked downstairs, her hand clutching the banister. She opened the front door and closed it gently behind her. The evening air was knife sharp. She pulled her coat around her as her silver heels clacked on the cement path that was already whitening with frost. The taxi looked black in the streetlights, but it could have been any dark color.

She opened the back door and slid in, murmuring a greeting to the driver.

"Just yourself?" he asked. He wore a woolly hat. The car was warm and smelled of apples. The radio was on, some trumpet music playing softly.

"Yes," she said, not looking back at the house. It occurred to her suddenly that she hadn't asked Patrick about the woman he'd met. How had she not asked? What if it was someone she knew? What if everyone knew about this other person except Hannah?

"Where to?"

"Oh...the Cookery."

She'd booked for eight people. She'd have to look at his empty seat all night; it would keep reminding her that he wasn't there. She dipped into her bag and fished out a crumpled tissue, and pressed it to her eyes. Her mascara wasn't waterproof: She had to catch the tears before they did damage.

Was he packing a bag right now? Were his suits laid out on the bed? Had he taken his orange toothbrush from the glass in the bathroom? Or was he on the phone to his other woman, telling her he'd done it?

Hannah took it badly, he might be saying. *She wouldn't listen. She kept telling me to get ready for the restaurant. I felt rotten.*

Saying he'd see her soon, saying he couldn't wait.

Hannah was frightened at the thought of going home and finding all the empty spaces he was going to leave behind, all the places he'd filled with his books and CDs and clothes and golf clubs when he'd moved in. His empty hangers rattling in the wardrobe. Maybe he'd spread out her clothes so it wouldn't look so bare when she slid open the wardrobe door. But she knew he wouldn't think of doing that.

And what about the things he'd forget? Because there was always something you forgot. Clothes in the laundry basket, books out of sight on top shelves, socks at the back of a drawer. What of the letters that would still come addressed to him? What of a voice on the phone asking for Patrick, someone he'd forgotten to tell?

And of course his smell would still be there, in the bed and on the towels, draped along the couch, seeped into the cushions, waiting to ambush her around the house. What was she to do with his smell?

She hadn't asked if he loved the other woman. She couldn't bear the thought of that, of the love he'd had for Hannah being gathered up and transferred to someone else. Maybe he'd never—But she stopped that thought before it could go any further. Of course he had. You knew when somebody genuinely loved you.

Didn't you?

She was glad the driver didn't try to talk. He probably knew there was no point, seeing her in his rearview mirror all hunched up. She was glad the radio was on, glad not to be sitting in a silent car with a stranger who might have felt obliged to say something.

They were getting near the restaurant. She found her little handbag mirror and dabbed with a corner of her tissue at the black smudges that had formed after all under her eyes. The driver turned on the overhead light.

"Thanks," she said. It didn't help much, such a watery wash of yellow, but another driver wouldn't have thought of it. She brushed on lipstick and ran her fingers through hair she hadn't had time to dry properly. Not that it would have made much difference—all the blow-drying in the world wouldn't take the kinks out, just as all the color rinses in existence didn't make the slightest difference to the boring midbrown color she'd been cursed with.

She tried smiling at herself in the little mirror. She'd have to smile for the next two hours at least. There'd probably be champagne. They'd all be toasting her, wishing her well in her new business.

"Patrick is sick," she said, smiling at the face that smiled back at her.

"Sorry?"

She looked up and met the driver's eyes for an instant in his rearview mirror. Had she really said it out loud?

"Nothing...just talking to myself."

They pulled up in front of the Cookery, and Hannah paid and got out. She moved toward the restaurant, practicing her smile.

"Hang on."

She turned. The driver was holding her scarf out the window. "You forgot this."

"Thanks." She draped it around her shoulders as he drove off in his woolly hat. Then she walked into the restaurant, her heart sinking as Adam spotted her from the corner table and stood up, as the others turned, smiling, toward her. As her mother began to applaud.

Patrick dropped the last of his cases onto the pale green carpet. "That's it."

"You're sweating." Leah reached up on tiptoe and ran her little finger across his forehead. "Ugh. Big sweaty man in my nice ladylike apartment."

He grabbed her wrist. "Hey, I've just lugged practically everything I own up a flight of stairs. You should be glad I'm not stretched out on your nice ladylike carpet with a coronary."

Leah laughed. "God, imagine that—after waiting for months to get you to myself, you go and die on me."

"Well, it's not going to happen tonight." Bringing her hand down and pressing it to his groin, holding it there until she felt a reaction. "Does that seem dead to you?"

"Darling, you're so romantic." She wriggled out of his grasp and moved toward the bathroom. "Come on, I need to scrub you clean before I can take advantage of you."

Hannah's face, when he'd told her, when she'd finally realized what he was telling her. Everything changing in it, the color draining away, even while she was still telling him to get a move on.

Saying she'd wait for him in the taxi, as if some part of her refused to hear what he was telling her—Christ, he hadn't expected that. He'd been expecting tears or maybe a few things pelted at him—some kind of unpleasant scene, certainly—but not that.

Leah undid his shirt buttons as the bath filled, as the air became warm and moist and scented. She unbuckled his belt and unzipped his trousers and eased off his shorts. She pulled out of his embrace, catching his hand as he tried to untie her wrap—"Not yet, you animal"—and he stepped over the side of the bath and lowered himself slowly into the foaming water.

"What are you thinking?" She reached for a pink sponge.

"Nothing—I'm too tired." Leaning his head back and closing his eyes, inhaling the musky scent of whatever she'd used to make the bubbles.

The meal in the restaurant would be over by now; they'd have moved on to a bar, probably. He wondered what Hannah had told them when they'd asked where he was. Of course they'd be all sympathy for her. They'd hate him for dumping her, despise him for his timing, so close to the shop opening. He imagined her mother's reaction, and his heart sank. He'd always liked Geraldine, and he knew that the feeling had been mutual.

"Happy?" Leah soaped his chest, his shoulders, the length of his arms, squeezing foam and warm water onto his skin. "No regrets?"

"No regrets." He opened his eyes. "Why don't you get naked and join me?"

She shook her head, smiling. "Bath's too small, babe."

But it wasn't too small, he was too big. Six foot four and wide as a rugby player. Beside him Leah was a nymphet, a five-foot-two slip of a thing with boy-short blond hair and the palest skin, weighing just over half his 210 pounds.

One time in bed she'd fallen asleep on top of him, one of the few times they'd managed to spend a whole night together, and the weight of her hadn't bothered him at all.

Hannah was more solidly built, edging always toward a plumpness she battled against but that Patrick had never objected to. He'd loved the small ripples of flesh around her waist, the heaviness of her breasts, the generous curves of her buttocks, the comfortable, dimply softness of her thighs.

Hannah's bath was bigger, too, an old cast-iron affair, stained and mottled with spidery cracks but roomy enough for both of them in a pinch. He had some fond memories of that bath—and what harm were memories?

"Right, I think you're clean enough." Leah squeezed out the sponge. "Up you get."

"Are you going to bathe me every night?" Standing on the blue mat drying his hair briskly as Leah wrapped another towel around his waist.

"Maybe. Depends on how you behave yourself." She turned toward the door. "Follow me in when you're not dripping anymore."

Patrick wiped steam from the mirror and checked his reflection. He raked fingers through the thick, almost black hair, rasped a hand across the stubble on his jaw. He should have shaved before he'd left Hannah's—Leah didn't appreciate the he-man look—but he'd been anxious to be off, nervous that Hannah might come home early from the restaurant, maybe to plead with him to stay. He brushed his teeth with Leah's toothbrush and dropped the towels into her pale blue wicker basket.

In the bedroom she'd lit candles and spread a fresh bath sheet on the fawn carpet. "Lie on your stomach," she ordered, and Patrick lowered himself to the floor. Leah undid the belt of her robe and knelt and straddled him, and he closed his eyes as he felt the warm massage oil trickling onto his back, as her hands began to spread it over his skin, as the scent of eucalyptus wrapped itself around him.

"I could really get used to this," he murmured.

"No talking."

Her fingertips drummed down his vertebrae, the sides of her hands chopped across his shoulder blades. She'd put on one of her salon CDs, all breathy panpipes and swishing waves, and he thought of the CDs arranged alphabetically on Hannah's bookshelves—Michael Bublé and Lady Gaga and Kylie Minogue and Paolo Nutini. He thought of the two of them sprawled on Hannah's deep red couch reading the Sunday papers, with Michael Bublé singing about stardust.

Hannah's bookshelves, Hannah's couch. Even after sharing it with her for more than a year, he'd never regarded the house as theirs, always hers. It was officially hers, of course.

She'd bought it three years before they'd met, and she'd taken in a housemate to share the costs. When Patrick replaced the housemate, he and Hannah had split the bills and mortgage repayments, and he'd repainted the entire downstairs, sorted out the garden, and bought the patio furniture she'd never gotten around to, but it was always Hannah's house. Maybe on some level he'd known that it wasn't his final destination.

"Roll over."

It had been Hannah who'd led him to Leah. He'd complained of aches and pains after a longer-than-usual bout in the garden, digging up her ancient box hedge and replacing it with willow fencing, and Hannah had dropped in to Leah's salon the following day and bought him a gift certificate for a massage.

She hadn't asked him about the woman he'd met, the woman he was leaving her for. He'd expected her to, he'd been ready to tell her the truth—it was the least she deserved—but she hadn't asked. She'd find out soon enough, of course: Like most Irish towns, Clongarvin was too small, and he was too well known. How would she feel when she heard Leah's name, knowing that she herself had been the one who'd brought them together?

Leah moved from his chest to his legs, stroking from knee to thigh in strong upward movements. For such a petite creature, she gave a massage that was deep and satisfying. She eased his legs gently apart and began to knead his inner thighs, using slow, circular movements with her knuckles. As she inched toward his groin, he felt himself stiffening pleasantly in response.

"Why, hello there," she smiled, and Patrick reached for her, sliding the robe off her shoulders, and Hannah was forgotten.

It was the longest two hours of her life, but she'd gotten through it with nobody having guessed. She smiled and thanked them all for their help—her parents and Adam, and Adam's two cousins, and one of their girlfriends whom she'd met for the first time a week ago—and she drank the champagne when they toasted her success, and she ate enough Dover sole not to arouse anyone's interest, although every mouthful of her favorite fish was an effort.

She told them that Patrick was in bed with food poisoning, and they all accepted it—why wouldn't they?

"Oh, the poor thing," her mother said. "I'll never forget how awful I felt after those prawns that time—remember, Stephen?"

"I certainly do," Stephen answered, winking at Hannah. "Not one of your finer moments, I'd have to say."

Geraldine shot him a stern look. "Very funny." She turned back to Hannah. "What did Patrick eat?"

"Er, sausages, I think." Hannah watched as Adam filled her glass, and willed the conversation to move on.

Near the end of the meal, when she was doing her best with a slice of lemon cheesecake, Adam leaned across and said quietly, "You okay? Anything up?"

She shook her head. "Just a bit stressed about the opening, that's all." Her face was rigid from smiling. She hated lying to him.

Of course she'd have to tell him. She'd have to tell her parents. But not tonight, when she'd hardly taken it in herself. Maybe it was good that she had this distraction while Patrick's bombshell was still so fresh and raw. Maybe by the time she got home, the first shock waves would be receding and the urge to smash something or have serious hysterics would have passed.

But the thought of the dark and empty house waiting for her, the thought of going home to nobody, the thought of all the unanswered questions, caused a new stab of despair. She lifted her glass and drank too quickly, splashing a little red wine onto the front of her horrible black dress. No matter, she thought, dabbing roughly at the damp patch. Who'd see a stain on black? And anyway, she wasn't planning to wear it again. She hated it, and now it was the dress she'd been wearing when Patrick had broken up with her. It was the breakup dress. How could she ever look at it and not remember?

He's gone. She said the words in her head, and a dart of pain shot through her. She pushed her glass toward the wine bottle. "More," she said to Adam. "Just a bit." Not too much or the truth might come out, and then the night would be ruined for everyone.

She shared a taxi home with her parents, having truthfully pleaded a headache when the others began talking about a nightclub. The driver with the woolly hat was still on duty, the same soft jazzy music still wafting from his speakers, the same appley smell in his cab. Hardly surprising, Hannah supposed, in a place the size of Clongarvin to have the driver who brought you out taking you home again. She sat beside her mother in the back, afraid suddenly that Patrick would still be in the house.

"I must say I really like that restaurant," Geraldine said. "The food is just right, and they don't give you huge portions like other places."

"Mmm."

How long did it take to pack up your half of a relationship? What if he were just leaving now, what if they met him on the doorstep, surrounded by cases? She should have stayed out longer, ignored her pounding head, and gone on smiling for another hour or two.

"And that waitress couldn't have been more helpful."

"No."

The house was dark, and there was no sign of a suitcase outside. Hannah's heart sank as she opened the taxi door, wanting him there now as fervently as she'd dreaded it moments earlier.

"We'll wait till you get inside," her mother said. "Have you your key out?"

The hall was warm. Patrick's leather jacket was missing from its usual hook. His keys, still attached to their fish-shaped key ring, were on the hall table. His golf umbrella was gone. She kept her coat on as she walked slowly through the house. His laptop, his books, his CDs—all absent. His toothbrush, his pajamas, his slippers, his clothes. His aftershave, his razor. His tortoiseshell comb. The toffee-colored bathrobe she'd given him for Christmas, less than two weeks ago.

She crunched on something as she crossed the bedroom and bent to pick up an earring. She remembered the biscuit tin falling to the floor earlier and now saw it sitting back on the dressing table with her jewelry inside. She dropped in the stray earring and sat on the bed, feeling bereft.

He was gone. He'd left her, and he was gone. He'd met someone else, and he'd packed up everything and left her. They were over. There *was* no "they" anymore.

She kicked off her shoes and pulled back the duvet and climbed into bed in her clothes. In her new black dress and black coat and blue scarf, in her foundation and mascara and eye shadow and blusher and lipstick. She curled into a ball and closed her eyes. She wrapped her arms tightly around herself, yearning for his. Wanting the warm weight of him on top of her, wanting his mouth tasting hers. Wanting to pull his pillow toward her but afraid of what that might do to her.

She wished she'd had more to drink.

Patrick lay on his back in the dark, wide awake. Leah was facing away from him, a faint asthmatic wheeze to her breathing. He moved his head and saw 2:35 blinking redly on the front of the clock radio. The room was brighter than Hannah's bedroom at night, the cream curtains no barrier against a streetlight directly outside. There was more traffic here, too, on Clongarvin's second-busiest street. He'd get used to it.

He was going to have to get used to a lot of things.

He turned onto his side and reached toward Leah, stroking the line of warm, naked skin from hip to rib cage. She made a soft sound as he moved his hand to rest on her breast. He suddenly found himself remembering Hannah's breasts, how much fuller they were. He pushed the image away and ran a thumb slowly across Leah's nipple, back and forth, feeling it stiffen in response to his touch. Leah stirred again, her breathing lengthening, and pressed her body back into his, her hand sliding onto his thigh. He reached past her flat stomach, and she drew a breath slowly as his hand found its way between her legs.

Hannah was sweating when she woke. The clock beside the bed read 3:11. There was a tightness around her throat, and something was bunched uncomfortably at her waist. She pushed the duvet back and groped for the lamp switch. As the room flooded with light, as she took in the empty space beside her, as she looked down at her rumpled clothes, it all came flooding back.

She swung her legs out and stood on the floor. She unwound her scarf and pulled off her coat, and let them both fall. She tugged at the black dress until the three giant buttons popped, one by one, and clattered across the wooden boards. She dragged the dress over her head, yanked off her tights and panties, and unhooked her bra. She threw everything in the vague direction of the laundry hamper and reached under her pillow and pulled out her gray tartan pajamas. She put them on and regarded her ruined face in the mirror.

He was gone. He was in another woman's bed now. After fifteen months together he'd left her—and she hadn't had a clue that anything was wrong.

"He's gone," she said aloud, her voice sounding surprisingly steady. "He's walked out on me."

The shock of it was still raw, the abruptness of his departure still hard to take in. But of course, if she were perfectly honest—and the dead of night was the easiest time to be honest—wasn't the real shock not that he'd walked out on her but that they'd ever gotten together in the first place?

He wasn't her type, and she certainly wasn't his. She'd been aware of him before they'd met—the man who had edited the local paper for several years wasn't averse to having his very photogenic features appear quite regularly in his own society pages. He was also known personally to Joseph Finnegan, who owned the bakery where Hannah worked—and if he wasn't exactly a regular customer there, he certainly put in an appearance from time to time.

All the same, he and Hannah didn't come face-to-face until she'd been working at Finnegan's for the best part of ten years—and that encounter might not have happened if she hadn't taken an hour off one day for a dental appointment.

She'd arrived back at the bakery to find Joseph behind the counter, as usual. He was serving a customer as she pushed the door open.

"Hannah, there you are. Do you know Patrick?"

His bulk took her by surprise; in the photos you wouldn't realize quite how big he was. His woody scent was pleasant, if a little overpowering. The smile came instantly and looked well practiced.

"I don't believe we've met," he said, his big, warm hand not so much shaking as cradling hers. Turning back to Joseph. "Where have you been hiding her, you scoundrel?" Hannah thought, *Flirt,* but felt the color warming her face all the same.

"Hannah works behind the scenes," Joseph said. "My best baker."

"Is that a fact?" Patrick released her hand. His navy tie was slightly crooked, his shirt very white. "I hope he pays you well then," he said.

She was aware of the numbness around her mouth, the dentist's injection only half worn off. Her lips bare of any color; no point in lipstick when you're going in for a filling. She attempted a smile, hoping it didn't look as lopsided as it felt. "Oh, he does," she said, uncomfortable under his scrutiny, waiting for him to switch his attention back to Joseph.

"I'm glad to hear it."

The effortless charm of him; he was well used, no doubt, to getting what he wanted. The echo of his warm grasp still on her hand. "Well..."

"Nice to meet you," he said. "Better let you get back."

Hardly an auspicious beginning—and their second meeting, three weeks later on the steps of the library, was equally uneventful.

"Well," he said, his arms full of books, "if it isn't Joe's prize baker."

She ignored the stab of pleasure—why shouldn't he remember her? "Hello there."

More casually dressed today in a gray flannel shirt and black jeans, a scattering of dark hairs at the open V of his shirt. The same thick, green scent as before. *Nelson Mandela*, she read on the spine of the uppermost book.

She held the door open for him, the top of her head barely reaching his shoulders. "Many thanks," he said, his shirtsleeve brushing her arm as he passed. She left him at the desk and wandered among the shelves, glimpsing him occasionally as he browsed through the history and politics sections across the room. By the time she'd selected her two novels, there was no sign of him.

In the weeks that followed, he rarely crossed her mind. She saw his photo in the paper once, standing among a group of similarly suited men and one red-haired older woman. *"At the Chamber of Commerce dinner,"* the caption read before listing their names. He was striking in a dark suit and a dazzling white shirt, the tallest in the gathering. Probably had his pick of Clongarvin's businesswomen.

His eventual approach, a couple of months after their initial meeting, took her completely by surprise. She was leaving the bakery at her usual three o'clock, and as she turned out of the doorway, she walked straight into him.

"Oh—" She gasped, the momentum causing her hands to fly toward his chest to steady herself.

He grabbed her wrists—"Oops—" and for an instant they

were entangled in an awkward sort of embrace, the intimacy of it, the shocking closeness of him, bringing a flush to her cheeks before she sprang back.

"Sorry," she murmured, flustered, half laughing, replacing her shoulder bag, smoothing her jacket. "Didn't see you there."

"Now, that's not something I hear very often."

He'd completely recovered his equilibrium—if indeed he'd ever lost it. Maybe the phenomenon of females flinging themselves into his arms was nothing unusual. "Actually," he went on, "it was you I was coming to see—looks like I almost missed you."

"Me?" She regarded him in astonishment. "Why?" She couldn't imagine what he might want her for.

He laughed. "Well, believe it or not," he said, "I've come to ask you out."

It was so totally unexpected, the last thing she thought she'd hear. He was practically the polar opposite of the men she'd been involved with up to this, the unremarkable but generally dependable handful of boyfriends she'd gone through since her teens. On the other hand, none of them had lasted beyond a few months.

But she hardly knew this man. Did he even remember her name? They'd met twice, for hardly a minute each time. It had been weeks since they'd even laid eyes on each other. He was too good-looking, too confident. She'd be playing with fire.

"You don't think it would be a good idea," he said, still smiling. Clearly he was amused by her. She didn't know whether to be offended. "Even after nearly running me down just now?"

It was impossible not to smile back. "I hardly know you," she said. "We've barely met."

"All the more reason," he said, "for us to go out. You can cross-examine me for the night and decide if I'm worth getting to know."

She wasn't glamorous. She'd never appeared in the society pages dressed in something long and spangly. Surely he could pick and choose—what on earth had made him choose her? And what could they possibly have in common?

"I'm quite eligible," he was saying. "I'm pretty solvent, I have all my own teeth—and the hair is real, too."

She laughed. "I did wonder about the hair."

Then again, why shouldn't he pick her? She might not be a raving beauty—and she certainly didn't have the kind of figure that stopped men in their tracks—but maybe he'd had his fill of those; maybe he was looking for someone with a bit more substance.

And really, what did she have to lose? Wouldn't she enjoy an evening in the company of a man who was well able to amuse her, even if nothing came of it?

"Where were you thinking of taking me?" she asked.

She should have known better. She should have trusted her instincts that day and resisted him. Because by the end of their first date, she'd already been half in love with him—and because she'd known all along, hadn't she, that he was going to break her heart sooner or later.

She pattered across the landing into the bathroom, hardly aware of the ice-cold tiles under her bare feet, oblivious to the tears that were trailing blackly down her face.

———

"I can't believe it," Alice said. "He walked out on her, just like that?"

"Just like that, no warning whatsoever." Geraldine pressed keys on the calculator. "I don't know how she kept it up at the restaurant." She turned the wine-colored stilettos upside down and crossed out *"€150"* on the sticker and wrote *"€100"* beside it in blue marker. "She said he'd got food poisoning; nobody suspected a thing."

"Well, why would you? It's the last thing you'd be expecting...Poor Hannah, though. How's she coping?"

Geraldine replaced the stilettos and picked up a pair of chunky black platforms. "Badly. She's very upset, naturally." She used the calculator again. "Less thirty percent is forty-eight ninety-nine. Will I round it up to fifty?"

"Do." Alice watched as Geraldine made the change. "But how could he leave her now, when she's just about to open the shop? Talk about bad timing. Is there someone else, is that it?"

Geraldine's mouth twisted as she turned the shoes right side up. "Apparently. He wouldn't say who."

"God, that's awful."

"Of course, I never trusted him," Geraldine said.

It wasn't true. They *had* trusted him, with his big job at the paper and his flowers every time he and Hannah dropped by, and going golfing with Stephen just like a real son-in-law would have done. But it felt good to say it now.

"He never appealed to me. He was too charming by half. I always felt there was always something underhanded about him."

"Mmm," Alice said. "Well, there must have been."

"Oh, there was. I mean, who's to say that this woman was the first? If he strayed once, you can bet he did it other times. Hannah's well rid of him." Geraldine replaced the shoes. "Have we the bottom row done?"

"I think so. What about the ones over there?"

"Anyway," Geraldine said, taking her stool across, "there's plenty more fish in the sea."

"There is, of course—and a nice girl like Hannah won't be waiting long, you can be sure."

Alice hadn't been at the dinner in the Cookery, and neither had her husband, Tom. Hannah had suggested inviting them, but Geraldine had discouraged it.

You know what Tom's like after a few drinks.

But Alice is your boss, Hannah had said, *and Tom works with Dad, and they've both been hearing about the shop forever—and they got me the clock. They might expect to be invited.*

Why would they? They didn't help get the place ready. They weren't up a ladder with a paintbrush, or sanding and varnishing floors like the rest of us were.

And that had been that, and Alice hadn't been a bit put out, as Geraldine had known she wouldn't. Alice would be the first to admit that while Tom was great company, he could be a bit of a pain after one drink too many. He'd have taken over Hannah's night, and Geraldine wasn't having that.

"I think it might be time for tea," she said now, putting the blue marker on the counter.

"Absolutely," Alice said.

———————

Neither of her parents had noticed anything strange about Hannah in the restaurant. Both had observed that she hadn't eaten very much, but Geraldine had put it down to nerves at the thought of the shop's opening at last, and Stephen had assumed that it was yet another of his daughter's inexplicable attempts to shed a few pounds.

So when Hannah had stopped by the following evening and told her mother in tears what had happened, it came as a complete surprise.

He's met someone else, she'd wept. *He didn't say who. He's in love with her. I hadn't a clue anything was going on.* Wiping her eyes with a paper towel, ignoring the plate of chocolate biscuits her mother had put out. *Can you believe it?*

Oh, love, Geraldine had murmured, *he doesn't deserve you. You're much too good for him.* Which probably didn't help in the least but was all her scattered thoughts could muster.

When Hannah finally left, still in tears, Geraldine had gone into the sitting room and broken the news to Stephen. *I hate to admit it,* she'd said, *but it's probably a good thing they didn't get married after all.*

Stephen had given her the look over his glasses that always reminded her of a professor.

Don't say it, she'd ordered. *I know what you're thinking. You wanted them to get married, too. It wasn't just me. You hated them living together without being married just as much as I did. I'm only saying, the way things have turned out, maybe it's as well they weren't married.*

It mightn't have happened if they'd been married, Stephen had pointed out mildly. *He might have thought twice about running around then.*

Or he might still have done it, which would make Hannah a deserted wife now. At least this way she can make a clean break. She's well rid of him, if you ask me.

I thought you liked him. You always said you did.

Well, I don't anymore, Geraldine had answered crossly. *Whose side are you on?*

Ours, of course.

Stop defending him then.

I'm not defending anyone. I was just saying you liked him. We both did.

Well, now he's gone, so we don't like him anymore, she'd said, and Stephen had wisely allowed her to have the last word.

Except, of course, that it wasn't the last word.

How dare he walk out just like that? She'd grasped the poker and attacked the fire angrily. *Hannah's devastated. How'll she be able to open that shop after this? It's less than a week away.*

Of course she'll open the shop. It's just what she needs to take her mind off things. And won't you be there anyway, to help out? She'll be fine.

Her heart won't be in it though.

Maybe not—but that won't stop customers from coming in.

She had her whole future planned around that man, Geraldine had said. *She's nearly thirty-three—most men her age are married.* She'd stared gloomily into the fire. *She'll have to get a new housemate in—she can't afford that house on her own, especially now with the shop.*

She'd replaced the poker and reached for the TV remote control. *Remember how happy she was when she signed the lease? I could kill that man.*

After several seconds of silence, Stephen had risked lifting his newspaper again, and Geraldine had thrown him an exasperated glance before pressing the "on" button.

———————

Hannah held out her glass and Adam emptied the last of the wine into it. "Should I open another?"

"No." She tilted the glass and watched the red trails slithering downward. "Not on my account. Mornings are miserable enough these days without a hangover."

She rested her head on his shoulder. It wasn't getting easier to do without Patrick, but she was getting more used to feeling horrible all the time. Maybe that was some kind of progress.

"I've nearly phoned him, you know," she said. "Loads of times. And I've typed umpteen text messages, but I haven't sent any of them."

"Good," Adam said. "Don't. Keep reminding yourself what a bastard he is."

She swirled the liquid again. "I'll try. But there's so much I want to know."

"Why? What good would it do? Just let him off."

"I know, I know. You're right." She set her glass abruptly on the coffee table and sank her head onto her knees. "Two days to go," she groaned. "I wish I'd never signed that lease—I'm dreading it now. Is it too late to change my mind?"

"Cut that out." Adam reached for her hand and squeezed it. "This is what you've always wanted, remember? Your own shop, selling all your own stuff. I've been listening to you going on about this for God knows how long, and it's finally going to happen. Don't let this guy take that away from you."

"It's not just Patrick—I'm still petrified," she said, her words muffled. "What if nobody comes in?"

"Of course they'll come in." He lifted her hand and counted on her fingers. "One: It's the first dedicated cupcake shop in Clongarvin. Two: It looks fantastic—no small thanks to me. Three: The location is perfect. Four: Nobody bakes cupcakes like you do. Five: You're giving them away free."

She raised her head and looked at him. "One complimentary cupcake with every order is hardly giving them away free.

And anyway, that's only on the first day." She nibbled a nail. "What if nobody comes back for more? Or what if someone says they got food poisoning? What if—"

"Stop that," Adam said. "I'm living proof that your cupcakes are impossible to resist, and not at all poisonous. You'll be the talk of Clongarvin within a week."

Hannah smiled faintly. "We'll see."

"A word of advice," he said.

"What's that?"

"Don't try selling leftovers the day after. They won't keep, and you'll lose your reputation."

She slapped his arm halfheartedly. "Nice try. You know very well they're good for at least three days. Leftovers will be half price, and that's that. For the last time, you will not be getting a steady supply."

"That's what I'm afraid of," he said gloomily. "You'll be so busy baking for the shop that I'll never get to taste them again."

"You could try buying a few, like everyone else. I'll see about giving you a small discount. Although I feel I should point out, darling" patting his generously proportioned stomach—"that you could do worse than laying off the cupcakes for a while."

He grinned. "That's better. You're beginning to sound like your old bitchy self."

"I'm going to be baking all night and selling all day—I'll be too wrecked to be a bitch." She rested her head on his shoulder again. "God, what possessed me to think of opening a shop? Why didn't you stop me?"

"Yeah, like you'd have listened to me for a second. Anyway, the one to blame is your granddad—it's all his fault for leaving you that money. But like I keep pointing out, you don't have to do it all on your own—you can take someone on part-time."

"And like *I* keep saying, pay them with what? Granddad's money bought the lease, and most of the paraphernalia, and not much else. You know I'm already up to my neck in debt..." She trailed off. "Did I tell you that the new stand mixer cost almost eight hundred euro—and that was on sale?"

"Yes, I've heard that more than once. You'll remember I nearly collapsed the first time." He shot her a stern look. "And I'm sorry, but I have no sympathy with your being broke when you still haven't put that ad in."

When Hannah said nothing, he added, "You haven't, have you?"

She reached for the remote and flicked on the TV and watched a herd of elephants thundering across some wide open space. "Stop nagging."

Adam took the remote from her and pressed the "mute" button. "Who's nagging? I haven't mentioned it in two whole days. When are you going to do it?"

She shook her head miserably. "I don't know—next week, maybe."

Too soon, too painful. "Person wanted to share house" meant accepting that Patrick was definitely gone, like bundling a dead person's clothes into black plastic bags for the charity shop. Like taking people's names off the company roster when they found other jobs. Six days without him felt like six years, even if he had been a bastard, but still it was much too soon for a new housemate.

There was a short silence. Adam stretched his arms above his head. They watched a man in a safari suit mouthing silently into the microphone he held, but Hannah's thoughts were miles away.

She'd lost count of the times she'd found Patrick's name in her phone and almost pressed "call." *Who is she?* she wanted to demand. *When did you meet her? How long was it going on? How dare you do this to me?*

But when she was lying alone in the middle of the night, the silent questions changed: *When are you coming back? Don't you know I'll forgive you? Can't we try again?*

"I suppose," she said sadly, "I'll survive. At least I'll be too busy to mope." She reached for her scarf. "I'd better be off. I'm trying to get to bed early these nights, so the new schedule won't be too much of a shock. You don't have to come," she added as Adam took his feet off the coffee table and reached for the leather jacket that was slung across the arm of the couch.

"Right—and when you're mugged, your father won't string me up for letting you walk home alone." He shepherded her toward the door.

"Come on, Kirby," he said, and the black Labrador lying in front of the fire raised his head and looked at him. "Come on," Adam repeated, and Kirby hauled himself to his feet and plodded after them.

The evening was clear, stars studding the sky. Hannah tucked her arm into Adam's as they walked the streets toward her house, Kirby padding along behind. Anyone looking at them would think lovers, or at least boyfriend and girlfriend—a couple of some kind anyway. It had taken Patrick, and most of Hannah's other boyfriends, quite a while to feel comfortable with her having a male best friend.

"You know what's just occurred to me?" Adam asked as they walked.

"What?"

"Today's the eleventh, so you're opening on the thirteenth, right?"

"Mm-hmm."

"And my birthday's on the thirteenth of August."

She looked at him. "So?"

"So it's exactly seven months from the day you open."

"And your point is?"

"My birthday," he said, "can be your deadline. Whatever happens in the meantime, give yourself at least seven months to make a success of it."

"Even if I go broke in the first week?"

"Yes. Even if you have to sell your house to keep it going."

She stopped dead and looked at him in horror. "Sell my house? You're kidding, aren't you?"

"Of course I am." He nudged her along. "I just think it would be good if you had that date as your watershed."

"My watershed?"

"You know what I mean. The date that you can finally say, 'I've made it.' The date that you renew your lease for another decade."

She laughed. "Actually, the lease is for a year, and it's not up till December."

"Forget the lease, then—you know what I mean. You agree not to give up before my birthday? Promise?"

"I...suppose so." She hesitated, then caught his eye and added, "I mean yes, I agree. I won't give up before your birthday."

"You promise?"

"I promise."

"Good. We'll have the mother of all parties then, two things to celebrate." They approached her house.

"I told you to leave a light on," Adam said, frowning at the darkness beyond the glass panes in the front door.

"I know—I forgot."

They were almost exactly the same height. They'd been friends for more than twenty years, since they'd signed up for the same swimming class at the local pool. Hannah still swam as often as she could, and while Adam's interest had waned somewhat around the time he discovered girls, he'd migrated by then to Hannah's circle of friends, and over the years the two of them had grown closer.

Funny how they'd never been drawn toward one another romantically. Hannah loved Adam, but he was a brother, not a potential partner. The thought of being in a physical relationship with him had simply never been an option for her, and she was fairly sure it had never occurred to him either, thankfully. If they were both romantically involved at the same time, they might go out as a foursome, but other than that, their love lives didn't intersect.

"You busy this week?" she asked.

"A meeting tomorrow, hopefully some new business. Other bits and pieces to finish off." He designed Web sites, working from the small flat he'd invested in around the time Hannah had bought her house. "I'll be in on Wednesday," he said, "to collect my free cupcake."

"Only if you buy some," she reminded him.

"God, you're hard. You'll go far."

They reached the door, and he put his hands on her shoulders. "Best of luck—not that you need it. You'll be great, I know you will."

She smiled. "Thanks."

He hugged her, enveloping her in the leathery scent of his jacket, kissing her cheek loudly. "Night-night. Put the chain on the door."

"Yessir."

The house was cold. Now that the heating bill was Hannah's alone, she had to economize. She filled a hot-water bottle and set her alarm for eight. The next couple of days would be busy; shopping for ingredients, organizing her kitchen, setting everything in place for Wednesday morning, when her new life would begin. When she'd rise at three in the morning to make and ice 144 cupcakes for the first time.

She'd practiced, she'd timed everything. Four trays into the big oven at a time, four dozen cupcakes baking for twenty minutes while she put the next batch of mixtures together. The first batch cool enough to ice by the time she'd filled the last of the second batch of paper cups and made up the various icings. Eight varieties each day, fifteen different tastes rotating as the week went on.

Five hours from start to finish every morning, breakfast grabbed somewhere along the way, as soon as she was awake enough to feel hungry.

Load the van, drive to the shop, and unload. Fill the cupcake tree that sat on the counter with one of each variety. Arrange half of the 136 others in the display cases, leave the rest in the back until they were needed. Open at nine, close at five. Bag the leftovers, drive home, eat dinner, and get to bed by nine at the latest. Up at three to start all over again.

Was six hours enough sleep? It would have to be. Could she keep that up for seven months, six days a week? What had possessed her?

She undressed quickly. This was the worst time, going to bed by herself—and waking up alone came a close second. Maybe she should get a cat, or maybe a small dog that would curl up at the end of the bed and help her to feel less unwanted.

She burrowed under the duvet, trying to think positive. Adam was right: This was what she'd always wanted, since she'd begun working in Finnegan's Bakery all those years ago. She used to imagine running her own place, selling exactly what she wanted to sell, answerable to nobody. If only she had the money.

And then Granddad had died, three years ago last August, and his house had been put on the market a few months later and had sold just before prices began to fall. And Hannah, his only granddaughter, had been given enough from the proceeds to realize her dream.

Last November a little corner unit on the main street had become vacant, the rent not too horrendous thanks to the recession. After dithering for a few weeks, she'd finally taken the plunge and signed the lease, and told Joseph Finnegan she'd be leaving at the end of the year.

She'd invested in a stove that took up twice the space of the old one—forcing a complete reshuffle of her other kitchen appliances, during which the tumble dryer had migrated to the shed—and she'd bought the frighteningly expensive stand mixer, along with the thousand other bits and pieces she hadn't realized she'd need.

Adam and his cousins had rallied, and the little shop had gradually been scrubbed and sanded, painted and fitted with display cases and shelves. And last week a man had painted CUPCAKES ON THE CORNER in bright blue letters on the yellow strip of wall above the front window.

The shop was tiny—not much room for more than three customers at a time—but there was space around the back to pull up with the van. Adam had set up a Web site and designed stationery and printed off leaflets that they'd pushed through mail slots, stuck on telephone poles and supermarket notice boards, and slipped under car windscreen wipers.

And a week before Christmas, Hannah's kitchen had been

visited by a health inspector and deemed a suitable place in which to produce the cupcakes.

So everything was set. She was poised at last to make her dream come true—and the one person she wanted by her side had just left.

She reached out in the darkness and found her phone on the bedside table. She opened a new text message and inserted Patrick's name on the recipient line, then typed "*I miss you.*" She held her thumb above "send"—and slowly moved it across to press "exit."

Save message? the phone asked.

No, she replied with her thumb, and the words vanished.

She replaced her phone, closed her eyes, and forced herself to begin measuring flour, sugar, and butter. For some reason mental baking usually sent her right to sleep.

"Mum?"

"Hello."

Leah's heart sank at the cool tone. "I'm just ringing to see how you are," she said, as brightly as she could manage.

"He's moved in, has he?"

Leah could picture her face, pinched with disapproval. "Yes, he's moved in—and his name is Patrick," she added before she could stop herself. "Mum," she went on quickly, "please don't be like this."

"Easy for you to say," her mother answered, "when you don't have to face Geraldine Robinson at bridge every Friday night."

"She can't possibly blame you."

"And who else would she blame, when it's my daughter

who stole her daughter's boyfriend? You should have seen
how upset she looked last Friday—I dread to think what she'll
say when she finds out who's responsible for all this."

Leah closed her eyes and took a breath. "Mum, let's not
get into this. Just please try to understand, nobody planned it.
I didn't set out to—"

"You knew he was involved with someone else. You should
have had some self-restraint."

"It wasn't like that. It's not something—"

"Imagine what that poor girl is going through right now,
and just about to open up a shop. Geraldine was telling us
all only a couple of weeks ago how nervous she was about it.
Remember how tough it was for you when you opened the salon? How would you have liked to be landed with something
like that on top of it?"

With an effort, Leah held her tongue. No point in arguing:
Nothing she could possibly say would make a difference. Not
when her mother had been in Hannah's very situation thirty
years earlier—only worse, because Leah's father had walked out
on his wife and small daughter. At least Patrick hadn't been married to Hannah, and no children were involved—not that there
was anything to be gained by pointing that out, of course.

And it was definitely not the right moment to break her
other news—although time was running out for keeping quiet
about it.

"Can we meet for lunch?" she asked instead. "My treat.
Maybe Wednesday?"

Her mother's sniff was perfectly audible over the mobile
network. "I might be busy. I'll have to check my diary."

Leah dug her nails into her palm. "Well, give me a ring,"
she said lightly. "I'll keep one o'clock free. Let me know,
okay?"

Hanging up, she opened the appointments book, took a pencil from the jar, and wrote *"Lunch with Mum"* in the one-o'clock slot on Wednesday. She lifted the phone again and made a reservation at Giovanni's; her mother liked it there.

Leah would wait until after the pasta to tell her what had to be told—and her mother would rant and rave all over again and probably not talk to her for another month.

Leah lowered her head into her hands and groaned quietly. It wasn't as if she'd set out to lure any man away from another woman—that had never been her intention. Not that she hadn't been attracted, right from the first time they'd met, when he'd walked into the salon to claim his massage. She remembered privately admiring the broad chest, the muscular arms. She remembered him flirting with her, warning her to leave his towel alone.

She'd been disappointed when he'd mentioned a girlfriend, but not surprised—the gift of a massage generally came from a woman. And that had been it as far as she was concerned. He was with someone else, no point in going there. Even after he'd made it plain that he was interested, she'd resisted him for as long as she could, insisting over and over that she didn't want an affair—particularly when she discovered the identity of his girlfriend and realized that they'd known each other, albeit slightly, at school.

But in the end he'd charmed his way into her bed. He'd said the things she wanted to hear, convinced her that it was over between him and Hannah in all but name. *She means nothing to me,* he'd insisted. *I just have to find the right time to leave her. I* will *leave her, I swear.*

Was it so bad then, that Leah had finally given him the incentive he needed to do just that?

The doorbell rang. She raised her head, pasted on a smile, and crossed the room to let Martina Hennessy in for her Indian head massage.

———

Alice spooned more peas onto her husband's plate as he lifted the wine bottle and refilled their glasses. She wouldn't finish hers—one glass was all she could manage comfortably—but if it was in her glass, it meant *he* couldn't drink it.

They never used to have wine with dinner; this was a new thing. Tom had received a case for Christmas from a patient who imported it, and they'd gotten into the habit of a glass or two in the evening. Alice could have lived without it quite happily—she'd never taken a drink until well into her thirties, apart from the odd brandy—but now it was a given. A bottle opened half an hour before dinnertime and, more often than not, gone by the end of the meal.

"There's more potatoes," she said.

"I'm all right, thanks."

He was well able to drink; he'd always been well able. There'd been times, mercifully few, when she'd had to put him to bed. But up till now he'd drunk only when they were out, and most of the time he managed to stop before it went too far, when he was still the life and soul of the party.

And it wasn't much, she supposed, a bottle of wine between two people. Where was the harm in his relaxing after a day's work? Except that he drank at least two-thirds of the bottle each night, and sometimes she noticed a slur in his words and worried about his condition the following morning—because who wanted a dentist with unsteady hands, or who smelled of alcohol as he bent over you?

"You heard about Hannah," she said. "I presume Stephen mentioned it."

Tom cut into his steak. "Mentioned what?"

"Her boyfriend left her."

"No, I didn't hear that."

Of course Stephen wouldn't have told Tom. Men didn't talk about those things the way women did. They probably discussed the latest soccer results or political shenanigans when they had a break at the clinic.

"Just walked out on her," Alice said. "About a week ago now."

"That's too bad." Tom chewed his meat and lifted his glass. "They were together a good while, weren't they?"

"Over a year. Geraldine was convinced he'd propose at Christmas."

"So where's he gone?"

Alice made a face. "Some other woman, apparently."

"Mmm."

His wineglass was almost empty, hers practically untouched. In a minute or two he'd raise the bottle and hold it out to her, and she'd shake her head and he'd empty it into his glass.

Six whites and six reds they'd gotten, all French. She wouldn't know one wine from another, they all tasted the same to her. By the time the case was gone, it had become a habit. Now he brought home two or three bottles every few days. "Six ninety-nine," he'd tell her. "Couldn't leave them behind at that price."

"Are you busy tomorrow?" she asked.

"Kept going. The usual."

"Will you have time to stop into the cupcake shop?" she asked. "I thought it would be nice to show our support on the first day, and I won't get a chance, with Geraldine gone."

"Right."

"Get half a dozen of whatever she has, a mixture. And don't let her give them to you for nothing."

"Okay."

He reached for the wine bottle. She put a hand over the top of her glass, and he emptied what was left into his own.

He was only relaxing. There was no harm in it.

A hundred and forty-four, twelve trays of twelve. Were 144 cupcakes enough for one day? There was no way of knowing. What if she'd made too many chocolate-orange and not enough lemon-lime? What if everyone wanted vanilla-coconut and nobody looked at the mocha? What if people hated the cream-cheese icing and only went for the ones topped with buttercream? Was Clongarvin ready for mascarpone frosting?

"Stop."

Hannah looked at her mother. "Stop what? I'm not doing anything."

"You're worrying. It's as plain as the nose on your face."

"I can't help it; my stomach's in a knot. I think I might get sick. I feel like I've been up for hours."

"That's because you have. Did you get any sleep last night?"

"Not much. And the kitchen looks like a bomb hit it."

"Don't mind the kitchen—I'll give you a hand to tidy up this evening. I hope you had some breakfast."

She shook her head. "Couldn't—I'd definitely have thrown up."

Geraldine regarded her daughter with concern. "I should

have brought sandwiches. I'll run out for some in a while. You have to eat, whether you feel like it or not."

"I know...maybe later." Hannah tweaked one of the cupcakes on the display stand. "Does this look okay?"

They sat in individual wire circles that curled upward from the central branch. Each cupcake was skewered with a wooden cocktail stick to which a brightly colored tag was attached.

"They look great, like a bouquet of flowers. All those lovely colors."

"I was sure I'd never get them all iced; it took much longer than I thought. Just as well I gave myself plenty of time." She darted a glance at the clock on the wall. "God, it's five to nine already."

"Which means we have five minutes." Geraldine disappeared through the door that led to the back. "I'm putting on the kettle," she called.

Hannah stared after her. "It's five to nine."

"And the place looks great, and it smells wonderful, and we're all set." After some splashing and clattering, Geraldine reappeared. "And you need a cup of tea, whether you want it or not. And so do I."

Hannah looked out through the plate-glass window. "There's nobody waiting outside," she said.

"Why would there be? You're open all day, aren't you? People don't normally have cupcakes for breakfast."

Hannah pushed a cocktail stick a fraction farther into the top cupcake on the stand. "These labels are too small. I told Adam they were too small."

"They are not too small. I can read them fine without my glasses. And I love that writing—it's so cheery-looking."

"Font."

"Pardon?"

"It's not called writing on a computer, it's called a font. That one is called Mufferaw. We couldn't decide for ages between that and Sybil Green. I wanted Sybil Green, but Adam persuaded me that this one is easier to read—" She broke off. "What? What are you smiling at?"

Geraldine stepped closer and put her arms around her daughter. "Relax, my darling—it'll be great. Your cupcakes will be famous in no time. You'll have such fun with this, wait and see."

Hannah nodded against her shoulder. "I know I will."

But she knew she wouldn't. She knew she'd made the biggest mistake of her life, taking her grandfather's money and throwing it into this liability, this tiny little cubbyhole on a corner that nobody else had been interested in renting. Why hadn't somebody stopped her? Why were they all letting her make this colossal, expensive mistake?

Geraldine moved toward the back again. "There's the kettle now. Are you tea or coffee?"

"Tea."

She didn't want tea, she wanted to go home. She glanced up again at the big orange wall clock in the shape of a sun that Alice and Tom had given her as an opening present. "It's two minutes to nine," she called.

"Deep breaths," Geraldine called back, and Hannah inhaled shakily. She must be the only idiot opening a shop in the middle of a recession, signing a twelve-month lease when she could be out of business in a week. It wasn't as if cupcakes were basic foodstuffs that people would keep on buying no matter how tough times got. They were one of the luxuries everyone was cutting back on. She shouldn't have set the prices so high—who on earth was going to pay €1.75 for a bun, no matter how fancy it looked?

"They're too dear," she called.

"Nonsense—they're worth every cent." Geraldine reappeared with two steaming mugs. "I think we're all set." She placed the mugs on the counter and smiled. "Now darling, why don't you open your shop for the very first time?"

Hannah walked to the door. She stopped, her hand on the key, and looked back at her mother. "Mam, what if nobody comes in?"

"And what if you open the door," her mother replied, "so at least they have a choice?"

Hannah smiled and turned the key. "There." She switched the sign that Adam had printed from SORRY, FRESH OUT OF CUPCAKES to COME IN—YOU KNOW YOU WANT TO. "We're officially open," she said. "I'm officially running my own business." She paused. "For however long it lasts."

"You'll be here for years. You'll become an institution." Geraldine blew on her tea. "People will travel from all over for Hannah Robinson's cupcakes."

"I don't know about that, but I'm here for seven months anyway—Adam made me promise to stick it out till his birthday in August."

"August? Didn't you sign a lease for a year?"

"Mm-hmm—don't remind me."

They watched the steady stream of pedestrians passing the window.

"Drink your tea," Geraldine ordered, and Hannah lifted her mug obediently. A minute went by. Geraldine rubbed with her sleeve at a smudge on the glass-topped counter. Hannah tweaked another label on the cupcake stand, then undid and retied her apron strings.

"I don't know about that chair on the wall," she said. "I'm not sure about it."

"Just you wait," Geraldine said. "It'll be a real talking point."

It was Granddad's rocking chair. They'd painted it bright blue to match the sign above the shop, and they'd gotten a man to hang it on the yellow wall to the left of the counter, since there was no room for it on the floor.

"What if it falls off and kills someone?" Hannah asked.

"Don't be silly, dear," her mother answered placidly. "The man said a hurricane wouldn't knock it off that wall."

Another minute went by, and another. The orange clock ticked steadily.

"I should have gotten a computerized cash register," Hannah said. "Nobody uses a drawer for money anymore. It's ridiculous."

"It's quaint, and people will be charmed by it. And the bell over the door, too, lovely and old-fashioned, really characterful."

"Mmm." Hannah wondered if there was such a word as "characterful" and decided that she didn't care.

At eight minutes past nine, a man's head appeared around the door. "You open?"

"Yes." A twin chorus.

"Nice bell. Blast from the past." He spotted the rocking chair on the wall. "Now, that makes a change from a picture."

Geraldine laughed, catching Hannah's eye triumphantly. "We wanted to be original."

"Well, you're certainly that." He approached the counter. "I believe it's your first day."

"It is—and you're our very first customer," Geraldine told him.

"Am I really?" He peered at the cupcakes on the stand. "In that case I'd better buy something. What's good?"

"Everything," Geraldine told him, resting her mug on the shelf behind her. "And I'm sure you saw our sign telling you about our opening offer of a free cupcake with every order, but since you're the first customer, we'll give you two free." She turned to Hannah. "That okay, love?"

Hannah smiled and nodded, because what on earth else could she do? "That's fine."

Two free cupcakes, and he might buy only one. She willed herself to relax. Who cared if he bought only one? It was still her first sale, wasn't it? And if he liked the one he bought, not to mention the other two, he'd surely be back for more. And it wasn't even ten past nine.

So what if she was so tired she could sleep standing up? So what if she still felt miserable whenever she found the time to feel anything? She'd just opened her own shop. People didn't stop eating cupcakes simply because there was a recession. They still needed treats—in fact, maybe they needed them now more than ever.

The man was studying the samples on the stand. "I'll take two chocolate, or my wife will never forgive me, and two of those coconut ones."

"Good choice—the coconut are my favorite," Geraldine said, reaching for a yellow box and almost knocking her tea off the shelf. "My daughter made them all, you know, earlier today. They're as fresh as they could possibly be."

"Excellent," the man replied, pulling a wallet from his jacket. "Tell you what, why don't you throw in a couple of those lemon-lime, too? Since it's your first day. And I'll leave the free ones up to you."

Six. He was buying six. Hannah watched as Geraldine arranged his purchases carefully in the box. Maybe it wouldn't be a complete disaster. Maybe she'd actually

make a small amount of money before her mother
bankrupted her.

––––––––––

The horror bloomed on Fiona's face. "Tell me you're not serious."

Leah tightened her grip on her water glass. "Mum, I'd
hardly joke about something like that."

"When?"

"June."

Her mother closed her eyes briefly. "You're four months
gone."

"Thereabouts, yes."

"And...you're obviously keeping it."

Leah looked sharply across the table. "Obviously."

"I assume," her mother said, "that it's the newspaperman's
child."

Leah's knuckles were white around the glass. "Of course it
is."

Their plates sat between them, the remaining pasta cooling, the sauces just beginning to congeal. Leah's two twenty-
euro notes were tucked into the bill wallet, waiting to be
collected.

"And I suppose he's delighted," Fiona said.

Leah met her mother's eyes steadily. "Yes, of course he is.
We both are."

Fiona's smile was bitter. "Well, isn't that nice? A happy
couple, and a baby on the way. Just what I always hoped for
my only daughter."

Leah stood up abruptly, almost knocking over her chair.
Forget the fifteen euro in change: nothing was worth this. She

grabbed her bag and pulled her jacket from the chair back. "I have to go now. I hope you enjoyed your lunch."

She didn't look behind her as she strode toward the door. Once again she'd let her mother get under her skin. She always swore it wouldn't happen, and it always did. It was unfortunate that Fiona played bridge with Hannah's mother, but it was hardly the end of the world. Relationships broke up all the time—Geraldine Robinson knew that as well as anyone—but Leah's mother was determined to make a song and dance about it.

The pregnancy of course had been a gamble, and Leah had hated lying to Patrick about the Pill not working, but it had paid off. He was with her now—and he *was* happy about the baby. He kept telling her how happy he was. Nothing her mother could say would change that, and in time she'd have to come around to the idea of being a grandmother.

Leah walked quickly through Clongarvin's busy lunchtime streets until she reached the pretty lavender-painted, window-boxed frontage of Indulgence. She let herself in and leaned against the door, breathing in the subtly scented air, her hands coming to rest on the stomach that was just beginning to swell.

———————

At ten minutes to five, Hannah untied her yellow apron and hung it on the blue, star-shaped hook behind the counter. She leaned wearily against the display cases and yawned as her mother counted the unsold cupcakes.

"Twenty-seven," Geraldine announced. "How many did you say you started with?"

"A hundred and forty-four. My feet are killing me."

"So that's...a hundred and seventeen gone on the very first day. That's just wonderful."

Hannah smiled tiredly. "Not bad, I suppose."

Not all sold, some given away—a fair few given away—but still, not bad for her first day in business. People, quite a few people, had actually come into the shop and paid money for her cupcakes.

Geraldine indicated the leftovers. "What do you want me to do with these?"

"Bag them in assorted sixes and put them in that basket."

"Six times four is twenty-four; there'll be three left over."

"You can bring them home."

Hannah emptied the money drawer—a few customers had remarked on it, and there had been lots of comments, too, about the chair on the wall—and bundled the cash into her satchel. Geraldine arranged the bags of leftovers in a green basket that announced, on another of Adam's signs, yesterday's bake—ALMOST AS NICE, HALF THE PRICE: 6 FOR €5.

They mopped the floor and wiped down the shelves. They unplugged the kettle and switched the door sign back to SORRY, FRESH OUT OF CUPCAKES. They loaded the van with the trays, and they turned off the lights and slid down the security grille before locking the front door.

And as they rounded the corner to get back to the van, they came face-to-face with Patrick Dunne, editor of the *Clongarvin Voice*.

It was the first time Hannah had seen him since he'd walked out, just over a week earlier. His pale green tie was new. Her heart turned over as she took him in. She looked a mess—she must look a mess after the long day, in her flat black shoes and wide gray trousers and black top. The outfit she'd chosen so carefully for her first day in the shop felt terribly dowdy now.

Her old brown satchel was slung across her body, not matching anything. No hint left, probably, of the lipstick she'd slicked on hours before—chewed off, no doubt, by nine o'clock. Her hair must be lying flat on her head, no time to do more than aim the dryer at it for half a minute this morning. And the skin under her eyes would be bagging, she was sure, with tiredness.

Her cheeks prickled with heat. Great—a red face was all she needed to look her absolute worst.

"Hannah." Patrick's smile was forced. "And Geraldine. How are you both?"

He carried the briefcase she'd given him for his last birthday. He smelled the same. He was horribly hearty. He was nervous. They'd shared hundreds of nights, she'd lain in his arms so many times. They'd made each other laugh and cry. She'd thrown a bowl at him once. He'd switched to boxers for her and taught her to play chess. And now he was nervous and hearty.

"Fine," she told him. "We had a good day." She was surprised at how normal she sounded.

His polite smile remained in place.

"Hannah's shop opened today," Geraldine said, her voice icy.

"Yes," he said immediately, "of course it did. It went well, I hope?"

He'd forgotten. Hannah had been planning this for months, he'd heard her talking about it forever, and he'd forgotten. She didn't matter to him anymore. Nothing she did mattered to him.

She turned to her mother. "Let's go."

"You're in a hurry," Patrick said, moving off. "Good to see you both. Take care." And he was gone, his aftershave lingering.

"Well," Geraldine began, "he's got some—"

"Don't," Hannah begged, and her mother was silent.

She drove to her parents' house, where her father, who'd left work an hour early, was under orders to have the shepherd's pie heated up by half past five. And somehow, miraculously, she managed to sit through the dinner she didn't want, listening to her mother giving her father an account of the day. She managed to answer his questions and nod and smile in all the right places. Somehow she managed to hold it all together until she got home and closed her own front door.

And then, before she'd taken off her jacket, she sank onto the bottom stair and put her head in her hands and cried bitterly at the thought that she'd been forgotten.

———

"Bestseller so far?"

"Chocolate-vanilla, easily."

"So you have those every day, as a staple. Write it down. Worst seller?"

She thought. "Not sure...maybe forest fruits, or apple-cinnamon; I definitely had a few of both left over."

"So you only do those once in a while. Go on, write it down."

They were in Hannah's kitchen. It was half past seven on a Friday evening, and pitch black beyond the big latticed window. Cupcakes on the Corner had been open for three days. Adam was making coffee, Hannah was scribbling in a notebook. Some woman was singing "Famous Blue Raincoat" on the radio.

"Mam's been brilliant," Hannah said. "I don't know how I'm going to manage on Monday when she goes back to Glass

Slipper and I'm on my own. She welcomes everyone who comes in, makes sure they know I'm just starting off and that I bake everything myself. She practically gets them to sign a contract promising they'll come back."

"Good. That's our Geraldine." Adam lifted the kettle off its base and poured water into mugs. "Now, are you making any money?"

Hannah shook her head. "Hard to say for sure—I haven't done a proper breakdown of outgoings and incomings yet—but I suspect I'm just about breaking even, if that."

Adam brought the coffee to the table. "Breaking even is fantastic. Time enough for profits. What you want to do now is keep your head above water."

"Well, I suppose I'm doing that, just barely. Nothing's been disconnected yet, and no sign of a bailiff, and I haven't gotten a bill in at least two days." She closed the notebook and lowered her head onto the table. "But, boy, I sure am tired."

"Poor you." Adam ruffled her hair. "I'd offer to help, but my cupcakes would close you down in a week."

"I've been making them in my sleep," she mumbled. "Did I tell you? Every bloody night, as soon as I nod off. You think I'd get a bit of a break in my sleep. If I never saw another cupcake, I'd be happy."

"Well," Adam said, selecting one from the plate that sat between them, "I'm still a big fan." He peeled off the paper and bit into the soft beige sponge and coffee-colored icing, decorated with pieces of lavender angelica. "By the way," he said, "I don't think I told you—Nora and Jackson are officially over."

Hannah lifted her head. "Oh, Adam, you're not serious?" She picked a piece of cherry from another cupcake. "I remember you saying they were having problems, but I didn't think it was that bad."

He shrugged. "I wasn't too surprised myself. Nora's been hinting that things weren't going well for a good while now." He and his twin sister talked several times a week, computer to computer.

"So they're definitely splitting up?"

"Yeah—she's going to come home for a while." He took another bite of his cupcake. "Pity. I liked Jackson."

Hannah sipped her coffee. Another relationship ended. "Is she terribly upset?" She wondered if Nora had been the one to finish it and guessed that she had.

"Doesn't seem too bad. She hasn't said anything to the folks yet."

Since their retirement Adam's parents had moved fifty miles away from Clongarvin, back to the tiny village where they'd both grown up and where Adam and Nora had spent all their childhood summers.

"D'you think Nora will settle back in Ireland?"

He shrugged again. "Dunno...hard to say. You never know with Nora."

"I forget how long they were married."

"Just over four years." He drank coffee. "Ah, she'll bounce back. My sister is nothing if not resourceful."

Hannah could think of plenty of words to describe Nora O'Connor (or Nora Paluzzi—wasn't that her married name?) and "resourceful" wouldn't have been the first to spring to mind. Adam's sister had been a year behind Hannah in school and had hung around with girls who didn't look twice at the likes of Hannah Robinson, since she wasn't pretty or slim enough to interest them.

Nora had her twin's green eyes and russet curls, and there

the similarity ended. She'd been spared his freckles, and her nose was smaller and her lips fuller. She was also half a head taller—and the last time Hannah checked, at least thirty pounds lighter—than her brother.

Adam was perfectly presentable, though not even Hannah could call him handsome, but Nora had always been striking—and blessed with the confidence to make the most of her looks. She'd moved to the States a week after her eighteenth birthday, much against the wishes of her parents and without a single qualification. In almost fourteen years, she'd been back just a handful of times.

Jackson Paluzzi, a pediatrician, was her second husband. Her first marriage, to an older university professor, had ended after less than a year. Whether by design or by accident, neither relationship had produced children. Hannah imagined that the news of another divorce wouldn't go down too well with Nora's parents.

Adam drained his mug and stood up. "Better get off and let you make tracks for bed. You'll be looking forward to a lie-in on Sunday."

"I sure will."

"What about coming out for an hour tomorrow night? A drink somewhere, just to relax you?"

Hannah shook her head. "Thanks for the offer, but I already have a plan—hot bath, face pack, good book. If I have any drink, it'll probably be warm milk."

"Just an hour," he said. "Why don't we check out that new wine bar?"

"What new wine bar?"

"Vintage, down by the quays. It's only been open a couple of weeks, where Delaney's Hardware used to be. Someone said there's live music at the weekends."

"Delaney's is gone?"

Adam smiled. "You definitely need to get out more."

"Maybe...I'll see how I feel tomorrow night." She pushed her chair away from the table. "There's something I haven't told you," she said, getting up.

Adam was pulling on his leather jacket. "What?"

"I met Patrick on Wednesday, on the way home from the shop." She took their two mugs over to the sink.

"You did? You never said. How was it?"

"Not good. Awkward." She turned on the tap. "He was so...formal, as if he hardly knew me. He'd forgotten that the shop was opening that day, can you believe it?"

"Bastard," Adam said lightly.

"My mother was there, which I suppose was just as well." She rinsed the mugs and put them on the drainboard. "I cried my eyes out when I got home."

"You know what?" Adam said. "That's the worst over. The first time you meet them is the worst."

She took the tea towel from its hook. "I know...There'd been flowers delivered to the shop in the morning, and the first thing that occurred to me when I saw them was that he was having second thoughts and wanted to come back." She tried to laugh. "How sad is that?"

"Who were they from?"

"Alice and Tom, sweet of them."

"All the very best with your new venture," Alice had written, and Hannah had buried her face in the hothouse roses that smelled of nothing and swallowed her disappointment. "I try not to think about him, honestly, but it's easier said than done."

Much easier said than done when she kept bumping into reminders around the house. Yesterday she'd thrown his half-full jar of Marmite into the bin. Last week it had been his prawns from the freezer. The handmade mug she'd brought him back from a trip to Dublin would be harder to let go.

She took the unsalted butter from the fridge and left it to soften. She set her utensils and baking trays on the worktop, all ready for the early hours. "You know, I thought his timing was horrible—dumping me just before the shop opened—but imagine how much worse I'd feel if I weren't so busy now. Maybe he planned it that way."

Up to her eyes in recipes and vanilla essence and poppy seeds and dried cranberries and chocolate chunks. No time to think about what he might be doing or whether he missed her at all. Asleep as soon as her head hit the pillow—which she'd moved to the middle of the bed.

"I deleted his number," she said quietly, "from my phone."

That had been hard. She didn't want to think about that, about his name disappearing. She searched for something different to say. "I'm considering getting a cat," she told Adam, filling the kettle again for her hot-water bottle, "to keep me company."

"What about getting a housemate," he asked sternly, "to keep you solvent?"

She sighed. "I know, I know. I must run the ad. I will, honest. Next week."

"Swear?"

"Swear...maybe."

Apart from all the negative connotations of replacing Patrick, she still shrank from the idea of sharing her house with a stranger. She'd been lucky with Annie, the housemate she'd had before Patrick, but who was to say she wouldn't end up with a monster this time around? Financially, though, she knew that it was unavoidable.

Adam crossed the kitchen and kissed her cheek. "Right, I'm off. I'll call you tomorrow evening to see if I can drag you out."

"Don't hold your breath—I probably won't go."

When he'd left, she took the hot-water bottle from its drawer and filled it. Not even eight o'clock and she was on her way to bed. At least it was dark—what would it be like in the summer, when she was going upstairs in broad daylight?

Time enough to worry about that. She switched off the light and left the room and plodded upstairs.

———

"It's Leah Bradshaw." Geraldine's voice floated in from the hall as she hung her coat.

Stephen didn't turn from the computer. "What is?" he called back.

Geraldine walked into the sitting room, rubbing her hands together. "God, it's chilly out tonight. Leah Bradshaw is the girl Patrick left Hannah for."

Stephen looked across the room at his wife. "Who is she? Do we know her?"

Geraldine poked the fire before tipping in coal from the scuttle. "I wish you'd keep this going when I'm out. She's Fiona Bradshaw's daughter." She waited for a reaction and getting none, she added impatiently, "Fiona Bradshaw, who I play bridge with. You know her—she has some environment job with the town council. You met her at Aoife's cocktail party in November. Tall, dyed red hair. Too thin. And she came here when I did the Alzheimer's tea thing—she brought those orchids that died. I remember you asking her about them."

"Oh, yes," Stephen said, knowing that it didn't matter in the least that he had absolutely no memory of Fiona Bradshaw. "So it's her daughter."

"And to think," Geraldine said angrily, pushing the poker through the fresh coals, "that I supported that girl when she opened her salon. I paid good money for a manicure, and I wasn't well out the door when one of my nails smudged; they weren't dry at all. I should have gone back, only I didn't want to embarrass her."

Stephen felt the conversation slipping away from him. "How are you so sure it's her? Did her mother tell you?"

Geraldine snorted. "Of course she didn't tell me—she hasn't come near me since it happened. Too ashamed of what her brazen daughter has done, no doubt. Maureen Hardiman told me, delighted to have a bit of scandal to report, as usual. Naturally, I let on I knew already."

"Good for you." Stephen's fingers crept back toward the keyboard, reluctant to abandon the first Scrabble game in ages that he was showing any signs of winning.

"Small slip of a thing," Geraldine said, settling onto the couch and picking up the remote control. "Don't know what he sees in her. Dyed hair, of course, like her mother. Can you see Hannah ever having to dye her hair?" She pressed a button on the remote, and the television flicked on. "Oh, not that fellow again—he's always on the *Late Late*. Must have written a book."

"Mm-hmm." Stephen typed in *"cousin"* as quietly as he could, and his score jumped to 176.

"I'll have to tell her," Geraldine said, still watching the television.

Stephen swung toward her again. "Tell who? Hannah?"

"Of course, Hannah. She'll have to hear it from me."

"Why? Won't that only upset her?"

Geraldine looked at him, incredulous. "Stephen, do you really think she wouldn't find out? In a place the size of Clongarvin, it'll be all over town in no time. I'd prefer she heard it from me than from some gossip like Maureen Hardiman."

Hannah's father returned to his Scrabble game. He'd long since given up trying to understand the workings of his wife's mind. Far easier to figure out what to do with a *q*, a *b*, three *e*'s, and a couple of *p*'s.

Vintage was Clongarvin's first wine bar. It was all dark wood, subdued lighting, and low couches arranged around candlelit tables. Not exactly what Adam was used to when he went out for a drink.

He sat alone on a barstool by the counter—at least they had a few barstools—having failed to persuade Hannah to accompany him. He hadn't pressed her too hard: maybe a night of doing nothing more strenuous than lying in warm, sudsy water was what she needed this weekend. And going out on his own had never bothered him. Clongarvin being the size it was, and this being Saturday night, he was reasonably sure of bumping into someone he knew before too long.

In the meantime he was content to drink his Guinness—thankfully, the stock wasn't limited to wine—and watch the woman who'd caught his attention pretty much as soon as he'd walked in.

She was the only female member of the group of four musicians performing on the small, slightly raised area—you could hardly call it a stage—in a corner of the room, diagonally across from where he sat.

It wasn't that she was beautiful—no, he really couldn't call her that. There was certainly something striking about the neat, pointed features, but she wasn't beautiful. Her hair, some pale color he couldn't determine, was pulled off her face by a wide black hair band and captured into some kind of low ponytail. No tendril escaped, so there was nothing to suggest the length or the texture of it.

Her eyes were hidden behind a pair of small, round, dark-rimmed glasses. From this distance he couldn't be sure, but he thought her hands were broad, the knuckles jutting sharply from her splayed fingers as they traveled over the keys of her instrument, which, from Adam's very limited knowledge of musical instruments, appeared to be a clarinet.

She was dressed entirely in black. A high-necked blouse fell in sharp pleats to her waist, where it was gathered into a wide belt made of some shiny material. A long, loose skirt stopped just short of her ankles, meeting a pair of black boots with pointed toes. The whole of her body was covered, apart from her hands and face. There was no clue to the shape that lay beneath the stiff folds of her top or the drapes below.

Not beautiful, no. Not in the least pretty. Unsmiling, wholly focused on the music they played. She sat hunched in her seat, her chair set back a fraction from her companions', giving the suggestion that she was trying to distance herself from the whole affair.

And yet Adam watched her. What drew him to examine that frowning face, to wonder what color the eyes were behind their glass barriers, to imagine undoing the ponytail, peeling off the black hair band, and watching the pale hair tumble downward?

The other three musicians were male, and casually dressed in white shirts and chinos. One played a keyboard, another an enormous version of a violin that could equally have been a cello or a double bass, and the third had what Adam was reasonably sure was a saxophone.

He enjoyed the sound they produced. They played old favorites—"You Go to My Head" and "Blue Moon" and "These Foolish Things"—and show tunes like "On the Street Where You Live" and "I Feel Pretty," and a few Beatles hits, and a couple of movie themes—and the treatment they gave each tune, the subtle rhythms they introduced, made the songs fresh and lively and interesting. It was music you couldn't help tapping a foot along to.

The female musician seemed unaware of her surroundings. The buzz of chatter in the wine bar didn't appear to bother her; she didn't react to the smattering of applause at the end of each piece. She flicked the pages on the stand in front of her and glanced now and again at one or another of her fellow musicians as they moved on to another tune, but she was distanced somehow from the warm, busy room.

"Adam, over here." A couple he knew were gesturing to him from the far end of the counter. He took his drink and joined them, and the next time he looked toward the musicians' platform, half an hour later, all that remained were two music stands and three chairs, on one of which was perched an empty half-pint glass.

———

"Leah Bradshaw," Geraldine said. "She opened a beauty salon on Russell Street a few years back. Not much of a place, if you ask me."

"I know it," Hannah said bleakly. "I was there."

"Small, skinny thing," Geraldine said. "Her figure isn't

half as nice as yours." She stopped. "You were there? When?"

"Oh...months ago, I don't remember exactly."

She remembered exactly. Eight months ago, early summer, when Patrick's back had been stiff after he'd dug up the hedge.

"Do you know her?" Geraldine asked. "Did you get something done there?"

"No...I bought a gift certificate for a massage. A present for someone."

A back massage, Hannah had said. *A gift.* She remembered Leah Bradshaw, remembered recognizing her vaguely from school, but they'd have been in different years.

"How did you hear?" she asked her mother. "Who told you?"

"Oh, just some old gossip at bridge with nothing better to do," Geraldine said. "I can't for the life of me see why he'd prefer her. Even if you are my daughter, there's no comparison. Some men need their heads examined."

Some men obviously preferred their women blond and petite, with the kind of boyish figure—small breasts, slim hips—that Hannah had always envied. Nails short and beautifully shaped, painted pale pink. Hannah had noticed the nails as Leah took her sixty euro and wrote *"back massage"* on the gift voucher, which was colored lavender like the walls of the reception area.

"Her mother plays bridge with me," Geraldine said. "Fiona Bradshaw. I don't think you know her. Not someone you'd warm to, bit of a cold fish."

I like the color of your hair, Leah had said to Hannah. *Very rich...and a lovely shine to it.*

"You're better off without him," her mother said, "although I know that's not much comfort now, love."

See you again, she'd said as Hannah had turned to leave the salon. *Thanks a lot, take care.*

"I felt I should tell you," Geraldine said. "I didn't want you hearing it from someone else. You didn't mind me saying it?"

Had Patrick known her already? Had Hannah innocently bought him forty-five minutes alone with his other woman? Had they laughed about that as Leah massaged his naked, oiled skin, her slender body leaning over his? Or had they bothered with the massage at all? Maybe they'd found something more interesting to do with each other.

Or—worse, much worse—had Hannah introduced them? Had she been the one who'd brought them together? The thought stopped her in her tracks, the awfulness of it.

"Are you still there?" her mother asked.

"Yes," Hannah answered. "Still here."

Confidence shattered, heart in bits, utterly miserable, but still there.

"You don't mind that I told you? You're not cross with me?"

"No, of course not...Look," she said, "I have to go. I'll talk to you tomorrow."

Leah Bradshaw. Was it better to have a name and a face? Did that make it any easier? Or was it worse to know exactly who had stolen Patrick from her? She flipped her phone closed and slid it into her pocket before grabbing the shopping cart again and pushing it toward the yellow van. What did any of it matter, when he was still gone and she was still alone?

As she unloaded the cart, piling bags into the back of the van, a man passed her wearing a navy jacket and a dark green woolly hat. A rucksack that looked heavy was hanging off one shoulder. "Hello," he said. "Nice evening."

"Hi," she answered, unsmiling because a smile was out of the question.

He seemed vaguely familiar. He unlocked a nearby taxi and slung his rucksack onto the backseat before getting in himself. He must have driven her somewhere, not that she took taxis too often.

As she negotiated the little van out of the car park a few minutes later, she turned abruptly back in the direction of the town and drove through emptying early-evening streets until she came to Indulgence. She pulled in to a space across the road and sat, engine idling.

She studied the prettily painted frontage. The downstairs windows were dark, the salon closed at this hour. On the first floor, a light shone faintly from one of the two tall, narrow windows.

Were they inside now? Was she cooking dinner for him—or were they sprawled in front of a television, the way she and Patrick used to do? Was she telling him about her day while he poured her a glass of wine?

If he looked out he'd see the van, with the shop name written clearly on the side. He'd know she was there, he'd realize she must have discovered Leah Bradshaw's identity.

The street was quiet, most workers gone home and cozying up for the night. Hannah glanced around, saw a few scattered pedestrians, a man dismounting from a bicycle, a dog sniffing at a lamppost.

She'd never had a massage. The idea of a stranger's hands moving over her naked skin, however competently, had never appealed to her. The subject had never come up between her and Patrick; neither had ever looked for one, none had ever been offered. Wasn't it odd, then, that she'd thought of getting him a massage when his back had been bothering him? Had she seen an ad?

Or maybe Patrick had suggested it. The idea jumped suddenly and unpleasantly into her head. No, surely he wouldn't have done that. But she couldn't remember exactly what had prompted her visit to Indulgence.

She regarded the salon again. She could come back when it was dark, lob a rock through the window, and drive off quickly. The notion came out of nowhere, filling her with a shocked thrill. She could get a can of black paint and fling it at the pretty lavender walls. Nobody would know. She could wear gloves so there was no evidence to point to her. She could—

A nearby door opened. A man and a boy appeared on the path and walked in the direction of the van. The man smiled briefly at Hannah as they passed.

What was she doing? What was she thinking? Was she completely mad? She put the van into gear and drove badly, her blood racing, all the way home.

February

I really want to pamper her this year."

Geraldine's hand hovered over the plate of assorted biscuits. She shouldn't—a biscuit was the last thing her midsection needed—but Lent wasn't far away, and she'd have to do without them then. "God knows the poor thing could use a treat."

"What about a gift certificate? You can't go wrong."

"Ah, no, not a gift certificate." Geraldine selected a pink wafer—not her favorite, but practically no calories, apparently. "Stephen thinks we should pay for someone to paint the outside of her house. I know it could badly do with it, but where's the pampering in that?"

"Mmm—and anyway, who would you get to do outdoor painting in February?" Alice watched a woman wheel a baby buggy along the rows of shoes and boots. "How old is she going to be?"

"Thirty-three, can you believe it?" Geraldine finished the wafer and took a shortbread finger. A finger couldn't hurt, even if it was loaded with butter. "I never thought she'd get to that age and still be single. How old was Ellen when she got married?"

"Twenty-eight."

"There you go. And she has three now."

"That's right." Ellen was Tom and Alice's only child, living for the past decade in Australia. "Wish we saw more of them."

The customer picked up a black patent boot, and Alice put down her cup. "I'll go."

The shop was quiet in February, the winter buying mostly over, too early for anyone to want sandals, no big occasions coming up that would call for new shoes.

Except Valentine's Day, a week from Sunday. A couple of men had bought gift certificates in the past few days, and some women had come in looking at heels. Geraldine would get her usual card and box of Thornton's chocolates, provided she made some reference to the fourteenth at least twice over the coming week.

"Are you doing anything for Valentine's Day?" she asked when Alice returned, having sold the boots and a pair of half-price slippers.

Alice considered. "Cooking pork chops, probably. You?"

"Roast beef, more than likely." Geraldine gathered up the plate of biscuits and the two empty cups. "And maybe apple crumble for afters."

"Very romantic."

In the small kitchen, she rinsed the cups and left them on the drainboard, and slid the biscuits back into their tin as her thoughts returned to her daughter. Hannah had been flown to Paris for her birthday last year, didn't know a thing about it until they'd arrived at the airport. Patrick had pretended he was picking someone up—his brother, was it? Some relation anyway.

Geraldine had been charmed when she'd heard; it had sounded so romantic. By then, of course, she and Stephen had had several weeks to get used to the fact that their daughter was living with a man who wasn't her husband. It had been a different story when Hannah had told them that Patrick was moving in.

You haven't known him a wet week, Geraldine had protested.

Three months, Hannah had said. *I know it seems soon, but it's what we both want. And with Annie being transferred to Cork, the timing is perfect.*

Annie had moved into Hannah's spare room three weeks after Hannah had bought the house, and she'd been with her ever since. She was the perfect housemate, paying her rent on time each month and going home to her family in Sligo every weekend. And now she was being transferred, and Patrick, whom Geraldine still regarded as Hannah's new boyfriend, was to be her replacement.

It's still so soon, though, Geraldine had said. *Couldn't you get another housemate, just for a few more months, even?*

But Hannah had been determined, and Patrick had moved in. And despite her parents' misgivings, it had seemed to be working out. Geraldine remembered the phone call from Charles de Gaulle Airport, how happy Hannah had sounded. She'd been convinced they'd come back engaged, but that hadn't happened. And look at them now.

She sighed as she replaced the lid on the biscuit tin. Just as well Hannah was worn out these days, with no time to brood. Up in the middle of the night to bake, bake, bake, and then standing behind that counter all day long. Thankfully, things seemed to be working out nicely in the shop so far. The cupcakes were selling reasonably steadily, and Hannah seemed to be enjoying it—at least that's what she told them. But she looked so tired and lost whenever Geraldine met her. Of course her heart was still broken.

Geraldine knew what her daughter needed for her birth-day—she'd known as soon as Hannah had signed her name on the lease, as soon as she'd finally committed to opening her own business. And much as Geraldine hated presenting her only child with a check on her birthday, that was what she and Stephen had to do.

She washed her hands and walked back out to the shop. She'd talk to Stephen this evening, decide how much they'd give. He'd be happy with her choice, always the practical one.

And tomorrow she'd parcel up the nice pink sling-backs that Alice would let her have for forty euro. Whatever else, a girl needed shoes on her birthday.

————————

"I have a proposition for you."

Hannah eyed him warily. "Go on."

"Don't look so suspicious. This could be mutually beneficial."

"Go on."

"Well, you know that Nora's coming home next week, for a while anyway."

"Yes?" Hannah's guarded expression slid up a notch.

"And you still haven't gotten around to advertising for a housemate, although you're probably living off beans on—"

"No," Hannah said quickly. "No. I'm sorry, Adam, but it wouldn't work. We...might fall out over something, and things could get messy, and...look, she's your sister and all, but I really don't know Nora that well. I mean, we're very different, and you'd be caught in the middle, and..." She trailed off, looking trapped.

"Hang on a sec," Adam said. "What do you think I'm suggesting?"

"That Nora move in with me. And while in theory the idea is fine, I just think—"

"Stop talking," he said. "Stop now."

Hannah stopped.

"I'm suggesting," he said, "that I let Nora have my place and *I* move in with you. Me. Adam."

"Oh." She sipped her red wine. "Right. You and me. Sharing my house."

"Just for a while, obviously," he said, his eyes on her face, "until you get your head together and see where you're going with the business."

"Right. Uh-huh."

"You know you need someone to share the bills, even though you keep putting it off."

She made a face. "I'm hardly likely to forget, with you going on about it all the—"

"And I just thought you might rather have someone you know."

"I would," she agreed.

"And if Nora decides to stay in Ireland, she'll find a place of her own—this would just be a stopgap for her—a few weeks, maybe. Couple of months at the most, probably."

"Right." Hannah nodded. "Uh-huh. Yes."

Adam lifted his drink. "You look like a rat caught in the headlights."

She smiled. "Don't you mean a rabbit?"

"Whatever it is, you look like it. You don't have to decide right now, obviously—and we won't fall out if you don't fancy the idea, although I might sulk for a few days. But while you're mulling it over, consider this: I never leave the toilet seat up, I always squeeze the toothpaste from the bottom, and I only drink from the carton when nobody's watching."

"Actually, I'm sure I've seen you do that."

"Never—and as you know, I'm a happy drunk."

"That's true. You go all mushy and tell me how great I am."

"And I can fix your computer when it breaks down."

"You do that already."

"Yes, but now I'd be on the spot. Instant repairs."

Hannah laughed. "I'll bear that in mind. And I presume Kirby would be part of the package."

"God, yeah—he'd have to be. But he's house-trained, obviously. And he loves you."

"And I love him too. But he sheds."

"Only a small bit." Then, seeing her expression, he added, "Okay, a big bit. But we can confine him to wherever you say."

"He wouldn't be allowed in the kitchen, ever. He could lose me my accreditation."

"Fair enough."

"Or upstairs. Or on my couch—he has yours destroyed. We'd have to get him a special chair. And he'd have to sleep in the shed at night. And you'd have to clean up after him."

"Fine. All fine. Fine on all fronts."

She considered. It just might work. And it would certainly ease her financial worries. But was it really what he wanted, or did he feel some silly responsibility toward her? She put a hand on his arm. "Look, if you're just trying to help me out, you really don't have to, you know. I was planning to put that ad in. I was just...working up to it."

"Are you kidding? Helping you is a very minor aspect—I'm trying desperately not to share my flat with Nora." He lifted his glass. "Anyway, enough of that. Think about it and let me know." He waved a hand to indicate the room. "So what do you reckon about this place?"

"It's great—just what Clongarvin needs." Hannah studied the band in the corner. "I like the funky music, too, really fits in. *She* looks a bit scary, though."

"Who?"

"The one with the clarinet. All those black clothes, and the hair scraped back. And the professor specs."

"Can't say I noticed," he said.

"And look at the frown on her. I wouldn't like to get on her wrong side."

"That's probably because she's concentrating."

"Mmm. The guy with the double bass looks foreign. Anyway, where were we?"

"We were just about to plan your birthday next week."

She groaned. "God, I was hoping you'd forget. Let's plan nothing, please—I really don't feel like celebrating this one."

"All the more reason. Sorry, but you have no choice. How about dinner on me, anywhere you fancy that won't bankrupt me?"

She picked up her glass again. "Honestly, Adam, I'd rather not." And as she sipped the oaky wine, her last birthday slid, unwanted, into her thoughts.

Sorry about this, Patrick had said, *There's no one else free to collect him. We'll still be in time for dinner, I promise.* And he'd dropped her at the arrivals door and gone to find a parking space. And even when she couldn't see a flight from London on the board, it hadn't clicked. She'd just thought his brother had gotten the time wrong and they'd be there all night, waiting for him to arrive, and the birthday dinner that they'd postponed till Friday night would be ruined.

And then Patrick had reappeared, pulling her weekend bag on wheels behind him. *Tell you what,* he'd said, smiling at her astonishment, *let's go to Paris instead.*

She set down her glass, pushing the memory away. "Anyway," she said to Adam, "my birthday's on a Thursday this year, so I'll be having my usual early night."

"We could wait till Saturday to go out."

She shook her head. "Let's just leave it. Really."

"Okay, I'll get you a surprise instead. What color scarf have you not got?"

She smiled. "Green. Not that awful touristy green, a nice sage." She hesitated, and then added, "Yes, by the way."

"Yes, what?

"Yes, I would like you to move in. You and Kirby."

"What?"

"I said I would like—"

Adam shook his head firmly. "No, that was too quick. You need to sleep on it."

"No, I don't. As long as you pay your rent on time, split the bills, and replace everything you break—and keep the dog hairs at bay a bit with the vacuum cleaner. And never, *ever* drink from the carton."

He regarded her closely. "You're totally sure about this?"

"Yes. I know you well enough to kick you out if you drive me mad."

"That's true." He clinked his glass against hers. "In that case—and only if you're absolutely, positively sure—it's a deal." He thought. "Nora arrives next Thursday, in fact. How would Wednesday suit for me to move in?"

"Wednesday's fine. Pop into the shop in the meantime and I'll give you keys."

Patrick's keys, which would now be Adam's keys. She turned her face quickly toward the band again before it gave her away—and Adam, bless him, launched into a description of an impossibly complicated Web site that he was setting up, which managed to drown out the whole of "Eleanor Rigby," and which required absolutely no response from Hannah.

———————

The buzzer sounded, its harshness making Patrick wince as always. A second later he heard Leah speaking softly on the intercom in the hall.

Then, as he was fastening his second cufflink: "She's here."

"Right," he called back. "I'm on the way."

He looked in the mirror and tweaked the knot of his tie and ran a hand over his hair. It wasn't his first meeting with Leah's mother. He'd been introduced to Fiona Bradshaw some years before at an art auction, and since then their paths had crossed occasionally at various functions. They nodded at each other when they met, shared the odd brief group conversation.

Her photo appeared quite regularly in the newspaper's social pages. She'd been featured once, about a year ago, in connection with her job as environmental officer with the local council.

Patrick had the impression of a cool, poised woman, at ease in social situations. Well able to hold her own, if not exactly someone he'd seek out for a friendly chat. And now their personal lives were going to intersect, and he wondered what lay ahead. If Leah's reports of her mother's feelings about their relationship were to be believed—and he had no reason to doubt them—the future looked interesting.

The fact that Fiona wasn't exactly over the moon about Leah's pregnancy was unfortunate but not unexpected—and in truth, remembering his own dismay when Leah had told him, Patrick could hardly blame the woman. But they were

all civilized adults, and he presumed they'd manage to get beyond it. For his part he'd be charming and pleasant and hope
for the best.

He smoothed his hair again and left the bedroom, at precisely the same moment that Leah opened the front door to
her mother.

"Mum."

It wasn't an embrace, more a brief connection, Leah's lips
barely touching her mother's cheek. Fiona was taller than her
daughter by about six inches. Her glance met Patrick's as Leah
drew back.

"So," she said. No hand outstretched.

"You know Patrick," Leah said, and he smiled and kept his
own hands by his sides and received a cool nod.

"We've met"—Fiona began unbuttoning her fawn
coat—"here and there." She wore a gray cardigan and skirt.
Her dark red hair gleamed, her lipstick a precise match. She
smelled of marzipan. The tips of her long nails were white.
A jewel flashed on her left hand as she gave Patrick her coat.
"Thank you."

"We're having fish pie," Leah said, walking ahead of them
into the apartment's tiny sitting room. "It won't be long."

She was nervous. She'd snapped at Patrick earlier over
nothing—he always left his shoes in the hall—and she'd spent
the past few evenings flicking through her cookbooks, decid-
ing on and rejecting any number of dishes. Patrick had had
the sense not to argue, to pretend to weigh up the advantages
of fish over chicken, to consider the wisdom of serving asparagus in February.

In the sitting room he poured drinks. Gin and bitter lemon
for Fiona, iced tea for Leah, single-malt for himself. He poked
the fire and added a couple of briquettes. Leah left the room

to check the fish pie and boil the water for the asparagus, and he sat across the fireplace from Fiona.

"Chilly tonight." He stretched his feet toward the blaze, itching to kick off the shoes he'd put on just minutes before.

Fiona sipped her gin and kept her eyes on the fire. "It is."

He became aware of the clock ticking on the mantelpiece. He put down his drink and crossed to the CD player. "Any preference for music?"

She didn't look in his direction. "I have no idea what you have."

"Right." He selected one of Leah's Lyle Lovett CDs and slipped it into the drive. "Let's take a chance on this one then."

The door opened, and Leah reappeared. Her face, he noticed for the first time, was slightly puffy. "Five minutes."

Lyle Lovett strummed his guitar and began singing about a porch, and Leah threw Patrick an exasperated glance before turning to her mother. "Are you warm enough?"

Patrick thought about the meals around Geraldine and Stephen's kitchen table. The roast chickens fragrant with tarragon and lemon, the rich casseroles, Stephen's tangy, oozing blue-cheese burgers. The mismatched crockery and the casual, relaxed conversation. Something Hannah had baked—raspberry roulade, apple strudel, sour-cream coffee cake—usually rounding off the meal.

He became aware that Leah was glaring at him and realized he'd missed something. "Sorry?"

"I said your father goes on a cruise every winter."

"Oh...yes. Yes, he does." They'd joked about bringing Bill Dunne and Fiona together. "He's sailing around Greece at the moment."

Since Patrick's father had been widowed more than twenty

years earlier, his tastes leaned to women considerably younger than fifty-eight and substantially less uptight than Fiona Bradshaw. The prospect of hooking up with her would probably have him heading for the hills.

"Mum's been on cruises, haven't you?"

Patrick did his best to look interested. "Oh, yes? Where have you been?"

Leah leaped up. "Sorry—I forgot something." She practically ran from the room. Patrick took a deep swig of his whiskey, welcoming its peaty burn.

"I don't approve of all this," Fiona said suddenly. Her voice was completely neutral. She might have been listing the countries she'd visited from her cruise ship.

"I gathered that," Patrick replied evenly. May as well give as good as he got. "I presume Leah explained that the baby wasn't planned."

"She did—which in my opinion makes it worse." She'd barely touched her drink. "It's not as if you're a couple of teenagers."

"No."

"And now my daughter is pregnant by a man who until a month ago was living with another woman."

"Yes." What else was there to say? He drank more whiskey. "That's true." He hesitated. "Not that it changes the way I feel about Leah." *Not that it's any of your damn business.*

Fiona didn't respond.

Patrick got to his feet again. "Can I freshen your drink?"

When she shook her head, he crossed to the cabinet where the bottles were kept and refilled his own glass. A buzz might help him to stay cool—and as long as she considered him a philandering bastard, he might as well be an alcoholic too.

Leah reappeared just then. "Okay, it's all ready. Bring your drinks."

Patrick watched Fiona leave the room, feeling that the battle lines had been well and truly drawn. Still, what could she do, other than rant at him whenever she got the chance? He gulped his whiskey and followed her into the small kitchen–cum–dining room, steeling himself against the next hour or so.

———

Hannah heard the front door bang.

"Honey, I'm home."

In the act of pulling the top off a can of tuna, she grimaced. A second later Adam's head appeared around the door.

"Shit, I'm sorry—what an idiot."

She forced a smile. "Don't be silly. I saw that you'd moved in. You don't have to pussyfoot around me, I'm fine." She drained the fish and spooned it into the saucepan. "And welcome, by the way. Presume you figured out which bedroom's yours."

"I took a chance on the one that wasn't full of your stuff."

"And where's Kirby?"

"In the garden, getting acclimated." He came into the room and took a small package wrapped in white tissue from his pocket. "I went out to get you a moving-in present."

She laughed. "But you're the one who's moving in."

"You know what I mean." He pressed the package into her hand. "Or maybe it's your birthday present—I haven't decided."

"You're a twit." She opened the bag and peered in. "Ah, Adam—you didn't."

"I did." He watched her lifting out the perfume. "As you can see, it's not a scarf."

She hugged him. "Thanks a million, but there was no need. That stuff costs a bomb."

"Don't I know it. Happy birthday for tomorrow. Does it make up for me putting my foot in it just now?"

"Of course it does—I mean, you didn't." She stepped out of his arms and turned back to her saucepan. "I'm glad you're here, really I am."

She'd been doing her level best all day not to dwell on the fact that Adam was moving in while she was in the shop—because thinking about her new housemate would remind her, inevitably, of the one who'd gone before him.

But of course her efforts were futile. Memories of Patrick refused to leave her alone. Listening to the soft ticking of the wall clock, or restocking a shelf after a customer had left, or cradling her lunchtime mug of soup as she watched the parade of pedestrians outside, she found herself returning constantly to the day he'd come to live with her.

You've got more luggage than a movie star, she'd complained as his bags had piled up in the hall. *Where's all this stuff going to fit?*

Pretending that the evidence of his moving in wasn't filling her with delight. Letting on that this wasn't the most thrilling day of her life.

Come outside a minute, he'd said. *I want to show you something.*

And he'd scooped her up, making her gasp, as soon as she'd stepped outside the front door, and he'd carried her back in over the threshold.

I'm too heavy, she'd protested with a giggle, hoping they were being observed, *and I'm already living here.* Hoping that the word was going to fly around that Patrick Dunne, one of Clongarvin's most eligible bachelors, was setting up home with Hannah Robinson.

She'd given him the fish-shaped key ring that first day, and he'd joked about the phallic shape of it. She'd slapped his arm, unable to keep the foolishly happy smile from her face. They'd gone upstairs and consummated the new arrangement before dinner. Afterward she'd made omelets, beating eggs and chopping tomatoes, wearing his T-shirt that almost reached her knees and that smelled of him. Later they opened the champagne he'd brought and drank it by the fire, and consummated again.

"I think your dinner's burning." Adam's voice pulled her back.

She whisked the saucepan off the burner. "Get plates," she said. "It may not be edible, but there's enough for two."

No more of that. That was over. Now it was her and Adam.

———

"Isn't it wonderful about Adam moving in?"

"It certainly is." Stephen set his knife and fork side by side on his empty plate. "Hannah will be glad of the rent."

Geraldine threw him an exasperated glance. "I hate when you pretend not to understand. You know very well what I'm talking about. He and Hannah have always been so close."

Stephen smiled. "Geraldine, stop matchmaking. They're friends."

She spooned apple sponge into two bowls. "Yes, and who's to say that that can't change? They're both single—and they'll be spending a lot of time together now. You never know."

Stephen poured custard over his dessert. "All the same, if it hasn't happened up to this point..."

Geraldine made no response. They ate in silence for a few minutes.

"I'm just saying not to get your hopes up, that's all," Stephen said finally. "Someone will come along for Hannah when the time is right."

"And *I'm* just saying," Geraldine answered firmly, "that I won't rule it out, that's all."

"Fine."

"By the way, I'm going to drop in to the shop tomorrow, over my lunch break. Just to wish her a happy birthday."

Stephen looked at her in surprise. "I thought we were going to see her later."

"We are, but I'd love to give her the check, not leave her waiting till the evening—would you mind?"

"No, of course not."

Outside the kitchen window the garden was almost completely dark, the yellow rectangle of light from the room capturing two of the arms of the rotary clothesline in the middle distance. Neither of them liked drawing the blinds until dinner was over.

"She's doing marvelously with the shop," Geraldine said, spooning up the last of her custard. "I'm so proud of her."

"So far so good," Stephen agreed. "She's making a great effort."

"The poor thing must be worn out though—it's an awful lot for one person to take on."

"It is—but she's young, and she has plenty of energy."

"And of course, even with Adam helping out, she still has to watch every penny until she finds her feet." Geraldine gathered their bowls and brought them to the dishwasher. "That can't be easy."

Stephen filled the kettle and took the French press down from its shelf.

"So," she went on, putting milk and sugar on the table, "I thought she could do with a little something extra this year. You know, just to give her a lift while she's struggling."

Stephen scooped coffee. "What have you done?"

She turned and smiled at him. "I got her a pair of shoes—Alice gave me a great bargain. I knew you wouldn't mind."

Stephen laughed. "I don't suppose it would make much difference if I did." He took cups from the press and brought them to the table. "Just as long as Hannah supports us when we're bankrupt."

As he drew near, Geraldine reached across and kissed his cheek. "Of course she will, dear."

———

Every day she was learning more and making fewer mistakes.

Through trial and error she'd whittled down her original fifteen recipes to ten, ditching some, replacing others, substituting ingredients here and there, experimenting when she had the time.

The cinnamon-apple simply hadn't worked, the honey-sesame had morphed into ginger-sesame, the poppy seed–key lime had been a slow starter but now sold steadily—especially, for some peculiar reason, on Mondays.

She didn't dare open without a good supply of at least two chocolate varieties. She'd learned to bag the leftovers in threes rather than sixes, and she'd introduced a special-offer variety each day. Thanks to Adam, she'd discovered an American Web site that sold discounted cupcake paraphernalia—themed paper liners, toppings, decorations—and she'd opened an account with them.

And she very quickly realized that mopping the floor at ten to five was practically a guarantee that she'd have a flurry of last-minute customers.

She was constantly tired. She dragged herself out of bed at three o'clock each morning and baked and iced and decorated solidly till just after half past eight, when she loaded the yellow van and drove to the shop. She fell into bed each evening, somewhere between eight and nine o'clock, to sleep soundly until the alarm beeped her awake again.

And on Sundays she regularly slept till midday, sometimes even later—a phenomenon that hadn't occurred since she was fourteen.

She'd lost track of her TV programs. She hadn't checked her e-mail in ages. She couldn't remember the last time she'd opened a book; the only reading she did these days was a flick through the local paper in between customers, or a rummage in her cookbooks in search of new recipe ideas.

She'd forgotten what a social life was. In the month since Cupcakes on the Corner had opened she'd had the sum total of one night out, when Adam had finally persuaded her to visit the new wine bar with him a couple of weeks ago.

And while she'd enjoyed the buzz in Vintage—and the feeling that she was actually out for the evening—she relished even more her precious Saturday nights at home, when she could laze around the house or soak in the bath for as long as she wanted.

She had a few regular customers already. The secretary from the office block up the road who came in every Friday around eleven with the same order: "One coffee-cream, one vanilla-chocolate, three peanut butter, and four chocolate-coconut."

The young man in a gray suit who stopped in every other morning for two of whatever was on special offer. One of Hannah's old teachers, Mrs. O'Neill, who appeared every Saturday for a bag of leftovers for the three grandchildren who visited her each Sunday afternoon.

A young woman had come into the shop one day who looked familiar, but Hannah hadn't placed her until the woman had smiled and said, *Hey, I know you. You used to baby-sit me and my sister, Claire.* She was Una Connolly, and she worked three afternoons a week in Clongarvin's library, down the hill from Cupcakes on the Corner. She'd taken to dropping in with an order from the library at least once a week since then.

She told Hannah that Claire waitressed in the town's only Chinese restaurant. *She has a little boy,* Una had said. *Jason, he's four. We're all mad about him.*

And every week Hannah made some money. Not much left over once the bills had been paid, not half enough to justify all her slaving, but it was *her* money, from *her* efforts. After running her own business for a month she was actually solvent, which seemed like a minor miracle.

And today, the eleventh of February, was her thirty-third birthday, and her feelings about this particular date were mixed, to say the least.

There was the memory of last year, of course. Boarding the Aer Lingus flight to Paris, still unable to believe what Patrick had arranged. Sharing a bottle of red wine in a tiny late-night bar, eating thick slices of rustic bread topped with peppery salami and gloriously pungent cheese. Dipping the crusts into the bowl of buttery, garlicky juice in which Patrick's *moules* had been served.

Not mentioning that he'd packed the wrong shoes for her

burgundy dress and not nearly enough woolens for the sub-zero temperatures, not caring that the shower in their hotel's ensuite bathroom trickled tepidly. They'd huddled together under blankets that smelled of grass, and they'd listened to the ancient pipes clanking, and to a woman holding a one-sided shrill conversation somewhere nearby, and the faint horns and sirens and shouts in the street far below their two narrow, shuttered windows.

She blocked out the image of the Parisian bedroom—the flowers on the wallpaper had been blue!—and thought again about Adam sharing her house. Of all the people she could have picked to be her housemate, Adam would have been her unhesitating first choice.

The trouble was, she didn't want a housemate. She wanted to share her home, and her life, with a romantic partner, like most women her age. Instead she had her best friend and an overweight black Labrador.

Still, it was better than living alone, wasn't it? Eating a solitary dinner night after night, putting on the TV purely to drown the sound of your cutlery clinking as you speared a bit of sausage or scooped a mound of beans. Washing up your one plate, your single knife and fork.

Buying a toothbrush you didn't need, because one on its own sticking out of the tumbler on the bathroom shelf was far too pathetic. Switching on the radio just to hear someone else's voice as you cracked your umpteenth egg into flour, butter, and sugar—

The shop door opened, and she blinked the thoughts away. "Hi there—I wasn't expecting you."

Geraldine approached the counter. "I wanted to wish my only child a very happy birthday."

Hannah regarded her with amusement. "You rang this

morning, and you and Dad are coming around for tea later."

"I know, but Adam will be there, and I just wanted to see you on your own and give you this, from both of us." Geraldine reached into her basket and produced an envelope. "Happy birthday, love. It's a check, I'm afraid, but we thought it was probably what you needed most right now."

Hannah smiled as she took the envelope. "It certainly is—thanks a million."

"And here's a little something extra," Geraldine added, taking a box from the basket, "because I couldn't let money be your only present."

"Ah, you didn't." Hannah opened the box and looked in delight at the pink shoes. "Oh, Mam, they're gorgeous—you always know exactly what I like."

As she slipped off one of her black pumps, her mother spoke again. "So how's the new arrangement going with Adam?"

Hannah took a shoe from the box and bent to put it on. "Mam, he moved in yesterday."

"I know, but you'd have some idea."

"We'll get on fine, I'm sure. He's threatening to cook dinner every evening though." She stuck out her foot. "Look—a perfect fit."

Geraldine didn't even glance down. "He's going to have dinner ready for you when you get home? Isn't that very thoughtful. Not many men would do that."

Hannah hid a smile as she slipped on the second shoe. "I know—I'm really lucky. I should snap him up before someone else does."

Geraldine looked sternly at her daughter. "I can't imagine why you find the idea so amusing—"

She broke off as the shop door opened again, making the bell ping loudly. They both turned.

"Hello there."

A man came toward them, his eyes traveling from one woman to the other. Hannah thought he looked familiar but couldn't for the life of her think where she'd seen him. He held a sheaf of pages.

"I was just wondering if I could leave these on the counter."

His accent wasn't Irish. He held out a page, and Hannah took it and scanned it quickly.

"Carpenter available," she read. *"Custom-built kitchen and bedroom furniture. All jobs considered. Free estimates, recession-beating prices. Quality guaranteed."* And beneath, in smaller lettering, *"John Wyatt"* and a mobile-phone number.

"I'm trying to spread the word," he said. "Would you mind?"

"Of course not." She took the bundle from him and placed it on the counter. "Are you just starting out?"

He didn't seem young enough to be starting out. He was her age, easily, or a few years older. His hair was cut tight into his head, so short it was hard to determine its color. His chin was dotted with dark stubble. He reminded her of a PE teacher she'd had in school—Mr. Flaherty, was it, or Flannery? Maybe that was why she thought he looked familiar.

"I've not been long in this area, just a couple of months," he told her, "but I've been a woodworker for quite a while, about fifteen years." He switched his attention to the cupcake display. "Now, these are interesting—who's the baker?"

"My daughter here," Geraldine said immediately, smiling brightly at him. "Hannah. She makes the most wonderful gourmet cupcakes."

"Well," he said, studying the display, "in that case I shall take two of the..." He scanned the colored labels. "Vanilla-chocolate, please."

"That's a Scottish accent, is it?" Geraldine asked as Hannah pulled on a pair of plastic gloves and put his order into a box.

He nodded. "But my mother comes from Tipperary, so we spent a lot of time here as kids."

"And what's brought you to Clongarvin?" Geraldine didn't see, or chose to ignore, Hannah's frown.

He didn't seem to mind the interrogation. "Change of scene."

"You like it here?"

"I certainly do. Nice, friendly place."

Hannah was terrified that her mother was going ask if his wife liked it too. "Three-fifty, please," she told him quickly. "I hope you enjoy them—the vanilla-chocolate is one of my bestsellers."

"Thank you." He took the box and pocketed his change. "And I notice," he said, nodding at the empty shoe box, still sitting on the counter, "that you also sell footwear."

Geraldine laughed. "Actually, they're a birthday present. It's Hannah's big day today."

"Happy birthday"—he smiled—"and many more of them."

"Thanks," she replied, willing him to leave. She wouldn't put it past her mother to tell him precisely how old she was, and how she was available if he fancied taking her out.

"Good luck with the work," Geraldine said. "We'll do our best for you here."

"I do appreciate it." As he turned away, the rocking chair on the wall caught his eye. "Well, now, that's what I call an original design feature."

"It belonged to Hannah's grandfather," Geraldine told him. "He made it possible for her to set up this shop, so she thought it would be nice to remember him in some way."

"Good—I like a bit of family history." He studied the chair, nodding. "Lovely workmanship. And the color is very...eye-catching."

"Hannah has extremely good taste," Geraldine said. "She has a way with color—you should see her house."

"Mam," Hannah murmured, throwing him an apologetic look.

He was amused; he could see exactly what was going on. "Well, I'd best be off," he said, heading finally for the door. "Bye for now."

They watched him walk out. "What a nice man," Geraldine said. "And works with his hands—I like that."

Hannah folded the plastic gloves and laid them aside.

"I love the Scottish accent, don't you?" Geraldine said. "It's so soft."

Hannah replenished the supply of vanilla-chocolate cupcakes.

"I think he liked you. I mean, there was no need for him to hang around admiring that rocking chair."

Hannah slid the full tray back into place.

"I wonder if he's married," Geraldine said. "He wasn't wearing a ring, but maybe men don't in Scotland." She took a leaflet from the bundle. "Wyatt—does that sound Protestant to you?"

"I just love these shoes," Hannah said.

At least Adam's eligibility, for the time being, had been forgotten.

———

The best thing you could say about Clongarvin, Nora Paluzzi decided, was that it wasn't as cold as New York in February. On the other hand, it was a whole lot wetter. It hadn't stopped raining since she'd arrived, and thirty-six hours of nonstop driving rain were every bit as bad, in her opinion, as cold that cut right through to your bones.

But at least it wasn't Dunmallon, where her parents had dragged her and Adam every summer, back to the farm where her father had grown up. Dunmallon with its single petrol pump, sub–post office, pathetically stocked supermarket, and scatter of pubs, all equally dreary. God, what a hole, everyone knowing everyone else's business, or letting on they did. Everyone looked for you at Mass on Sunday, and woe betide you if you were missing without good reason. Ma and Da delighted to be back there now, God help them.

At least Clongarvin had some semblance of life about it, however parochial. The clothes in the few boutiques weren't bad, there was a halfway decent deli—although the prices had shocked her; had Ireland always been so horrendously expensive?—and the two-screen cinema (two whole screens!) was actually showing movies that she'd seen in New York just a few months ago.

Not that she intended to make Clongarvin her home for any length of time—perish the thought. But it would do while she caught her breath and planned her next move. And it might be fun to look up some of the old gang from school—Francine, Jojo, Leah, Dee. She assumed at least one or two were still living here.

She walked into Adam's tiny kitchen, which smelt of dog. The whole damn place smelt of dog—what had possessed him to get a huge Lab in this tiny apartment? She took the box of Cheerios from the shelf above the refrigerator—the fridge, the fridge—and shook out a handful. She shouldn't eat, with dinner at Hannah's just over an hour away, but her body clock was still all screwed up from the trip, so mealtimes were either forgotten or totally confused, and she was starving right now.

As she crunched, the calendar on the wall caught her eye. Valentine's Day coming up—big freaking deal. She was finished with love and romance: been there, done that, got the divorces to prove it.

Mind you, she was a damn sight better off now than before she'd met her exes, neither of whom could live with the knowledge that everyone fooled around in New York. Nora only wanted a bit of fun on the side; where was the harm in that? But the professor had run for the hills before the ink was dry on the marriage license, and Dr. Paluzzi couldn't hack it either, couldn't turn a blind eye, more fool him. At least she'd had the sense to marry men with lots of cash—and Nora had enjoyed her share from the first divorce, and was looking forward to the next.

She wondered about the men of Clongarvin. She wondered if she'd find what she wanted among them while she was here. Just because she was done with love didn't mean she was done with men—far from it.

She closed the Cheerios box and replaced it on the shelf. She left the kitchen and went into the doggy-smelling bedroom to make herself pretty for dinner.

———

"Does he look like you?"

Patrick shook his head. "Not in the least. He's shorter and balder, and his eyes are blue."

"And you said he's younger."

"Yeah, by three years."

Leah's hand rested on his thigh as he drove, her fingers stroking absently. He enjoyed how tactile she was—presumably from force of habit, since her job involved so much physical interaction.

"I'm dying to meet this brother of yours," she said. "The first of your family to check me out."

"That's right."

The surprise trip had been more awkward to arrange than last year's. Getting time off for Hannah had been easy—a phone call to Joseph Finnegan at the bakery, and it had been sorted. With Leah he'd had to plan his strategy more carefully.

The reason for his brother's imaginary visit home from London became a cousin's imaginary fortieth-birthday celebration in County Offaly the following day, Saturday, to which he and Leah had also been invited. "They want us there by lunchtime," Patrick had told her, "so you'll have to take the whole day off. I've booked us into the local hotel for the Saturday night."

"And what about Valentine's Day?" she'd demanded. "Am I spending that in Offaly too?"

He'd assured her that he'd made plans for Sunday. What she didn't know was that his plans were due to begin that very evening. He was assuming that the discovery that they were headed to Paris as opposed to Offaly would cancel out any annoyance Leah might feel at having been duped into thinking she was going to meet some of Patrick's family. She'd met none of them so far, since Patrick's father had left for his Greek Islands cruise just before Patrick and Leah had become an official couple, and now she wasn't meeting his brother either.

He hoped she'd be pleased with the hotel he'd found for

them on the Internet, which had better live up to its impressive description. No way could he risk ending up in a dump like last year's—Hannah might overlook faulty plumbing and erratic heating, but Leah liked her comforts. Patrick had paid considerably more this time around, and he expected to be well rewarded.

"What time did you say his plane is in?"

"Ten to eight."

Interesting how easily both women believed his lies. Hannah, of course, had had no reason to doubt him—until Leah, he'd covered his tracks well, been discreet on the few occasions he'd wandered. But Leah, who'd been party to his deceiving Hannah, who had seen him covering his tracks and telling his half-truths, still happily trusted him. Interesting how easy it was.

Interesting, too, how intoxicating deceit could be. Until Leah had managed to get pregnant and Patrick's cover had been forcibly blown, the excitement of having both women, each so different from the other, had been wonderful. Sex, regardless of whom he was with, had been amazing.

And if Leah hadn't gotten pregnant, who knew how long the situation might have gone on, despite her constant urging him to tell Hannah, to leave Hannah? *Soon,* he'd said, *when the time is right,* knowing, even as he spoke, that he was repeating the mantra of so many men—and indeed women—before him. Knowing that he would happily have lived with the situation long-term. What man wouldn't, for Christ's sake? And was it really so bad, trying to keep them both happy for as long as he could?

He couldn't believe it when Leah had dropped her bombshell. *I'm sorry, darling,* she'd whispered, clinging to him. *Don't be angry, it was nobody's fault.* Naturally, after that everything had changed, and Hannah, unfortunately, had suffered in the fallout—something Patrick had never intended to happen.

He couldn't imagine being a father. He'd never envied friends with children, never wondered when his turn would come. Hannah had hinted gently now and again—inevitable, maybe, when they were living together, and she'd been in her thirties by the time they'd become a couple—but Patrick had managed each time to postpone what he'd regarded as the inevitable. *Someday,* he'd said, *when we're both ready. When the time is right.*

He pulled in by the arrivals building. "Why don't you go in," he said, "and I'll find a parking space. Won't be long." Ignoring, as he spoke, the faint echo of his identical words a year ago.

He watched Leah walk toward the automatic doors. Her waist had begun to thicken—and didn't her hips seem slightly wider? She'd also started to develop the tiniest suggestion of a double chin, and her ankles weren't quite as slender as before. She was still beautiful, of course. He wondered what other changes were in store, what pregnancy would do to her body as the months went on.

He found a parking space and unloaded the case he'd packed the previous night while Leah was in the bath. The thought occurred to him as he made his way back to the arrivals building that maybe he should have chosen another destination: Leah might not be too pleased if she ever discovered that she was following so closely in Hannah's footsteps. But it had to be Paris for Valentine's Day, didn't it? Women expected Paris.

And technically, of course, Hannah's trip had been for her birthday rather than for Valentine's Day; it was just a happy coincidence that the two dates were so close together. But Leah might not see it like that.

The doors to the arrivals hall slid open, and he walked through. Too late to change anything now—and anyway, the past was in the past. He watched Leah's expression as he approached her, smiling.

"Tell you what," he said. "Let's go to Paris instead."

———————

"Another slice?"

Nora shook her head. "Not for me, thanks." One slice of decidedly unexciting shop-bought quiche was more than enough. Her brother seemed to be in charge of the cooking this evening, worse luck. She picked up an oven-baked french fry—talk about ruining a potato—and slid her glass toward Adam. "I'll have a top-up, though." Eighteen euro she'd paid for the wine, and it was just about drinkable. Eight dollars would get you a decent Chablis in New York.

Adam filled her glass. "So how're you settling in? Anything you can't find in the apartment?"

"Just the Jacuzzi," she told him. "And the pool. But I'm sure they're there somewhere."

He grinned. "You're not in Amerikay now. None of that posh rubbish in Clongarvin."

"Don't I know it." She smiled so they'd think she was joking. "I'd forgotten how much it rains here too."

"So what d'you think you'll do?" Hannah asked. "Are you moving back to Ireland?"

"Not sure yet," Nora replied. Better be diplomatic, since they both still lived here and presumably liked it. "I'm considering my options."

It still amused her, how her brother and Hannah Robinson had hung around together for as long as she could remember and had never, as far as she knew—and she was pretty sure she'd know—had any kind of a romantic fling with each other, never even a wham-bam-thank-you-ma'am night after a couple of drinks too many.

And now here was Adam, moving in with Hannah right after her big relationship bust-up. Was he secretly hoping to be her rebound guy? Had the thought of getting together really never occurred to either of them? Weird. Definitely weird.

And then there was the whole cupcake-shop business. It might work in New York—it *did* work in New York—but who opened a shop that sold nothing except cupcakes in a small Irish town in the middle of a serious recession? And Hannah baking everything herself, getting up in the middle of the night, according to Adam—was she nuts? Nobody could keep that up for long.

She and Hannah had never hung around together at school. For one thing, they were a year apart—but even if the two of them had sat beside each other for five solid years of secondary school, Nora was willing to bet that they'd hardly have known each other's last name at the end of it. They were programmed differently, your original chalk-and-cheese combo.

Nora wondered idly what Hannah's ex was like. She'd never met Patrick Dunne; their paths hadn't crossed before she'd left for the States. Adam had said something about his being involved with the local newspaper, but she knew nothing else about the man, apart from the fact that he'd apparently done the dirty on Hannah.

Of course, neither of their breakups, hers or Hannah's, had been mentioned over the quiche. Nora certainly didn't feel like talking about Jackson Paluzzi, and Hannah was probably just as anxious to put the newspaperman behind her.

Nora looked without appetite at the cheese selection Adam was putting on the table—insipid white cheddar, blue that wasn't half blue enough, Camembert that looked too firm to have been out of the fridge for very long—and thought with yearning of chunks of Monterey Jack scattered with toasted pecans, melting slices of Swiss draped over prosciutto, Neufchâtel spread thickly on a warm bagel, scamorza drizzled with olive oil and sprinkled with black pepper.

Hannah cut into the cheddar. "D'you see a big change in Clongarvin?"

Nora pretended to consider. "I suppose so . . . yeah, quite a few changes." Which, of course, was a lie—apart from the odd unfamiliar building and a scattering of boarded-up premises, the place was depressingly pretty much as she'd left it more than a decade ago. She remembered how impatient she'd felt then, how desperate she'd been to finish school and get on a plane—any plane—and leave behind the same old faces, the boringly familiar cafés and shops and narrow streets.

And now she'd had enough of small talk with her brother's friend. She emptied her glass and got to her feet. "Thanks a lot, you two—I guess my body clock is still screwed up. I'd better leave before I fall asleep on the table."

"No coffee?" Adam asked, and Nora, imagining the instant horror she'd probably be served, shook her head. "I'll pass, thanks."

"Drop by anytime," Hannah told her, "now that you know the way."

"Yeah, I might just do that." Both of them knowing quite well that she wouldn't be dropping by. How ridiculous were social conventions?

Adam walked her back to his apartment. The earlier rain had cleared, leaving the air damp and clean.

"I was thinking today, I must look up some of the old gang," Nora said as they skirted the puddles. "That's if they're still around."

"Like who?"

"Like Francine Kelly, or Jojo Fitzpatrick. Or Leah Bradshaw."

Adam shrugged. "Can't say I remember any of them."

Nora grinned. "If Francine heard you—she fancied you like mad for ages."

"Did she? You might have told me. Any idea what you want to do otherwise?"

"You mean a job?"

"I suppose I do."

She shrugged. "Don't really need one, bro—the advantages of alimony."

"I know, but don't you want something to keep you from being bored while you're here?"

"Yeah, maybe. Depends what's available, I suppose." In the States she'd worked behind the scenes in a radio station, and before that she'd divided her time between PR and various jobs with fashion magazines. She was adaptable, if not exactly qualified. "I get the impression work is fairly thin on the ground here right now."

"Depends what you're willing to do," Adam told her. "If you don't set your sights too high, you'll probably pick up something. Hannah was talking about taking on a part-timer in the shop."

"No thanks," Nora said swiftly. "Not my scene." She could think of few less appealing prospects than standing behind the counter in a cupcake shop. "I'd rather something a bit more...challenging." Glamorous was what she meant, but he'd probably laugh.

They reached the apartment block. Adam hugged her. "Night, sleep well."

"I intend to. Call me tomorrow." She turned toward the door.

"Hey," he said, "want to come out for a drink with me and Hannah on Sunday? Can't leave you all on your own on Valentine's night."

She considered. Any excuse to strut her stuff was better than none, even if they'd be surrounded by loving couples all night. "Yeah, sure—why not? Gimme a call."

"And do me a favor," he said.

"Yeah?"

"Lose the Yankee accent."

She laughed. "I'll do my best. See you." She turned the key in the lock and went inside, checking her watch and realizing that she was in time for *Grey's Anatomy*. Chances were she'd seen the episode before, but what the hell.

———

Hannah weighed flour and sugar and put them into the bowl of the stand mixer. Get as much done as you can the night before, ease the pressure when you stumble, half asleep, into the kitchen at three in the morning.

Once she woke up a bit though, once she got into the routine of mixing and chopping and stirring and icing, she had to admit that it wasn't so terrible being up when the rest of the country was asleep. There was something peaceful about moving around the warm kitchen, radio playing softly so Adam wouldn't hear it, surrounded by the scents of new sponge and vanilla and roasting nuts.

Not that she wouldn't choose to be tucked up in bed, given the option, of course, but someone had to produce the cupcakes for the shop—and until her fairy godmother appeared and waved a wand, that someone was going to be Hannah.

The front door opened and closed, and Adam put his head around the kitchen door. "I'm back—and I'm off upstairs. I have stuff to do for the morning, so see you when I see you."

"Okay. By the way, I should warn you that my mother has her heart set on you marrying me—now that we're living together and all."

He considered. "Well, I'd hate to disappoint Geraldine—we'll discuss it on Sunday night, when we're painting the town red."

Hannah shook her head. "I told you, count me out. I have work on Monday."

"We'll see. I can still have you home by ten." He vanished, and a few minutes later Hannah heard Neil Young's voice drifting faintly downward.

She opened the fridge and took out butter and eggs and left them on the worktop. She filled the cups of four muffin trays with pink paper liners decorated with red and white hearts. She refused to dwell on the fact that Sunday was Valentine's Day, and that whichever customers bought one or more of her special sweetheart cupcakes tomorrow (strawberry center, white chocolate icing, sugar-paste heart on top) would in all likelihood be spending Valentine's Day with someone they loved, and who loved them back.

She especially didn't think about last year's Valentine's Day or the man she'd spent it with, didn't torture herself thinking about how he might spend the day this year. She didn't dwell on the breakfast of warm croissants and *chocolat chaud* in bed last year, the film in the darkened French cinema that evening, the shared bath afterward. No, not for a second did any of that cross her mind.

And while she wasn't recalling any of that, Neil Young was telling her that only love could break her heart. What, he asked, if her world should fall apart?

She tipped what was left of Nora's wine into her glass and concentrated on how overly made-up Adam's sister had been, how bored she'd seemed all evening, how ridiculous her American accent had sounded. How relieved Hannah had been when she'd left.

Much safer to keep on thinking about Nora, as she assembled strawberries and chocolate chunks and little pink hearts in bowls on the counter.

And when she'd finally made all the preparations she could, she took off her apron and filled the kettle for her hot-water bottle. Then she went into the sitting room and sat on the floor beside Kirby, who was slumped in his usual spot beside the radiator, his head resting on his paws. She bent and put her arms around his warm neck and buried her face in his smooth black coat, and listened to the soft thump of his tail on the carpet.

"Quiet tonight," Adam said. "Thought you'd be busier on Valentine's Night."

The barman shook his head. "All the loving couples are out to dinner," he said. "Be in later, I'd say." He tilted his head in the direction of the musicians. "The band is here special tonight. Normally they only play Saturdays."

"Is that so? I hadn't noticed," Adam replied, pocketing his

change and turning his attention to the female musician. Her hair was completely hidden, swathed in some kind of black turban. Below it she wore a black turtleneck sweater and a pair of black tailored trousers over shiny black ankle boots. Her legs were thin, her knees pressed together. Her feet were slightly parted, toes turned inward.

She made eye contact with nobody, as far as Adam could see from where he sat, apart from the keyboard player, who stood more or less in her line of vision. She didn't smile between numbers. Occasionally she pushed her small, round glasses farther up her nose. During the livelier tunes, one of her feet tapped along sporadically. Her back was hunched a little. Now and again a frown creased the skin between her eyes.

She was his own age, or close enough. As far as he could make out, she wore no rings—did musicians take rings off before they played? Her fingers flew over the keys of her clarinet. The backs of her hands might be freckled—the pale tone of her skin suggested freckles—but from this distance, and in this light, it was hard to be sure.

Adam couldn't for the life of him figure out why she fascinated him. She didn't remotely resemble any of his previous girlfriends. There was nothing he could put a finger on, nothing charming about her. Nothing he could point to and say—

"Hey."

He turned to see Nora walking toward him. "There you are. What'll you have?"

"I might chance a vodka martini, if they can manage it." She glanced around. "No Hannah?"

Adam shook his head. "Couldn't persuade her. Work tomorrow—but I think it's really that she's still cut up about the ex."

Nora shrugged. "She needs to get back in the saddle—no point in moping around." She scanned the room. "Not a bad little place. About time Clongarvin got a wine bar. Let's grab a couch while we can." Her gaze fell on the musicians in the corner. "Get the secret agent with the clarinet," she said.

———————

Hannah lay back, closed her eyes, and breathed in the scented, steamy air. From the attic above her came the faint, comforting sound of water gurgling through pipes as the tank refilled. In her bedroom next door, Seal sang soulfully of love and loss. She lifted a hand languidly and watched its coat of bubbles sliding slowly from her skin.

This had become the new high point of her week, this hour or so of pampering she allowed herself on a Saturday or Sunday night. A bath as hot as she could bear it, piled with foam. A face mask, a hair-conditioning treatment. No phone, no book, the only light a soft, flickering glow from two fat, white candles that sat by the taps.

Thoughts drifted lazily into her head as she lay there—and annoyingly, despite her best efforts, a lot of those thoughts still concerned Patrick Dunne.

Almost six weeks after his departure, and the loneliness and regret hadn't gone away. But the pain was slowly dulling, her tears less frequent these days, and the world continued to turn. She hadn't laid eyes on him since that first encounter, the day she'd opened the shop—which was hardly surprising, given that most of her waking hours now were spent stuck behind the counter.

Business had been brisker than usual yesterday, and the sweetheart cupcakes had sold well. She'd thought of her profits and smiled determinedly at the customers, refusing to feel an ounce of self-pity, refusing to dwell on the fact that nobody would be buying her any kind of Valentine gift this year.

And now the bathwater was beginning to cool, so it was time to rinse off her masks, put on pajamas, and sit in front of the fire that Adam had lit earlier until her hair dried. She'd watch an episode of his box set of *The Office*, share a bag of Aged White Cheddar Kettle Chips with Kirby, and be in bed by half past nine—and probably asleep minutes later.

Not exactly the Valentine's night of her dreams, but not the worst in the world either.

———

Alice bundled the envelopes together and brought them into the kitchen. Two for Tom, the gas bill and a bank statement. Three for her—a Visa bill, a postcard from Sheila Barrett, home from the Canaries for the past week, and one with a catering-company logo in the top corner that she vaguely recognized.

She laid the envelopes on the table before fishing Tom's boiled egg out of the simmering water and setting it into one of the yellow pottery eggcups with chicken feet that Ellen had given them years ago as an anniversary present.

She put the butter dish into the microwave and cut two slices of brown bread. She dropped three tea bags into the teapot, waited for the kettle to click off, and made the tea. She took marmalade and milk from the fridge and went to the kitchen door and called "Tom?"

She sat at the table and turned the postcard over. *"Having a lovely time,"* Sheila had written. *"Very warm. Bit of a trek to the beach, so we're staying put by the pool. See you soon."*

The picture was of a platter of seafood on a blue-and-white-checked tablecloth.

She opened the envelope from the catering company. Its director turned out to be a woman she knew slightly from meetings of local businesswomen that took place each month, which Alice attended sporadically. She was invited to purchase tickets to a dinner-dance that was being organized to raise funds for a dialysis machine for Clongarvin's hospital. *"I'm sure you'll want to support this very worthy cause,"* the director had written, *"and if you can rally your friends, too, so much the better."* The event was scheduled for a date in late March and would be held in a local hotel. *"Sponsorship is generously being provided by various local businesses, which means that all proceeds on the night will go directly toward the cost of this vital machine."* The letter went on to mention a champagne reception before the meal and spot prizes throughout the evening.

A champagne reception—and no doubt plenty of sponsored wine with the dinner, and more alcohol available at the bar afterward. Alice heard Tom's footsteps on the stairs and pushed letter and envelope under the others.

"Morning, love," she said. He'd never been at his best in the first few hours of the day—that was nothing new.

"Morning." He sat and topped his egg. He didn't normally shave till after breakfast. She hated the stubble: it made his face look dirty.

"It's nice out today," she said. They had to chat a bit at the table; she couldn't sit there in silence, even if Tom's end of the conversation was mostly grunts. "The forecast says no rain, so I'm going to chance putting out the clothes before we head off."

She wouldn't say anything about the dinner-dance. She'd

have to support it—she'd buy two tickets and ask Geraldine if she and Stephen would go instead. She'd say Tom wasn't feeling his best, a bit run-down at the moment. She'd be quite happy to pay: She'd call it an early Easter present.

He eyed the saltcellar on her side of the table, and she passed it over to him. A bottle of wine every night, par for the course now. And more often than not, a gin and tonic before dinner for him too. The other evening when he'd gone to answer the phone, she'd taken a sip of the gin and tonic. It had been hard to taste the tonic.

And he snored every night—when had that started? He snored, and his breath was sour in the morning.

"You're not eating," he said, and she picked up her knife and began to butter her toast.

"Miles away," she said, smiling at him.

———————

You wouldn't call the trip a disaster, exactly, but it hadn't gone quite as Patrick had hoped. It had begun on the flight to Paris, when Leah's asthma had acted up slightly.

"Did you pack an inhaler?" she'd asked him, and of course he hadn't. It hadn't occurred to him, because she hadn't had an attack in months, not since shortly after they'd met. So their first hour in Paris had been spent finding an all-night pharmacy and trying to explain about the pregnancy and about the medication her doctor had recommended in the event of an attack. Hardly the most romantic of starts.

The hotel was a disappointment too. Farther from the city center than Patrick had understood and distinctly lacking in friendliness. They'd made the best of it, of course. They'd taken advantage of the large Jacuzzi bath, and they'd ordered breakfast in bed from the unsmiling concierge, and Leah had bought horrendously overpriced but wonderfully saucy underwear in the small, dangerous gift shop.

The weather was very cold, which he'd been expecting from the previous year. He'd packed plenty of woolens, and they made frequent stops for *chocolat chaud* during the day, but Leah still shivered violently after just a few minutes outdoors. Patrick made a mental note to go south for any future winter breaks.

The restaurant they picked for dinner on Valentine's night was unremarkable. Leah's pot-au-feu was fatty and Patrick counted three mussels in his bouillabaisse. The violinist who wandered among the tables stared openly at Leah's breasts as he played, making her uncomfortable. Patrick consoled himself with the thought that only he was aware of the silk-and-lace confections that lay underneath the black wool dress, and only he would have the pleasure of removing them later.

In the plane on the way home, her hand stole under his blanket, but for once her touch had no effect. "Never mind," she said, taking out her magazine, but Patrick did mind. He minded that he'd spent far too much on a mediocre few days. He minded that her mother despised him. He minded how terrifying he found the notion that in four months or so he'd be a father.

"I'm just tired," he told her, and closed his eyes.

"Hello again."

He wore a pale blue denim shirt under a rust-colored V-necked sweater. Hannah decided that the almost-shaved head suited him. His eyes were halfway between blue and green. She was glad her mother wasn't there to see him turn up again, to put two and two together and come up with eighteen.

"I called to say thank you," he said. "I got a phone call yesterday from someone who'd picked up one of my leaflets here."

"That's good. I've seen a few people taking them. Well, I'm glad to have been of assistance." She still thought she'd seen him somewhere else, and she still couldn't remember where.

"You certainly *were* of assistance. And while I'm here," he said, scanning the samples on the stand, "let me take some more of these delicious cupcakes off your hands."

"You mustn't feel obliged to keep buying them," she said. "Really, you don't have to." If her mother could hear her.

"Not at all. They're a lot cheaper than taking out an ad."

"I suppose they are." She liked the dimple in his left cheek when he smiled. "In that case, what can I get you?"

He selected three and watched as she arranged them in a box. "Do you really make them all yourself?"

"I certainly do, in the small hours. I have it down to a fine art."

"I'll say—you must have tons of energy."

She laughed. "More like gallons of coffee—and the knowledge that if I don't bake them, I'll have nothing to sell."

"Aye, that would do it." He took his wallet from his jeans pocket. "I see you don't have your trusty assistant with you today."

Hannah made a wry face. "My mother—sorry about that. You were lucky to escape alive."

He grinned. "Ah, no, she was fine."

"She doesn't work here. She has her own job. She just happened to drop in that day. But I am going to take on someone part-time, when I can get around to it." She handed him the box and took the bill he held out. "Whereabouts in Scotland are you from?"

"A wee island called Bute, off the west coast," he told her. "I daresay you'll not have heard of it."

"No."

She wondered what had brought him to Ireland. He'd mentioned that his mother was Irish—maybe he was simply exploring his roots. Or maybe he'd met an Irish girl in Scotland and followed her back here. She counted out his change. "Thanks a lot. Enjoy them, now."

"I will." He tucked his wallet away and put out his hand. "We've not been properly introduced. You know I'm John Wyatt, and I think your mum mentioned your name, but I'm afraid I've forgotten it."

"Hannah Robinson," she said. His hand was warm. "Nice to meet you."

When he'd gone, she checked the time. Ten past four—still most of an hour to go. She must get some music for the shop. Even a little radio would do to kill the awful silence between customers.

And she must definitely take on a part-timer. Now that Adam was sharing the house and helping out financially, she could manage to pay someone for a couple of hours, two or three mornings a week. The bliss of being able to walk out at ten and just sit somewhere with a coffee, or wander through the shops or down by the river. A chance to do nothing—that was all she wanted. And she thought she had found someone who might make a good assistant.

The shop door opened.

"I don't believe it," Hannah said. "I was just thinking about you."

Una Connolly smiled. "Were you really?"

"Good news," Geraldine said. "We're going to a dinner-dance."

"A dinner-dance?" Stephen eyed her over his glasses. "How exactly is that good news?"

"Well, for one thing it's to benefit a very worthy cause—a dialysis machine for the hospital."

"Which is good news for dialysis patients." He poured sauce over his chicken breast. "I'm waiting to hear how it's good for me."

Geraldine spooned cabbage onto their plates. "It's good because we got the tickets for free."

"I see. So we personally are not, in fact, helping to provide the hospital with a dialysis machine."

"Well, no—but that's beside the point. Have you enough mash?"

"Yes, thanks. So who's giving us this wonderful treat?"

"Don't be sarcastic. Alice bought the tickets. She got a letter about it and felt obliged to buy some, but apparently Tom isn't feeling up to it, so she asked if we'd go instead."

Stephen frowned. "Tom isn't feeling up to it? Since when?" He reached for the butter dish.

"I've already added butter to those potatoes. Well, that's what Alice told me. Apparently he's run-down. She's going to put him on a tonic."

"He didn't look run-down to me today. He hasn't been off sick for as long as I can remember. He's as healthy as I am."

"Well, that's what I thought too, but I didn't like to contradict her. Maybe he's just putting on a brave front." She sprinkled black pepper on her chicken.

"Maybe he just doesn't want to go, more like it. When's it on?"

"Not for ages, the end of March. The last Thursday, I think." She refilled their water glasses. "I'll drop your dinner jacket into the cleaner's tomorrow." She set down the jug. "Stephen, don't say anything to Tom—there might be another reason that Alice isn't telling me."

"Like what?"

"I don't know—maybe they're going through a bad patch or something. I just think it might be better if you said nothing."

Stephen sighed heavily and added a wedge of butter to his mash, and Geraldine decided that it might be wise to let it pass.

———————

"PA required," Nora read. *"Experienced, flexible, highly organized & efficient individual with an excellent attitude toward work and the ability to adapt and function under pressure."*

Nothing about qualifications. Nora read on.

"Responsibilities will include diary management, compiling PowerPoint presentations, organizing travel, accommodation, and meetings, and providing PA support at senior management level."

Piece of cake—apart from the PowerPoint presentations, which Adam could coach her in. She skimmed down to *"Professional Qualifications"* and read *"Leaving Cert"* and *"Secretarial Qualification."* Was that it? She had the Leaving Cert, and the secretarial qualification could be arranged with a phone call to Sonia at one of the fashion magazines. A letter on headed paper from New York would surely do the trick with the hicks of Clongarvin.

No mention of what kind of company it was, not that it

bothered her. Not when she was doing this purely for laughs, when she could leave anytime she felt like it. She'd apply to the box number, see what happened.

"Here we go."

The taxi driver pulled up to the curb. Nora folded the newspaper and looked in amusement at the lavender walls, the pink window boxes filled with the little vividly colored flowers—something beginning with *c*, she thought—that everyone seemed to grow in Ireland in February. "Indulgence," the ornate gold letters over the window spelled. Pure Leah Bradshaw, as girly as ever.

"How much?" He mightn't be bad without that horrendous woolly hat. Probably hiding a bald patch. Sexy green eyes, though, and decent-enough teeth.

"Four-thirty, thanks."

Nora pulled out a note and checked that it was a fiver. "Keep the change."

"Thanks a lot."

Nice music too—she was partial to a bit of Miles Davis. But of course a taxi driver didn't interest her. She stood on the path and rang the bell outside the salon, smoothing her leather jacket as she waited.

"Surprise," she said when the door was opened.

Leah's eyes widened. "Nora O'Connor? Is that you?" She stepped forward and put her cheek against Nora's. "Bloody hell, you look fantastic. It's been years."

"I'm here for a massage," Nora told her. "I booked under the name Jackie Collins."

Leah laughed. "That was you? I should have known." She stepped back into the hallway and held the door open. "Come in. How did you find me?"

Nora walked past her, taking in the deep blue carpet, the

white reception desk, the framed certificate on the wall behind. "You're kidding, aren't you? This is Clongarvin."

Leah Bradshaw had put on weight. Her face was heavier.
Hard to see her figure with the loose, flowery thing she wore,
but her ankles had thickened too. Maybe she had kids now.
No ring on the wedding finger though.

"Come on." Leah walked ahead of Nora down the narrow
corridor that led off the hall. "We have lots to catch up on."

"We certainly do."

Nora was led into a small treatment room that contained
a massage table, a cart piled with various bottles and pots, a
sound system on a shelf, and a single chair. "You can strip
down to panties and lie under the towel," Leah said. "I'll be
right back."

"Hey, no need to disappear—I'm not shy." Nora unbuttoned her jacket and slipped out of it. The room was warm
and scented. Some elevator music wafted softly through the
speakers. "Nothing under here that you haven't seen plenty of
times."

She was aware of her still-youthful body as she undressed—and well aware, as she listened to Leah's voice, while
she laid her clothes on the spindly-legged turquoise chair and
unhooked her Agent Provocateur bra, that her school friend
was checking out the full breasts, the flat stomach, the firm
thighs.

Jackson Paluzzi's obsession with his wife's figure—he'd
happily paid for the personal trainer, the yoga and Pilates
classes, the regular spa treatments—had served some purpose.
And his first-anniversary present of a boob job hadn't hurt either.

"Right, let me have it." She swung her legs onto the massage table and rolled onto her stomach, knowing that her

thong made it quite clear that Nora Paluzzi didn't have an ounce of cellulite. "I like it good and deep—as the actress said to the bishop."

She closed her eyes and prepared for an hour of gossip and pampering.

"What's today's special offer?"

"Red velvet—it's a basic chocolate mix with red coloring and a classic cream-cheese topping. It's one of our most popular varieties."

In between customers she found her thoughts straying to John Wyatt. His accent was very attractive; all those soft, rolling *r*'s made the Clongarvin dialect sound very flat in comparison.

"Have you any chocolate-coconut today?"

"Sorry—they're all gone. What about orange-coconut?"

She refilled the shelf and rubbed at a mark on the glass counter. She'd never been to Scotland. Her parents had honeymooned there, and Geraldine's abiding memory was that it had rained solidly for five out of the seven days.

"I'll take two of the strawberry and one peanut butter, please."

She stirred her lunchtime soup, minestrone today. She didn't think he had a wife. It felt like he had an interest in her—you always knew when someone had. She wondered if he was planning to ask her out and hoped he wouldn't. It was much too soon, after Patrick.

"My husband goes mad for your ginger-sesame—he kills me if I bring home anything else."

She switched channels on the little radio she'd bought and

found something that wasn't sports. Yes, definitely much too soon.

"A chocolate-vanilla, please—oh, and a double chocolate, too."

"Any lemon left?"

At ten to five, she began to mop the floor. Pity, though. It would have been nice.

––––––––––

John Wyatt took his saxophone from its case and thought about the treacle-haired woman behind the counter of the shop that sold nothing but cupcakes. "Hannah." He said the name out loud, liking the soft roundness of it. It suited her.

The lie about his sweet tooth was forgivable. How else was he going to get to know her? She was never at Vintage on Saturday nights, or anywhere else he'd been to. And Patsy at the woodworking store was delighted to take the cupcakes off his hands, so he was making someone happy, which surely canceled out the lie.

He was lonely, and it had been quite a while. The only ring Hannah Robinson wore was on the middle finger of her right hand. Enough grounds for asking her out? Maybe he should bide his time, get to know her a bit more.

Or maybe he should go for it, take a chance. Not much to lose if she turned him down. A minor embarrassment, a small disappointment. Easy enough not to put himself in the way of meeting her again.

He opened the sheet music and began to play around with "Penny Lane" for Saturday night.

––––––––––

Hannah turned the key again and pumped the accelerator. The little yellow van shuddered, coughed, and went silent. She groaned and leaned her head against the steering wheel. This was all she needed after a slow day, with a thumping headache and a big wash on the line that Adam had probably forgotten to take in when the rain that had been threatening since noon had finally arrived at four o'clock, the only time she'd been too busy with customers to phone him.

It was still lashing now, but at least the thunder and lightning had stopped. She'd always been terrified of lightning; it had taken all her resolve not to put the Closed sign on the shop door and hide in the back until it passed. And now the van had broken down, and who knew how much it would cost to get fixed?

She pulled out the keys and grabbed her satchel and umbrella and stepped into the rain. She'd hail a taxi and go home. In this rain, and with her busy schedule, waiting for a bus wasn't an option—and anyway, the trays were too awkward to manage on the bus. Her shoes were completely sodden by the time a taxi pulled up. She closed her umbrella and opened the door.

"Can you come around the corner? I have to get some trays from my van."

"Sure—hop in and I'll drive you."

"Thanks."

He helped her shift the wooden trays from the van to the back of the taxi. Hannah gave her address and sank gratefully into the passenger seat, closing her eyes. A hot bath when she got home, even if she couldn't spare more than ten minutes in it. Hopefully Adam would have dinner waiting. And a couple of aspirin might get rid of this damn headache.

She opened her eyes and fished her phone from her bag, and called Adam.

"The van broke down," she told him. "Will you call your friend?"

"Do you need me to come and get you?"

"No thanks, I'm in a taxi. I'll be home in a few minutes."

As she hung up, she caught the driver's eye. "Sod's law," she said, smiling bleakly.

"Bummer," he agreed.

The music was pleasant, something mellow and jazzy. She was dangerously close to nodding off in the warm car. He wasn't wearing the woolly hat today, but she was pretty sure it was him.

She remembered him driving her to the restaurant the night Patrick had broken up with her, then home again later that evening, with her parents in the car. And hadn't she seen him since somewhere? . . . Yes, getting into his taxi in the su-permarket's car park. She hadn't recognized him that day, but now she was sure it had been him.

His hair was muddy blond and curled around the edge of his collar. His left hand rested on the gearshift as he negoti-ated Clongarvin's rush-hour traffic. He wore a green pullover. She couldn't be sure without looking directly at him, but she thought his eyes were green too.

He caught her glance. "Thought you were asleep."

"Nearly. I've been on my feet since three this morning." Yes, definitely green.

He grinned. "In that case, feel free—I'll wake you when we get there."

Nice even teeth. She turned to the window and noticed that the rain had finally stopped and been replaced by a pale lemon sun that was doing its best to shine.

March

Did you know that Leah is the woman Hannah's ex left her for?"

Adam poured boiling water into the mugs. "I wasn't sure of the name, but I had heard, yes."

"Does Hannah know?"

"Yes. She's the one who told me." He handed her a mug. "Nora, it's in the past—leave it alone. Hannah's moved on." He offered her a biscuit but she waved the packet away. "She's doing fine now."

She sipped her coffee and grimaced. "What's the deal with you two anyway?" she asked. "You and Hannah, how come you never got together?"

Adam bit into his custard cream. "You're such a drama queen. You know quite well that Hannah and I are just friends. It is possible, believe it or not."

"Right." She tapped a nail against the side of her mug. "Do you remember Leah?"

"Not really. She was one of the princesses you hung around with, that's all I know."

"Leah was the small dark one. She's the small blond one now."

Adam shook his head. "Nope, nothing. Did she fancy me too?"

Nora laughed. "Oh, no, Leah was immune to your charms. She went for the studs."

"Thanks."

Hannah had told him about dropping in to Leah's salon and getting the gift voucher for Patrick. *I probably brought them together,* she'd said, trying to smile. *Isn't that a good one?*

"I got a massage from her the other day," Nora said. "Wasn't the best I've ever had, but it wasn't bad."

"You don't say."

"Stop looking like that. I didn't know about Hannah till Leah said it—how could I, when you tell me nothing? And anyway, like you say, it's all in the past and nothing to do with me."

"Yeah . . . so you two had a good gossip?"

"Of course we did. I had to find out what everyone else was doing. Get this—Jojo married a widower with six kids."

Adam took another biscuit. "Fascinating. I just can't believe it. Good old Jojo."

"Shut up." Nora pulled an envelope out of her bag. "Here's the real reason I came round—have a look at what I got in the post this morning."

Adam took the envelope. "What is it?"

"Read it."

He pulled out the single sheet and scanned it. He looked back at Nora. "You're joking."

She giggled. "Isn't it a scream? Talk about a small world, even for Clongarvin."

He stared at her. "You're not going to go?"

She took back the letter and folded it. "Of course I'm going to go. The first job I apply for and I'm called for an interview—you should be pleased. And why the heck shouldn't I go?"

"Because you'd be working for him."

"So? Just because he did the dirty on Hannah, who I hardly know, I'm not allowed to work for him?"

Adam frowned. "Well, no, but—"

"Look," Nora said, "I might not even get the job. But if I do...well, like you keep telling me, Hannah's moved on, right?"

"Have you told Leah about this?"

Nora paused. "No. Why should I? She said nothing when I told her I was looking for work, although she must have known that lover boy was in the market for a PA. Anyway, she'll find out soon enough if I get the job."

"Jesus." Adam lifted his mug. "I'll never figure women out."

He wouldn't mention it to Hannah; it might come to nothing. On the other hand, if Patrick Dunne decided to take Nora on as his PA, it might be awkward explaining to Hannah why he'd kept quiet about his sister's applying for the job. He sighed.

"Don't worry, bro," Nora said, "I didn't tell you anything, okay? Wouldn't want you getting into trouble with Hannah. You know nothing about this job interview. Right?"

Adam nodded slowly. "Right."

He might never figure her out, but his sister had him completely sussed.

———————

As Geraldine slid the grill pan toward her and lifted the lamb cutlets onto the warmed plates, she heard her husband's key in the lock. After thirty-five years of marriage, their timing was impeccable. "Yoo-hoo," she called, and a second later

Stephen's head appeared. "Just in time," she said. "I'm dishing up."

"Smells good. Won't be long."

He thumped up the stairs while she uncorked the red wine that they'd opened the night before and emptied what was left into the two glasses on the table. She drained the broccoli and transferred the potatoes from the steamer to a bowl. She turned the oven down to low so the apple crumble would keep warm.

She knew exactly the kind of meal Stephen would serve up if their working hours were reversed and he was the one who got home earlier. On the very few occasions he'd cooked dinner in the past, he'd taken several hours and used more saucepans than she'd thought they possessed. He wasn't a bad cook—the end results were generally very palatable—but for the time and effort involved, Geraldine could have cooked for the week. Just as well she was always home ahead of him.

"Guess what," she said when they were sitting opposite each other, he having splashed his face and exchanged his work shirt and shoes for sweatshirt and slippers. "Alice and Tom are coming to that dinner-dance after all."

"I know," he said. "Miraculous recovery."

"Tom mentioned it to you?"

"He asked if we wanted to go. I told him we already had tickets."

Geraldine looked sharply at him. "You didn't say Alice gave them to us, did you?"

"No—I said as far as I knew, you'd got them from someone who'd bought them and couldn't go."

"Good."

Alice had been strange, that was the only word for it. *You won't believe this,* she'd said to Geraldine, *but Tom was asked to buy tickets to that dinner-dance by one of his patients, so it looks like we're going along after all.*

There'd been an expression on Alice's face that Geraldine couldn't put a name to, a smile that wasn't a smile, and she didn't meet Geraldine's eye as she spoke.

Of course, Geraldine hadn't asked how Tom was feeling—clearly that story hadn't been true. Just as well she'd told Stephen to say nothing to Tom at the dental clinic. There was something going on between Alice and her husband, but whatever it was, Alice wasn't saying.

Geraldine had offered to pay for her and Stephen's tickets, but Alice had firmly refused. *They're a present,* she'd said. *I won't hear of it.* So now they were all going, the four of them.

They hadn't often gone out together in the past, even though she and Alice got on fine in the shop, and Tom and Stephen would go for a drink after work every now and again. For whatever reason, they rarely went out as a foursome.

Alice and Tom were older than Stephen and Geraldine—at almost sixty, Alice was around seven years older than Geraldine, and Tom's sixtieth had already come and gone—but that in itself wouldn't have stopped them from meeting up socially. Maybe it was the fact that they worked side by side every day.

We can share a taxi, Geraldine had suggested, and Alice had agreed. So on the last Thursday in March, they were all dressing up and heading off to the Dunmurray Arms Hotel for a night out that probably none of them wanted.

Stephen hated having to wear his dinner jacket and eat much later than they normally did, and he danced only when it was completely unavoidable. Geraldine would miss *Dexter,* and she didn't fancy having to get up for work after a late night. And Alice and Tom had whatever was going on be-

tween them, so they were probably looking forward to it with
even less enthusiasm.

But it was for a good cause, so that was that.

And who knew? They might even enjoy it. Geraldine had
that navy dress she'd worn only once, to Aoife's cocktail party
last autumn. Hopefully, she'd still fit into it, with everything
else feeling a little snug these days. She'd cut out all treats till
the dinner-dance—Lent was next week anyway—and maybe
desserts too.

"I saw that Leah Bradshaw today," she told Stephen. "She
walked past the shop, all done up."

Fiona Bradshaw was still avoiding her at bridge, and Geraldine was pretending not to notice. All a bit awkward, really,
but she had no intention of giving up her weekly game, and it
wasn't as if she and Fiona had ever been close in the past.

"I phoned Hannah at lunchtime," she said, "to see how
Una's first day went."

"Oh, yes?"

"She did fine, apparently. Hannah will stay in the shop
with her this week while she learns the ropes, and then she'll
let her off on her own after that."

"Good."

Geraldine vaguely remembered the Connolly girls, for
whom Hannah had baby-sat in her teens. The parents still
lived across the park in Larch Crescent, although the father
rarely left the house—Parkinson's or MS, he had—and the
mother was a bit odd, would say hello to you one day and ignore you the next.

Claire, the older girl, had had a baby a few years back. Geraldine recalled the minor scandal it had caused, remembered
seeing Claire and a boy—the father, she presumed—pushing a
pram, both looking like children themselves.

But Claire was always pleasant, would smile at you when she passed, not like her mother. And Una, the younger sister, was a nice little thing too. Hannah seemed happy with her choice of assistant.

"It'll be great for her to have a bit of time to herself," Geraldine said. "Take some of the pressure off her."

"Certainly will. Did she mention the van, how it's running now?"

"I forgot to ask. She would have said if it was still acting up."

"Hope it wasn't a bad buy."

They'd gotten it cheap from one of Stephen's patients, who had a small garage out in the country. Patrick had organized the spray-painting, and the fitting of the wooden brackets in the back to hold Hannah's trays in place.

They ate apple crumble—Geraldine allowed herself a small portion, now that it was made—and in due course the dishes were washed up, the fire lit, and the television switched on. Stephen played Scrabble against a virtual opponent on the computer, and the evening passed in the same way that most of their evenings did.

And when she went upstairs, Geraldine slipped the navy dress out of the dry cleaner's plastic sleeve and tried it on in the bathroom, and decided that desserts were definitely out for at least the next three weeks.

———

Hannah sprinkled blue cheese onto her tomato soup. "I can't believe I'm actually someone's boss."

Adam took a chunk of bread from the basket. "I wanted to warm this, but I didn't know how."

"Wrap it in tinfoil and put it in the oven. Did you hear what I said?"

"About what?"

She slapped his wrist. "Pay attention. About my having an assistant. About me being the boss."

Una had arrived ten minutes early. Hannah had explained how to record sales in the hard-backed notebook by the cash drawer—*just put a tick in the appropriate column*—and shown her where the gloves were kept—*don't forget to take them off before you handle any money*—and provided a list of the main ingredients of each variety, in case anyone asked—*and make sure you mention when you're selling anything with nuts in it.*

Una had listened and nodded, and swept the floor without being asked, and insisted on making tea when Hannah mentioned that she usually had a cup around eleven.

That's what I'm here for, she'd said. *The assistant always makes the tea.*

Adam dunked bread into his soup. "So you think you chose well?"

"I do—she'll be fine."

"And the soup?" he asked. "You think I did okay? Not too chunky?"

She grinned. "You did very well, dear. Maybe your best meal so far."

They were getting more like a married couple every day.

"Nora O'Connor is back in town."

It was something to say, another sentence to cut through the disapproving silence that rushed to fill any gap in their lunchtime conversation these days.

"Who's Nora O'Connor?" Fiona wasn't happy with her tagliatelle today—too much sauce—which didn't help.

"You remember Nora, we hung around together at school. She was often in the house. She went to the States straight after doing the Leaving. She hasn't been back since—or rather, she's been back the odd time just to visit her parents...You don't remember her?"

"Can't say I do. So she's home for good?"

"She's not sure. Her marriage just broke up." As soon as the words were out, Leah regretted them. "She's thinking of staying in Clongarvin for a while," she added hurriedly. "She's looking for a job. I said I'd keep an eye out."

Leah hadn't told Nora that Patrick was looking for a PA. She had instinctively kept quiet about it. Nora O'Connor had looked after herself in America. Her skin was clear, her body toned and smooth. Leah, remembering Nora's teenage single-mindedness when it came to getting a boyfriend, had decided there was no point in inviting trouble.

Not that she didn't have complete trust in Patrick—those people who said that if a man is unfaithful once he'll do it again didn't have a clue what they were talking about. *You're the one,* he'd told her. *You're my soul mate. I need you like I need food.* It wasn't Patrick she didn't trust, it was Nora O'Connor.

Fiona pushed her half-eaten lunch aside. "Your face is puffy," she said to her daughter. "It'll get worse. I went the same way on you."

"My ankles are swollen too," Leah said, grateful that her mother was at least acknowledging the pregnancy. "And I'm getting heartburn a lot."

And I've gone up a bra size, and I can't close the zip on my jeans, and for the past fortnight I haven't been able to keep my hands off Patrick, she thought. *And my breasts have become incredibly sensitive—he has only to look at them.* Leah felt a ribbon of desire flutter through her and took a hasty mouthful of lasagna. Not the time, not the place—and certainly not the company—for such confidences.

"What's going to happen to the salon when you have to stop working?" Fiona asked abruptly.

"I'll get someone to keep it ticking over until I can go back," Leah answered. "Just for a month or so."

"Can you afford to pay someone?"

"Oh, yes," Leah said. "Part-time anyway."

Preferably someone who'd work for peanuts and not lose all of Leah's remaining customers. The salon hadn't been doing much more than ticking over for some time now, but there was no need to admit that here.

"And who'll look after the baby when you go back?"

Leah decided that a joke about Fiona's taking on the role of child minder wouldn't go down too well. "We'll find someone," she said. "There are plenty of young girls who'd welcome the job, I'm sure. And I'll just be downstairs."

Fiona raised her hand, and immediately a waiter appeared. Leah's mother had always been good at attracting the attention of waitstaff. "I'll take an espresso," she told the waiter. "And kindly let the chef know that my tagliatelle had far too much sauce."

The waiter took her plate, murmuring apologetically and glancing at Leah.

"Nothing more for me, thanks," she told him, laying down her fork. She and Patrick often ate here when neither of them felt like cooking in the evening. The food was good and not too pricey, the chef first-generation Italian. You'd think Fiona would have kept her mouth shut, allowed them one little slipup.

"Seen any good films lately?" Leah asked. "Any new books?" Stick to the safe topics, avoid the personal.

Fiona shrugged. "A couple of interesting Booker nominations," she said. "I'll pass them on. Nothing worth mentioning at the cinema—I lasted twenty minutes at the one that got the Oscar for best director. Can't imagine why, complete rubbish."

She didn't acknowledge the waiter as he put her coffee in front of her. "So," she said, dropping a sugar lump into the tiny cup, "have you any plans to marry this man?" Looking impassively at Leah, as if she'd asked her for the time.

The heady smell of the coffee wafted toward Leah. She resisted an impulse to fan it away as she searched for the least incendiary answer. "We're taking things slowly," she said eventually. "One step at a time." Under the table she crossed her swollen ankles.

"Slowly?" Fiona's eyebrows raised. "You weren't with him a wet week when you got pregnant."

"You know very well," Leah said tightly, "that we didn't mean it to happen." She pressed her feet together. "And I'd hardly call ten months a wet week," she added—and immediately realized her mistake.

Fiona frowned. "Ten months? You told me you met him in October."

Leah forced herself not to look away. "We met last May, actually. I didn't feel it was something you needed to know."

"So you lied to me. I see." Her mother sipped coffee. "Your little affair was going on for—what?—eight months or thereabouts. You were the mistress all that time, with him going home to Hannah Robinson every night." She dabbed her mouth. "No wonder you were so evasive anytime I asked if you'd met anyone new."

"I *couldn't* say anything. How could I?" Leah asked angrily. "It's not exactly something you share with your mother."

She wished she'd ordered green tea—the pasta was sitting uncomfortably in her stomach—but it was too late now. All she wanted was to leave.

"I wonder how long it would have taken him to finish with her if you hadn't got pregnant," Fiona said then in the same bland voice, her eyes on Leah's swollen, blotchy face.

Leah scanned the room for their waiter and of course didn't find him. "I need to get back," she said, her voice quivering. She rummaged in her bag.

"There's no need for you to be like that," Fiona said. "I know I sound unsympathetic—"

"You sound bitchy." Leah found her purse and pulled it out. She'd just called her mother a bitch. Her fingers shook as they fumbled with the clasp.

"I'm only telling it like it is." Fiona reached across the table and grasped Leah's hand. "How do you know he'd ever have left her? How do you know he wasn't just stringing you along, saying what you wanted to hear?"

"He *loves* me," Leah said angrily. A couple of heads at the nearest table swung in their direction. "We love each other," she said more quietly, pulling her hand from her mother's grip. "He left Hannah, he's with me now, and we're having your first grandchild, whether you like it or not. Nothing you can say will change that."

She pulled a twenty-euro note from her purse, but Fiona waved it away impatiently. "I'll pay—you paid last time. I'm only looking out for you. I'm only trying to make you see—"

But Leah was gone, hurrying past the tables toward the door, the money fluttering onto the white tablecloth.

Fiona watched her only child rushing away from her. Then

she lifted her cup and calmly finished her espresso, oblivious to the furtive glances from adjoining tables.

"Remember to take off the gloves when you're handling money. Maybe I mentioned that already...Did I show you where the spares are in the back?"

Una nodded. "You did, yeah."

"Not that you'll need them, but just for future reference. Oh, and if anyone looks for the apple-cinnamon, make sure you tell them that they're made with organic apples."

"Okay."

"And don't forget to mention the nuts if anyone goes for the chocolate–peanut butter or the coffee-pecan. I know it's on the sign, but I always say it, too, just to be on the safe side."

"Yes."

"And will you make a note if anyone looks for a variety that's not here? Tell them we rotate the stock but that you'll let the baker know what they were asking for."

"Okay." Una smiled.

Hannah stopped. "Am I fussing too much?"

"No, you're just making sure I get it right—but you've already used up ten minutes out of your two hours."

"Right, I'm off." Hannah walked toward the door. "You have my mobile number."

"I have."

"Don't be afraid to use it for any reason—I won't be far."

"Okay. See you later."

Ridiculous how reluctant she was to leave Cupcakes on the Corner in anyone else's hands. Una was well able, and she had a lovely manner with the customers—after just a few days she was as confident as Hannah behind the counter. What was the worst that could happen?

And as if waiting for its cue, her imagination instantly supplied all the options. An armed robbery, someone who'd taken note of the cash drawer and come back to help himself. Someone who might be watching the shop right now and seeing a young girl left in charge.

Or a fire in the launderette next door—how ancient were those machines? Imagine the state of the wiring, a disaster waiting to happen, if ever there was one.

Or a burst pipe, water cascading down the walls, ceiling collapsing—

With a major effort of will, she kept walking in the direction of the coffee shop where she'd arranged to meet Adam. She pushed the door open, and there he was.

"Welcome to the world." His cup was half empty.

"Sorry, I know I'm late." Hannah perched on a chair opposite him. "I shouldn't be here."

He laughed. "Let me guess. You're feeling guilty for deserting your ship. For leaving your baby with a stranger."

"Don't make fun—what if something goes wrong? What if there's a . . . a burst pipe or something?"

"A burst pipe—Jesus wept. You should bottle your imagination and sell it along with the cupcakes."

"Well, a robbery, then."

"A robbery is always possible, I suppose. But let's assume, just for fun, that it's not going to happen today." He turned to the waitress who had appeared. "A large brandy for my friend here please, and a couple of horse tranquilizers."

"Very funny. This is my livelihood I've just left a twenty-year-old in charge of. Just a pot of tea, please," she added to the waitress.

"You said Una was well able," Adam pointed out. "You were singing her praises the other night."

"She is well able—when I'm standing beside her."

"And how will she be less able when you're not there? She can still put cupcakes in a box and tote up the bill, can't she?"

"Yeah, I know..." Hannah unbuttoned her jacket slowly.

"She can still take money and make change."

"I know, I know. You're right."

"And I assume she has your number in case anything does come up."

"Yes, of course she has. Everything's under control." She took off the jacket and laid it on the chair beside her. "Any chance of a packet of Kettle Chips with that tea?" Since she'd become the proprietor of a shop that sold nothing but confectionery, Hannah had developed a craving for all things savory.

As Adam walked toward the counter, she took her phone out of her bag, checked again that it was on and charged up, and set it beside her on the table.

Just in case.

———————

"Now, Geraldine," Maureen Hardiman said, lowering her voice and leaning in, "there's something I think you should know, and I'd rather you heard it from me."

Geraldine's heart sank. Bridge was over for the night, and they'd been shepherded into Aoife's kitchen for tea and nibbles—Aoife didn't like getting crumbs on the Axminster. Maureen had made a beeline for Geraldine as soon as she'd walked in, which was never good. Geraldine armed herself with a chocolate macaroon from a nearby plate, stifling the inner voice that reminded her of the navy dress. "What is it?"

No point in saying she'd rather not know—with Maureen that was never an option. And anyway, she *did* want to know, whatever it was.

"Well, of course," Maureen went on, brushing imaginary flecks from her green cardigan, "it shouldn't make much difference really. I mean, things have moved on, haven't they?"

Geraldine noted with satisfaction that the broken veins scattered across Maureen's cheeks were especially vivid in the fluorescent light of Aoife's kitchen. "What is it?" she asked again, staring pointedly at Maureen's roots, which were overdue for a touch-up by at least a fortnight.

"It's just," Maureen said, patting her hair and glancing around at the little knots of women, "I saw Leah Bradshaw this afternoon."

Geraldine bit into the macaroon and chewed. Fiona Bradshaw was safely across the room.

"And I'd *swear*," Maureen said, lowering her voice a notch further, almost mouthing silently now, "that that girl is expecting. She has all the signs of it. Her face is swelled up, and she was wearing—"

"You don't say," said Geraldine briskly. "Isn't that lovely? Fiona must be thrilled." She put down the macaroon that had suddenly begun to taste of cardboard.

Maureen's eager face fell slightly. "Yes, I'm sure she is," she said, "but poor Hannah will be very upset, I'd say."

"Oh no, not at all," Geraldine said. "Didn't I mention? She has a lovely new man, a master carpenter from Scotland. He's totally smitten—and he's loaded, from what Hannah tells me." She lowered her voice to match Maureen's. "Now, say nothing to anyone—Hannah would kill me—but he owns an island. Quite a substantial one, apparently."

It was worth the risk of the story's getting back to Hannah

to see the look of pure deflation that spread across Maureen's powdered features.

"Oh." She took a second slice of Aoife's Victoria sponge from a nearby plate. "Oh, isn't that great. Oh, I'm delighted to hear that."

She could easily be mistaken—what had she to go on but a puffy face and some baggy clothes? Didn't all the young ones wear baggy clothes these days? And, anyway, what difference could it make to Hannah now? Geraldine would say nothing. Maureen probably had it all wrong.

She picked up her macaroon again. "You have jam on your chin, dear," she told Maureen, a little too loudly.

She was in black again. The same long skirt, he thought, that she'd been wearing the first time he'd seen her. A long-sleeved black top that showed a couple of inches, no more, of her throat. Flat black shoes, black tights. Her pale hair gathered up and caught high on the back of her head.

She played with the same ferocious concentration, barely looking up from the music on the stand in front of her, not acknowledging in any way the scattering of applause between numbers. He wondered what her smile looked like, what it might do to her face.

Small Change they were called, according to the barman. *Know anything about them?* Adam had asked, but the barman didn't. And here came Nora, threading through the knots of drinkers toward him, wearing a tight-fitting green top he hadn't seen before and a pair of loose, faded jeans.

"Hi there," she said, kissing his cheek. "Oh, nice after-shave; who are you trying to impress?" She turned to the barman as he placed Adam's pint in front of him. "Martini, very dry." She perched on a stool beside Adam. "I have news," she said. "I got that job."

"The one with the paper?"

"Yeah, the one with the paper."

Her eyes were dramatic, all dark-ringed and long-lashed. Her curly hair was loose and smelled of coconut. She grinned. "You should see your face."

———————

He was better-looking than she'd been expecting. She'd assumed that any man who'd go for nice-but-boring Hannah Robinson couldn't be up to much, so Patrick Dunne had come as a pleasant surprise.

Lovely to meet you, she'd said, when they were introduced. Gripping his hand firmly, meeting the dark brown eyes. Reacting to a handsome man the way she always reacted, with undiluted charm. *So you're looking for a new PA.*

She'd BS'd her way through the interview. She'd skirted her lack of qualifications, she'd deflected questions with more questions, she'd made him laugh more than once. She'd pulled out all the stops to make him feel that she was the PA he wanted, that what she lacked in credentials would be more than made up for with enthusiasm and initiative, and it had worked.

But of course she'd known that it would work. Nora O'Connor had always known what men wanted.

———————

"Leah wasn't exactly over the moon when I told her," Nora

said. "Probably thinks I'll seduce Patrick—as if." She flashed a smile at the barman as he brought her drink. "Did I mention that she's pregnant, by the way?"

Adam stared at her. "What?"

"She told me the other day, when she was giving me the massage. Don't know if you want to say anything to Hannah."

"She told you she's pregnant?"

"Yeah—she's due in June." She sipped her drink. "You know, the martini in here isn't half bad."

Adam watched as she pulled the olive from its cocktail stick. "Say nothing to Hannah when you meet her."

Nora looked at him in amusement. "Wouldn't dream of it, bro. Not that me and Hannah have any plans to—"

"Back in a sec," he said then, slipping abruptly off his stool and making his way across the room. The music had finished, the musicians packing up. The woman was turning away as he approached.

"Excuse me," Adam said, but she didn't seem to hear above the chatter. She moved off and began threading her way rapidly around the low tables, toward the back of the pub. Adam hurried after her.

"Excuse me," he said again, more loudly, but she didn't react, seemingly unaware that she was being followed. Just before she reached a blue door that led, he presumed, to some kind of rear exit, he caught up with her.

"Excuse me."

Finally she stopped and turned, a quick swing of her head—and even in the dim lighting, Adam could see the dark flush that spread rapidly upward and covered the pointed, elfin face. She was almost exactly his height. She clutched her clarinet to her chest.

"Yes?" Her voice was breathy, hardly more than a whisper. She regarded him as if he were about to attack her.

He had absolutely no idea what to say; the impulse that had pulled him toward her hadn't supplied him with words. He hunted for something, anything, to break the silence between them. "Sorry to bother you," he began, and then he stopped again, with no clue as to what should follow. He tried to make eye contact, but her gaze seemed to be fixed on the lower half of his face.

The flush deepened on her cheeks. Tiny, dark freckles were scattered across her nose. She blinked rapidly behind her little round glasses as she waited for him to continue.

And finally, when she must surely have been on the point of turning away, Adam thought of something. "Er...I just wondered what the title of that last piece was."

"'I've Got a Crush on You,'" she said all in a rush, in the same breathy, whispery voice that he almost didn't hear.

"I really like your music," Adam said, but she was gone, vanished abruptly through the blue door, leaving behind a faint powdery, flowery scent. Adam stood there for a second or two, and then he walked back slowly to where Nora sat.

She eyed him curiously. "What was that all about? What did you want with that woman?"

Adam leaned against the counter and picked up his drink. "I thought I knew her," he said. "I thought she was somebody's sister, but I was wrong."

"I've Got a Crush on You." He wasn't superstitious, and he didn't believe in signs. There was no significance to be attached to the title of a song; it had no bearing on anything.

The way she'd blushed when he'd spoken to her. The frightened look she'd given him, the tense set of her body, as if she expected him to pounce at any minute.

Her hair was paler in color than straw. Her lips were too thin, and her nose was too pointed, and she never smiled, and the glasses hid what might be her best feature. She had large hands and feet.

But she lost herself in the music when she played. And the thought of unpinning her hair, of taking off her glasses and looking into her eyes, of putting his palm against her pale face—the thought of all that was inexplicably tempting.

I've got a crush on you.

"I have a new PA," Patrick announced, undoing his tie.

"I heard," Leah answered. "I know her. We were at school together."

"You were?" He looked at her in surprise. "She never mentioned that."

Sorry to drop by unannounced, but I had to tell you, Nora had said, dressed in her yellow wrap top that was probably cashmere, her black skirt, and her oh-so-soft black boots. *You'll never guess,* she'd said, standing in the doorway of Indulgence, and straightaway Leah had guessed.

Haven't a clue, she'd said, heart sinking.

As he walked in, John Wyatt noted that the shop was empty of customers. So far so good. Hannah turned at the sound of the bell, and he saw that she held a mop.

"Hello again." He smiled.

Her cheeks pinked charmingly. "Hi there, I was just—"

"You're cleaning up?" He glanced at the clock on the wall. "You finish at five?"

"No, no—I mean yes, I do finish at five, but it's not quite that yet." She replaced the mop in its bucket and began to peel off her rubber gloves. "Actually, it's part of my cunning plan: start to wash the floor and customers come in. Works every time."

She didn't look unhappy to see him. He decided to take her slight loss of composure as a positive sign.

"In that case," he said, "I'd hate to disappoint you. I'll take a couple of whatever's good. You choose."

"No preferences?" Sliding a tray toward her, reaching for a chocolate-lime.

"Not really." It wasn't a lie: He was immune to them all. "How do you resist them, surrounded all day?"

She laughed. "Believe me, if you spent as long as I do baking them, you'd soon lose the taste." She closed the lid of the little yellow box. "Sometimes I think if I never see another cupcake, it'll be fine. In fact," she continued, sliding the box toward him, "these days I'd much rather have a bag of Aged White Cheddar Kettle Chips."

"Do you never get a break?" Feeling his way toward an opportunity, waiting for his moment.

"Funny you should ask. I've just taken someone on who does a couple of hours three mornings a week. It's heaven."

He passed her a five-euro note—now or never. "And what about evenings?" he asked. "Do you ever get a free one of those?"

Hannah looked at him. Her half smile didn't disappear, but something changed in her face all the same. She blinked once, her mouth opening slightly. She seemed to be trying to come up with a response, but none came.

"I thought," he went on—because he had to go on, one of them had to say something—"you might like to meet up for a drink, or...whatever, really."

She was going to turn him down. He was sure, all at once, that she wasn't going to say yes.

Decidedly uncomfortable now, she held his money, her eyes slipping from his face to the cash drawer. "Actually—"

Yes, she was turning him down. He wished himself anywhere but where he was.

"I'm really sorry," she said all in a rush, "but I've...recently broken up with someone." Her face going pink again. "It was a long-term relationship, and it happened suddenly—the breakup, I mean, and I don't think—"

Her embarrassment dismayed him. "That's fine," he cut in quickly, smiling to show he didn't mind in the least. "You don't have to explain. It was just a thought. No harm done."

"I'm sorry," she said again, rummaging for his change. "If the timing were different or—"

"Really, it's fine. You've done nothing to be sorry for." He took the money and pocketed it. "You need time to yourself—I understand perfectly." He turned to go, his knee banging against the counter in his haste.

"Thank you," she said, "for...being so nice about it." She smiled faintly. "If it weren't such a cliché, I'd say it's not you, it's me."

"No problem. Be seeing you."

But of course he wouldn't be seeing her again. The four steps to the door seemed to take forever.

———

When she got the answering machine for the third time, Fiona knew that her daughter was avoiding her.

"You've reached Indulgence," Leah said in her salon voice. *"Sorry we can't come to the phone at this time, but if you leave your name and number, we'll return your call at our earliest convenience."*

Fiona waited for the beep, and then said, "Leah, it's me. Please get in touch." She paused. "There's no need for us to fall out. I didn't mean to upset you. Give me a ring when you get this message."

She hung up and walked to the window, looking out at the long, narrow back lawn that her neighbor's fourteen-year-old son mowed every fortnight in the summer, in return for twenty euro. Fiona remembered when a youngster would have cut a neighbor's grass for nothing, but that time was long gone.

She leaned against the windowsill and thought of how her plans for Leah were all going terribly wrong, and she wondered bitterly about the unfairness of it.

Look at the salon she'd financed when Leah didn't have two cents to rub together, fresh out of beauty school and no notion what to do next. Hadn't Fiona sorted her out? Hadn't Leah been happy to take her mother's money? How many mothers would have done as much and asked nothing in return?

Look at the men she'd had in mind for Leah, sons of friends with qualifications and good jobs and excellent prospects. The lengths she'd gone to introduce Leah to them, the efforts she'd made. The few dates that had come out of such meetings, the hopes Fiona always had, and then, a week or a month later, Leah's saying it hadn't worked out. But someone would have turned up eventually, Fiona was certain.

And now look at her daughter. Pregnant and unmarried, living with a man who'd been happy to string her along for months, who might never have left his cozy setup with another woman if Leah hadn't been careless enough to get caught.

A man who'd made small talk with Fiona whenever they'd met socially, all the time running around with her daughter on the quiet. Who looked at Fiona defiantly now, not a scrap of shame for having behaved despicably. Proud, probably, of his bastard on the way.

And Leah avoiding her. Screening her phone calls because Fiona showed concern, because she said what she was thinking instead of smiling and pretending she was pleased with how things had worked out.

The salon would inevitably suffer with the disruption, Leah's whole future suddenly uncertain, because who knew how long this man would stay with her, how long before his attention was caught by another pretty blonde? How was Fiona to remain silent? What mother could?

History was repeating itself in a horribly ironic way, with her own daughter playing the part of the other woman. Leah was inflicting the hurt now that had been visited on Fiona thirty years earlier, the bitterness and shock of it every bit as vivid today as they had been then.

I'm sorry, he'd said as Fiona had stood dumbfounded, the tea towel still in her hand. *I didn't mean it to happen, it just did.* Leah babbling in her baby talk, sitting on the kitchen floor, banging a wooden spoon on the tiles. *I'm so sorry.*

Fiona's heart thudding in her chest, a prickle of cold sweat on her forehead. Bending to pick up her daughter, needing something to hold on to.

How long? All she could manage to say, with her throat

closing up and her abdomen clenched so tightly she could hardly breathe. *How long?* Her legs had begun suddenly to tremble, forcing her to put Leah down again in case they both crashed to the floor.

And the desolation after he'd gone, the chasm he'd left behind. The torture of having to face him when he came by to see Leah. The protective shell forming around her, so that after a while it became—not easy, never easy, but not quite so impossible to smile and pretend that he hadn't destroyed her heart.

And worst of all, on hearing of his aneurysm less than a year later, the fresh grief, the hurt on hurt that had almost caused a complete breakdown. No satisfaction, no sense of justice being done, none of that.

She'd stayed away from his funeral, not trusting herself to come face-to-face with the woman who'd caused it all. It had taken her five years to visit his grave, to stand in front of his headstone and read his name in the granite and realize that she felt nothing anymore, nothing at all.

She sighed impatiently, not seeing the long strip of lawn beyond the window, the neat shrubs running up either side. Wasn't she entitled to be angry now? Wouldn't any woman be angry in her position, with her history?

She turned from the window and went to run a bath—and to pour a large gin and bitter lemon to accompany it.

"Something happened today," Hannah said.

"What?"

Adam was poaching eggs to sit on top of their smoked haddock. Smoked fish had never done much for Hannah—and she certainly wouldn't have chosen an egg as an accompaniment—but she was starving and not about to quibble when it was being served up to her.

"Someone asked me out," she said.

"Who?"

"I think I might have told you about him. He's a carpenter. He asked if I'd put his leaflets on the counter a few weeks ago."

"The one Geraldine tried to set you up with—I remember." Adam cracked the second egg and dropped it carefully into the swirling water.

"He's been in a few times since," Hannah went on. "I didn't mention it because, well..."

"And now he's asked you out."

"Yes."

"And you said?"

"No."

"Blast—why do they always break up? I'll have that one." Adam lowered the heat under the saucepan. "So you turned him down."

"I did." Hannah set the table with cutlery and glasses. "The problem is...I'm wondering now if I did the right thing."

Adam lifted out the eggs and laid them on the fish. He brought the plates to the table. "What's he like?"

"Nice." She poured water into their glasses. "He seems nice," she said, "what little I know of him." She picked up her fork. "Thanks—this looks interesting."

"But you're not sure that you're ready."

"Yes—I mean no. I'm not sure."

"I wouldn't worry. If he's keen, he'll be in again."

"Maybe...if I haven't scared him off."

Adam grinned. "Ah, men aren't that easily scared. Nobody would ever get together if they were."

Hannah cut a corner off her fish. "When he asked me out, I sort of...froze. I wasn't expecting it—at least I didn't think he'd ask so soon—and my instinct was to say no without really thinking about it."

"Right."

"I know I have to move on. I do realize I can't lock myself away..." She sighed. "Oh, let's change the subject, it's too depressing. What about you? You haven't been on a date in ages."

He looked skeptically at her over his fish. "You think my love life's less depressing than yours?"

"Good point. Well, what about Nora, then? Has she put her eye on anyone?"

"Not that she's told me." Adam paused. "Actually, speaking of Nora, there's something I'd better tell you, before you hear it from someone else."

Hannah looked at him quizzically. "Sounds very mysterious."

"Ah, it's nothing really—it's just that she's got a job."

"Has she? That's good, isn't it?"

"Well, yes...The thing is, it's with the paper."

Hannah stared. "Nora got a job with the paper? Doing what?"

He poked at his fish, separating the pale orange flesh into sections. "She's going to be Patrick's PA, of all things. She starts on Monday."

"Oh." Hannah digested the information. "That's weird." She cut a piece of egg white. "Not that it makes any...It is a bit weird though, isn't it?"

"It's nothing," Adam said. "She probably won't last longer

than a week. Anyway, what do you care? I just didn't want you hearing it by chance, that's all."

Hannah wondered what had happened to Patrick's last PA, super-efficient Andrea with her peanut allergy and her English husband and her son in the army. Andrea who never forgot a meeting or missed an appointment, Andrea who set up golf tournaments and organized business lunches—and who had reminded Patrick, probably, when Hannah's birthday was approaching.

And now Andrea was gone, for whatever reason, and Patrick had taken on Nora O'Connor, who'd presumably remind him when Leah Bradshaw's birthday was drawing near. Nora would organize his schedule and arrange his day and book his flights when he traveled. Nora would be spending a lot of every day in his company.

"She knows who he is, right?" she asked Adam.

"Yeah, turns out she's friendly with Leah—apparently they used to hang around together at school, but I don't remember her."

"Of course, they'd have been in the same class...So Leah must have got her the job."

"Yeah, maybe...I'm not sure." Adam looked uncomfortable. "Han, you know what Nora's like. It probably never crossed her mind that it might be a bit...awkward."

Like hell it didn't. Hannah smiled across the table at him. "She's right, why should it be awkward? It's all in the past now. It really doesn't bother me."

"I don't think I'll be doing this dinner again," Adam said, regarding their plates. "It hasn't exactly been a roaring success."

"You know what I like?" she said. "Your chicken-and-sweet-corn soup. Let's have that tomorrow night, with those nice seeded rolls that you got last time."

She would put it out of her mind. It didn't matter in the least.

———————

Maybe Alice was the only one who noticed. It wasn't as if he were falling around the place, and he hadn't thrown up or disgraced himself in any obvious way. He was slurring his words a bit, certainly, and his eyes were bloodshot. He looked like someone who'd had a few too many, and he was louder than usual, monopolizing the conversation, like he always did after too much alcohol.

But maybe it was more obvious to her; maybe it didn't really bother anyone else. And so what anyway, if he'd overdone it a bit? They were out for the night, weren't they? They were helping a good cause, and it wasn't doing anyone any harm. And there were plenty of others who'd had more than a few; you only had to look around to see that.

It was useless—her excuses failed to reassure her. The knot in her stomach wouldn't budge. Her armpits felt horribly damp, her hands kept making fists. She wanted to go home; she wanted them both home and out of sight, before everyone started talking about Tom Joyce, who was making a bit of a fool of himself at the charity dinner-dance.

The band switched to a slow waltz, and Stephen extended a hand to her. "Come on," he said, pulling her up. He wasn't 100 percent sober either, she told herself—he didn't volunteer to dance when he was—but he was still well able to hold his own, and Geraldine didn't seem in the least concerned about him.

Alice tried to will her tension away as she let Stephen lead her around the stifling, perfumed room. "Isn't it hot?"

she said, but he wasn't listening, his head tilted toward a neighboring couple, the man saying something that made him smile.

I'm worried about Tom's drinking, she wanted to say to him. *Maybe you could have a word.* But of course she kept quiet. Tom would hit the roof—and it wouldn't be fair to Stephen, who was more a work colleague and a casual friend than someone you could expect to get involved in something like that.

There was nobody she could talk to. Not Tom's family, such as they were: a priest brother in Colombia, a pair of sisters—one married, one separated, both living in England—a ninety-two-year-old uncle in a nursing home at the other side of the country whom they visited a handful of times a year.

Alice wasn't close to either of her own siblings, not in that way. And of course she wouldn't dream of mentioning anything to Ellen—what could their daughter do so far away, except worry about her father?

At half past twelve, Alice told Geraldine she had a headache, and Geraldine immediately said, "I'll get Reception to call us a taxi," so Alice suspected that she'd been wanting to go home too. The taxi arrived remarkably quickly—they were still gathering coats and bags when the porter came and found them.

Tom stumbled getting into the back, and Stephen put a hand on his arm and said, "Easy there, fellow," and Alice's face burned in the darkness. She sat between Tom and Stephen, and before they were through the gates of the hotel, Tom's head had drooped toward her shoulder. She prayed he wouldn't snore.

Geraldine turned in her seat. "The dinner was nice, I must say."

"My beef was tough," Stephen said.

"How long till we have to get up for work?" Alice asked, so neither of them would look for Tom's opinion of the beef.

They both groaned, and Geraldine said, "Oh, don't think about that."

Tom's mood would be black in the morning. Alice dreaded the drive in to work. He usually dropped her, since Glass Slipper was on the way to the dental clinic, and it made more sense than to take the two cars. She made her own way home, relishing the half-hour walk after her day in the shop, unless the weather was very bad, in which case she took a lift from Geraldine.

"That's nice music," Geraldine was saying to the driver.

"It's Herbie Hancock," he told her. "One of my favorites."

"Do you play yourself?"

"I do, a bit."

Tom's head was heavy on Alice's shoulder. She shifted slightly, and Stephen immediately moved to allow her more room. "I'm fine," she said quickly. Here was the roundabout. Up the hill and two more left turns and they were home.

She dug her elbow into Tom's side when the car stopped, and he snuffled awake. "Money for the taxi," she hissed—she had only a fifty-euro note in her wallet—but Geraldine said, "Alice, forget it—we'll sort it out tomorrow." Stephen walked around the car and opened the back door and shepherded Tom out onto the path.

"Maybe he needn't bother coming in tomorrow," he murmured to Alice as she climbed out. "Let him sleep in. We can manage."

"We'll see," she answered. "Thanks very much."

If Tom missed a day's work because of drink, they'd be talking about it at the clinic. She dug into her bag to fish out the door key, and grabbed Tom's arm as he lurched toward her.

"Will I go to the door with you?" Stephen asked.

"No, we're fine. You head off."

Tom leaned heavily against her while she walked as quickly as she could up the driveway, which had never seemed so long. The taxi sat there, idling, long after Stephen had gotten back inside. She willed them to go, to stop watching Alice Joyce supporting her drunk husband.

Lying alone in bed later—she hadn't been able to get Tom past the living-room couch, so she'd pulled off his shoes and lifted up his legs and left him there—she imagined the conversation in the taxi after they'd been dropped. About how Tom had been knocking it back, about poor Alice having to put up with that. Maybe a remark about a dentist needing a clear head and a steady hand.

Or certainly they'd be thinking it, even if it were left unsaid.

She'd wake him in the morning. She'd do her best to get him up. If he was grumpy she'd put up with it. She turned onto her side and read 1:14 on the clock. She closed her eyes and tried to sleep.

———

Leah couldn't sleep. If it wasn't the constant urge to pee, it was the horrible acidic lurch of heartburn that had her lying awake next to Patrick at almost three in the morning.

And if it was neither of those, it was Nora O'Connor. Oh, it was stupid to think Patrick was going to be seduced by the first attractive woman who looked at him, or flirted with him. It was stupid and insecure, and she despised herself for thinking it.

She was pregnant with his child; he'd left his long-term partner to be with her. She was pretty and confident and independent. He loved her, and she satisfied him in bed, she was sure of it. What possible reason would he have for straying?

Except that he'd done it to Hannah. He'd been with her for over a year, he'd been living in her house, and then he'd met Leah, and that had been that. And Nora was very, very good at attracting a man. And she'd be working closely with Patrick—every day, probably. She thought about Nora's lean, well-kept body, her sexy lingerie.

So you were at school together, Patrick had said. *In the same class?*

Yes, but I hadn't seen her in years until the other day, Leah had told him. *We were never that close, really. And she went straight to the States after school and lost touch with everyone. She was married twice—neither of them lasted.*

She should have said something to him when Nora had told her she was job hunting. She should have realized that there was a possibility Nora would apply when she saw the ad for the PA. She should have said, *If you see an application from Nora Paluzzi or Nora O'Connor, dump it. I know her, I was at school with her, and she's hopeless. She's been sacked from every job she ever got, and now she's back here looking for work. Don't touch her with a barge pole.*

And Patrick would have believed her and thrown Nora's application into the bin. She should have said something, but she hadn't.

Now she turned toward Patrick. Maybe sex would put her to sleep. She leaned across and touched her lips to the side of his neck, to the spot he liked. She opened her mouth and pressed her tongue to his skin. She bit the flesh gently, her hand moving slowly down his chest, past his stomach, her fingers burrowing into the coarse hair below.

He stirred. "Hey," he whispered thickly, "can't sleep?"

She moved closer and took his nipple into her mouth and sucked. He groaned sleepily and reached for her hips, pulling her against him.

He loved her. There was nothing to worry about.

———————

Hannah cut butter and added it to the mixing bowl. She switched on the stand mixer and began to weigh coconut. He'd been so nice about her rejection, but the smile hadn't reached his eyes. She'd felt cruel.

She cracked eggs into a smaller bowl and whisked them briskly. It must be terribly difficult to ask someone out, to put yourself in that vulnerable position. Then again, not all men were the same. She remembered Patrick's confidence the first time he'd approached her, no discomfiture that she could see, even when she'd been a bit hesitant. But she'd made John uncomfortable, and she regretted it.

She opened the oven door and slid out the top tray and shifted the others up. Outside, the sky was just beginning to show slivers of gray. She loved this predawn time, the silence in the garden broken only by the occasional chirps of the earliest birds. In another month or so, she'd be able to open the window as she baked, to hear them more clearly.

She beat cream cheese and orange juice together, then added soft butter and icing sugar. The carrot-ginger cupcakes were a big hit, well worth the extra effort they took. Maybe she could grate the carrots in bulk, keep them in the freezer.

But she'd been right to turn him down; it would have been

crueler to start anything that probably wouldn't have gone anywhere. Shame, though. Tragic timing, to meet someone who seemed so suitable while she was still shaky after Patrick.

She slid another tray into the oven and closed the door gently. As she began to spread the cream-cheese icing over the cooled cupcakes, Adam's revelation of the other evening slipped abruptly into her head. What had Patrick been thinking of, taking Nora on as his PA? Even if her looks had impressed him—which they surely had—what on earth had possessed him to take on someone so inexperienced?

The impression Hannah had gotten from Adam over the years was that Nora was well able to find jobs where qualifications came a poor second to looking good. Did she somehow imagine that she could sit outside Patrick's office and file her nails all day? Surely PA to a newspaper editor was a job that required considerable organizational skills, not to mention being able to run an office?

And even if Patrick truly loved Leah Bradshaw, what would he do if Nora decided to make a play for him? What would any man do?

She iced the last carrot cupcake and submerged the empty bowl in the sink. None of her business what any of them got up to. As the sky brightened, she filled the kettle for her first cup of tea.

Adam slept on his stomach, as he always did, legs splayed, arms flung out, duvet falling sideways off the bed. Oblivious to his landlady's movements in the kitchen directly underneath.

He dreamed about the clarinet player. He dreamed about

her fair hair flying about her head as she made music on a much bigger stage than Vintage's, all by herself. He sat in an empty auditorium and listened to her. She wore red, a long dress that showed him the white gleam of her shoulders and the curves of her body, and that ended in a silky pool around her ankles.

And when she had finished playing, he stood and walked toward her, and she laid her clarinet on the chair and smiled and opened her arms to him, hair streaming around her pale, pale face.

"Thank you," he said, climbing the steps and pulling her to him, hands sinking into her hair as his mouth found hers, as his tongue eased her thin lips apart.

———————

John Wyatt sprinkled brown sugar and splashed milk onto his porridge and ate it standing by the window as he always did in the morning. He liked that his third-floor flat had a view of Clongarvin's main street, even if the traffic at night had taken some getting used to after the peace of Kerrycroy, the tiny coastal village where he'd spent most of his life. Now that he was sleeping through the night again, he was able to appreciate his central location, his bird's-eye view of the comings and goings of Clongarvin's residents, especially first thing in the morning.

Today was Friday. He should finish the kitchen cabinets for Carlton Road by lunchtime, if he put his mind to it, and then he'd head across town to check out a new inquiry. He was lucky to have anyone showing any interest, with the recession as bad as it was. Hopefully he'd manage to keep body and soul together until he'd built up enough of a business to relax a bit.

The gigs helped, of course—and that was thanks to Wally, whose cousin Patsy stood behind the counter in the wood-working store where John bought most of his supplies. Funny how things turned out: a chance remark one day about the fact that he played the sax and Patsy was saying, *Oh, you should meet my cousins, they're in a band.* And before you knew it, John was practicing with Small Change, and then they were playing in the newly opened Vintage every Saturday night, which helped with the rent on this place and on the tiny workshop he'd found by the river.

He took another spoonful of porridge and watched the early-morning bustle in the street below. A man sprinted toward a red van that was causing an obstruction, waving apologetically at the driver in the car behind it before climb-ing in and moving off. A woman in a green jacket walked slowly past a shoe-shop window, her relaxed pace contrasting with the scurry of the people around her. A bus pulled in to a stop, engine chugging as the straggle of waiting passengers disappeared inside.

I'm leaving, he'd told Lara, and she'd shown no surprise. The only surprise, maybe, that he'd waited so long. Nineteen years in a marriage that should never have taken place, that had been entered into when they were both too young to lis-ten to anyone's advice.

And eight months after the wedding, when both of them had already realized their mistake, Danielle had turned them into a family—Lara unknowingly pregnant as they'd walked down the aisle—and there was no leaving then, no grounds for walking out, because lack of love wasn't enough, was it, when a child was part of the picture?

No animosity on either part, no harsh words, no bitter quarreling between them. But no romantic love either, the initial fierce blaze extinguishing itself almost as quickly as it had ignited, leaving behind a friendship, you could call it, but without any deep warmth or feeling. Nothing to have you rushing home in the evenings, nothing to have you aching for the other's touch. They tolerated each other amicably, was the best you could say.

And occasionally, when loneliness caused him to reach out to Lara in the night, she responded, but it was an empty, mechanical coupling that left him even more bereft, if anything.

Danielle helped. The poor girl had held them together for years. It had been harder, much harder, to tell her. *Your mother and I are separating,* John had said. *Nothing has happened, we haven't fallen out, there's nobody else involved. We just feel there's no point in staying together anymore.*

Now that I'm moving out, you mean, Danielle had replied. Her expression had been difficult to read, her feelings kept to herself, as they always had been, even when she was a young child.

We've decided it's best, John had told her. *I'm going to Ireland for a while. I think a change of scene might be good. I'll be back as often as I can to see you.*

It was okay, he told himself. With Danielle starting college in Edinburgh, there would have been a parting anyway; they'd have been separated for weeks at a time.

It's a change, he'd said, *that's all. You're still as important to both of us as you always were.*

They'd still meet, either in Edinburgh or at his parents' house on Bute whenever both of them could make it back there. They'd be like so many other separated families across the world, living under different roofs most of the time, seeing each other when they could.

But of course something had been lost between father and

daughter, something John had sacrificed by choosing to leave the family home, and he mourned it bitterly. Danielle had always been closer to Lara; he supposed it was inevitable with mothers and daughters.

He'd gone back twice. He'd met Danielle as planned, and they'd spent Boxing Day together at his parents' house. Danielle had talked quite cheerfully about college; she seemed to be enjoying it. She'd cut her hair, which John had privately mourned, and she'd grown thinner, which he didn't approve of either. He'd teased her about boyfriends, and she'd laughed and given nothing away, as ever. They'd had a good day.

But all the same, something was lost, and they both knew it. *You might come to Ireland in the spring,* he'd said to her. *I'm in a nice little town. You could stay a week in the holidays.* And Danielle had said, *Maybe,* but nothing had been fixed and no more had been said.

A couple walked hand in hand down the street, a rolled-up newspaper tucked under the strap of the man's briefcase, an umbrella swinging from the woman's free hand. It was hard to be sure from this distance, but John put them in their twenties.

Hannah Robinson was in her late twenties or early thirties. Maybe a decade younger than his thirty-eight. Her skin was beautifully fresh, like a young girl's, but her body was all womanly curves, the same solid build as her mother. Her eyes were the color of early-morning sea, and her hair was dark and wavy.

He'd acted too soon. He should have dropped in to the shop a few more times, maybe worked music into a conversation. He could have mentioned the gig in Vintage and suggested casually that she stop by some Saturday night. He'd been too impatient, and she'd turned him down.

But at least he knew she was unattached, even if she wasn't over her ex. Unless, of course, the ex was someone she'd made up to let him down gently. All the games people played...he'd forgotten the games. He had no time for games.

He finished his porridge and left his bowl in the sink, on top of last night's dinner dishes. He brushed his teeth and grabbed his keys. He left the small flat and took the stairs two at a time, as he always did.

Busy. Keep busy.

————————

Alice stood at the cooker and waited for the eggs to boil. She didn't feel a bit like eating—she was deathly tired, and her stomach wasn't the best—and neither, she was sure, did Tom, but they had to eat something if they were to put down a day's work.

She'd opened the sitting-room door when she'd come downstairs and said, "Tom, time to get up," loudly. She'd repeated it, and he'd grunted. She'd crossed the room and yanked the curtains open and turned to him, sprawled on the couch.

"Get up," she'd said, "or you'll be late. I have breakfast on." She'd left the door open and gone into the kitchen, and a few minutes later, when she'd been on the point of going in again, she'd heard him plodding upstairs.

Now she spooned the eggs out of the bubbling water and set them into eggcups, and as she brought them to the table, the kitchen door opened and Tom walked in. His face was waxen, and he looked exhausted, but he'd shaved and put on a tie.

"Your egg is ready," she said, setting it at his place.

He pulled out a chair and sat heavily. "Is there tea in the pot?"

She poured for him. She cut brown bread and arranged the slices on a plate in the middle of the table.

Underneath his eyes there were heavy pouches. She supposed they must have been there for a while, but this was the first time she'd taken notice of them. He'd cut himself shaving—a fragment of tissue he'd stuck on the cut was red in the middle.

"I can drive, if you like," Alice said. "I could leave the car at the clinic and walk back to the shop." She'd be late, but she could phone Geraldine on the way to let her know. Geraldine had often opened up; she had her own set of keys. "Or I could park at the shop and you could walk the rest." The fresh air might do him good, put a bit of color in his cheeks.

"I'm fine," he said. "I've slept it off." He poured milk into his cup and drank thirstily. He ignored his egg and took no bread. "I overdid it a bit last night," he said.

Alice made no response. She couldn't contradict him, but this wasn't the time to talk about it. "I was thinking we might go out for an early bird this evening," she said. "I could meet you in town after work. We could go to Giovanni's, save the cooking."

He probably wouldn't feel like drinking this evening. They could have a quiet chat maybe, in neutral surroundings. She topped up his tea.

"I don't think I'd be up to going out," he said, watching the tea as it flowed into his cup. "I'll get a takeaway if you don't feel like cooking."

"It doesn't matter," she said. "Just a thought."

The morning air was sliced with frost. The car was cold.

Tom turned the heater on full, and the fan whirred loudly, drowning the radio. Alice pulled her coat tightly around her and clicked her seat belt into place, and rubbed her hands together. She kept forgetting her gloves, in the drawer of the hall stand. She should leave them out where she'd see them.

Tom reversed out of the driveway—too fast, it seemed to Alice, but again she held her tongue. The road glittered, and the paths on either side were full of children and mothers on their way to school. They turned onto Carbert Road, and Alice made a list in her head for a lunchtime shopping: milk, toothpaste, washing-up liquid, eggs, nail-varnish remover. Something else she couldn't think of.

"Do you need anything?" she asked Tom. "I have to go to the supermarket at lunchtime."

"No," he said, and just then she remembered: batteries for the remote control.

The air in the car got marginally warmer, and Alice turned the heater down a couple of notches, and the radio became audible again in the middle of someone's sentence: "...causing a tailback from the Red Cow Roundabout."

She was glad they didn't have a long commute every morning. On a quiet day, the drive to the shop took ten minutes, and even in the heaviest traffic it was still well under half an hour.

Afterward, trying to remember the sequence of events—because she kept trying to remember, she couldn't stop trying to remember—all she could see was the color of his jacket. All that was there, when she sent her mind back to the minutes leading up to the accident, was the small, bright blue patch of his jacket, the flash of bright blue that was suddenly there, suddenly, sickeningly, *there* in front of the car, and she shouted something—Tom's name? something else?—and she

was thrust against her seat belt, she felt the tug of the strap
across her body, the nylon taut against the side of her neck,
her hands flying out to smack against the dashboard, the blue
gone, no more blue now, and the thump as she was flung
back against her seat, as the car skidded to a stop, swerv-
ing in an arc across the road, *no, no, no, no, no, no, no, no,
no, no, no,* unable to stop repeating it, *no, no, no,* her fists
beating against her thighs, *no,* her head shaking from side to
side, *no, no,* pulling at her seat belt, struggling to get it off,
no, and someone screaming and screaming, and people running and shouting and crying, and Alice still repeating *no,
no, no,* the blue hidden now behind all the other colors, the
reds and the purples and the browns, *no, no,* and at some
stage the new, shrill scream of a siren, and doors opening and
closing, and her door opening, and someone unbuckling her
seat belt, and someone slapping her face, slapping it hard, the
new shock jolting her into silence, her words stopped, her
mouth gaping dumbly, her whole body shaking violently as
she was helped from the car, guided toward the open doors
of an ambulance, clutching at the hands that supported her,
a blanket wrapped around her, the smell of wool and anti-
septic as she was hoisted up into the ambulance, and all the
time the screaming, someone shrieking, voices shouting—and
stretching her arms toward Tom, the blanket dropping off her
shoulders as he put something, the end of a stick, a pipe, into
his mouth, Tom's face so white, the man beside him laying
a dark blue arm on Tom's shoulders as Tom's cheeks puffed
out and turned pink, as he took the stick from his mouth
and the man took the stick from Tom and looked at it, his
arm still on Tom's shoulders, his fingers curved around them,
and everything was sharp and hard, and a man was talking
to her, she could see his mouth moving, but the words made

no sound, as the blanket was wrapped around her again, as she was eased down onto the trolley in the ambulance, as her handbag appeared on the floor beside her, and when she looked toward Tom again, he was gone, and she wanted to ask for him, she wanted to call out for him, but the words made no sound—

And afterward, she had no idea how long afterward, the curly-headed guard at the station put a blue-and-white mug of too-hot, too-sweet tea on the table in front of her—her lashes stiff with salt, her eyes hot and stinging, the ball of her sodden tissues lying next to the mug, her skirt creased—and then he sat on the wooden bench beside her and said quietly, "Now, Alice, there's something I have to tell you."

And as he spoke, as he told her, her face crumpled and the screams and the tears began all over again.

———

Geraldine unlocked the grille and slid it upward into its casing. She opened the shop door and stepped in, inhaling the robust, leathery scent. She locked the door again and walked through to the rear of the shop, where she hung her coat on the back of the door and stowed her handbag in the small green cupboard that held the accounts ledgers and the petty-cash box.

She filled the kettle and plugged it in, then lifted the two red mugs from their hooks. The mugs said OXO in fat white letters. She took the milk carton from the tiny fridge and sniffed it. She dropped tea bags into the mugs and added half a spoonful of sugar to hers before she remembered she'd given it up for Lent. She took out the tea bag and poured the sugar into the sink.

She switched on Alice's transistor and let the ads wash over her as the kettle began to sing. She didn't care for the local radio station, but Alice liked it. At a minute to nine, she went out to the shop and unlocked the front door and wheeled out the display of boots on sale. She went back and poured boiling water into her mug, adding milk as the newscaster reported on the latest political scandal, and the shelving of plans for a new motorway in the west, and the protests over the cancellation of another route out of Shannon Airport, and the closing of Carbert Road in Clongarvin following a traffic accident. An accident—that would be what was delaying Alice, who came by Carbert Road.

At ten past nine, she called Alice's mobile and got her voice mail. "I presume you're stuck in traffic," she said. "No rush—it's quiet here. See you in a while."

At twenty past nine, when there was still no reply from Alice's phone, she called the house. Maybe they'd both slept it out after last night, or maybe Alice's mobile was stuck in her handbag, out of earshot.

But the phone rang and rang, and she finally hung up.

At half past nine, she phoned the dental clinic. "Is Tom there?" she asked Suzie, the receptionist.

"No—Stephen says he's not coming in," Suzie told her.

"Has he phoned? Or Alice?"

"No, I've heard nothing."

"Will you put me through to Stephen?"

Stephen had heard nothing either. "He's not here, so he must be sleeping it off. I thought Alice would have rung, but she didn't."

"Alice hasn't arrived here either—and she'd definitely let me know if she wasn't coming. I've tried phoning, but there's no answer."

"Maybe they *both* slept it out, then. I suppose we'll just have to wait and see."

At a quarter to ten, Geraldine phoned Hannah, who told her that Una Connolly's four-year-old nephew had been knocked down on his way to school.

"I'm waiting to hear how he is," Hannah said. "Una just rang me on her way to the hospital."

"Oh, Lord, the poor little thing."

"Why were you ringing me?"

"Alice never showed up for work," Geraldine said, "and Tom isn't at the clinic. I can't contact her."

"They could be stuck in traffic. Maybe the accident caused a delay."

"But Alice would let me know. It's not like her at all."

"The battery could be gone on her phone—you know how easily that can happen."

"Mmm." But still Geraldine was anxious.

The main item on the ten-o'clock news was an accident on the Carbert Road in Clongarvin, in which a young boy had been knocked down and fatally injured.

———

Alice couldn't stop crying. She leaned her elbows on the table and buried her face in her hands and sobbed loudly, the tea forgotten.

"Oh, God," she wept, thinking of the small blue boy flying upward. "Oh, Jesus, God. Oh, God Almighty."

And sometime after that, with the tears finally over and her throat aching and her eyes burning and her head throbbing, Tom walked into the room, chalk-faced, and said quietly, not meeting her eye, "We can go home now."

And all Alice could think was how desperately she wanted to hit him.

———————

"Mum, it's me. I'm afraid I have bad news."

Geraldine's hand flew to her chest. "Is it Stephen? What's wrong?"

"No, it's not Dad...It's Claire's son. He died. Una just rang me."

"Oh, Lord." Geraldine sank onto the stool, her eyes filling with tears. "Oh, the poor little thing—what age did you say?"

"Four. He was only four."

"Oh, that's so..." She pulled a tissue from her sleeve. "Oh, I can't believe it."

The shop door opened just then. "Someone's here, I have to go," she said hurriedly, hanging up and slipping her phone under the counter. She dabbed her eyes and blew her nose and tried to put the news from her mind while she dealt with the customer.

And after the woman had decided against any of the three pairs of shoes she tried on, after the shop door had closed behind her, after Geraldine had tried Alice's mobile again and again gotten no response, a terrible suspicion began to dawn slowly inside her.

———————

Nora strolled along the rails of clothes, running a hand over the different fabrics, occasionally pulling something out to have a closer look.

"Can I help you at all?"

She smiled at the assistant, who could lose half a stone, easily. "Not really, thanks—just looking."

She wasn't just looking: She knew exactly what she wanted. In the dressing room, she removed her top and jeans and tried on her selection, turning to see as much as possible in the floor-length mirror. She got dressed again and walked to the checkout desk with a high-waisted purple skirt, a fitted cream top, a black wool wraparound dress, and a deep crimson jacket.

"Hang on to these," she told the assistant. "I need to pick up some lingerie."

A bustier, maybe—she hadn't bought a new one in ages. Stockings, of course, and suspenders. A cream bra for under the top, one that gave serious cleavage. A couple of lace thongs.

And it was so satisfying, as the assistant folded her purchases and wrapped them in tissue, as Nora slid her credit card across the counter, to remind herself that Jackson Paluzzi was paying for lingerie that some other man, with any luck, would get a lot of pleasure from.

Not that she had any specific man in mind, of course. But with her new job, and meeting all those newspaper employees, somebody would surely come along.

And if he happened to be out of bounds...well, so much the better. The last thing she needed was another husband.

"What d'you fancy?"

Leah, full of heartburn, didn't fancy anything. She looked for the least offensive dish on the menu. "The poached salmon."

"Me, too."

Patrick closed his menu as Leah stifled a yawn and eased her swollen feet one by one out of her stilettos. She'd barely made it from the car to the table in them. "No sauce on mine," she told the waiter as he took their order.

What she wouldn't give to be stretched out on the couch in front of the telly, a cushion under her back. What she wouldn't give for a foot massage—except that Patrick wasn't talented in that department. His attempts at massage left her more frustrated than relieved.

He reached across the table and covered her hand. "Good day?"

She pushed her hair out of her eyes with the other hand. It needed a cut, but she hadn't the energy. "Fine. You?"

"The usual." He filled their water glasses. "Did you hear about the accident on Carbert Road?"

"I did. Horrible. A child, wasn't it?"

His wine arrived, and her apple juice. She was sick to death of apple juice. She hoped to God he wouldn't say cheers.

He lifted his glass toward her. "Cheers."

Irritation flooded through her. She knew that it was her hormones gone haywire, but the knowledge didn't stop her from wanting to wipe the smug look off his face, whatever it took.

She looked for something to rattle him, and found it. "By the way," she said, "did I mention that your new PA is Adam O'Connor's sister?"

Patrick's smile faded. "You don't say."

"Twin sister, actually." She watched him assimilate the knowledge that he'd just employed the sister of his ex's best friend. "Not that it matters," she added, daring him to contradict her. "I mean, now that you and Hannah are history."

He shrugged. "Of course not. Why would it? I'm just surprised, that's all." He lifted his glass again. "Mind you, she did say she came from around here, so I suppose it shouldn't surprise me if I know someone belonging to her, in a place this size."

"I'd be a bit careful all the same, if I were you," Leah said. "She probably tells Adam everything. You know how twins are."

Patrick smiled, his equilibrium restored. "I hardly think Adam would be interested in the comings and goings of a newspaper office."

"Probably not." Leah sipped apple juice. "They've moved in together—did you know that?"

"Who?"

"Adam and Hannah—he's moved into her house." She laughed lightly. "I assume it's just to help her out financially."

He studied her. "I would imagine so."

"On the other hand," Leah said, "I wonder if he was just waiting for you and her to break up."

Patrick sipped his wine. "And I wonder," he said mildly, "why you're being such a bitch."

Leah looked innocently at him. "I have no idea what you mean," she said. "I'm just making small talk."

And for the next forty minutes, while they played with their food and made more small talk, he didn't take her hand again or touch her foot with his under the table.

———————

"He ran out in front the car," Tom said. "There was no way I could avoid him."

It was the first thing he'd said to her since they'd left the police station. Alice had refused the guard's offer to drive them home, dreading their arrival in a squad car, the twitching net curtains all along the road. Not that, on top of everything else.

But the taxi they'd gotten instead just reminded her of the night before—only one night ago!—and she'd sat rigidly on the backseat, gripping her handbag and trying to think of nothing at all.

They'd let themselves into the house, and Tom had gone straight upstairs, and she'd let him. She hadn't called him when the kettle boiled, and he hadn't appeared by the time Geraldine showed up an hour later, having closed the shoe shop early for the day.

And only when Geraldine had left and the sky was almost completely dark, did Alice hear his footsteps on the stairs. She picked up the tea towel as the kitchen door opened and he walked in.

"He ran out in front of the car," he said immediately, his voice low and broken. "There was no way I could avoid him. It happened in a second—there was nothing I could do."

Alice finished drying the cups she and Geraldine had used. She put away the banana bread that neither of them had touched. She kept her back to him as she took potatoes from the vegetable rack and brought them to the sink.

"You saw it too," he said. "You saw how he ran out. You were there too."

Alice began to peel the potatoes, noticing with some surprise that her hands were shaking.

"Alice," he said, "didn't you? Didn't you see how he ran out?"

She faced him then, a half-peeled potato in her hand. "You shouldn't have been driving," she said, trying not to make the words too loud. "You should have let me drive. I *offered*, I *said* I would—" A wobble on the last word made her stop and take a breath. "You were drunk last night," she said more quietly, "and you were still under the influence this morning, and a little boy—"

Her voice cracked again, and she turned back to the sink and tried to finish peeling the potato, but she could hardly see it with her eyes full of tears.

"I felt okay," Tom said. "I didn't feel that I couldn't drive. I would have let you if I had."

Alice wiped a sleeve across her face and went on peeling.

"I'm sorry," he said. "If you knew how bad I feel—"

She whirled then, the potato flying from her hand and thumping onto the floor between them, skidding across to rest by the fridge. "*You* feel bad? *You* didn't lose a child today, did you?" The words bursting out of her now, flying from her mouth. "You have no idea how those people feel, no *idea*, because you're too busy feeling sorry for *yourself*!"

She clamped her mouth shut. She crossed the room and grabbed the potato, her heart thudding, the breath gasping out of her nose in sobs.

She heard, or sensed, Tom leaving the kitchen. She dropped the potato and the peeler into the sink and held on tightly to the edge, trying to calm herself.

A file will be sent to the prosecutor, the curly-haired guard had told her. *Because your husband failed two breathalyzer tests, he will be charged today with drunken driving. As this is his first offense, we can release him on station bail, and he'll be summoned in due course, probably in a few months, to appear at the district court and be formally charged with whatever the prosecutor decides.*

And what then? Alice had asked, her hands twisted together around the fresh tissues he'd given her. Terrified of his answer, and terrified of not knowing his answer.

He'll be summoned to the circuit court for trial. That'll take another few months, probably in the autumn sometime. He'd seen the next question in her face and added, *Sentencing will depend on the charge, and on how the case goes in court—it's impossible to anticipate the outcome at this stage.*

But he could go to prison?

The guard had met her terrified eyes calmly. Her situation probably meant nothing to him. He must hate Tom, another drunk driver who'd mowed down and killed a little child.

He could go to prison, yes, he'd said. *Quite possibly.*

The worst of all, the part that wouldn't leave her head, was that she'd made him go to work. She'd forced him to get up, too afraid of what people might say if he hadn't gone in. She could have left him asleep, she could have phoned Stephen and said he wasn't well, and everyone would have gotten over it. They'd have dealt with it. And a little child would still be alive.

After a while Alice pried her hands from the edge of the sink. She went to the cupboard and took down a can of beans. She opened the can and spooned the beans straight into her mouth, standing by the window, looking out into the blackness and seeing nothing except the little flying blue boy, whose life they had ended.

———————

"He was only four," Hannah said. "He was in Junior Infants. His mother was walking him to school."

They sat at the table, their dinner plates stacked but not removed. She should have been making her usual preparations for the morning, but instead she cradled her coffee.

"And the driver was Alice's husband?" Adam asked. He and Alice had talked some years before about setting up a Web site for Glass Slipper, but in the end it hadn't happened.

Hannah nodded. "Tom...You'd have met him at Mam and Dad's twenty-fifth. They'd all been out the night before, and apparently he was quite drunk going home." She sighed. "He was breathalyzed when it happened, and he was still over the limit, imagine."

"It can happen. And Alice was with him in the car?"

"Yeah...She's in an awful way, Mam says."

Adam reached for a cupcake and peeled off the paper. "That would wreck your head. I've often thought I'd rather be run down myself than do it to someone else."

Hannah shuddered. "God, don't talk like that. Mam was in the shop on her own all day. She didn't hear from Alice till the afternoon, when they got home from the police station."

"He wasn't kept in after failing the breath test?"

"No—he was released on bail."

They sipped their coffee in silence. The rain lashed in sheets against the window. Hannah imagined the little boy's parents listening to the same pelting rain, the same howling wind. Or maybe they didn't hear it, maybe they were beyond hearing it.

"Una was so upset when she rang me, poor thing. Imagine, she was apologizing for missing work. I told her to take as long as she needed."

"What did you say he was? Her nephew?"

Hannah nodded. "Her sister Claire's son. Remember I told you I baby-sat for them. He was the first grandchild, on both sides—they all doted on him, apparently."

She remembered Claire as a youngster, all wiry and long-legged, mad into sports, couldn't care less about clothes or boys or anything unless it involved a field and a ball. But it was Claire, and not prettier, quieter Una, who'd gotten pregnant at seventeen, just a few years after Hannah had given up baby-sitting. Everyone had been convinced that the boy, the father, was going to disappear, like so many before him, and that Claire's parents would be saddled with the child's upbringing.

But Dave hadn't done what everyone expected. He'd stayed around, eventually managing to provide a home for his small family. Hannah had lost touch with the girls by this time, but Una had brought her up to date.

Dave's a house painter. He works with his cousins. He and Claire rent a house in Springwood Gardens. It's nothing special, but Dave has it looking lovely. He's got an eye for color. You should see Jason's bedroom—it's brilliant. The kind of room every boy would love.

She'd taken out her wallet and shown Hannah a photo of a round-faced, earnest little boy with an unevenly cut, pale-colored fringe and the full Cupid's-bow lips of the very young.

He's a bit older than that now—this was taken last summer. His hair is getting darker, too. Claire hates that. She wants him to stay blond.

He's gorgeous, Hannah had said, and Una had smiled.

Isn't he? He's spoiled rotten, but he's not a bit cheeky.

And now he was dead, and his hair would never get darker. Hannah cradled her coffee mug and chased a crumb with her finger. "God, I can't imagine what his mother is going through right now. Life's so unfair, isn't it?"

"Sure is."

"Anything funny on the telly?"

They moved into the sitting room and searched around and eventually found *Curb Your Enthusiasm*, and sat watching as Larry got into an argument in an ice-cream shop, but for once Hannah found it all terribly pointless.

———————

The church was packed. It might have been Christmas Day. Most of the pews were full, people shuffling along to make room for still more. The atmosphere was thick with the smell of damp clothes and waxy flowers and furniture polish.

The little white coffin sat in front of the altar, a single wreath laid on top, spelling out JASON in red carnations. Someone was playing a tune on the organ that sounded familiar to Hannah.

Cupcakes on the Corner was closed, the first time in its twelve weeks of existence that she'd closed it outside normal working hours. *"Back at one,"* she'd written on the sign she'd stuck to the door. Two hours off to mourn Una's nephew, Claire's son.

"God, it's warm."

Beside Hannah, Geraldine fanned herself with a hymn booklet. Glass Slipper was closed, too, had remained closed since Friday, three days before. *"Closed until further notice"* was what Geraldine had written on the sign that went up on that door, the day after the accident. *God knows when we'll reopen,* Geraldine had told Hannah. *Poor Alice is in an awful state. I've told her I can manage on my own, but she hardly hears what I'm saying, she's so distracted.*

There was a rustle among the congregation, and Hannah looked up to see a priest walking onto the altar. She got to her feet with everyone else. The priest told them in a soft voice that they were about to take part in the Mass of the Angels. He said that he had baptized Jason, that he had met him often in the Junior Infant class when he visited the school. He remembered Jason's cheerfulness and love of drawing pictures, and he said a terrible cross had been given to Jason's loving family.

Somewhere behind Hannah a woman began sobbing bitterly. Feet shuffled, people coughed and sneezed and blew noses and cleared throats, and a woman cried her way through the Mass of the Angels.

A choir from Jason's school sang "He's Got the Whole World in His Hands" at the offertory. A teenage girl played Eric Clapton's "Tears in Heaven" on the violin while everyone filed up to Communion. Jason's Aunt Una walked onto the altar and struggled through a terribly maudlin poem about little angels that caused a renewed rustling and sniffling.

And all through the ceremony, Hannah felt a desperate sadness that she knew to her shame was only partly in response to the little boy's death. She mourned Jason, of course, she deeply regretted the shocking waste of his passing, but kneeling in the too-warm church, responding automatically to the familiar litanies, she realized that she was also mourning Patrick's absence, and the children they might have had if things had gone differently. She wanted to howl at the tragedy of her ruined relationship, the death of the dreams that seemed so foolish now.

She glanced at her mother, kneeling beside her, whispering prayers. Imagine if she knew what was going through her selfish daughter's head.

And then the Mass was over, and they all got to their feet again and shuffled toward the top of the church to pay their respects to the bereaved family. When she eventually reached the front pew, Hannah took Claire's limp hand in hers and said, "Claire, it's Hannah Robinson, I'm so sorry," and the girl looked emptily back at her, and the man beside her, who Hannah assumed was Jason's father, shook with sobs, head bowed, as she pressed his hand.

She sympathized with Mrs. Connolly, dry-eyed and haggard, and shook hands with the next two people, whom she took to be Jason's other grandparents, and a couple of distraught teenage girls who might have been aunts. She hugged Una, weeping at the end of the pew, and she shook hands with Claire and Una's father in his wheelchair in the aisle.

On her way back down the church, Hannah saw her mother with an arm around the shoulders of the woman who was still crying helplessly, and she realized it was Alice.

Nora Paluzzi had been a PA for three hours and twenty-seven minutes. She'd made coffee for her new boss (strong, black, two sugars) and met some of the journalists and secretaries who worked for the newspaper, none of whose names she remembered now. She was given a desk in a kind of anteroom outside Patrick's office and shown by one of the other females (Hilary? Andrea?) where Patrick's filing cabinet was and how he liked his files to be organized.

She'd been introduced to the diary in which she was to record Patrick's schedule, and she'd been shown the database of contacts she'd need when arranging meetings, making hotel reservations, and the like.

She'd been brought to the staff room where they could make coffee or tea and eat lunch; the toilets had been pointed out to her on the way, and the password to access the newspaper's computers had been divulged.

An e-mail address had been assigned to her. She'd had

her photo taken for an identity card, and she'd been given forms to fill in, looking for tax numbers that meant nothing to her—Adam would help there.

On her desk were a dark green phone, a computer, an intercom pod, a spiral-bound notebook, the hard-backed diary, and a selection of pens. In the top desk drawer, she found a stapler and a half-full packet of staples, a solar-powered calculator, a bottle of correction fluid, a box of paper clips, a pair of scissors, a roll of sticky tape, a safety pin, a box of rubber bands, a three-pack of highlighter markers—one missing—and two brand-new yellow pencils with pink rubber tips.

Behind her desk there was a wooden cabinet on which sat a coffeemaker, coffee and filters, a bowl of sugar lumps, and six mugs, with a bundle of spoons poking from one. Presumably, if Nora wanted to make coffee for herself, she'd have to go hunting for milk.

Nobody had complimented the black wraparound dress or the crimson jacket. Patrick's eyes had flicked over her, but he'd made no comment. He'd disappeared at ten—"Off to meet a colleague, back later"—and she hadn't seen him since. She hoped nobody would come looking for him, as she'd forgotten to ask him where he'd be or what "later" meant. She hadn't thought to get his mobile number, which surely his PA should have.

Nobody had rung. For three hours and twenty-seven minutes, the green phone had sat silently on her desk, except for when she'd phoned Adam.

What's happening? he'd asked, and she'd told him, *Not much,* and they'd arranged to go for a drink that evening.

She debated ringing Leah and decided against it. Leah was being cool, no doubt about it. She needed to get used to the idea that Nora was working for her partner, that was all. Give her a week or two.

She wondered if Leah's pregnancy had been deliberate or accidental. Had Leah engineered it so Patrick would leave Hannah? And what would Hannah make of this news, coming so hot on the heels of his leaving her? She wondered without much interest if Adam had told Hannah about the baby yet.

"I'm bored," she said aloud, to the empty room. She leafed through the diary, reading past entries in some other woman's handwriting. She got up and opened the door of Patrick's office and wandered in. If he came back, she'd say she was looking for anything that needed filing.

His office smelled of his aftershave, which she found a bit heady. An orange scarf dangled from a coat stand in one corner, and a black umbrella hung from a lower hook. A silver-framed photo of Leah and himself in what looked like a hotel lobby stood on his desk—she wondered if Hannah had occupied the silver frame originally. A jumble of papers was scattered across the walnut surface, but she had no notion of sorting them.

His first-floor window overlooked the street. Not much doing out there, as usual. She wondered if her impulse to leave the United States had been a bit premature. Of course, now that she had her green card, she could go back anytime. Maybe she'd try the West Coast next. L.A. might be interesting, or San Francisco.

She checked her watch: a quarter to one. Nobody had mentioned lunchtime, so she assumed it was up to her when she took it. She wasn't particularly hungry, but it would be something to do. She left Patrick's office and ripped a page from the spiral-bound notebook. She wrote, *"Gone to lunch—Nora,"* and left it on his leather swivel chair. He might miss it on the desk, with all those papers.

She took her bag and jacket from her desk drawer—no coat stand for the PA—and walked headlong into Patrick as she turned the corner for the elevators.

"Oops—" He caught her arms to steady her. "Had enough already?"

His aftershave swept over her. "I thought I'd go to lunch," she said, "since there isn't a lot to do right now."

"Good idea." He turned toward his office. "Hang on a minute and I'll join you—I was going to take you out anyway, for your first day."

"Lovely."

As she waited, she pulled out her lipstick and her handbag mirror. That was more like it, a decent lunch with a good-looking man across the table. She was glad now she'd chosen the wraparound. He'd enjoy a bit of cleavage when she leaned across to tell him what she and Leah had gotten up to as teenagers. He'd enjoy that too—she'd spice it up a bit for him. And if he told Leah afterward, what could she say? Wasn't Nora only having a laugh, sharing a few harmless memories with him?

She tucked her lipstick back as he reappeared. Yes, things were definitely looking up.

———

"She's riddled with guilt, poor thing," Geraldine said. "She says she'll be into work tomorrow, but I can't see her being able. I told her I'd open up and she could play it by ear."

Hannah sipped her tea and made no reply.

"And those poor parents," Geraldine said. "Completely

brokenhearted, the two of them. I don't think they knew what was going on." She shook her head. "It's just terrible, the whole business, isn't it?"

"Yes."

"There was no sign of Tom when I dropped Alice home after the funeral. I haven't seen him since it happened—he's probably ashamed to face anyone. God, imagine being responsible for the death of a child. It doesn't bear thinking about, does it?"

Hannah shook her head.

"Of course I knew he liked a drink—we all knew that. But I never would have taken him for a drinker—not a serious one, I mean. He was definitely a bit...the worse for wear at the dinner-dance, but you'd think by the next morning it would have worn off, wouldn't you?"

"Mmm."

"He's taken leave from the dental clinic. They're looking for someone to replace him for a few weeks. Alice says he'll have to go to court. That'll be awful, for both of them."

"It will, awful."

Geraldine paused and studied her daughter. "Are you all right, love? You seem a bit quiet. Are you upset about the funeral?"

"Sorry," Hannah said. "It's not the funeral—I mean, of course that's terrible, but that's not what's bothering me right now." She lifted her cup and drank again.

"What is it then?"

"Ah, it's nothing really..." She laid down her cup and laced her fingers together, and regarded them. "It seems so trivial, compared to..." She took a deep breath. "It's just that I saw Leah Bradshaw today."

Geraldine made a dismissive gesture. "Oh, what do you care about—"

"I think," Hannah broke in, lifting her head to look at her mother, "at least I'm pretty sure, that she's pregnant."

"Oh," Geraldine repeated more softly, putting a hand on Hannah's arm. "Oh, love, I'm so sorry."

"It's okay," Hannah said quickly. "I'm fine, really. I just got a bit of a shock, that's all."

It had taken her a minute, on her way back to the shop from the funeral, to recognize the slight, blond-haired woman across the street. She'd glanced at her and then away—and something, some flash of memory, had made her look back. And there she was, the woman Patrick had left her for. Standing at the edge of the path, scanning the oncoming traffic.

And as Hannah stared, the anger rose in her, so palpable she could taste it. She glared across the street, willing the other woman to see her, on the point of storming across the road and slapping her—and then Leah raised her arm to signal to an approaching taxi, and the movement stretched the fabric of her jacket against her body and clearly outlined the swelling underneath her bust.

Hannah watched, incredulous, as Leah got into the taxi and disappeared. *Pregnant,* Hannah thought. *She's pregnant with his child.* Trying to assimilate this startling new discovery as she made her way slowly back to the shop. Leah was pregnant; they were going to have a baby. Sometime in the next few months, Patrick was going to be a father. He might have known—he must have known?—before he'd left Hannah. Each fresh realization causing another shiver of disbelief.

And as the clock on the wall crawled toward five, she remembered with mortification all the times she'd almost texted him, craving his return, ready to beg him to come back. Imagine if she'd done it, imagine that.

"It's just so soon," she said to Geraldine now. "It seems so quick." Reaching for a ginger nut, cracking it in two. "Doesn't it?"

It's early days, Patrick had said every time the subject had come up. *We're in no hurry, are we? Plenty of time.* And Hannah had accepted it: no point in arguing if it wasn't what he wanted. So they'd taken precautions, and no babies had happened, and she'd waited for him to be ready.

"She must have been pregnant when...he was still with me," she said, tapping the half biscuit against the side of her cup. "She wouldn't be showing yet if..." She searched her mother's face. "Do you think it was an accident?" she asked, knowing as the words were uttered that it was wishful thinking, not wanting to accept that maybe Patrick had wanted children after all—just not with her.

"Well—" began Geraldine.

"Doesn't matter," Hannah broke in swiftly. "No point in ifs and buts. It was just a shock, that's all."

"I know, love," Geraldine said quietly. "Of course it was." She took a ginger nut. "I'm supposed to be off these for Lent, but, really, what's the point?" She dunked it in her tea. "Where did you say Adam was gone?"

Hannah cradled her cup. "Out for a drink with Nora. It was her first day at work today."

"You never told me she got a job. Where's she working?"

And just like that, they were back to Patrick.

———

Wally slapped John on the back. "Hey, Johnny. Fancy meeting you here. Can I get you another one?"

John shook his head. "I'm okay, thanks. You working tonight?"

Wally nodded. "Probably be quiet, but I'll do a few hours."

Monday nights at Vintage were very different from Saturdays. At almost ten o'clock, barely a dozen drinkers were about, soft piped music replacing the band.

The barman set a small bottle of water in front of Wally. "Thanks, Neil." He touched it against John's glass. "*Sláinte.*"

They sometimes ran into each other on Mondays. John had developed the habit of dropping in for a pint on his way home from the rented workshop, just down the road. He liked the quietness of Monday nights, liked the chance to kick back and do nothing for an hour or so. And Wally, whose work brought him all over Clongarvin, sometimes found his way to Vintage on Mondays, too.

We could use a saxophonist, Wally had said when he'd rung John, his cousin Patsy having passed on the number of the carpenter-musician from Scotland. *That's if you're any good, of course.*

No sign of a smile in his voice, so John couldn't tell if he was joking. *I'm not bad,* he'd replied. *No complaints so far.*

Why don't you come round when we're rehearsing, Wally had suggested. *Try out a few pieces with us, see how it goes.*

So he'd gone to Wally's house and met the three of them, and they'd played together for an hour or so. The pieces were popular ones that John knew well, and he soon adapted his playing to suit their quirky style. He knew he fitted in well so he wasn't surprised when Wally, the unspoken leader of the outfit, invited him to join them.

We play here and there, wherever we can pick up a gig, he told John. *As it stands, we've got no regular slot, but there's a wine bar just about to open down by the river, and I've heard that the owner wants some live jazz, so I'm going to have a word with him.*

Carlos, the Portuguese double bassist, had heavily accented and quite broken English, and Wally's sister Vivienne, who played the clarinet, was so shy she barely spoke, so it was Wally whom John felt he knew best after almost four months of playing with them.

Wally finished his water. "Better get going. That taxi won't drive itself. See you Wednesday." Wednesday was rehearsal night, usually in Wally's house.

"Good luck, now." John raised his pint and drank, and wondered, as he often did, what his daughter was doing right then in Edinburgh. For some reason, since Hannah Robinson's rejection, he was missing Danielle more.

"Hannah saw that Leah Bradshaw today," Geraldine said.

Stephen tried in vain to remember who Leah Bradshaw was. "Really?"

Geraldine stirred her tea. "It appears," she said, "that Maureen Hardiman was right."

"About what?"

Geraldine threw him an exasperated look. "You never listen to me. I told you she told me Leah Bradshaw was pregnant. I distinctly remember telling you when I got home from bridge."

"Sorry."

"Poor Hannah got the shock of her life today. She knew the minute she saw her." When he made no response, Geraldine looked at him sharply. "Which means, of course, that she was already expecting by the time Patrick broke up with Hannah." She shook her head. "And to think that trollop did my nails."

Stephen raised his cup. Sometimes silence was the safest option.

Geraldine sighed. "I wish Hannah and Adam would give it a try." And as Stephen opened his mouth, she added quickly, "I know you say they're just friends, but can't friends become something more? At least they could try."

"Maybe they're afraid of ruining their friendship if it didn't work out," Stephen said.

Geraldine flapped an impatient hand at him. "Why are you always so sensible? And there was that other lovely man from Scotland—I told you about him, but you probably don't remember that either."

Stephen smiled. "Actually, I do. Isn't he the one who makes kitchens?"

"Yes—he was just lovely, and I'm sure if she'd encouraged him, he would have been interested."

"She's trying to get a business off the ground," Stephen pointed out. "That doesn't leave a lot of time to socialize."

"I know, I know—especially now with that awful accident and Una gone again."

"But she'll be back in a few days, won't she?"

Geraldine lifted her shoulders. "Who knows what'll happen now? That whole family must be devastated."

They drank in silence for a while. It was twenty past eleven, and they were having their usual nighttime cup of tea before going upstairs to bed.

"We were talking at work today," Stephen said after a minute.

There were four male dentists working in the clinic—three now, without Tom. Geraldine had met them all. The other two were in their thirties, both with young families. Tom had started the clinic more than twenty years before, with another man who had since died. Stephen had worked there for more than a decade. The younger men had joined in the last five years.

"About Tom," Stephen added. He lifted the spoon in the sugar bowl and let the sugar spill off it.

"Oh, yes?"

"We were thinking that he doesn't have that long left to work," Stephen said, digging the spoon in again.

Geraldine stared. "What do you mean, he doesn't have that long left? Tom is barely sixty."

"He'll be sixty-two next birthday," Stephen said. "He could take early retirement now if he wanted."

Geraldine frowned. "Early retirement? Has he ever talked about it?"

"Well, no, but that doesn't mean—"

"I wish you'd stop playing with that sugar," Geraldine said sharply. "I can't see Tom wanting that at all. He's much too active to give up work. What would he do with himself all day?"

Stephen lifted the teapot and refilled their cups. "Well, maybe after what's happened, he might change his mind."

Geraldine's hand, reaching for the milk jug, stilled. "Stephen, you're not going to hound him out, are you? Have you forgotten that it was Tom who started the clinic? He got *you* in there, for God's sake."

Stephen put his hands up. "Of course I haven't forgotten, Geraldine. But it's not entirely up to me—I'm just one voice in there."

"You're the senior voice. You and Tom are the seniors. The others haven't been there long enough to be having those kinds of discussions."

"Look, it wasn't an official discussion. It wasn't anything

like that. The subject just came up casually over lunch, that's all."

"It was an *accident*," Geraldine said angrily, "and he'll be well punished for it. The man could go to jail, for heaven's sake. The rest of his life could be ruined."

"I know it could."

"We're his friends. He'll need us to be there for him."

"I know," Stephen repeated. "We *will* be there for him."

"So there'll be no more talk of him having to leave work?"

"Geraldine, I told you it wasn't like that."

"But if the subject comes up again, you'll defend him?"

"Yes."

Geraldine reached for a biscuit.

"I thought you'd given them up for Lent," Stephen said mildly.

"Oh, who cares about bloody Lent?" Geraldine snapped. "There are more important things than *Lent*!"

She dropped the biscuit and put her head into her hands. Stephen reached across the table and stroked her arm.

"Sorry," he said.

"No, *I'm* sorry," she said, and he could hear the tears in her voice. "I'm not cross with you, it's just... What a horrible thing to happen. It's just horrible."

"It is," Stephen said, squeezing her arm gently. "It really is horrible."

They sat opposite each other, the tea cooling in their cups, the clock on the wall every now and then giving a soft electronic whirr.

———————

Patrick lay back in the hot, scented water and closed his eyes.

We had this password, Nora had said, leaning across the table toward him, *for when we fancied a boy.*

Waiting for Patrick to ask, so of course he'd asked.

It was "climax," she'd said, watching his face. *If one of us worked it into a sentence, the other knew to lay off whoever it was, or else.*

The dress she wore crossed over her breasts, and when she leaned toward him, it revealed quite a lot of them. He'd found it hard to avoid looking. She'd caught him once, more than once. It didn't seem to bother her.

Did you ever fall out over boys? he'd asked.

It was just talk, there was no harm in it. It was just harmless talk about two schoolgirls and what they might have gotten up to.

Nora had grinned. *A few times we shared, if he was too good to resist,* she'd said. *Not at the same time, of course.* Poking her fork into the pasta she'd barely touched. *Although there was this one guy...* Trailing off then, laughing softly. *Leah would kill me,* she'd said. *She'd have my guts for garters.*

Go on, Patrick had said, smiling. *Your secret's safe with me. I won't tell.*

She'd put a finger to the side of her mouth, pretending to consider. *Well,* she'd said, *let's just say he got a very tasty... um, sandwich one night. We were all a bit drunk... but it was great fun.*

Twirling a fork through her pasta, smiling. *He was older, so he knew a thing or two about keeping us happy.* Bringing her fork to her lips, sliding it out slowly. *Oh, my.*

Patrick lay in the warm water and pictured two teenage girls peeling off their school clothes—unknotting ties, unbuttoning white shirts, stepping out of pleated skirts. Teasing him, giggling as they undressed. Lying on a bed, or on a floor, maybe—yes, let's put them on the floor, in front of a log fire, with their firm bodies and their lacy white panties.

He was an older man, someone Patrick's own age, probably. Watching as they shed their uniforms, smiling at their antics, egging them on, maybe, before taking off his own clothes and joining them.

He knew a thing or two about keeping us happy. Oh, my.

He lifted himself quickly from the bath, patted himself dry, and walked naked into the bedroom.

Leah looked up from her book and glanced at his erection. "Oh, God," she said. "Sorry, Patrick, not tonight. I'm totally bushed."

April

Sooner or later it had to happen.

After several Friday nights of successfully managing to ignore the events that had taken place in the lives of their daughters, matters between Fiona Bradshaw and Geraldine Robinson finally bubbled to the surface—in Maureen Hardiman's house, of all places.

The bridge itself was played in the drawing room. Maureen called it the drawing room, but as far as Geraldine could see, it was identical in both size and layout to her own sitting room. Typical Maureen, putting on airs, with her collection of spindly-legged two-seaters that really seated only two very good friends comfortably—what was wrong with fold-up chairs?—and ridiculous little coffee tables that were far too low and that barely held their cards and score sheets, never mind a handbag.

There was nothing disastrous in itself about Fiona and Geraldine meeting up. Hadn't they been in the same room several times since Patrick's defection? Hadn't they sat opposite each other for a set time each evening? They were both mature women; they could handle a sensitive situation with the dignity and tact it required. There was no reason for any loss of face or sharp words of any kind. No blame whatsoever need be attached to either party, for indeed both women were entirely blameless.

Geraldine took her seat opposite her partner as usual at the start of the evening, and play commenced. In due course a new game was announced, and the partners who were moving found their new positions and began again. The cards were dealt, the usual discussions ensued. Games were won and lost, scores were entered. The evening wore on.

As usual, Geraldine and Fiona eventually found themselves playing against each other. At no time over the course of that particular bridge game did Geraldine address Fiona directly, or vice versa, unless communication was strictly necessary. The two women's eyes never met, and their hands remained resolutely apart, despite the limited space on Maureen's tables. So far so normal.

Such a shame, then, after successfully negotiating their way through most of the proceedings, after keeping to separate sides of the room during the ensuing tea and nibbles, that Geraldine happened to overhear a chance remark in Maureen's hall at the end of the evening, when the bridge players were maneuvering themselves into coats and retrieving umbrellas. When, in fact, all danger of a contretemps of any kind between the two women in question might have been assumed to have passed.

"Fiona," Dolores Mulcair was heard to say in her unmistakably strident tones, "I hear that your Leah is expecting."

In the act of buttoning her coat, Geraldine froze.

"Yes," Fiona replied, "in June."

Geraldine turned slowly to regard her enemy and discovered Fiona to be looking directly across the hall at her, a tight smile on her face, even while Dolores was congratulating her loudly, even as Maureen Hardiman was saying triumphantly, "I knew it!"

And if she'd seen the slightest hint of remorse, the tiniest sign of regret in Fiona's expression, Geraldine might possibly have found it in her heart to remain silent and let the moment pass. Sadly, she saw nothing of the sort as she gazed across the hall. Fiona's smile wasn't one of triumph, but it held no repentance either. Not, of course, that Fiona was personally responsible for Hannah's desertion, but her daughter had behaved despicably—surely the woman could pretend she was even a small bit ashamed of that?

So Geraldine decided to react. "That was quick," she said loudly, over the buzz of conversation, every bit as loudly as Dolores. "Weren't you saying just at Christmas, Fiona, that you wished Leah would find some nice man?"

Fiona frowned. "No, I—"

"Oh, yes, I definitely remember you saying that," Geraldine continued, "and now she's due in June, which means she got pregnant"—pretending to calculate, aware that the conversations had trailed off around them—"way back in October, it must have been. Now, don't you tell me," she went on, "that you had no idea, you sly old thing."

A dead silence. Eyes swiveling from Geraldine to Fiona. A slight flush in Fiona's cheeks the only sign that her composure was slipping. She opened her mouth, then closed it again. Geraldine waited.

"So who's the lucky man?" someone asked finally, into the silence.

"Yes, Fiona," Geraldine said, the smile rigid on her face, "who is this mystery man that nobody knew about?"

Fiona met her gaze squarely. What else could she do?

"Patrick Dunne is his name," she said evenly, "as you well know, Geraldine."

A collective indrawn breath. Eyes back on Geraldine now,

waiting for her reaction. They all knew that Patrick had been with Hannah: Hadn't Geraldine often mentioned him, saying how good he was to her daughter? Hadn't she expressed the hope to quite a few of them that he'd propose at Christmas? And now they all knew that it was never going to happen, that he'd moved on to Leah Bradshaw, who was pregnant with his child.

Mind you, they'd probably known it all already; when had anything stayed private in Clongarvin for more than five minutes? Hadn't Maureen Hardiman herself been only too delighted to share the juicy details with Geraldine? But here it was, in the public domain at last.

Geraldine turned without another word and opened Maureen's teak front door. She stepped into the damp night air and closed the door on the silence, and walked on shaking legs to where she'd parked the car.

Already she regretted her impulse. It had been irresistible, baiting Fiona like that, so satisfying to throw her off balance. But now they'd all look at Geraldine in pity, and they'd be careful not to mention Hannah. And, of course, she and Fiona would be watched furtively anytime they came face-to-face in the future.

Still, it was out in the open now, no more avoiding to be done. She and Fiona would carry on as usual, she supposed. They'd be polite and cool and never, ever friendly. And naturally, the other women would be sensitive to Geraldine's situation, and Leah's pregnancy wouldn't be discussed in front of her, which was a blessing.

She started the engine and drove home, trying to remember if there was any custard. She could do with a bowl of custard—which was perfectly allowable as long as you made it with skimmed milk.

Hannah raised her glass and sipped. The Spanish wine had a creamy taste that hinted at apples. "Mmm, this is a good one, must remember it."

"Now aren't you glad you came out?"

"You didn't give me a lot of choice."

But she *was* glad, happy to escape her gloomy thoughts for a couple of hours. Here in this dimly lit wine bar it was easier not to think about little dead boys, and eaiser to push ex-boyfriends out of your head, to stop endlessly calculating, counting back the months to figure out when he might have made a baby with another woman.

She sighed, resting her elbows on the bar. Not for the first time, she wished that she and Adam could just fall in love. How simple that would make everything, how happily-ever-after that story would be.

Or would it? Would they drive each other mad within a week? Would romance mess things up between them, ruin the brilliant relationship they had now? She shook her head; what a foolish notion. She hadn't the slightest intention of falling in love with her best friend. Things like that only happened in books.

"To happy times," she said, lifting her glass again, "that are just around the corner."

"I'll drink to that."

A movement caught her eye then, and she turned to see three men and one woman assembling on the little stage, setting up instruments, settling into their seats. "Hey, I forgot about the music."

She watched them preparing for their performance. She saw the woman in black taking a seat, leaning forward to set pages on the stand in front of her. The keyboard player, his back to her, sorting wires and pressing switches, the enormous double bass being positioned on its stand. The man with the closely shaven head raising the saxophone to his—

"I don't believe it," she said softly, lowering her glass.

"What?"

"The man on the far side, with the sax."

"What about him?"

"He's the one who asked me out—John Wyatt. He's John Wyatt. Remember I told you, and I said no."

He hadn't been back to Cupcakes on the Corner. Almost three weeks now without a sign of him, and she kept telling herself that she was relieved, that she'd done the right thing.

"I thought you said he was a carpenter," Adam said.

"Well, he was a carpenter—I mean, he is. I had no idea he did this too."

She was sure he'd never mentioned playing a musical instrument. But they'd spoken so little—two or three times altogether, a few minutes at the most. She knew virtually nothing about him. She remembered thinking he looked familiar, the first time he'd come into the shop, and now she realized it was because she'd seen him here.

She sipped her drink. The band played "'Round Midnight" and "Moonglow" and "At Last," the slow old tunes wafting over her, perfectly suited to the intimate, candlelit surroundings.

He wore a white shirt open at the neck, its sleeves rolled to the elbows. He looked relaxed as he played, perfectly at ease with his instrument. She loved the idea of a man who could make music. Patrick hadn't even been able to sing.

She drained her glass and turned to Adam. "Same again?"

She hadn't been going to stay long: She'd been planning an

early night—or at least not too late a night. But what was the rush, with a Sunday lie-in to look forward to? It had been so long since she'd had a night out. One more drink wouldn't hurt.

They had two more. By the time the music stopped, Hannah's head was buzzing pleasantly. "He's coming this way," she said as John approached the counter in conversation with the man who'd been playing the keyboard.

"Say hello," Adam ordered.

"Hello there," she called immediately, loudly, and they both looked across.

"Well." John smiled as he came over. "Hello to you. Still selling your cupcakes?"

"Of course."

She'd forgotten how attractive his accent was. He showed no embarrassment. There was no awkwardness meeting him again. She introduced him to Adam.

The men shook hands, and then John turned to indicate his companion. "Wally O'Toole."

"Hi," he said, lifting a hand.

"I know you," Hannah exclaimed. "You drive a taxi. You brought me home the day my van broke down." *And the night Patrick left me,* she added silently.

She hadn't even looked at him up to this, too preoccupied with her discovery of John in the band to notice anyone else.

"I remember that," he said. "Presume you got it sorted."

"Oh, yes, all better now."

"Glad to hear it."

He was definitely Irish, no trace of a foreign accent there. He had a nice smile, with very even teeth, and tousled, muddy-blond hair.

"Hannah sells cupcakes," John said, his eyes on her. "She makes them herself."

"Cupcakes," Wally said. "They're some kind of fancy buns, are they?"

Hannah laughed. "That's exactly what they are. 'Cupcakes' is just a sexier name."

"Well, I'm all for sexy buns. Can't have too many of those."

John turned toward the counter and signaled to the barman. He pointed at Hannah's almost-empty wineglass questioningly, but she shook her head. She didn't fancy ruining her one day off with a hangover.

"What's your shop called?" Wally asked, nodding as he accepted a bottle of water, setting aside the accompanying glass.

"Cupcakes on the Corner," Hannah told him.

He considered. "Yes, I remember it now. It's yellow, isn't it?" Raising the bottle to his lips.

"It is."

"That's good," he said. "Yellow's a good color for a cupcake shop."

"I like your music," she could hear Adam saying to John. "A nice mix of instruments, and you play well together."

She threw him a mocking smile—trying to sound as if he knew the first thing about music—but he ignored it.

"I'm afraid I'm just the blow-in," she heard John reply. "The other three are the real musicians—especially Vivienne."

"'And now you'll have to excuse me." Wally waved his half-empty bottle at them. "She'll be waiting for me to drive her home. Nice to meet you both. Johnny, see you next week." And he was gone, weaving his way through the tables toward the rear of the pub.

John turned back to Hannah. "So what do you think of our music?"

"I love it—I had no idea you were a musician."

He really was quite good-looking. And it wasn't as if there were the smallest hope that Patrick would be back now. She wondered if there was any chance she'd be asked out again, or if she'd burned her bridges with John. Maybe she should take the initiative—but even as the thought occurred, she knew she didn't have the courage. She'd never had that confidence around men, could never imagine putting herself into the vulnerable position of asking someone out and risking rejection—just as she'd rejected him.

"I've always wanted to play an instrument," she told him. "Anything really, I wouldn't mind."

Which wasn't true at all, of course—the thought of making music had never, as far as she could remember, crossed her mind. She'd never pressed the keys of a piano, or plucked a guitar string, or even put a tin whistle to her lips. But he wasn't to know that.

"You should take lessons," he said. "Vivienne's a music teacher."

"Oh—is she?" Her bluff was being called. She searched for an excuse and found one. "The trouble is, I'm just so busy with the shop." Thank goodness for the shop.

"Where does she teach?" Adam asked.

"In her own home, as far as I know."

"She looks a bit fierce," Hannah said. "I'm not sure I'd want her teaching me anything."

John laughed. "I can't think of anyone less fierce than Vivienne—she's as timid as a deer. And she's a beautifully sensitive player, totally focused."

"I might take a few lessons myself," Adam said. "I fancy the clarinet."

Hannah looked at him in astonishment. "You, take lessons? You've no interest in music."

He shrugged. "Maybe I'd like to give it a go."

She laughed. "I'd love to see that—as long as you practice in the shed." She turned to John. "Adam is my housemate," she explained. "He moved in to keep me solvent. We've known each other forever."

"And your shop is going well?" John asked. Giving no sign at all that the status of her relationship with Adam was of the slightest interest to him.

"Fine," she said. "It's hard work, some weeks better than others, but I'm still there and managing to pay the bills, just about."

"Well done," he said. "That's pretty good going, these days."

"And how's the carpentry business?"

"Could be better, but I'm surviving too."

"How did you get to be in the band?" Adam asked him.

John told them about Patsy in the woodworking store, who'd put him in touch with Wally. "I was lucky—it's a good group. I think we play well together, and everyone gets along."

Yes, she had definitely been too hasty. He was probably exactly what she needed to help her forget about Patrick Dunne.

The lights went up in the bar just then.

"Will we hit the road?" Adam asked, pulling on his jacket.

"I suppose so." She didn't want to go, but there was no excuse to stay.

"See you again," John said, addressing both of them, "when you want to hear some good music."

She smiled. "And if you ever need a cupcake, you know where I am."

That was as much as she could do to try to reopen the door she'd shut in his face a few weeks ago. He might or he might not be willing to try again, but at least she could encourage him a little.

"Safe home," he said, lifting a hand.

She wondered if he watched them walking out.

Nothing had changed. Everything had changed. They slept in different bedrooms now.

Ah, don't, Tom had said when Alice had taken her night-dress from under her pillow, her toothbrush from the ensuite bathroom. *Ah, don't do this.*

But she'd been raw. She'd been angry and heartbroken and still full of tears, and she hadn't answered him. Now she slept in the bedroom they still called Ellen's, although it was years since their daughter had spent any time there.

That first night Alice had lain awake in Ellen's bed, afraid to close her eyes, afraid of the pictures that might appear. In the morning she'd gotten up at twenty to eight like she always did on a workday. She'd gone downstairs and put bacon and tomatoes under the grill, and when they were cooked Tom had appeared, and they'd sat down and eaten breakfast, and no mention had been made of the accident.

She'd gone back to work the day after the funeral. It was a relief to have somewhere to go, something to set the alarm for—not that she'd needed an alarm, wide awake long before it had gone off. Tom hadn't appeared for breakfast that morning, and she hadn't called him.

In the shop she watched the faces of people coming in, looked for a sign that they knew. Waited for them to spit in her face and call her a murderer—because wasn't she as guilty as Tom, when you thought about it? Shouldn't she have driven, shouldn't she have insisted, knowing the state he was in?

Geraldine was her savior. Geraldine chatted away when the shop was empty and smiled at customers when Alice couldn't. Geraldine followed her into the back when she disappeared, and held her while she wept, and told her that there was nothing she could have done, nothing at all.

When Alice got home in the evenings Tom was there, reading the newspaper or watching daytime television. She still cooked dinner, although he was the one with the free time now, but he'd always been hopeless in the kitchen so she didn't push it. God knows what he'd serve up.

They made small talk as they ate. The weather might be mentioned, the days getting nice and long now. He'd say if he was out of shaving foam or if next door's dog had gotten into the back garden again. She'd offer more potatoes, another spoon of rice pudding.

No mention was made, by either of them, of his returning to work. Geraldine had told her they'd gotten a temporary replacement for him at the dental clinic, but Alice didn't pass this information on at home. She had no idea whether Tom was in touch with Stephen, or with either of his other colleagues, and some instinct stopped her from talking about it. She had to believe that he'd go back when he was ready.

They had a visit from a guard who'd played golf with Tom occasionally. *Your solicitor will be working away on your behalf,* he'd said. *Keep the spirits up, keep busy, that's the thing,* and Alice thanked him and cut more coffee cake.

She found it amazing that Tom hadn't lost his license. The car had been returned to them a couple of days after the accident, and no mention had been made of taking Tom's license away. He'd killed a child and failed a breath test, and he was still legally entitled to get behind the wheel of a car and drive.

But he hadn't driven since the accident. It had been Alice who'd taken his car to the garage to have the dent in the bumper straightened. She hated doing it—her fingers were white on the wheel, her body clenched so tightly she could hardly breathe—but the sight of the dent had been unbearable to her.

She had no idea what Tom did all day. She didn't know what time he got up or how long he stayed in his pajamas. He didn't have to go out for the paper—they had it delivered. She was pretty sure he hadn't been near a golf course, even with the nice mild weather they'd been having lately.

But he went out sometime. Alice found the bottles by accident, searching in the trash for a receipt she'd thrown away. They'd been pushed right to the bottom, three empty Powers Gold Label whiskey bottles. She'd taken them out and brought them to the recycling bins at the roundabout, ten minutes' walk away. She'd keep an eye out for others, because of course there would be others, and whenever she found them, she'd recycle them.

She'd decided to say nothing to Ellen. Why worry her, so far away? Ellen might feel she should come home, which Alice dreaded. Imagine their daughter seeing Tom in this state, imagine her walking into this nightmare. Time enough to tell her when things began to happen, when telling became unavoidable, as it surely must do.

So when Alice wrote her weekly letter, the day after Jason's funeral—they phoned only on special occasions—she made no mention of a dead child. She didn't talk about a court case, didn't bring up the failed breathalyzer tests.

She was convinced that Tom would be sent to jail. Why would anyone let him off, after what he'd done? Even if he hadn't meant to do it, a child was dead and it was his fault. He'd have to be seen to be accountable.

With every night she passed in Ellen's room, moving back across the landing became more of an impossibility. She discovered that she liked the compactness of the single bed, after years of sharing a double. She was beginning to forget what it felt like to have another body lying beside you at night, to have someone else's odor mixing with yours in the morning.

She used a hot-water bottle in place of Tom's warmth. She left the window open more than he would have liked. One night she left the curtains open, too, and stared out at a scattering of stars till morning. She slept little, some nights not at all, but during the days she seemed full of restless energy.

She thought about the boy's parents. They filled her head as she climbed the stepladder to take down a shoe box, as she peeled carrots, as she brushed her teeth. She thought about the grief Tom had visited on them. She imagined the mother taking little clothes off the line, knowing that there was nobody left to wear them. She thought about a football lying forgotten under a bush, the father remembering the last time they'd kicked it around the garden together.

They filled her head, these two people. She'd never seen them—she'd been in no state to sympathize at the funeral, even if she'd felt she had any right to shake their hands. She didn't know a thing about them, apart from their names and the fact that they'd once had a son.

And she knew where they lived.

"Springwood Gardens," the death notice read. No house number, no name. Alice knew roughly where Springwood Gardens was, behind the town hall.

"Beloved only son," the notice said, *"of David and Claire."*

O'Brien was the surname. Jason O'Brien was the boy Tom

had killed. It shouldn't be too hard to find David O'Brien in Springwood Gardens. If there was confusion, she could say she had a Mass card to deliver.

She folded the death notice and put it back into her bag. She took an onion from the vegetable rack and cut into its creamy, wet center.

Vivienne. He loved the name. He was reasonably sure he'd liked it before he knew that it was hers, but now he loved it. Vivienne, who played the clarinet.

He'd been thrown by the other man's saying he was driving her home after the gig on Saturday night. What did that mean? Were they together? Was her home his home, too, or did they just live in the same direction and travel to the bar in one car simply because it made sense?

Adam had no way of knowing—so he decided to assume she was single and proceed with his new plan.

The intercom buzzed. Nora dropped the emery board and pressed the "receive" button. "Yes?"

"Can you come in?"

She heard the words in stereo as usual. Patrick's actual voice on the other side of the door behind her was almost as audible as the more mechanical words that issued through the machine. She'd pointed out to him that he only had to raise his voice slightly to call her into his office and thereby do away with the need for the intercom, but he'd laughed.

"On the way," she replied.

She released the button and got up, taking her pad and pen from the desk, smoothing her purple skirt, checking that her lipstick was in place.

He sprawled in his chair, hair tousled, tie askew. She crossed to the window, dropping her pad and pen on his desk as she passed. She slid the window open, aware of his eyes on her as she leaned against the sill and reached upward.

"Stuffy in here," she said. "You need air-conditioning."

He waited until she'd taken a seat. "Like I keep telling you, you're not in New York now."

"Don't I know it." She hitched up her skirt a fraction and crossed one knee over the other. "Am I taking a letter, sir?"

Ten days down she was reasonably sure she wouldn't spend the rest of her life—or even the rest of this year—working for the *Clongarvin Voice*. But it would do to pass the time for a while—and really, apart from the lack of any trace of glamour, she had no serious objections to the job.

The paper was a weekly, which meant their only really busy day was Thursday, and even that had been easy enough last week, with the others still regarding her as the new girl who wasn't expected to know her way around yet. Patrick's schedule wasn't too hectic most of the time, which suited her just fine—and compared to some of the scumbags she'd come across in New York, he was pretty much the ideal boss.

He fancied her, of course. Men were rubbish at hiding that. He couldn't keep his eyes off her chest, he watched her mouth when she talked, he probably lusted after her rear view when she walked away from him. And she fueled the attraction, enjoying the attention of a good-looking man while well able to keep him at a distance.

The clothes she wore to work were carefully chosen to tease, to give just enough away without being too revealing.

Her skirts were figure-hugging, but long enough to look suitable for the office. Her tops showed cleavage, but not too much—unless she leaned in and allowed a better view. Her blouses weren't exactly sheer, but sufficiently fine to hint at what lay beneath. She kept a bottle of perfume in her desk drawer.

She knew, as she scribbled down his words, that he was looking at her. Slouched in his chair, he was taking her in. Maybe even fantasizing a little. She felt his eyes on her body as she brushed a stray hair from her face, as she bit her bottom lip gently.

"That's it," he said after two letters had been dictated. "Will you get those out before lunchtime?"

"Of course." She closed the pad and stood. "How's Leah? I haven't seen her in a while."

She'd sent a text a few evenings ago, just to say hello and see the reaction. Leah's reply, when it came, had been brief: UP TO MY EYES, HOPE ALL'S WELL. MUST MEET UP SOON.

"She's fine," Patrick replied. "A bit tired, naturally."

"Naturally...When's she finishing up?"

"Oh, not for another month or so." His eyes strayed to the neckline of her pale gray top. "No maternity leave when you work for yourself."

"Ain't that the truth." She pushed her hair behind her shoulders. "Well, I'd better get back to work."

"What about lunch?" he said as she reached the door. "Have you plans?"

She turned, her face full of regret. "Actually, I have, sorry. Some other time."

She had no plans, of course. But it was fun to keep him at a distance—until he was gagging for it.

Always such fun, the foreplay.

———————

Una came back to work a week after Jason's funeral.

Hannah took in the pale face, the determined smile. "Are you sure you're ready for this? You can have longer."

Una shook her head. "Thanks, but I need to get back to some kind of a routine...And I think Claire and Dave would like to be on their own for a while. They've been surrounded by people since—"

She broke off, pulling a tissue from her bag and pressing it to her eyes. "God, sorry—I'm not going to do this all morning, I promise."

"Go in and put the kettle on," Hannah told her, "and make yourself a cuppa. I'm afraid there's only boxed milk, I forgot to get fresh."

But Una pushed the tissue back into her bag and began to unbutton her jacket. "No, I'm okay, honestly. Just give me something to do and then you head off."

Hannah glanced around the shop. "Well, I didn't get a chance to sweep the floor this morning," she lied, "so you could do that."

Una hung her jacket and got the broom from the back room. "They're devastated," she said as Hannah began to untie her apron. "Completely in bits, the two of them." She pushed the broom around the clean floor. "Dave told me Claire cries all night, just lies in bed all curled up and cries." She gathered up nothing in the dustpan. "She sits in Jason's bedroom for hours in the day. Dave hasn't been near it—he says he just can't bring himself."

Hannah made no move to put on her jacket. "Listen," she said, "there's nothing I have to do in town today. Why don't I stay around here? Why don't the two of us—"

Una straightened up, holding the empty dustpan. "No, no, don't do that—if you stay here I'll just feel useless. I'll be fine, honest."

"But maybe," Hannah said gently, "you'd like to talk."

Una shook her head. "No...thanks, Hannah, I really appreciate the offer, but I think I need a distraction."

"You're sure?"

Una nodded. "I'm sure. See you at twelve."

"Ring me if you need to."

So Hannah left the shop, for once not relishing her two hours of freedom. As she walked down the street, a taxi drove by, the driver lifting a hand in greeting. Hannah waved back, not recognizing him until he'd passed.

Wally, the taxi-driving keyboard player. Maybe nobody could afford to be a full-time musician anymore. She remembered him making some remark about sexy buns, and she smiled.

She turned a corner and saw with a sinking heart that Nora O'Connor was walking rapidly in her direction, too close for Hannah to pretend not to have seen her and duck into the nearest doorway.

"Hi there," Nora said as she approached. "I was just on my way to your little shop, actually."

Dark green skirt that hugged her hips and fishtailed out beneath. Black fitted jacket over snow-white blouse. Black boots, snug on her calves.

Dressing up for Patrick Dunne. The thought popped, completely unbidden, into Hannah's head. She wished she were wearing something slightly more fashionable than her old blue top and gray trousers. "Did you want me for some reason?"

Adam never talked about his sister's job at the newspaper.

Hannah couldn't imagine that working for the *Clongarvin Voice* held too many attractions for Nora O'Connor—apart from its editor, maybe.

"I wanted to pick up some of your cupcakes for a meeting," Nora said now. "Thought they'd add a nice fancy note."

"Oh..." Hannah immediately felt ashamed. Why should she assume that Nora would make a play for Patrick? Who was she to judge Adam's sister—whom she hardly knew, after all? "That's nice of you. Una is in the shop, she'll look after you."

"Yes, Adam mentioned you'd taken on an assistant. Business must be going well."

"Not bad," Hannah said. "It's hard work, but it's keeping me solvent—more or less." She began to edge away. "Well, I'd better..."

"Me, too—catch you later." And Nora was gone, leaving behind a whirl of something that smelled expensive. Off to buy cupcakes for a meeting that Patrick would most likely be attending. Hannah wondered if he'd notice them, if he'd recognize them as hers. Surely he'd remember her cupcakes, after all the sample recipes she'd presented him with once she'd made up her mind about opening the shop.

They'd still had only one encounter in the months since they'd parted, but she'd caught sight of him a few times. Across the aisles in a supermarket as she stood in the queue with her cart. Sitting in the front seat of a taxi once, thankfully not looking in her direction. Flicking through the pages of a golfing magazine in the barber's as he waited for the hot-towel shave that was his weekly treat to himself.

And once with his arm curved around Leah Bradshaw's waist as he shepherded her across the street. Hannah couldn't be sure if they'd spotted her and chosen to avoid a meeting.

Probably—and under the circumstances, she supposed quite understandable—but it had hurt nonetheless.

She still felt a lurch when she saw him. She still loved the look of him, the thick, dark hair, the wonderfully deep brown eyes, the stubble that crept back a couple of hours after he'd shaved, the tallness of him, the solidity of his body. She remembered his smell, the musk of his aftershave, the sharp tang of his sweat.

She turned another corner and realized she'd walked toward Glass Slipper without intending to. Might as well check out the new stock—not that she could afford a pair of tights, let alone shoes, but a look wouldn't hurt.

A sign on the window read EVERYTHING 10% OFF. Another read ALL STOCK REDUCED. Geraldine sat alone on a stool behind the counter, reading a magazine. She looked up as Hannah walked in. "Hello, love—nothing wrong?"

"No—I'm just at a loose end. Una came back this morning."

"Yes, you were saying. How is the poor girl?"

"Still very upset, of course, but I think it'll do her good to be back at work." Hannah looked around. "It's quiet here, isn't it?"

Geraldine closed the magazine. "There's been nobody in yet today."

"Nobody at all? Even just looking?"

"Not a soul." Geraldine lifted her shoulders. "We've been blaming the recession, but..." She shook her head. "I'm wondering now if that's all there is to it."

Hannah stared at her. "You think people are avoiding the shop, after what happened?"

Geraldine shook her head. "I really don't know what to think, love—but in a place the size of Clongarvin word doesn't take long to get around."

The shelves were filled with brightly colored shoes and sandals. There was an assortment of boots labeled FINAL REDUCTIONS—UP TO 70% OFF. There were two rows of slippers and a selection of sports shoes.

"Where's Alice?" Hannah asked.

"Gone to the doctor. She says she's having trouble sleeping."

"I'm not surprised...How is she in general?"

Geraldine considered. "Well, she's improved a bit since she came back, and she's doing her best to put a good face on it, but she looks terribly worn out—she must be worried sick about what's ahead of them. No wonder she's finding it hard to sleep. I've tried inviting them round to dinner, but she keeps making excuses."

"What about Tom?"

"He seems to have gone to ground—Alice changes the subject whenever I ask her about him, and Stephen says he's made no effort to contact the clinic about going back to work." She got to her feet and walked toward the back of the shop. "Will you have tea?"

"Only if you want some yourself."

But the shop door opened just then, and Geraldine stayed to attend to a woman who entered and began walking slowly past the footwear on display. Hannah drifted around the shop, picking up and trying on various shoes. A red peep-toe sandal with a woven wedge sole, a lime green stiletto that would probably look a lot better below Nora O'Connor's slender ankles.

"You'll come for lunch on Sunday, won't you?" Geraldine asked when the woman had left, empty-handed. "I'm doing lamb."

"I'll be there."

Sunday was Easter Sunday. Last year she and Patrick had spent Easter in a small house on Achill Island. They'd driven up early on Good Friday and stayed till Easter Monday evening. By prior agreement he'd given her a gold-wrapped Lindt chocolate rabbit, and she'd given him a six-pack of Walkers Cheese & Onion crisps. They'd eaten Easter Sunday lunch in the local hotel and walked it off on the beach afterward.

"When do you expect Alice back?" she asked as they were drinking their tea.

"Not for another hour, I'd say. It was after ten when she left, and you know what doctors' waiting rooms can be like." Geraldine paused. "Anyone nice come into your shop?"

"Not really, no one out of the ordinary."

Hannah knew that her mother was thinking about John Wyatt. She wondered if he was traveling to Scotland for Easter. If not, they could well have been spending Easter Sunday together, or part of it at least. He hadn't been back to Cupcakes on the Corner since they'd met in Vintage. Of course it didn't matter, she hardly knew him—but still it irked, this feeling that she'd been hasty, that she'd thrown something away without considering its worth. Maybe she'd visit Vintage again sometime with Adam.

When she got back to the shop, Una reported that a woman had bought two dozen cupcakes and asked for a written receipt.

"Curly auburn hair, well dressed, American accent?"

"Yes. You know her?"

"I know her."

Two dozen cupcakes, easily their biggest order to date. It occurred to her suddenly that Patrick might specifically have asked his PA to shop at Cupcakes on the Corner. Salving his conscience, maybe, by throwing some business her way? Not that it mattered a damn whose decision it had been—an order was an order, wherever it came from.

Still, it would be nice to know.

———

"I've invited my mother for lunch on Sunday," Leah said. "I couldn't leave her on her own at Easter."

"Fine," Patrick answered, thinking about the way his PA's fingers trailed across the skin of her throat as she spoke on the phone. Back and forth, back and forth, across that smooth, polished-looking skin.

"Will you pick up some antacid tablets on your way home?" Leah asked him. "The original ones, not flavored."

"No problem."

He bet she wore stockings, the ones with lacy tops that Leah used to wear. An inch or so of tanned, bare skin above them, before the other lace began.

"What time will you be home?" Leah asked.

"Around six, I'd say. Maybe a bit later."

He wondered if she'd had a job done on her breasts. He wondered if you'd be able to tell by touching them. She certainly took every opportunity to show them off. Not that he was complaining. He'd always been a breast man. It had been the first thing he'd noticed about Hannah—and the only positive effect Leah's pregnancy was having on her body was that her breasts were fuller and more sensitive to his touch.

"I'm doing lasagna," Leah said.

"Lovely."

After he'd hung up, Patrick sat for a few minutes behind

his walnut desk. Then he pressed the intercom and said, "Can you come in?"

There was always a letter that needed to be written, if you thought about it for long enough.

It took Alice less than fifteen minutes to drive from Glass Slipper to Springwood. She pulled in to the curb on the first road of the estate—Springwood Park—and opened the Mass card she'd bought and wrote *"Jason O'Brien"* on the empty line and *"Alice"* in the space for her name. She slipped the card back into its envelope before getting out of the car.

Springwood was a mix of terraced and semidetached houses with low iron railings separating their narrow front lawns. Some residents had replaced the grass with cement or paving to create a driveway, while others had bordered the lawn with flower beds. A few were terribly neglected—rented, probably—but most were fairly well cared for.

"I'm looking for the O'Briens," she told a woman with long blond hair who turned out of a gate and came toward her, but the woman shook her head.

"They're in Springwood Gardens," Alice said. "David O'Brien."

But the woman said, "Sorry," in a foreign accent and walked on.

"The O'Briens," she said to a man walking a small black-and-white dog. "Springwood Gardens." The dog sniffed at her shoes, his tail wagging.

"Dave and Claire, the ones who lost their little boy?"

Alice nodded, heart thudding. "I have a Mass card," she said, but he'd already turned away to gesture up the road.

"Second next left is Springwood Gardens," he told her. "They're on the right, about halfway down."

"You wouldn't know the number?"

He shook his head. "Anyone will tell you," he said. "Ask anyone up there."

But when she took the second left turn, there was no one to ask, except two small boys around seven or eight, sitting on the edge of the path eating crisps, a grubby white football trapped between the feet of one.

"Do you know where the O'Briens live?" Alice asked, and they stared at her, still crunching. She didn't want to say, *Where the little boy was killed.* "Dave and Claire O'Brien?"

One of the boys took his hand out of his crisps packet and pointed. "That house," he said, "with the flowers," and Alice followed his finger and saw the red bunch of wilting roses tied to the gatepost with a faded white ribbon.

"Thank you," she said, crossing the road, feeling their eyes on her as she approached the gate. There was a plastic-covered note attached to the bouquet. Alice bent and read *"To Jason, all our love forever, from the McCarthys"* in a child's careful script.

She straightened and regarded the house. It looked much like its neighbors, the middle one in a terrace of five. The lawn was neatly mowed, the flower bed studded with hard-pruned rosebushes. The windows were bare except for an upstairs one whose curtains were drawn. The front door was dark green with a brass 37 on it.

She walked up the cement path, pulling the Mass card from her pocket. She pushed it quickly through the letter slot and walked away, out the gate and back onto the path, past the two boys who were still eating crisps.

When she returned to the shop, Geraldine told her she looked pale. "Are you all right?"

"I'm fine."

"You had a long wait."

"I did."

"Did he give you a prescription? Did you get sleeping pills?"

"Yes...I'll make us a cuppa."

Alice filled the kettle, seeing the wilted roses tied to the gate, the carefully pruned rosebushes in the garden, the green door with 37 in brass screwed onto it. She'd felt resistance as she'd pushed the card through, a draft excluder on the other side. She hadn't heard the card falling onto the floor.

She thought about the mother picking it up, taking out the card, and reading *"Alice."* Showing it to the father, who'd shake his head when she asked if he knew anyone by that name.

The previous evening Alice had found two empty whiskey bottles pushed to the bottom of the bin. She'd pulled them out and brought them to the recycling station.

She'd lied to Geraldine about going to the doctor. It was the first time she'd lied to Geraldine.

Adam typed *"clarinet"* and pressed "search." After a few seconds, the screen changed, and he read *"2,234 results."* He scrolled slowly through clarinet mouthpieces and sheet music for clarinets and clarinet cases and the odd actual clarinet. He went back to the home page and typed *"clarinet instrument"* and searched again, and this time eleven results showed up.

He studied an ebony clarinet that was being sold by

George4234. The price quoted was forty pounds, which was considerably lower than the ones he'd seen scrawled on the tags attached to clarinets in Clongarvin's one and only musical-instrument store, which also sold sound systems, TVs, and DVDs. George4234 was in the United Kingdom, which seemed close enough. There was a bid of forty-two pounds on the clarinet. Adam typed in a bid of forty-four and pressed "enter."

NOT AN EBAY MEMBER YET? the screen asked. REGISTER HERE. Adam chose a user ID and a password and filled in all the boxes with the information required for him to get his hands on a clarinet for forty-four pounds.

However shy she was, a music teacher could hardly refuse a would-be eager pupil. If she said she was fully booked, Adam would ask to be put on a waiting list. He'd tell her that he'd just bought a clarinet and he was desperate to play it and that she'd been recommended to him. It wasn't a complete lie—John Wyatt had called her a beautifully sensitive player, which was surely a recommendation. He'd also said she was as timid as a deer, which Adam liked.

He'd be patient. He'd be gentle and nonthreatening, and he'd gain her trust, however long it took.

And who knew? He might even learn to play the clarinet.

———————

In number 37 Springwood Gardens, a woman sits on a single bed, on top of a Spider-Man duvet. The curtains in the room are drawn, although it's still early afternoon. Enough light filters through the unlined fabric—zoo animals on a yellow background—to pick out the small white wardrobe and matching chest of drawers, the red wooden toy chest, the shelf full of Mr. Men and Dr. Seuss and Thomas the Tank Engine books. The row of small footwear—his white runners, his red wellies, his blue slippers—underneath.

The woman sees none of these. She sees him soaring on a swing, shouting *Higher! Higher!* and laughing delightedly as she pushes him. She sees him squatting on a beach, filling a bucket with sand as the tip of his tongue pokes from his mouth, his blue trunks slipping down in the back to show an inch of his bottom.

She sees his cheeks puff as he blows out four candles on a blue-and-white cake, a dribble of saliva plopping onto the icing.

She feels his hand slipping out of hers as he runs onto the road because he's just seen his friend Paul on the other side. She feels the terror, she sees the car, she hears the scream bursting out of her as he flies into the air.

Higher! Higher!

He is all she sees now.

———

Adam handed her a boxed chocolate egg. "Happy Easter."

"Oh, yummy—thanks very much." Hannah produced a similar box. "And for you, the usual."

"Ta."

They made coffee and settled at the kitchen table. "So," she said, peeling the gold paper from her egg, "when are you off?"

Adam and Nora were traveling the fifty miles to their parents' house for Easter Sunday lunch.

"I'm collecting Nora in an hour." He broke a curved slab from his egg. "I suppose I should be working up an appetite."

"Me, too." Hannah dipped a shard into her coffee mug. "We'll just have half now."

"Listen," he said then, his mouth full of chocolate, "guess what I did the other day."

"What?"

He licked the tips of his fingers one by one. "I bought a clarinet."

Hannah turned to him, the melting chocolate halfway to her mouth. "What?"

"I said—"

"A real clarinet that you play?"

He grinned. "Yes, a real clarinet. I bought it on eBay. It should be arriving in the next few days."

Hannah stared. "I don't believe it. You were serious the other night, about wanting to play? But you're about as musical as an elephant."

"Thank you." He crunched chocolate loudly. "I'll have you know I intend to take lessons."

Hannah's eyes narrowed. "Not from the woman in the bar?"

"Well," he said, dipping another shard into his coffee, preoccupied all at once with the task at hand, "since she's the only one I know who teaches, I thought I may as well ask her." Raising and lowering the softening piece of chocolate into the steaming coffee, head bent. "Of course, there's no guarantee that she'll agree."

Hannah put down her mug. "Look at me," she demanded.

Adam turned an innocent face toward her. "What?"

"You fancy her. You fancy the scary woman."

He laughed incredulously. "You're such a drama queen. Just because I decide that I'd like to—"

"You fancy her. It's written all over your face."

"Look, I don't know what you—"

"You bought a clarinet because you fancy her, and you're going to pretend you want to play it."

"I won't be pretending," he protested. "I think it might be...interesting, learning to play a musical instrument."

"You know how I know?" she demanded. "Because I did the same with John Wyatt. I pretended to be really interested in learning how to play something, just because I...sort of fancy him."

His eyes widened. "You fancy the Scotsman? You sneaky thing."

"Don't change the subject. You haven't a note in your head. You haven't a musical bone in your body."

"That's got nothing to do with—"

"I bet you didn't even know what a clarinet was until you started fancying her. I bet you thought it was a flute she was playing."

"Of course I knew what a clarinet was," he said. "As a matter of fact, I'm familiar with all the woodwind instruments."

"Woodwind instruments," Hannah said triumphantly. "You've been cramming so you'll sound as if you know about them in case she asks you."

He stopped. "Damn," he said, a bashful grin spreading over his face. "You're good."

"So you do fancy her."

"Yes," he said, replacing his remaining half egg in its cardboard box. "I do. I'm not sure how it happened, but I find myself quite...taken with this woman." He got up and brought his mug to the sink. "And just for the record, she's not a bit scary. She's very shy, and quite sweet, I'm sure."

Hannah stood, too, brushing chocolate crumbs from her clothes. "Well, I have to say I think it's terribly romantic, buying a clarinet just to get to know someone. Terribly foolish, of course, and extremely wasteful, but very romantic." She put her mug in the sink. "So when are you going to ask her about lessons?"

He ran water. "Soon. Next time I go to the bar. Probably next weekend."

"I have to be there."

"Fine."

"But what if she says no? What if you have to have some kind of musical qualification or something before she'll take you on?"

He looked at her in dismay. "I never thought of that."

"What did you pay for it?"

"Forty-eight pounds sterling. I had to bid a bit."

"Wow." Hannah picked up the tea towel. "But could you not have tried asking her out? It might have been slightly less trouble than buying a clarinet on eBay." She giggled. "Sorry, but it's funny."

"Go on, laugh. I did consider asking her out, but to be honest I think she'd run a mile. I think I'll have to take the softly-softly approach."

Hannah looked fondly at him. "Have you ever actually spoken to this woman?"

"Not as such, no—except for asking her the name of a piece they played one evening, and I think I nearly gave her a heart attack."

"So in fact you don't even know if she's single."

"Well, not exactly—"

"She could be married. She could have half a dozen kids."

Adam threw her a pained look. "I've decided to assume otherwise, until I know for sure."

"I see." Hannah dried a mug. "I have to say, though, she's nothing at all like the ones you usually go for."

"I know." He smiled as he lifted the second mug from the water. "Maybe I've been going for the wrong ones."

"Maybe we both have," she said thoughtfully.

"So tell me more," he said, "about you fancying the Scotsman."

Hannah considered. "Ah, maybe I don't really," she said. "I mean, I didn't even buy a saxophone—how serious can I be?"

"Very funny."

———

Alice gave her husband new pajamas, handing them across the table when they'd finished breakfast. Sunday was the only day they had breakfast together now.

"Happy Easter," she said. "It's just pajamas. You needed a new pair anyway."

Tom's hand trembled slightly as he took the brown-wrapped package. "I got you nothing," he said. "I'm sorry." Other years she'd been given chocolate eggs, Terry's or Toblerone.

"It doesn't matter."

She should tell him to pull himself together. She should be trying to get help for him, maybe urging him to talk to their doctor about his drinking. But the rage was still there, keeping her immobile. The rage had made her buy the pajamas, knowing she would get nothing in return. Another little portion of guilt for him to carry around.

He'd stopped shaving every day; now it was two or three times a week. He looked worse after he shaved, his chin littered with cuts. No way could he do any dental work with those shaking hands.

She'd stopped going into his bedroom—*his* bedroom now, not theirs anymore—apart from once a fortnight when she took the old sheets off his bed and put clean ones on. The room smelled of whiskey, although he was keeping it fairly clean.

"I'm going to eleven Mass," she told him.

"Are you?"

She didn't think he'd been to Mass since the accident, unless he went during the week when she was out at work.

"I'll go for a walk by the river afterward," she said. "It's a good day for walking." Sunday mornings they'd often have gone for a walk after Mass if the weather was good.

"That'll be nice," he said. "You'll enjoy that."

"I'm doing lamb chops for dinner," she said. Not the stuffed turkey crown that she usually got at Easter. Chops would do him this year.

"Lovely," he said. "I look forward to that."

———

Fiona brought a bottle of Glenfiddich for Patrick and a set of bath oils for Leah, and she was presented with a string of chunky lilac beads that Leah had bought with Patrick's credit card.

"It's from both of us," she said as Fiona opened the long gray box. "Happy Easter, Mum."

No hug. They didn't hug each other these days, Patrick noticed.

"Thank you, darling," Fiona said, glancing at the beads before snapping the box shut. "They're delightful. And thank you, too, Patrick," she added. "It's thoughtful of you both."

She was making an effort. Patrick poured her a generous

gin, added bitter lemon and a lemon slice. "Cheers," he said, raising his glass.

This would be all right. Fiona was getting over her resentment of how he and Leah had gotten together. Somewhere along the way, she'd learned to live with the idea of the baby. Maybe she was even beginning to look forward to the arrival of her first grandchild.

The conversation over the drinks was formal, as he'd expected. They talked about the abrupt closure of Clongarvin's only music store, and the helicopter crash in Donegal, and the changeable weather. Leah asked her mother about the garden, and Fiona talked about kerria and forsythia and pyracantha and other names that didn't mean a thing to Patrick.

Lunch was chicken, Fiona's meat of choice. Patrick opened a bottle of sauvignon blanc from New Zealand that had cost him more than thirty euro, and he poured a glass each for himself and Fiona. They talked about an exhibition in the National Gallery that Fiona had visited on a recent trip to Dublin and a reiki course Leah was planning to do after the baby arrived. Patrick mentioned an upcoming trip to France, to attend a journalists' convention in Lyon. The main course passed peacefully.

And then, as they were just starting on the crème caramel, Fiona said, "May I ask again if you two have any plans to get married?"

Leah shot Patrick a look—warning? pleading?—before turning to her mother. "It's not something we've talked about."

"I see." Fiona rested her spoon on the side of her plate. "And I take it you're going to continue living here after the baby is born."

"Mum," Leah said quietly.

"We'll find a bigger place when we get the chance," Patrick said quickly. "One thing at a time."

"As I understand it," Fiona said coolly, "you have no property of your own."

"Please, Mum," Leah said, "don't ruin this."

"I'm just attempting to establish the facts, darling." Fiona's eyes didn't leave Patrick's face. "You lived in your parents' house, didn't you, until you moved in with Hannah Robinson?"

"That's true," he said tightly, resisting the impulse to pick up the wine bottle and bring it down on her immaculately coiffed head. "My mother died when I was young, and I lived with my father up to a year and a half ago."

"And then you moved in with Hannah," Fiona said, "and now you've moved in with Leah."

"Mum." Leah's voice held a note of desperation, but her mother didn't even glance in her direction.

"Mrs. Bradshaw," Patrick said evenly, "I find your attitude quite offensive, and I suspect it's entirely deliberate."

Fiona smiled thinly. "Oh, don't be silly," she said. "I'm not trying to offend anyone. I'm just concerned about the future upbringing of my grandchild, that's all—and your present circumstances don't seem particularly...stable to me."

Patrick said nothing. He felt a pulse throbbing in his forehead.

Fiona turned to Leah. "Geraldine Robinson put me in a very embarrassing position at bridge last week," she said. "She demanded, in front of everyone, that I name the father of your baby, knowing full well that everyone there knew that Patrick had been with her daughter until recently. You can imagine how that went down, can't you?"

"So you were embarrassed," Patrick said tightly, ignoring

Leah's hand on his arm, "and now you're taking it out on us."

Leah stood up abruptly, clumsily. Her face had flushed deeply, and her eyes were filled with imminent tears. She turned and left the room.

Patrick watched her go, then forced himself to turn back and meet Fiona's gaze. She was Leah's mother. Like it or not, she was part of Leah's life—and part of his now.

"I'm sorry if you've been put into an awkward position with your friends"—he emphasized the last word slightly, imagining the bridge contingent, delighted to have a bit of a scandal to chew on—"but Leah and I will not be pushed into making any plans simply to spare your blushes. We'll do things in our own time, as we see fit, and I hope you can accept that without causing Leah any more distress."

Fiona held his gaze for what seemed like an awfully long time. Her face was as devoid of expression as ever, and Patrick suddenly wondered if she'd had something done to it to prevent any movement, any alteration of her features that might cause lines to develop. Then she got up and unhooked the strap of her bag from her chair back.

"Thank you for lunch. I'll see myself out."

She left the room, and Patrick made no attempt to follow her. He didn't get up when he heard Leah's raised voice in the hall and her mother's inaudible replies. He didn't move when the bedroom door was slammed or when the front door was opened and closed quietly shortly afterward.

Eventually he poured what remained of the wine into his glass and sipped the tepid liquid unhurriedly while he finished his dessert. Then he got up and began to clear the table.

———

"And how's the new job going? I wish you'd come out to see us more often."

"I would, Ma, if I could hop on a bus, but you know there's none to Dunmallon, so I have to wait for Adam to take me." Nora shot an apologetic glance at her brother, who glared back. "The job is okay, although I probably won't stay there too long—it's not me, really. I'm trying to decide what my next move should be."

"I hope you're not thinking about going back to America," her mother said quickly. "Daddy and I wouldn't like that at all. Would we?" she demanded, turning to her husband.

"No," he said through a mouthful of roast potato.

Adam smiled to himself. They probably thought she'd get married again the minute she set foot on American soil.

"You picked up the accent," their father said to Nora.

"I did, didn't I?" Nora helped herself to another spoonful of garden peas. "Ma, this lunch is amazing—I forgot how much I missed your roast lamb."

"Three hours in the oven, a hundred and sixty," her mother said. "Forget twenty minutes to the pound, it'd come out half raw. Three hours, isn't that what I always do?" she asked her husband.

"Three hours," he said, forking up more lamb.

"And Adam, what's your news?" their mother asked. "Any nice young lady?"

"No, Ma," Adam said. "I'm between nice young ladies right now. But I'm keeping an eye open."

Every time he saw her, she asked. He presumed that the question was programmed into every woman who gave birth to a son. He debated briefly telling them about the clarinet but then decided to wait until he'd at least gotten the lessons set up.

His mother sighed. "I'll never be a grandmother," she said, "with the pair of you. Nora keeps getting divorced, and you're doing nothing at all. I can't for the life of me see why you and Hannah wouldn't get together and have done with it."

"Yes, bro, I think you and Hannah would be perfect for each other," Nora put in, grinning.

"Ma, you're far too young to be thinking like that," Adam said, shooting his sister another dark look as he tried to calculate his mother's age. Sixty-three or thereabouts. "There's lots of time."

"There is not lots of time. Everyone your age is married or getting engaged. I'm the only one I know with no grandchildren. There'll be nobody left to choose from if you wait much longer."

"True... I'll set my mind to it. Would I put an ad in the paper, d'you think?"

As his mother sighed exasperatedly, Adam wondered what Vivienne's home was like. He imagined a small cottage—a single woman's house, he thought firmly—filled with things made of china and flowers in vases. Rugs in muted colors on the floors and maybe a wall hanging of birds that she'd made herself.

A small room where she gave her lessons, her clarinet on a polished wooden table next to a music stand. Narrow attic stairs to her bedroom, the bed covered with a white crocheted spread.

"How's Hannah's shop doing?" his father asked.

"Good," he said, relieved at the change of subject. "She's kept busy, but it's going well. She's taken on a part-time assistant."

"We must take a trip up to see it," his mother said, turning to her husband again. "Mustn't we?"

"Oh, we must, sometime soon."

A dreadful squawking erupted just then outside the back door, causing them to abandon the roast lamb. They rushed out to find the hysterical chickens being chased joyfully around the yard by Kirby, who'd somehow managed to wriggle free from his rope.

He was reattached more firmly to the yard gate, well out of reach of the fowls, who soon recovered from their fright and began pecking the ground again.

"He's full of energy," their father said, regarding the dog sternly.

"I might take him for a bit of a walk after lunch," Adam replied. "Tire him out."

They went back inside and followed the lamb with tea and fruitcake, and then their father disappeared to listen to the second half of a football match on the radio, and Nora and her mother tackled the washing-up while Adam escaped with his dog and strolled along country roads for an hour.

"God, nothing changes there," Nora said on the ride home, Adam steering the car carefully between the potholes that lined the laneway to their parents' house.

"No, but it suits them." He longed suddenly for that life, the comfortable coexistence with the person you chose, and who chose you.

Nora yawned. "The boredom of it, though. Miles from anywhere, nothing going on. I'd slit my wrists. You can have my cake," she added. "I'm watching my fabulous figure." Ma never let any visitor leave without a generous slab of whatever she'd been baking.

Adam hadn't mentioned the clarinet to Nora. He could imagine her reaction. It was a daft thing to do—he knew exactly how daft it was. But there was the hope within him that this daft action, this illogical plan of his, would lead him to where he wanted to be.

His clarinet should have arrived by next Saturday, and then everything would be in place. He'd intercept Vivienne on her way out and ask if he might please have a word. He would make every effort not to sound like a crazed stalker.

She couldn't possibly turn him down. He was only looking for music lessons. Where was the harm in that?

May

J ohn Wyatt passed the yellow-fronted shop on the opposite side of the street. He walked half a block, and
then he retraced his steps, crossing the road when he saw
a gap in the traffic. He pushed the shop door open and
walked in.

The woman behind the counter wasn't Hannah. It threw
him for a second—he hadn't been expecting that.

"Hi," she said, smiling.

She was younger, hardly out of her teens. Her skin was
pale, her hair tied back. She wore the same apron he'd seen
on Hannah, with wide white and navy stripes overlain with a
yellow smiling sun. Her shade of lipstick was too light against
her pale face. Her eyes were the green of the glass marbles he
remembered from childhood.

"Hi there," he said, glancing at the displays under the
counter. "I'll take a couple of cupcakes, please—you can
choose."

"No preferences?" she asked. "With or without nuts? Chocolate chip?"

"Not fussed," he said. "They're all good."

"That's true." She selected a peanut butter and a rum-
raisin and put them into a small box.

"Hannah not around today?" he asked as he handed her a fiver.

"She's gone out for a bit—she'll be back at noon."

He remembered then, her saying that she'd taken on someone part-time. "Tell her John Wyatt was in, would you? Just to say hello. Sorry I missed her."

"I will. Thanks, now."

"See you."

At the woodworking store, he handed over the two cupcakes and was thanked and scolded in equal measure by Patsy, who was trying, as ever, to lose weight. "You're the devil, John Wyatt, you know that?"

Hannah hadn't been back to Vintage for the past two Saturdays. She'd seemed pleased to see him the last time, and she'd made a point of letting him know that she and her companion, whose name John had forgotten, were just friends. But she hadn't been back. Wouldn't she have shown up at the bar again if she'd been at all interested?

She might come this weekend, if the part-time girl remembered to pass on his message. If she thought he still wanted to keep up the contact, she just might appear.

———

Alice pulled in three doors up on the other side of the street. There was no sign of the two little boys from the last day, but the red flowers were still there—or rather their remains, hanging forlornly from the gatepost of number 37. And the curtains were still closed in the upstairs room.

There was no car outside the house, but maybe the father had gone to work in it, or the mother. Would they be back at work, barely a month after their only child had been buried?

They probably wouldn't have had a choice—life went on, and bills needed to be paid.

She wondered if they were married, if they had gotten around to that. She guessed they hadn't been married when Jason had come along four years earlier. The sister saying the poem on the altar at the funeral had looked in her teens still; Jason's mother probably wasn't much older.

Two girls in blue school uniforms walked past the car, both heads bent over a mobile phone. A small dog pattered across the road in front of Alice, sniffing at something on the edge of the far path, lifting a leg briefly against a streetlight before trotting away rapidly.

A car drove past, coming up behind her unnoticed, making her start. Someone cycled by, whistling. It began to drizzle, settling silently on the windscreen. A man came out of the house beside number 37 and walked past it buttoning his coat.

She sat for fifty minutes, a magazine open on her lap in case anyone looked at her, in case anyone approached her to know what she was doing there. The front door of number 37 remained closed; nobody came or went from the house. She thought she saw a movement once, in the uncurtained upstairs window, but it might have been her imagination, or a trick of the light.

At twenty to four, she started the car and drove back into town.

The dark brown UPS truck stopped outside the house, and Adam watched a man in a matching brown uniform get out, slide open a side door, and remove a package that didn't look long enough to house a clarinet. He thought maybe it wasn't for him, that it was a delivery for a different house, but then the man turned in to the driveway and walked up the path.

Adam waited until the doorbell rang. He got up, walked downstairs, and opened the front door. "Morning."

"How do?" The man looked at the label on the package. "Adam O'Connor?"

"That's me." The man handed him the clipboard, and Adam signed along the dotted line. "Thanks."

He brought the package into the sitting room, where Kirby was dozing. "Look what I got," he said, tearing off the paper to reveal a black case. He opened it and saw that it was lined with dark blue velvet, and contained five pieces of clarinet.

He took his phone from his pocket and called Hannah.

"It's here," he said.

"What is?"

"The clarinet."

"Well? What's it like?"

"It's in bits."

"So you have to put it together. Try not to break it."

"Hang on, I'll call you back."

Ten minutes later, when he had finally figured out how to assemble it, he put the clarinet's mouthpiece between his lips and blew.

A low sound squawked out, like the honk of a seal. Kirby pricked his ears.

Adam called Hannah again. "Listen," he said. He laid the phone on the arm of the couch and pressed the keys one by one, blowing furiously, honking and squeaking in equal measure. Kirby lifted his head and regarded Adam, ears still cocked.

He lifted the phone, breathless. "What do you think?"

"Brilliant," she said. "You don't need lessons at all. Is Kirby there?"

"Yes."

"Put him out, or I'm reporting you to the animal-welfare people."

"Good-bye," he said, and hung up.

He raised the clarinet to his lips again and pressed keys at random, blowing as forcefully as he could manage. Midway through this performance, Kirby shuffled to his feet, padded to the sitting-room door, and sat looking pointedly at it.

In less than a minute, Adam was completely out of breath. He lowered the clarinet and waited for the feeling of light-headedness to pass. "It's okay," he told Kirby, "I won't be doing any more of that for a while."

He had a long way to go. Maybe he should have started with a tin whistle.

"I'm worried about Alice," Geraldine said, folding her glasses.

Stephen entered *"biscuit"* using a triple-word square, and his total shot up to 215. "You're worried? Why?"

"She's not herself." Geraldine slid the glasses into their soft tartan case. "She seems to have no interest in the shop any-more. Last week we made less than three hundred—I don't ever remember a week that bad—and it didn't seem to knock a feather out of her."

Stephen tried to find a word that contained *l, x*, two *a*'s, and a *t*. "Don't forget, we're in a recession. All businesses are suffering."

Geraldine unplugged the television. "It's not that,

though—this is different. I'm really wondering if there's some kind of boycott going on."

Stephen gave up and tagged *"axl"* onto the *e* of *"fable,"* which earned him a pathetic eleven points. "Hardly a boycott. Surely everyone appreciates that the accident wasn't Alice's fault—what would be the point in taking it out on her?"

Geraldine bundled the newspaper sections on the coffee table into a neat pile. "You'd be surprised. I'd swear Sheila Barrett crossed the street when she spotted me yesterday—she never misses the new stock, and there hasn't been a sign of her lately." She straightened the rug in front of the fire with her foot. "And another thing—Alice has started disappearing in the middle of the day."

"Disappearing?"

"Well, she doesn't say where she's going, just that she has things to do, very vague. She was gone for over two hours yesterday. Normally she just does the weekly run to the wholesalers or takes half an hour around the town now and again."

"She's got a lot on her mind," Stephen said, eyeing the *"excel"* his virtual opponent, Stanley, had just entered.

"She certainly has—half the time she doesn't seem to hear me when I talk to her." Geraldine walked to the door with her newspaper bundle. "Will I make tea for you?"

"I might be another while," Stephen said, determined not to let Stanley, described only as adept, beat him. "Have your own, and I'll be up when I finish this."

In the kitchen Geraldine poured water into the kettle and put a tea bag into her cup. No point in a pot for just one. She took a single ginger nut from the pack and left the rest in the press.

If you need to cut my hours, that's okay, she'd said to Alice.

Just while things are slow. She and Stephen would manage fine—if she had no income at all, they'd manage on what he made. But Alice had shaken her head and said, *Ah no, we needn't do that.*

She must be losing money now, must be out of pocket. Ridiculous for Geraldine to be there all the time, when some days only half a dozen customers came in. Some days they didn't sell a single pair of shoes.

How's Tom doing? she'd asked a couple of times since the accident, and Alice had said, *He's fine,* or *Bearing up,* in the kind of tight voice that had kept Geraldine from saying any more.

Come to dinner this evening, she'd suggested more than once, *you and Tom. Four is as easy to cook for as two.* But Alice had shaken her head and found an excuse each time, and Geraldine had eventually given up.

The kettle boiled, and she made tea and brought it upstairs with her biscuit. Just as well she had John Grisham to distract her when she went to bed.

———

"She's getting up," Hannah said. "Head her off at the pass."

Adam turned and moved swiftly through the tables of drinkers, advancing diagonally toward the back door. He reached it as Vivienne approached from the opposite direction, clarinet clutched to her chest. Tonight she wore a long black dress with sleeves to her elbows and black suede ankle boots.

It was now or never. "Excuse me," Adam said, smiling. At least he hoped it was coming out as a smile.

Vivienne stopped, the color flooding into her cheeks like before. She gave no sign of remembering his earlier approach.

Adam stood between her and the door. There was nowhere for her to go—unless she bolted back the way she'd come.

"Sorry to bother you," he said, "but I wanted to say I really admire your clarinet playing."

She blinked and pushed her glasses up her nose, the tiniest of smiles flitting for an instant across her flushed face. "Thanks," she said quickly, her eyes darting to the door behind him.

"I believe," he hurried on, "that you give lessons, and as I've recently come into possession of a clarinet, I was wondering if you would—"

"No," she broke in, shaking her head rapidly. "Sorry." Pushing her glasses up again, looking beyond him to her escape route. "I don't."

"Pardon?" She couldn't be turning him down out of hand. "But I was told that you're a music teacher, and I would really love—"

"I don't teach adults," she said in a rush. "Children, I just teach children." Her voice was low, and he strained to hear it. She looked more pointedly at the blue door. The blush was receding, leaving her face blotchy. She blinked repeatedly behind her round glasses.

Children. The one thing Adam hadn't anticipated, that at thirty-one he'd be too old. It was a blow, but he held his ground. "Well, would you consider making an exception?" he asked. "I don't know any other clarinet teacher, you see, and I'd really like to learn. And I promise I'm as ignorant as any child."

But she shook her head again. "Just children," she repeated. "I'm sorry." She shifted the position of her clarinet slightly and took a small sideways step toward the door.

"Please," Adam said, nothing left to lose. "I've just bought it, you see, and if you don't teach me, it'll sit in my house gathering dust and nobody will ever get to play it. It'll be a terrible waste of a clarinet. You don't want that, do you?"

She was clearly uncomfortable. She opened her mouth and closed it again. She'd run out of ways to tell him no. He could feel her anxiety, her whole body tense with it, but his determination drove him on. Out of the corner of his eye, he spotted the keyboard player approaching.

He decided to make one last attempt. "How about you just try me out for two or three lessons, and if you're not happy, you can send me on my way and I'll never bother you again? Would you consider that? Please? Just a few lessons?"

She sighed, a frown creasing the skin above the bridge of her glasses. "Half eight on a Thursday," she said, her eyes fixed on the blue door.

"Sorry?" Her sudden surrender caught him unawares.

"Half eight on a Thursday," she repeated, in precisely the same resigned tone.

"Okay. Great." Adam stepped aside at last and pushed the door open for her. "Where do I go?"

She moved toward the blue door, close enough for him to smell the lemony scent that rose from her tightly bunched hair. "Ten Fortfield Avenue."

"And your name?" he asked, wanting to hear her say it.

"Vivienne O'Toole." Over her shoulder as she disappeared.

The keyboard player arrived, and Adam held the door open, struggling to remember his surname—was it O'Toole too? Were he and Vivienne married? Was Adam's enterprise doomed before it started?

"Thanks, mate."

Nodding at Adam but not recognizing him, by the look of it. No curiosity evident, no suspicion as to what Adam might have been saying to Vivienne. Surely a husband or partner would want to know.

"Great gig tonight," Adam told him, and the man thanked him again as he walked through the blue doorway.

She hadn't asked Adam's name. She didn't want to teach him—he'd bullied her into it. She was more comfortable, probably, in the uncritical presence of children. Chances were, she was dreading next Thursday already.

But she'd agreed, and in five days Adam was going to see her house and be in her company for at least an hour. He was going to be her very first adult pupil.

And he was finally going to discover whether or not she was single.

Ten Fortfield Avenue. Vivienne O'Toole. *Baby steps,* he thought, still hardly understanding what drove him on but knowing he wanted to persevere. Baby steps and lots of patience.

As he made his way back to the bar, he noticed that the Scotsman was talking to Hannah. He managed to retrieve his drink without either of them seeing him, and he moved farther up the counter and replayed the conversation in his head.

"You didn't have to leave us alone," she said as they walked home.

"But I did," Adam replied. "And you look like the cat that got the cream, so my cunning ploy worked."

Hannah smiled. "I'm meeting him for coffee on Wednesday morning. I decided I'm tired of being a hermit."

"Good for you." They turned onto the bridge.

"And you?" she asked. "What did she say?"

Adam ran his hand along the smooth, cold surface of the metal rail. "Get this—she teaches children, not adults."

"Oh." She threw him a sympathetic look. "Oh, Adam, that's too bad—and after buying the clarinet as well. Will you try selling it again?"

"Actually, I won't—because she's agreed to take me on. She tried her best to turn me down, but I nagged a bit."

Hannah laughed. "Are you serious? You're going to a children's music teacher?"

"I am."

"You do realize that she'll probably have you playing 'Baa, Baa, Black Sheep'?"

Adam regarded her sternly. "We may well begin with that, yes. But I'm confident that I'll progress to more adult material in due course."

Hannah tucked her arm into his. "Of course you will. You'll be giving recitals by Christmas."

"Very funny." They turned off the bridge. "But now that you mention it," he added, "maybe I could do a bit of busking."

"Why not? You could be like that fellow in the Kit Kat ad—remember? Everyone throws money at him the minute he stops playing. You could make a fortune."

"Ha ha." After a pause he added, "What was the keyboard player's surname, can you remember?"

"Who? Oh, you mean Wally, the taxi driver. Can't remember what his surname was. Why?"

"Well, the night we met him, he said he was driving her home."

"Did he? I don't remember."

"So they might be together. A couple, I mean."

Hannah considered. "Or he might just be doing her a favor. Maybe they live near each other."

"Mmm...She's O'Toole, but I can't remember what his surname is."

"Tell you what," she said, "until we know for sure, let's not dwell on it. Let's plan your busking career instead."

They walked on, both in high good humor. Both hopeful of happy outcomes.

———

"So," Nora said after they'd ordered, after their menus had been replaced with her martini and Leah's tonic water. "How are things?"

The puffiness she'd seen in Leah's face the last time they'd met was more pronounced, the earlier suggestion of a double chin now a distinct reality. Leah was still attractive—or rather the echo of her attractiveness was still there in the dark brown eyes, the regular nose, the full lips. But the overall effect was blurred now, as if her original elfin prettiness had been diluted. Little wonder that Patrick's thoughts were straying.

Leah sipped her tonic water. "Just wish it was over at this stage. I am so sick of being bloody pregnant."

"How long more?" The martini was ice cold and delicious. Nora pulled one of the olives from its cocktail stick with her teeth.

"Four weeks, about. Seems like forever."

Nora smiled. "Poor you. Soon be over."

Leah grimaced. "Yeah—and then I'll be up to my neck in Pampers while Patrick swans out to work every day."

"Ah, he'll help though, when he's around." But Nora

couldn't see Patrick holding a baby with any degree of comfort, let alone changing a nappy.

Leah nodded glumly. "Hope so. This baby..." She hesitated. "Well, it wasn't exactly his idea. I mean," she added hastily, "he's thrilled, of course, but..."

The baby hadn't been Patrick's idea—what a surprise. "He'll rise to the challenge," Nora said. "Just wait and see. As soon as he sets eyes on it."

"Of course he will." Leah looked far from convinced. "Anyway," she said, shifting her position, adjusting her weight on the chair, "enough about me. How's the job going? Patrick tells me you're settling in well."

A new note of horribly false brightness in her voice—but as far as Nora could tell, nothing more. No hint of suspicion, no sign of jealousy.

They hadn't met since Nora had begun working for Patrick, well over a month ago now. The occasional text had been exchanged, each mentioning vaguely a future lunch date, but until the previous evening nothing had been arranged. And then, out of the blue, a text from Leah: LUNCH 2MORO? MY TREAT. And here they were.

"The job is fine," Nora said. She hadn't missed Leah's look when she'd walked in, the envious glance her lilac wool top, silver-gray pencil skirt, and black stilettos had earned. "Nothing I can't handle."

She wouldn't mention Patrick directly. She was still feeling her way toward the reason for today's lunch. "The people are nice. A few of us went out for drinks the other night."

She'd spent the first twenty minutes trying to escape from Evan in Accounts, who clearly fancied his chances. In the end she'd gone to the toilet and joined another group when she got back, where the talk was of babies and teething and weaning. She'd excused herself after ten minutes, pleading stomach cramps. Back at the flat, she'd watched an episode of *Law & Order* she'd seen six months ago in the States.

"It's interesting, working for a newspaper. I haven't done it before."

"And you'll stay in Clongarvin?" The waiter appeared, and Leah regarded her plain pasta without appetite.

"For the moment," Nora replied, plucking a cube of feta from her Greek salad as it was placed before her. "I'll have another of these," she told the waiter, holding up her martini glass. "I'll do the drinks bill," she added to Leah, "since you're not having any."

"Don't be silly," Leah said. "You can pay next time. We mustn't let it go so long before we do it again."

"Absolutely not," Nora replied.

Leah envied her, that much was obvious. She probably wasn't entirely happy still about Patrick's being in close proximity with Nora, whose looks and figure were so much more attractive than her own right now. But as far as Nora could see, Leah's only motive for inviting her out to lunch today was that she needed someone to talk to—or possibly, Leah being Leah, she might have decided that by keeping Nora close it would make it more difficult for anything to happen between her and Patrick.

She had no idea, none at all, that she was too late. Shame, really.

Why don't you lock the door? he'd said as soon as she'd walked in.

Why don't I leave it open? Nora had replied.

Not surprised, not in the least, by his suggestion. It was what she'd known would happen, very soon after she'd started to work for him. Sooner even, his eyes lingering on her crossed thighs, on the V of her top, at the interview. His hand holding hers a second too long as he'd thanked her for coming, as he'd promised to be in touch. She'd thought, *You're up for it.* They were always so obvious.

Leave it open, then, he'd said. Watching her as she'd crossed the room that smelled of the drinks he'd had at his three-hour lunch. Better sober up before he went home to Leah. Nora hadn't minded that he was fairly well on—it usually added to the fun. Got rid of the inhibitions.

Come in for a minute, he'd said as he'd passed her desk on his way back. She'd smelled the alcohol, and she'd known.

She'd made her way unhurriedly around the desk to where he was slouched in his big leather chair. She'd swiveled the chair around to face her.

Are you ready for this? she'd asked softly.

Take your panties off, he'd replied thickly.

She'd stood in front of him and opened the buttons of her blouse one by one, taking her time. She'd reached behind and unhooked her bra and lifted the cups off her breasts, all the time looking at his face. She'd hiked up her skirt and slid her underpants slowly over her hips, letting them drop to the floor and stepping out of them.

Now me, he'd said, and she'd undone the button of his trousers and slid down the zip and reached inside before straddling him in her lace-topped stockings, in her black stilettos, in her bunched-up skirt and open blouse.

No need to talk, both of them knowing the rules. His mouth had found her nipple, she'd guided him into her with his office door unlocked, anyone liable to knock and walk in without waiting for a response, as she'd seen people do plenty of times, as she did herself all the time. His huge hands on her bare buttocks, her hands in his hair, watching people passing in the street below.

Moving against each other, the leather chair creaking in rhythm, anyone liable to walk in, her excitement mounting as he gripped her buttocks, as she bent her head and found his mouth and took his tongue between her teeth, as he moaned, as she lifted her head again, drawing breath sharply, and arched against him—

Yes, she thought regretfully, *much too late for Leah to be taking me out to lunch, to be buying me a Greek salad and two martinis.*

———

Fiona Bradshaw took particular care with her preparations. She stroked on liquid eyeliner, resting her elbow on the dressing table to keep her hand steady. She blended cream shadow carefully and dotted concealer under her eyes. She brushed on powder and blotted two coats of lipstick with a tissue.

She dressed in linen, a suit of duck-egg blue that Leah said brought out the color of her eyes. She added pearls at her throat and in her ears. She replaced her everyday gold watch with the white-gold one that had a diamond in place of the number twelve. She slipped her feet into new dove-gray suede shoes, sprayed scent at her wrists, neck, and cleavage.

Imagine her disappointment then, when she walked into Frances Mitchell's sitting room looking as good as she could possibly look and saw Frances's daughter Cathy sitting with Geraldine Robinson's usual partner.

A wasted effort. Geraldine was too embarrassed, probably, to face her after the showdown two weeks before. No bridge game last week because of Easter, plenty of time for Fiona to plan her outfit—and all for nothing.

No mention was made, during the game or over the coffee and cakes afterward, of Leah's pregnancy. Nobody asked Fiona how her daughter was doing; nobody wanted to know what baby names were being considered. Nobody at all, thanks to Geraldine Robinson, seemed the slightest bit interested in how Fiona felt about becoming a grandmother for the first time.

She helped herself to a sliver of Frances's chocolate rum cake, smiling at Aoife's account of her niece's honeymoon in Mauritius, admiring the bracelet Maureen's husband had given her for her birthday. Accepting graciously the compliments on her own appearance. Showing no sign at all of her resentment, giving no indication that she'd even noticed their lack of curiosity.

Keeping up appearances. Which, of course, was what it was all about.

—————

"She hasn't gone back to work yet," Una said. "Dave is doing a few bits and pieces, but Claire's still not ready. And with Jason's memorial Mass coming up next week, that'll bring her right back down again."

Hannah slipped off her plastic gloves. Hard to believe it was time for the memorial Mass, that a month had gone by since the little boy's death. "They're keeping Claire's job open?"

"For the moment, yeah, but for how long? You couldn't blame them if they gave it away—they can't wait forever."

Hannah took her phone from the shelf behind the counter and slotted it into its pocket in her bag. "Maybe when the memorial Mass is behind her..."

"Maybe." Una watched as Hannah slung the bag onto her shoulder. "So where are you off to this morning?"

"I'm meeting someone for coffee," Hannah said—feeling, to her great surprise, a rising warmth in her face. Making a great show of rummaging in her bag as she made for the door. "See you at twelve."

The café was dotted with people. John sat at a table by the far wall reading the *Irish Times*, a blue mug in front of him.

"Hello," she said. Her stomach was fluttering ridiculously. "I hope I'm not late."

For her first date with Patrick, they'd had an early supper and gone to the theater to see *The Faith Healer*. He'd taken her hand and tucked it around his arm as they reclaimed their seats after the interval, and the tips of her fingers had tingled with pins and needles for the last twenty minutes. She'd rested her calf against his and hoped to God her breath wouldn't be stale by the end of the night. The following morning, kneading dough in Finnegan's Bakery, she couldn't remember how the play had ended, but the memory of his good-night kiss, the lick of desire it had caused in her, had been vivid.

She ordered cappuccino, and John got a top-up for his tea. He wore a faded blue sweatshirt that looked very soft. His nails were bitten, his fingers slender for a man. *Musician's fingers,* Hannah thought, picturing him sitting with the other band members, playing his saxophone.

He told her he'd come to Ireland after walking away from his marriage. He spoke of his wife without bitterness, mentioned a divorce pending. He told her about a daughter studying law at Edinburgh University.

He asked her about the cupcake shop, how it had started, if she'd always been interested in baking. He moved his hands as he talked. He smiled a lot. His teeth were even and cream-colored.

Hannah spoke briefly of Patrick but didn't explain how they'd broken up, made no mention of Leah. She talked about Adam's moving in with her to help with the bills after Patrick had left, about his twin sister, Nora, home from America after her second divorce. "She works for the local paper now."

She told him about Kirby the black Labrador who shed hairs everywhere. She talked about the awful brown tweed armchair Adam had brought home from the charity shop to protect Hannah's red couch from the black hairs. "It's like Frasier's dad's chair, only a whole lot tackier."

She spoke of her dentist father and her mother who worked in Glass Slipper, one of Clongarvin's three shoe shops. She drank a second cappuccino. He ordered a black coffee. And by the time she thought to check her watch, her two hours had ended twelve minutes earlier.

Number 10 Fortfield Avenue wasn't in the least what Adam had been expecting. Instead of a cozy cottage for one, he found a two-story redbrick semi, attached to its identical opposite number in an area of Clongarvin he knew only slightly, never having had occasion to visit it in the past.

Fortfield Avenue was one of several similar roads in the neighborhood—Fortfield Park, Fortfield Drive—all lined with redbrick houses, most of them semidetached, all two-story.

Vivienne's house looked big for a woman on her own. Adam locked his car and slipped the keys into his pocket, gripping the clarinet case firmly. *Here we go,* he told himself.

Time to find out, once and for all, if there was a man in her life. He walked up the short paved path, noting the dark green six-year-old Corolla parked on the gravel beside it, and pressed the white button on the doorframe.

A loud, harsh buzz sounded from within, causing a little brown bird perched on a nearby cable to flutter away. When nothing further happened for almost a minute, Adam began to wonder if he had the right house. She *had* said number ten, hadn't she? He lifted his hand to press the bell again but lowered it when he heard someone approaching.

The door was opened, not by a man.

"Yes?"

Adam offered his most charming smile. "Good evening," he said. "I've come for a music lesson."

"Yes," the woman repeated. Unmoving. Unsmiling. A pair of what looked like gardening gloves in the hand that hung by her side.

"With Vivienne," Adam added. Maybe the house was full of music teachers. Maybe he'd come to the smallest music school in Ireland.

"You know she only takes children," the woman said. "Up to twelve. No adults."

"Right." Adam shifted his clarinet. "She did mention that, yes, but after some discussion she agreed to try me out—to give me a few lessons," he amended hastily.

"Yes." Mouth set in a thin, disapproving line. Clearly not impressed with Vivienne's first grown-up pupil.

Adam put her somewhere in her late fifties or early sixties, her short, silvering hair pulled off her face with what looked like a child's hair band. Large, fading freckles were scattered across her face. "You'd better come in then."

She stood back not quite far enough, forcing Adam to

squeeze past her, holding the clarinet case awkwardly above his head to avoid a collision. The hallway was narrow and dimly lit and smelled of turnip.

"Wait in there," the woman ordered, and Adam stepped into a room that contained a green tweed couch covered with clear plastic and two matching armchairs similarly protected. A portable television was perched on a high stool in the corner, to the left of a small fireplace, in front of which dried plants were arranged in a tall glass vase.

As the woman disappeared, Adam became conscious of piano music coming from somewhere in the house, a complicated piece that meant nothing to him. He wondered again if the house contained more than one music teacher.

He sat in one of the green tweed armchairs, plastic crackling loudly as it accepted his weight, and let the distant notes wash over him as he checked out his surroundings. The carpet was biscuit-colored with maroon swivels, the walls were papered with embossed cream. A painting of men pulling a low black boat up onto a beach hung over the fireplace. Adam spotted photos in frames on the mantelpiece. He crackled to his feet and walked across to study them.

There was Vivienne, maybe ten years old, standing solemnly by a five-bar gate, hair twisted into two thick plaits that hung at either side of her bespeckled face. Gray pullover, plaid skirt that stopped above her skinny knees, long white socks, black-laced shoes. A book tucked under one arm. A boy of about the same age was sitting on top of the gate, grinning at the camera in his gray trousers and gray pullover, feet tucked behind the third bar.

And there Vivienne was again—early twenties, he guessed—mortarboard topping her tied-back hair, sitting formally in blouse and skirt, hands resting in her lap, one holding a rolled-up piece of paper. No glasses this time, her blue-gray eyes looking somewhere to the right of the camera, the smallest hint of a smile on her unpainted lips.

As he moved to the next photo—a black-and-white family group—he heard footsteps in the hall. He turned just in time to see Vivienne passing the doorway, followed by a boy of about twelve. The boy had a booklet of some sort under his arm. The front door opened and closed, and then Vivienne reappeared, two red spots in her cheeks. "This way," she said, and promptly vanished again.

Adam grabbed his clarinet case and followed her into the hall, in time to see her stepping through a doorway farther down. He walked along the dim corridor, wondering what the next hour would bring.

The second room was smaller than the first and held only a piano with a long bench beneath, a small folding table, a wooden kitchen chair, and a music stand. A wooden clock on the wall showed half past eight precisely.

"There's a cat on the piano," Adam said, standing in the doorway.

An enormous marmalade cat was sprawled along the top, staring fixedly at Adam with its yellow-green eyes, the tip of its tail flicking languidly.

Vivienne was riffling through a bundle of papers on the table, her back to the door. "He likes music," she murmured, without turning around. "But if you'd rather I put him out..."

"No, no," Adam answered. "It can...I mean, he can stay. I don't mind."

Cats did nothing for him; he felt no affinity with them whatsoever. Give him a dog any day. On the other hand, he had no serious objections, as long as they kept a reasonable distance from him. He hoped fervently that the current one would respect his boundaries.

That unblinking stare was unnerving though. Adam shifted his attention to the window next to the piano and saw the woman who'd shown him in. She was kneeling on a green pad beside a flower bed, a pale blue basin on the ground next to her, a supermarket plastic bag covering her hair. The gardening gloves were back on her hands.

"Is that your mother," Adam asked, "in the garden, with the bag on her head?"

"Yes," Vivienne replied shortly. She wore a dark gray cardigan over a black top and black trousers. Her hair was pinned up tightly.

She lived with her mother. No sign yet of anyone else. She wasn't wearing a ring. Adam's hopes rose a notch.

"Sit down," she said softly, still not looking in his direction. She added something under her breath that he didn't catch.

"Pardon?"

"Eighteen," Vivienne repeated, selecting another sheet and scanning it. "Euro. For the lesson. Per lesson."

"Oh." Adam hadn't given a thought to the cost. Eighteen euro seemed reasonable to him; he must be getting the child's rate. "That's fine. Where do you want me to sit?"

His voice sounded too loud. The room smelled faintly of mints, with a musty undertone that he guessed was coming from the cat.

Vivienne lifted her head then and regarded him, her cheeks deeply flushed now. "Chair," she said, the faintest suggestion of surprise in her voice. "The bench is for the piano."

"Oh...right. Of course. Silly me."

He stepped across and took his seat, feeling the cat's stare following him all the way. Outside the window the older woman got awkwardly to her feet, crossed the lawn with her basin, and upended it into a round green container. On the way back to the flower bed, she glared into the room, and Adam hastily shifted his gaze.

Vivienne placed a sheet of music on the stand. Adam read "Mary Had a Little Lamb" and imagined what Hannah would say.

"Jacket," Vivienne murmured, pulling the long bench out from under the piano and sitting on it. She was about three feet diagonally across from Adam, with the music stand between them. "You need to take your jacket off."

"Right." He placed the clarinet case on the floor, shrugged off his leather jacket, and hung it over the back of the chair. "I've a lot to learn," he added, rolling up his shirtsleeves.

Vivienne made no response.

"I heard someone playing the piano," Adam said, just to put something into the silence, "while I was waiting." He picked up the clarinet case and opened it.

Vivienne reached an arm across and turned over the front page of the sheet music.

"Was that you?" he asked, determined to have some kind of conversation as he twisted the pieces of his instrument together. "Were you playing the piano earlier?"

"No," she murmured, her eyes on his hands. "That was a pupil."

"Oh? You teach piano, too?"

"I *only* teach piano," she said, the color rising in her face again.

"You only teach piano?" Adam stared at her. "But you're teaching me the clarinet."

She lifted her eyes and met his for an instant. "I said no," she reminded him, her voice holding a hint of impatience now, her gaze dropping back to his hands. "I *tried* to say no. You kept asking." She was clearly ill at ease, her hands pressed between her knees, her shoulders hunched.

"Sorry," Adam said. "It's just that...er, I've always wanted to play the clarinet, and I assumed, since you played it..."

She only taught piano. She only taught piano to children. He tried to feel remorseful—he'd badgered her into it, hadn't allowed her to refuse him—but his delight at being so close to her, at having her all to himself, didn't allow for remorse.

"Sorry," he repeated. "And thanks again for taking me. I'll behave, I promise. I'll be a model student."

She didn't smile, but her expression relaxed slightly as she gave him a tiny nod before turning to look at the sheet music again. He wondered how many lessons it would take for her to be at ease in his company.

"We'll begin with the scales," she said, "and move on to this simple tune"—indicating the page—"which you can practice at home for the next time."

The next time. She was almost close enough for him to reach out and touch her face, to take off her glasses and unpin her hair. He smelled flowers, and the musty animal scent. Her face was covered with pale freckles that blended into one another.

"What's the cat's name?"

"Pumpkin," Vivienne answered, looking pointedly at the sheet music. "So we'll start with the positioning of your fingers."

"Mine's Adam," he told her as he raised the clarinet. "My name, I mean. I don't think I mentioned it before."

Another tiny nod. Clearly, the name of her only adult pupil wasn't of great interest to Vivienne O'Toole.

"The memorial Mass is on Sunday," Alice said. "I'm going."

She hadn't mentioned the funeral to Tom; she'd slipped out of the house that morning and said nothing. She'd walked to the church, still afraid to get behind the wheel of a car, any car, and Geraldine had ended up driving her home, such a state she'd been in. No comment had been made regarding her red eyes at the dinner table later that evening, which had been a relief.

But now she was annoyed at his lack of involvement. How could he just detach himself when he'd been the cause of it all? "I think you should go," Alice said. "It would be the right thing to do, to go to the Mass."

He made no response, and Alice felt her anger rising. "You can't avoid people forever," she said sharply. "You can't just stop everything because of what happened."

Tom put down his knife and fork. "I can't go to that Mass," he said. "I just can't. You can't expect me to."

"You have to face up to things," Alice persisted. "You have to move on, like I'm trying to do."

"How can I move on," he said, "when I don't know if I'm going to jail or not? You're expecting too much of me."

"Well, I know one thing," she said, the irritation scratching inside her. "Drink isn't going to help. Drink is what caused all this."

He pushed his chair back abruptly and walked toward the door.

"Oh, finish your dinner anyway," Alice said impatiently. A sausage and a half and two bits of white pudding, still lay on his plate. "You can eat your dinner without anyone seeing you."

He made no response as he left the room, and she listened to his steps on the stairs. She laid her cutlery down and put her head into her hands. After a while she took the two plates and scraped what food was left on them into the bin.

———————

At nine o'clock precisely, as Adam was still trying to grasp the concept of breathing from his abdomen—which made no sense to him, when everyone knew your breath went in and out of your lungs—the door was pushed open and Vivienne's mother, whom he hadn't noticed leaving the garden, walked in with a small tray that held a glass of milk and a plate of biscuits.

"Break," Vivienne said, taking the tray. No attempt at introductions was made. The older woman didn't look in his direction.

Adam got to his feet and put out his hand as the woman turned to go. "Adam O'Connor," he said clearly. "Delighted to meet you, Mrs. O'Toole."

For a second he thought she was going to ignore him and keep going, but after the briefest of pauses she offered him her hand. "We're not used to catering for adults," she said flatly. "I only have Jammie Dodgers."

"They'll do fine," Adam assured her, trying to remember the last time he'd been presented with a plate of childrens' biscuits. "I wasn't expecting anything at all."

She looked scandalized. "We always do a break," she told him. "The children find the hour too long."

"I can understand that," Adam said gravely. "Thanks very much."

She left the room without another word. Adam turned

back to Vivienne, who had set the tray on the windowsill. She held the glass of milk out to him. He took it and accepted a Jammie Dodger when it was offered. "Thanks."

He never drank milk, apart from a drop in tea or coffee—it affected his sinuses—but he suspected that a refusal would cause more discomfiture. He wondered if he could find a way to give it to the cat, who was watching the proceedings intently from above. Vivienne hadn't taken a biscuit; it looked as if the three Jammie Dodgers were all his.

He decided to give conversation another try. "Have you been teaching music for long?"

"Eight years," she answered. "You'll need to practice your abdominal breathing at home, every morning and evening. It'll take the strain out of playing the notes." As usual she didn't meet his eyes; her gaze seemed to be focused now on his left ear.

"I will," he promised. "And how long have you been playing the piano yourself?"

She shifted on her bench. Personal questions were clearly a problem. "Eighteen years," she said, examining a speck on her cardigan sleeve.

"Wow, that's—"

"Twelve years the clarinet and oboe," she went on, as if he hadn't spoken. "Eleven years the violin. Six years the saxophone."

Adam looked at her in amazement. "You play all those instruments?"

Vivienne nodded and looked pointedly at his glass, and Adam drained it—no hope at all of palming it off—and finished his biscuit.

"Now," she said, turning back to the music stand, and Adam brushed Jammie Dodger crumbs from his shirt and lifted the clarinet again.

"Mam?"

"Hello, dear. Everything all right?"

Hannah smiled. Her mother's first question whenever she phoned her, maybe every mother's first question.

"Everything's fine...I just thought you might like to know that I met John Wyatt for coffee the other day."

Foolhardy, really, putting her mother in the picture so soon. Nothing might come of it; she might be ringing again in a few weeks to say it was all over. But Geraldine needed some good news. They all needed something positive to focus on.

"Oh, love, I'm delighted to hear that, I really am—he seemed so nice that day in the shop. So he called back?"

"He did." No need to go into the details, the roundabout route they'd taken.

"And how did it go? Did you get on well?"

"Very well—he's actually in a band in his spare time. He plays the saxophone."

"Oh, a musician—that's wonderful." Her mother's voice bubbled with enthusiasm. "Oh, I just knew there was someone much better waiting for you."

Hannah smiled. Geraldine had her walking down the aisle with him, at the very least. But listen to how upbeat she sounded.

"So when are you meeting him again?"

"Saturday night—he plays in the new wine bar by the river."

"Yes, I know it—at least, I know of it. I'm sure it's full of young ones. Can you imagine me and your father turning up?"

Hannah grinned. "Actually you'd love the music—they

play all the old songs. But yes, the crowd would be a bit younger."

"We'll stick to Dillon's," Geraldine said. "But I'm delighted with your news."

"Of course it's early days."

"Early days, of course."

Hannah glanced at the wall clock. "I should go," she said. "It's nearly time to tidy up."

"Let me know how Saturday night goes," Geraldine said. "I presume I can tell your father."

"You can."

She hung up and slipped her phone back into her pocket. Saturday night, two nights away. She began planning what to wear.

Take me to a hotel, Nora had said. *I want to do it on a king-size bed.* So he had.

It hadn't been hard to organize. Nora had booked the hotel room in Galway for one night in her name, paying in advance with Patrick's company card. In the morning she'd called in sick and taken the bus to Galway. She'd booked in at noon and gone upstairs.

He'd arrived at one and walked past the reception desk, briefcase in hand, business-suited, attracting no attention at all when he'd taken the lift to the third floor and knocked on the door of Room 324.

They'd ordered a room-service lunch. They'd run a bath and made full use of the generously proportioned bed before and after. They'd left at five and driven the hour back to Clongarvin.

We must do it again, she'd said, squeezing his thigh in the car when he stopped to let her out on a side street, well away from prying eyes. *You're full of energy.*

You're not so bad yourself, he'd said, glancing around before slipping a hand under her skirt.

Next time she might bring him to Adam's flat, make him pass within three blocks of Indulgence to get there. Nothing like a bit of danger to keep things interesting.

"But you're playing in the wine bar," Hannah said.

"I'm not on till nine," he pointed out. "We could get an early bird—which, of course, would suit a cheap Scotsman perfectly. Would seven o'clock give you enough time to get home from work and out again?"

"I suppose it would," she said, a slow smile blooming on her face.

"How do you feel about Indian?"

He made her laugh. He listened when she spoke; he wasn't only waiting for her to finish so he could say something else. He smelled of soap, nothing fancy. She liked the clothes he wore. She liked his shoes.

After she hung up, Hannah wiped her hands on her apron and walked through to the sitting room, where Kirby was curled in his awful charity-shop chair. She stood for a minute, listening.

"What do you think, Kirby?" she asked. "Is our boy showing promise?"

The dog lifted his head and thumped his tail against the side of the chair as the first two lines of "Mary Had a Little Lamb" floated down from upstairs for the umpteenth time.

Hannah settled on the couch and reached for the remote control, humming along. Half an hour later, as the closing credits of *Coronation Street* were rolling, Adam walked in.

"I heard you practicing," she said, switching off the television. "Very promising."

"Do you know how to breathe through your abdomen?"

"No."

"That's what I have to do, apparently. Look." He placed the flat of his hand below his waistline. "You have to feel the breath coming from down here." He inhaled. "I think I'm getting it."

Hannah smiled. "That's good. Your teacher and her mother will be so proud. Have you discovered yet if she's single?"

"Not exactly—I couldn't very well come out and ask her—but there's no sign of a man around the place."

"Sounds promising." She let a beat pass, and then said, "I'm going out to dinner tomorrow night."

"I thought you were going to Vintage."

"I am, but I'm going to dinner first. With John," she added. "We're getting an early bird."

"Good for you—I'll see you at the bar afterwards, then." He picked up the remote control and sat next to her. "I might ask Nora along."

"Fine," Hannah replied.

Adam scanned the Aertel screen, humming as he checked that night's program schedule. After a few seconds, Hannah recognized an out-of-tune version of "I've Got a Crush on You."

Alice hadn't planned to go to the cemetery after the memorial Mass. She sat a few rows back from the front of the church and recited the prayers, and stood and knelt when everyone else did. She watched the parents and their families standing and kneeling in front of her, the father's head bent, the mother's blond hair tied in a low ponytail.

She stayed in her seat while people came up to them afterward.

She waited until they filed down the aisle past her pew, the father's hand cradling the mother's elbow. So thin, she looked, the mother. So pale and empty.

Outside the church Alice got into the car and drove to the cemetery, having made no conscious decision to do so. She walked along the rows of headstones until she found them. Ten of them stood around the grave. Four older people, one of the men in a wheelchair. The grandparents, she guessed. The mother's sister there, too, dressed today in a gray jacket and a denim skirt. A youth with a shaved head, two other teenage girls.

A small-enough family, the newest member wiped out now.

Alice stood three graves away and kept her eyes on the headstone in front of her in case they turned around. There was a murmur from them that she couldn't make out. It didn't sound regular enough to be praying, but she couldn't be sure.

They left eventually, walking past the spot where Alice stood. When they were out of sight, she approached the grave.

He was buried in a family plot, the granite headstone already covered with O'Brien names dating back to 1939. A small wooden cross had been stuck into the ground just in front of the headstone, flanked by two fat, creamy-white candles burning in glass jars. A photo in an oval brass frame was attached to the top of the cross, and a little metal plaque underneath read simply JASON O'BRIEN 2006–2010.

Alice said an Our Father and a Hail Mary and a Glory Be, her eyes on the photo. His smile was wide. His teeth were tiny and perfect. He had a chubby, baby face. She said an Act of Contrition, her lips moving silently.

Back home she stuffed a chicken, roasted potatoes with garlic and rosemary, and mashed carrots and parsnips. At dinner Tom didn't ask about the Mass, and she didn't mention it, or her trip to the cemetery.

"I'm going to have to reduce Geraldine's hours," she said. "Just temporarily, till things pick up."

"I'm sorry to hear that," Tom answered. "I didn't realize things were that bad." He was still on full pay from the clinic—"extended leave," they were calling it—but that couldn't go on much longer.

"I'd like you to think about going back to work," she said. "It's not good to be staying out so long. You're only making it harder for yourself in the long run."

He chewed his chicken, and she waited for his response, and it was quite a few seconds before it became clear to her that none was coming.

They met at the restaurant. He'd offered to pick her up, but Hannah had refused. *It's only a ten-minute walk,* she'd said. *I need the exercise.*

The weather was fair. The warming air smelled like the beginning of summer. Hannah sprayed on a citrus scent and chose a gray dress with tiny pale blue polka dots whose folds played down her curves. She realized she was happy. She smiled at people who came toward her, and most returned her smile.

"You look sunny," John said. He was waiting outside, leaning against the restaurant wall, hands in the pockets of the chinos he wore when he was performing.

Hannah laughed. "I think that sounds like a compliment." She looked at the gray sky, streaked here and there with washed-out blue. "D'you think we've any hope of a summer this year?"

"Absolutely." He held the door open, and she walked ahead of him. "By September we'll be wishing for a drop of rain."

They weren't the only early-bird diners. Waiters scurried around, depositing baskets of pappadams and dishes of chutney, uncorking bottles of wine, whisking away the remains of meals. As they were shown to a table, Hannah was suddenly reminded of her last meal out, the night Patrick had dropped his bombshell and she'd taken a taxi alone to the restaurant. Trying her best, as each course was set before her, not to bury her face in her hands and howl. And here she was with someone new, who she didn't think would sleep with another woman behind her back.

"Tell me about the band," she said as they sat, determined to push all negative thoughts away tonight. "The man who plays the double bass doesn't look Irish."

"No—he's Portuguese, but he married an Irish girl."

"I see. And I assume," she went on, thinking of Adam, "that Wally is with the clarinet player."

John smiled. "No—they're brother and sister. Both single, in fact."

"Oh—my mistake." Adam would be pleased.

"Fancy some wine?" John was scanning the list.

Hannah reached for her menu. "Why not? You choose—I'm not fussy."

He was good company, as she'd known he would be. He described the village where he'd grown up, and she saw the narrow shingle beach, the whitewashed houses cradling the shoreline, the fishing boats moored along the pier, the lobster pots bobbing on the water. He told her about his parents, his fisherman father battling arthritis as fiercely as he battled the elements, his volunteer meals-on-wheels driver mother. "Her apple jelly wins first prize at the village fete every year—I'm sure the others are fit to throttle her."

Hannah told him about her grandfather. "He was the one who got me interested in baking. He taught me how to make rock buns and almond cookies when I was seven or eight. He got me my first apron and electric mixer. His father was a baker, but I never knew him."

"Was it frightening," he asked, "opening your own shop, all by yourself?"

"Terrifying—and in the middle of a recession too. I'm sure people thought I needed my head examined." She smoothed a small crease in the tablecloth. "Even with Granddad's legacy, which helped a lot, there was still a fair bit of expense involved, and I also have a mortgage to pay, and all the other bills that go along with a house. My parents didn't say it, but I know they were worried I'd go belly-up in a week."

"It's their job"—he smiled—"to worry about you."

"I suppose so. Luckily, I've proved them wrong so far and I'm still here—if not exactly raking it in." Their waiter brought pappadams, and she reached for one. "And I haven't collapsed from exhaustion—yet."

When the wine arrived, John filled their glasses and lifted his. "I have every faith in you. This time next year, you'll be counting the profits, mark my words."

Hannah touched her glass against his. "I'll drink to that."

Her mother's perfume these days smelled terribly cloying to Leah. In the past few weeks, she'd completely lost her taste for anything sweet—developing instead a craving for salted crackers topped with cheese and sprinkled with soy sauce—so it was hardly surprising that Fiona's heady, almondy scent made her want very much to gag.

"Thank you," she said when her mother handed her a jar of verbena hand cream, knowing that it was the nearest Fiona would come to an apology.

They hadn't spoken since the disastrous lunch on Easter Sunday, when Fiona had practically called Patrick a gigolo, not until Fiona had rung the other night and suggested she call in for a short visit on her way home from bridge, using exactly the same tone of voice she always did, as if they hadn't parted in anger almost three weeks earlier. And Leah, caught unawares, had found herself agreeing.

Patrick wasn't there. Leah had suggested he make himself scarce, and he'd been happy to oblige. When the baby came, he and Fiona could put their differences aside. Once Fiona realized that Patrick was as committed to parenthood as Leah was, she couldn't object to him anymore, and a silent truce would come into force. It had to.

In the meantime Leah would have to be the buffer. "Coffee?" she asked her mother. "Or tea? Earl Grey?" She was determined to keep this meeting neutral, had resolved to be polite and hospitable and no more.

Patrick hadn't once referred to Fiona's implied accusations; no mention had been made of the Easter Sunday encounter. After lunch had ended so abruptly he'd left the apartment without coming into the bedroom where Leah lay.

She'd heard the front door closing softly, and she'd turned her face to the wall. She hadn't heard him return, but had woken some time later to the sound of the television, and walked out to find him asleep on the couch, his jacket still on, the remains of a pizza in a box on the floor beside him.

"Your baby cot is still in the attic," Fiona was saying, "and I think a playpen. Of course, you may prefer to buy new ones."

She was trying, as much as Fiona could try. Leah should meet her halfway; she'd probably need her mother around when the baby arrived. Need, not want.

"Thank you," she replied, in the same neutral tone. "I'll think about it. Did you say tea or coffee?"

She and Patrick had made love twice in the past fortnight, both times at her instigation. Patrick hadn't looked for it. He hadn't once turned to her in bed, hadn't woken her up in the middle of the night the way he used to.

It was the baby, of course. He was wary of doing anything so late in the pregnancy, that was all. Once the baby arrived, things would sort themselves out.

"Have you seen much of Nora O'Connor?" Fiona asked as Leah began to lay out cups and saucers.

"A little."

Nora had dropped by the salon out of the blue a few days earlier. She'd brought a toy white rabbit and a bottle of jasmine-scented bath salts. *How're you feeling?* she'd asked, leaning against the doorjamb in her cream linen cardigan and blue linen trousers. *We must do lunch again,* she'd said. *My treat this time. When you get a chance.*

Leah hadn't asked Nora about her job. She'd shifted her weight and told Nora she had a customer waiting. *I'll give you a call,* she'd said. *Thanks for these.*

She'd phone Nora at some stage, and they'd go to lunch, and Leah would hope, as she'd been hoping now for weeks, that Nora would look past Patrick for a diversion. That Patrick wouldn't consider being unfaithful, even if Nora did set her sights on him.

"You look tired," Fiona said. "Are you getting enough sleep?"

Three weeks, give or take, and Leah and Patrick would be parents. He hadn't once asked about names, even though she'd left the book where he couldn't miss it. He never wondered aloud if they'd have a boy or a girl, hadn't asked her which she'd prefer. He'd gone along to the classes when she'd asked him and taken part like all the other expectant fathers, but he didn't mention the baby the rest of the time, ever.

Surely when it arrived, he'd change. Surely he'd take one look at his son or daughter and fall in love.

"I think I'm having a girl," Leah said suddenly, wanting someone to share it with. "I've just got this feeling."

Fiona regarded her above the rim of her cup. "A girl," she said, without expression. "You could be right—although I was convinced *you* were going to be a boy."

Leah squeezed lemon into her tea. "How did you feel," she asked then, "when you saw me? How did you and Dad feel?"

Fiona lowered her cup. "We were happy to have a healthy baby, of course," she answered placidly. "Just as you will be."

Just as you will be. As if Leah had made this baby all on her own. She hoisted herself from the chair. "I need the toilet," she told her mother, and walked heavily from the room.

"Hi there."

Hannah smiled. "Hello. This is a surprise." His accent was even more pronounced on the phone.

"Can you talk? Are you busy?" he asked.

"Yes I can, and no I'm not."

"I have something to confess," he said then, and her smile faded. She waited, looking at the cupcake tree. Reaching out to straighten the coconut-lime sample.

"I'm not sure how to say this," he went on. "I haven't been completely honest with you."

He was still with his wife, they hadn't separated. His conscience was at him now, and he'd decided to come clean.

"Are you still there?" he asked.

"Still here," Hannah answered lightly. "Just wondering what's coming." *Say it,* she thought. *Say it and get it over with.*

"The truth is..." She heard his indrawn breath and closed her eyes. "...I don't really like cupcakes."

Her eyes snapped open. "You what?"

"I haven't really got a sweet tooth, you see," he said. "It's not just cupcakes, it's chocolate and biscuits and...well, anything sweet really."

Hannah let out the breath she didn't know she'd been holding.

"Are you mad at me?" he asked.

"I am," she said, her smile returning. "I'm shocked at your deceit. I'm not sure that I'll be able to forgive you, really."

"I was afraid you'd say that," he answered, "so I thought I'd make it up to you."

"How?"

The shop door opened and there he was, holding a bag of Kettle Chips. Slipping his phone back into his shirt pocket.

"Aged White Cheddar, right?" he asked, approaching the

counter. "See? I'm not the only one who likes savory things."

Hannah laughed. She'd mentioned Kettle Chips in passing, weeks ago, and he'd remembered. She hung up and took the dark blue bag from him.

"You're forgiven," she said. "Let's open them right now."

She was being wooed, and it was wonderful.

He'd mastered "Mary Had a Little Lamb" and "Sur le Pont d'Avignon." He'd eaten the Jammie Dodgers when they'd appeared for a second time and drunk the milk—and suffered the consequences the following day. He'd attempted small talk with Vivienne's mother when she'd appeared—he'd admired the garden, remarked on the fine weather they'd been enjoying—even though the older woman was clearly suspicious of him. (And who could blame her? If ever someone's motives were suspect, Adam's were.)

He'd even reached out to pat the giant marmalade cat, which seemed to live on the piano—but to his relief it had shrunk away from him, and Vivienne had murmured that he was shy around strangers.

I wonder where he gets it from, Adam had thought.

Any attempt at personal conversation on his part brought a fresh flood of color to her face—if she could have shrunk away from him as the cat had, Adam suspected she would. So he stuck to questions that related to the pieces they were looking at, and he did his best to be patient and bide his time.

But all the same, he was inching toward her, absorbing a fraction more about her with each visit. She had a habit of rubbing her middle finger as she listened to his efforts and closing her eyes briefly now and again. Her teeth weren't quite straight and not perfectly white. She wore no jewelry, not even a watch. Her ears, surprisingly small, had never been pierced.

She dressed only in dark colors—black and gray and navy, mostly. Her clothes were modest and unremarkable. Her hair was always pinned up, never loose. Her breath smelled minty. She used no makeup, as far as his untutored male eye could tell.

Her feet were long, her calves—what he could see of them—slender. He was reminded of a scene from *The Piano* when Harvey Keitel had lain on the floor and poked a finger through a hole in Holly Hunter's stocking as she played. Vivienne's eyes were fringed with surprisingly long, pale lashes.

And thanks to Hannah, he now knew for sure that she was single.

He decided, during his third lesson, that the time had come to risk tiptoeing a little further toward her. He waited until her mother had delivered the usual tray—tiny Iced Gem biscuits tonight, which he'd last eaten more than twenty years ago—and left them alone again.

"How did you get involved with the band?" he asked. A musical question: She could hardly object.

She blinked rapidly twice, a nervous gesture he was becoming accustomed to. He wanted to reach out and touch her arm and tell her that she had nothing to fear.

"My brother," she said quickly, bending to riffle through the pages of sheet music for a new piece for him.

Adam bit the pastel pink swirl off an Iced Gem. "He's a member?"

She nodded. "Keyboards."

"I see." Adam crunched his biscuit. Imagine admitting that he knew all this already, that his friend had pumped the saxophonist to discover her marital status. Imagine her reaction if he said that.

"And your brother only plays one instrument? That's a bit lazy, isn't it?"

She looked up, the tiniest of smiles flashing across her features. "He can play the guitar, too. And the flute."

"Right," he said. "So you're a musical family."

A short nod as she pulled a sheet from the bundle and placed it on the stand. Beethoven, Adam read. Bit of a step up from "Mary Had a Little Lamb." Hannah would be impressed.

"What's the name of the band?" Another question he knew the answer to.

"Small Change."

"And how long—"

"We'll try Beethoven next, a lullaby," she said. "When you've finished."

Adam downed the rest of his milk and returned the glass to the tray. "What's your brother's name?"

Vivienne shifted on her bench, her smile gone. For a second, Adam thought she wasn't going to reply, and then she said, "Walter. Wally."

"And he's a full-time musician?" Aware that he was pushing but reluctant to return to the formality of the lesson just yet.

"No—he drives a taxi." She looked pointedly at his clarinet, lying on the floor by his chair, and Adam picked it up. "Beethoven," she said again, turning toward the stand, and Adam put the mouthpiece to his lips and awaited further instruction.

And then she said, keeping her eyes fixed on the sheet music, "You're improving a bit." The familiar flush reappearing, drifting slowly up her cheeks. "With the clarinet."

It wasn't much. It was hardly anything. She probably said that to all her pupils to keep them trying. Silly, really, the effect it had on him.

When the woman came out of the house, Alice nearly missed her, scraping with her nail at a stain on her skirt. As she raised her head, a movement caught her eye on the other side of the road. The woman walked rapidly, head lowered, shoulders hunched, hands thrust into the pockets of a green jacket.

Alice grabbed her bag and got out, no thought in her head but to follow. She locked the car and walked after the woman, suddenly aware of her quickening heartbeat, her dry mouth, her grotesquely loud footsteps on the quiet afternoon street.

After crossing a number of intersections and turning a few corners, they came to a bus stop. The woman stood next to the pole, ignoring the shelter. An elderly man sat on the wooden bench inside, his hands wrapped around the knobby handle of a wooden stick.

Alice approached, slowing her pace. No plan, no clue what to do.

She stopped a foot or so from the woman and rummaged in her bag. She never traveled by bus, had no idea how much it cost. She emptied coins from her purse into her palm—roughly two euro. Surely that would be enough.

She closed her bag and hung it on her shoulder, then turned her head slowly toward the mother, who was staring fixedly at the ground. She looked tightly clenched, standing there. Alice could see the shape her fist made in the near-side pocket. The thin strap of a small brown bag lay across her body. Her blond hair was pulled back into a blue rubber band.

"Excuse me," Alice said, and the mother turned toward her and regarded her dully. "I wonder," Alice went on, struggling with an unexpected lump in her throat, "if you know when the bus is due?"

Nothing in the woman's face suggested that she'd even heard the question. As Alice was about to repeat it, she said in a low voice, "Ten past," and turned away again.

"Thanks."

The man on the bench pulled a hankie from his pocket and blew his nose noisily. A younger man approached the bus stop and sat, rattling change in his pocket, tapping one shoe on the ground, presumably in accompaniment to whatever was coming out of the earphones he wore. A woman arrived from the opposite direction, pulling a smallish suitcase on wheels. A siren sounded faintly in the distance.

Alice was acutely aware of the mother's presence, so close she could have reached out and taken her arm and told her how terribly, terribly—

The bus appeared and slowed to a stop. The two men got to their feet, the older man's knuckles white around his stick as he hauled himself upward.

Alice stood unmoving as the others filed on. Her hand tightened around the coins she held as she watched the woman boarding. She waited until everyone was on, and then she turned and retraced her steps to the car.

She drove slowly out of the estate and through streets full of people, past shops and parks and schools. On the far side of town, she pulled into a small car park attached to a church she'd never been inside. She switched off the engine and sat there, watching the few who came and went from the church. Eventually she started the car again and drove home.

In the kitchen, as the dinner was cooking, she stood at the window looking out at the lawn spotted with dandelions, the flower beds that were more weeds than flowers, the mint that was running riot in the herb box.

She opened the cutlery drawer and took out her daughter's last letter, and she read again the news of kindergarten graduations and birthday parties, and a camping trip to the mountains. She looked at the photos Ellen had sent, of grandchildren Alice hardly knew jumping into swimming pools, eating pizza, laughing for the camera. Healthy-looking and tanned, with such white teeth. She longed to be there with Ellen, to leave this hellish place behind.

When the shepherd's pie was ready, she spooned a serving onto a dinner plate. She put it on a tray with a glass of water, a butter dish, and the smaller of their two saltcellars. She brought the tray upstairs to her husband, who had taken to going to bed in the late afternoon and not rising again till the following morning was almost over.

"Guess what," Adam said. "Nora has a man."

"Has she?" Hannah closed the door of the washing machine. "What's he like?"

Adam draped his jacket over a kitchen chair. "Well, I didn't actually meet him."

She turned a dial, and water started rushing into the drum. "So what did she tell you about him?"

"Nothing." Adam hesitated. "The thing is, I think she was hiding him. Just now, when I called over."

Hannah frowned. "Hiding him?"

"I'm pretty sure someone was there." He filled the kettle.

"Nora couldn't wait to get rid of me. She said I should have phoned before coming over—"

"I told you—"

"—and she said she hadn't time to make coffee because she was getting ready to go out, but she was definitely cagey. Barely let me get the books I wanted before shoving me out the door."

Hannah crossed to the fridge and took out a pound of butter. "So you've no proof anyone was there?"

"No, but I'm pretty sure." He got mugs from the cupboard. "I'd bet anything there was a man there."

"But why would she hide him? I mean, it's not as if she's forbidden to have men in your flat."

"Dunno." He spooned coffee into the mugs. "Maybe he's married."

In the act of unwrapping the butter, Hannah paused. "Married?"

"Hey, I could be wrong," Adam said. "There might have been nobody there, but I just got a feeling."

Hannah made no reply.

"No doubt we'll find out soon enough if there's someone on the scene," Adam said. "Coffee's made."

"Thanks..." Hannah took eggs from the fridge. She got sugar and flour from a cupboard and lay them next to the eggs. She attached the beaters to the stand mixer and filled four baking trays with paper liners.

"Look what I bought today."

She turned back to Adam, who was holding out a little plastic bag. She peered inside. "Iced Gems—I haven't seen them for years."

"Yeah—I'd forgotten how much I like them." He tipped a scattering of the brightly colored little biscuits into her hand

and turned toward the door. "And now you must excuse me—I have to practice my Beethoven."

"Now that's a sentence I never thought I'd hear you say. You have half an hour before I go to bed."

"Plenty. See you tomorrow."

Hannah bit into a pink-iced biscuit. Just because Adam thought there'd been a man in his apartment didn't mean there was. And even if there was, it didn't mean he was married, or with someone else—there could be a totally different reason for Nora to not want anyone to know about him.

She filled the kettle for her hot-water bottle.

"Jesus," Patrick said, "that was a bit close."

Nora ran a fingernail along his back. "Imagine his face if he'd walked in and found you in his bed."

Patrick laughed shortly. "Actually, he's really not my type." He winced. "Hey, easy with the claws—no marks, remember?"

"I thought you said Leah wasn't interested." Continuing her slow trail down his spine. "So I'll only leave my mark where she won't be looking." Bending and nipping his buttock with her teeth.

He jerked out of her reach. "Cut it out—we can't take chances like that." He rolled over, pinning her beneath him and trapping her arms. "We can still have our fun—we just need to be careful not to get caught."

She smiled. "But darling, the risk of getting caught is where all the fun comes in."

June

I can't get hold of Tom," Stephen said. "I've tried ringing him, several times—his mobile is switched off, and the landline just rings out."

"Can't you leave a message?" Geraldine asked.

"No—there's no answering machine on the house phone."

"Oh, that's true. I forgot that."

"It's like he's trying to hide." Stephen pushed his plate aside. "It's been nearly ten weeks now. The clinic can't keep paying him indefinitely for not showing up."

Geraldine set her fork down. "Stephen, I don't know what I'd have done if it had happened to you."

"Don't think like that." He rubbed a hand across his face wearily. "I'll have to call around there."

"It seems like you will." Geraldine stacked the plates and brought them to the sink. "Should I say anything to Alice?"

Her hours had been cut. Now she didn't go to work till two, and then usually held the fort on her own till closing time.

"No," Stephen said slowly, getting up. "Best say nothing to Alice." He took the salt- and pepper cellars back to the shelf above the fridge. "Tom might lie low if he thinks I'm coming."

Geraldine spooned ice cream into dishes. "Poor Tom. Poor Alice."

Stephen thought, but didn't say, *At least they're both alive.*

———————

"I'm trying to get my daughter to come over for a visit," John said, "as soon as she gets holidays at the end of the month."

"That's good." Hannah put a hand over her glass as he lifted the brandy bottle. "Better not, thanks. You said she's in college?"

John topped up his own drink. "Yes, in Edinburgh. She's just finishing first-year law."

"And she's been to Ireland before?"

"Yes. We often came to visit my mother's family in Tipperary when Danielle was growing up. But she hasn't been over here in years, and it would be her first time in Clongarvin."

"Wonder what she'll make of us." Hannah took a tiny sip of her remaining brandy. "Well, I must say that dinner was most impressive."

"So my cooking hasn't scared you off."

"Not in the least—I love spare ribs. You're a far better cook than I am."

"Oh, I doubt that very much." He set his glass down on the coffee table. "But maybe I'll have the chance to compare our cooking skills sometime."

"You never know."

He moved closer and bent his head and put his lips against her throat. "I'm glad I met you," he whispered. "I'm glad you're here."

"Me, too." She closed her eyes as he moved his mouth to

the opening in her blouse. She felt her way to his shirt buttons and began to undo them.

His skin was warm. His hands were gentle. And his mouth, when he finally found hers, tasted of brandy.

———————

Vivienne was not herself.

"You're not yourself," her mother told her at the dinner table. "You never say no to apple sponge. It's not a bit like you."

"I'm not hungry," Vivienne replied.

"That's what I mean," her mother said. "It's not like you not to be hungry."

"You're miles away," Wally said when he called around as usual for Saturday tea with his sister and mother. "You haven't heard a word I've said, have you?"

"She's not herself," their mother told him.

"You forgot to give him the new piece last week," Robbie O'Donnell's mother told Vivienne on Tuesday. "You were going to give him that new Debussy piece to practice, and you forgot."

"She's not herself these days," Vivienne's mother said to Mrs. O'Donnell as she showed them out. "It's not a bit like her to forget something like that."

"Maybe she needs a tonic," Mrs. O'Donnell said. "Maybe she's coming down with something."

"When can I stop having piano lessons?" Robbie asked, and his mother shushed him and pushed him ahead of her out the front door.

Vivienne bought a lipstick. It was called Candy Floss, and it cost her €8.99. She had no idea if this was expensive, as lipsticks went. She brought it home and sat in front of her dressing table and pulled off the top and ran the color across her lips. She turned to Pumpkin, who was sprawled on the chest of drawers. "What do you think?" she asked him.

He purred gently and flicked his tail.

"I'm wearing lipstick," she told him, and he closed his eyes and went on purring.

She studied her face in the mirror. She took off her glasses and peered at her shiny mouth. She made it smile at her, and then she stopped smiling. "No," she said. She pulled a tissue from its box and rubbed away the lipstick and threw the tube into her wastepaper basket.

Ugly, Specky Four-Eyes, Freckleface. The size of those feet, they're gross. What color is red, Four-Eyes? Look at her, she's puce.

Nobody to walk her home from school. Nobody to ring and ask her out. No cards on Valentine's Day, no flowers, ever, for Specky Four-Eyes O'Toole. Nothing but music to lose herself in, to block out the cruel voices, to take her away from them all.

Music helped her to forget. Music filled her empty spaces. Music was all she needed, until Pumpkin had appeared in the back garden one day six years ago, shivering and thin, as unwanted as she'd been. Now they had each other. It was enough.

Wasn't it?

"Dinner is on the table," her mother shouted up the stairs.

"Coming," Vivienne called back. She pushed the lipstick deeper into the wastepaper basket. No more of that silliness. She would be herself again.

She lifted Pumpkin into her arms and left the room and walked downstairs.

———————

"Can't you stay a bit longer?" he asked. "It's not even nine."

Hannah buttoned her blouse. "Nine is my bedtime. Actually, nine is late for me—I have to be up in six hours, remember. Anyhow, the taxi's on the way."

John watched as she slipped her arms into her jacket. "You don't regret what happened?"

She smiled, put a hand to his face. "Of course not. It was as much my doing as yours."

He kissed her palm. "Good."

It had been different. It had been strange, being with another man after Patrick. But John had been tender, and she'd felt comfortable with him—not, she suspected, that "comfortable" was a word a man would like to hear used to describe his lovemaking.

"What's funny?" he asked.

"Oh, I'm just amused at the way things turn out," Hannah answered. "You never know, do you?"

"No." He started to say something else, but just then a car horn sounded in the street below—and for a second, Hannah was back in her bedroom, scattered jewelry at her feet, listening to Patrick telling her he'd fallen in love with someone else.

John crossed to the window and looked down. "That was quick." He came back and took her into his arms.

"I like how you smell," she said against his shoulder. "Nice and soapy."

He laughed. "I'm glad to hear it. I'll walk you down."

"No need," Hannah said, drawing back. "You haven't got shoes on—I'll be fine."

"I'll call you in the morning," he said as she let herself out and hurried down the two flights of stairs to where the taxi waited. She opened the door and slid into the backseat.

"Not you again," the driver said, watching her face in the rearview mirror. "We'll have to stop meeting like this."

Hannah smiled. "I think you must be stalking me."

His eyes crinkled in the mirror. "How's your yellow shop?"

"Still there, thank goodness." She leaned back in her seat. "Will you turn up that music a bit?"

"So you don't have to talk to me?" But he raised the volume, and Hannah closed her eyes and let the soft, mellow sound settle around her.

The evening had gone pretty much as she'd imagined it would. They'd both known how it was going to end. She'd sensed John's attraction, and she'd been happy to let it take its natural course. And if the earth hadn't exactly moved, so what? It had been perfectly pleasant, and she was happy with that.

And earth-moving experiences didn't last anyway. Her first time with Patrick, at the end of their third date, had been intense, her climax leaving her trembling and limp—and look how that had turned out. Maybe the slow burners were better.

She opened her eyes and studied the back of Wally's head. His hair needed a cut. Funny how they kept meeting up. "How long have you been in the band?" she asked him.

"Couple of years," he answered, "give or take. I started it." There was a short silence, and then he said, "So you and Johnny are an item then?"

"Kind of," Hannah replied, meeting his eyes again in the rearview mirror.

"He's a good man," Wally indicated as he changed gears. "Even if he is from Scotland."

Hannah laughed.

"I assume, by the way, that I'm taking you home."

She started. "Sorry—did I forget to give you my address?"

"I know where you live," he said. "I'm your stalker, remember?" Turning to flash her a grin.

"Of course." She smiled. "I'd forgotten that."

When they reached her house, she opened her bag. "How much do I owe?"

He turned to face her again. "On the house," he said, "in return for a free fancy bun when I eventually make it into the yellow shop."

"Oh, no, I can't—"

"Oh, yes, you can," he said. "You're a friend of Johnny's. Don't worry," he added, "you'll pay the next time. I'm not made of money, you know."

She laughed again. "Well, if you insist, thanks very much—but do call into the shop. You know where I am."

"Indeed I do—good night, now."

She watched him drive away, and then she took her key from her bag and let herself into the house.

———

She smelled sweet, she smelled of vanilla ice cream. She reminded him of something in bloom. He remembered her crying that night, months ago. He remembered turning on the light for her when she was dabbing at her eyes, how she'd said thank you. How he'd called her back to give her the blue scarf she'd left behind. How he'd wondered about why she was crying.

So Johnny had gotten her. Fair play.

———

Every afternoon Alice left Glass Slipper soon after Geraldine arrived at two. They had tea together first, both pretending that everything was still as it always had been, and when the mugs were washed and put away, Alice left. She'd stopped inventing reasons for leaving, and thankfully, Geraldine had stopped asking if she'd be back.

She varied her routine. Sometimes she went straight to the cemetery, other days she drove directly to Springwood Gardens.

The flowers were finally gone from the gate of number 37. One day she saw Dave mowing the lawn, up and down, up and down. Wearing a dark blue hat with a brim, stopping every now and again to pull it off and wipe his brow with a bare forearm.

Once Claire came out and walked right past Alice's car. Alice sat and watched her until she turned a corner.

She thought of them as Claire and Dave now.

A green plastic rectangular planter had appeared on the grave, about a foot and a half long. It lay on the earth in front of the wooden cross, filled with real violas and pansies.

She wondered if they were planning to add Jason's name to the big headstone, or if the cross was going to stay. The oval frame of his photo was spotted with tarnish that she couldn't get off, even with Brasso.

She left him flowers every few days. She signed the cards "A."

At half past ten Fiona ran her usual evening bath, adding plenty of lavender salts. Lying in the scented water, she read one chapter of the Gandhi biography and drank a tall glass of warm milk. Afterward she toweled herself dry before applying her nighttime body lotion.

She cleansed, toned, and moisturized her face, applied

hand cream and massaged it in. She adjusted her clock radio so the display was turned away from the bed; nothing like watching the time pass to encourage insomnia. She pulled on the white cotton gloves she wore in bed.

And just before she lay back on her down pillows, she felt a sudden impulse to talk to her daughter, after almost a week of no communication. She lifted the cordless phone off its cradle and reached a gloved finger toward the keypad—but as she was about to press the first key, she paused to turn the clock radio back to face her.

She saw that it was 11:18, too late. She replaced the phone. She'd call Leah tomorrow afternoon. They had nothing much to say to each other these days anyway.

———

Stephen pressed the bell again. After several more seconds had passed, he stepped back from the door and looked up toward the first-floor windows.

"Tom?" he called. The car was in the driveway. The curtains were drawn back. "Tom?"

He put a hand over the side gate, slid the bolt, and walked around to the back of the house. He rapped loudly on the door, calling Tom's name again. There was a plastic bag by the wall. Stephen glanced in and saw empty bottles with the gold labels of Powers whiskey on them.

He walked up the side passage again, bolting the gate after him. He opened his wallet and found an old receipt. He wrote on the back of it and posted it through the mail slot. He checked the upstairs windows again before walking down the short driveway to his car.

He got in and drove back to the dental clinic.

———

"Hi."

"Well, hello." The pleasure in his voice was evident. "What's up?"

"I got the flowers," she said. "You shouldn't have."

"Sorry; I'll try not to do it again."

She smiled. "Thank you, they're lovely."

They were big orange daisies, six of them in a long-stemmed bunch. She had no vase in the shop, so she'd filled her tiny sink with water and propped them in it.

"Thank you for last night," he said. "Are you tired?"

"A bit," she admitted, watching a man push open the door. "I have to go."

"Okay—I'll call you later."

He was perfect on paper, he was doing everything right. She loved being in his company, she enjoyed the way he treated her. Her feelings would deepen, given time. She was sure of it.

———

She should have said something to Patrick before he left for work. She should have mentioned the ache in her back that had woken her a couple of times in the night, sliding dully through her and then easing. She should have said something as he was getting dressed, as she was struggling into the shower, as he was drinking coffee in the kitchen, standing by the window. As she was dabbing concealer under her eyes, smoothing foundation onto her swollen face.

I have this pain, she should have told him. *It comes now and again, down my back. It's a new pain. It's different.*

But she'd said nothing, because Patrick must be sick of her complaints, tired of hearing about her constipation and her heartburn and her constant need to pee, weary of her indigestion and her nausea and her craving for salt.

So he'd gone to work, kissing her cheek briefly, his aftershave making her want to gag. And that had been three hours ago, and the pain in her back was worse now, much worse, and she'd rung her two appointments and canceled them until further notice. And the pain was slicing through her now, easing for a while before returning and making her gasp with its intensity.

She waited until the latest one had passed, and then she picked up the phone and called Patrick's mobile. When it went straight to his voice mail, she disconnected and tried again, and when the same thing happened, she waited for the beep and then said rapidly, "Patrick, it's me—please ring. It's urgent."

She hung up and tried Nora's mobile, but it rang and rang and remained unanswered. She called directory inquiries and got the number of the newspaper offices—the first time she'd needed the main number—and the receptionist told her that Patrick had left for a meeting and no, she didn't know where. Could she give Leah his mobile number?

"I have that," Leah said, "but I can't contact him. I can't get through to him. Is his PA there?" Surely Nora would have a number where he could be reached.

"I'm sorry," the receptionist, whom Leah had yet to meet, replied, "but she called in sick this morning. Can I take a message at all?"

The pain came again then, and Leah hung up and bent double, gritting her teeth. When it faded, she called her mother. "I need you," she said, her eyes closed. "I think the baby's coming."

As she hung up, she felt a warm gush of wetness between her legs and looked down to see a puddle seeping into the pale green carpet.

The first thing Alice saw when she opened the front door was a brown envelope on the floor and a scrap of paper lying next to it. She picked up the envelope and saw Tom's name, and the government harp above it. She tore it open and pulled out the page and read that Tom Joyce was summoned to appear at the district court on Friday, the eighteenth of June, at half past eleven.

She bent and picked up the scrap of paper and saw that it was a receipt from Boots for some toiletries. She turned it over and read *"Tom, please get in touch—Stephen."*

"Right," she said aloud in the empty hallway. She walked to the stairs and sat on the third step, holding the letter and the receipt. After a while she got up and climbed the rest of the stairs to her husband's bedroom. She walked in and crossed to the window. She pulled the curtains apart and shoved the window open.

"Tom, get up," she said, turning to him. "You need to get up now. I have to talk to you."

As Nora pulled on her top, she heard a soft beep. She turned to see Patrick switching on his phone.

"Well," she said, "can't wait to get back to the real world, can you?"

"Shit," Patrick said, looking at the screen. "Shit." He

jabbed buttons rapidly and raised the phone to his ear.

Nora reached for her skirt. "What's all the—"

"Shh," he said, listening, holding up a palm to Nora. After a few seconds he snapped the phone closed and grabbed his briefcase. "Come on," he said, "we have to go."

"What's the big panic?" Nora asked, zipping up her skirt.

"Leah," he said, already halfway out of the room. "She's having the baby."

"Jesus." Nora stepped into her shoes, snatched up her bag and jacket, and hurried after him. "I thought it wasn't due for a fortnight."

He didn't answer, stabbing at the lift button, checking his watch, tucking his shirt into his trousers. "Come on, come on," he muttered.

"Calm down, would you?" Nora struggled into her jacket. "A few minutes aren't going to make much difference at this stage."

Patrick shot her a look she hadn't seen before, and then he turned back and banged his palm against the lift button. *"Fuck."*

The journey back to Clongarvin was mostly silent. Patrick drove fast, passing other cars recklessly, hooting impatiently at anyone who got in his way.

Nora hung on, enjoying the ride. "Is she in the hospital?"

"Yes," he answered shortly.

"What did her message say? How long ago was it?"

He made no response, and Nora gave up. When they approached Clongarvin's outer limits, forty minutes later, Patrick pulled in to the curb.

Nora looked at him. "I hope you're not expecting me to get out here," she said. "It's miles—"

"Call a taxi," Patrick said, leaning past her and opening her door. "Do it, Nora. I haven't got time to argue." He yanked his wallet from his jacket and shoved a twenty-euro note at her. "Here."

She took the money and got out. "I don't believe—"

But he was gone, screeching toward Clongarvin's maternity hospital.

"Charming," Nora said aloud. She took out her phone. "Absolutely bloody charming." She couldn't walk ten yards in these shoes, and he knew it. She dialed a number and said, "You couldn't come and pick me up, could you? Long story."

Adam sighed. "Where are you?"

Where are you? Leah had said in her second message. *Patrick, please ring me—I need you.* Her voice tight with tension.

And Fiona's message, less than an hour later. Calmer, much calmer. *Patrick, in case you're at all interested, my daughter is having your baby. We're at the hospital.*

And no other messages, just twelve missed calls. Leah, Leah, Leah, Leah, Fiona, Leah, Leah, Fiona, Fiona, Fiona, Fiona, Fiona.

He ran through the sliding doors. "Leah Bradshaw," he snapped to the girl behind the glass screen. She tapped her computer and asked if he was a relative.

"I'm the father," he answered shortly, his gut a tight knot, his shirt stuck to his back, the urge to urinate nagging in his bladder.

Fiona met him at the entrance to the labor ward. The skirt of her navy suit was creased, but otherwise she was as unruffled as ever.

"You have a son," she said, looking at him as if he'd just spit on the floor in front of her. "Congratulations."

John looked at his mobile and read DANIELLE.

"Sorry," he said to Patsy. "Better take this."

"Hi, Dad," Danielle said.

"Hey there. What's up?"

"Nothing..." Danielle's voice sounded far away. John pressed the phone closer to his ear. "I just got your letter."

"Yes?" He preferred writing. He was never good on the phone. "When will I see you?" He'd suggested a week, longer if she wanted. He'd have to invest in a camp bed of some kind, but they'd manage.

"Dad...I don't think I'll be coming over. Not this summer," she said.

John transferred the phone to his other ear and moved farther from the counter. "You're not coming?"

"No." A short silence, and then she said, "I think I should be here, with Mum."

"I see." He hesitated. "Maybe you could come later in the summer? Don't you have a few months off?" He heard the neediness in his voice, so of course she'd hear it too.

"I think it's better that I stay here," she said, and then he understood. She was choosing, and she'd chosen Lara. She'd taken sides, when he'd thought there was no battle.

"Okay, love," he said. "That's no problem. I'll see you next time I'm home. How's everything else?"

When he hung up, he turned back to Patsy. "Sorry about that," he said again.

"That's all right, dear," Patsy said. "No bad news, I hope."

"No," he said. "Not bad."

He'd go back for a few days as soon as he could organize it; he'd see her in Scotland instead. Maybe she'd have a change of heart if they spent some time together on Bute. Maybe she'd come over later on. And until then he had Hannah.

The thought of her lifted his spirits. After so many years, he'd forgotten the pleasure of affectionate physical intimacy. The warm feel, the scent of a woman's body next to his, the whispered words, the soft sounds of her reaction to his touch—

"Your change, dear," Patsy said. "You're miles away."

"So I had to rescue Nora today," Adam said.

"Rescue her? How?"

"She was stranded on the Galway Road. She said she'd had a row with the driver of the car she was in, and she'd made him stop and let her out."

"Whose car? Where was she coming from?"

"She wouldn't tell me. She said it didn't matter, it was over now. I presume it was the mystery man she was hiding from me when I called round that time."

Hannah emptied chopped walnuts from the scales into a bowl. "Shouldn't she have been at work, instead of gallivanting around the place with some man?"

"I didn't ask." He picked a cherry from an open tub. "Nora will do as she pleases, as always."

"That job won't last," Hannah said. "Stop eating those cherries."

"I don't think she cares about the job, to be honest. I wouldn't be surprised if she heads back to the U.S. soon. There's nothing for her in Clongarvin. She's grown out of it."

Hannah said nothing.

"Well, time for my clarinet practice," Adam said, moving toward the door.

"I like that little piece you're learning now."

"It's Chopin. I'm getting a musical education, if nothing else."

Left alone, Hannah wondered again about Nora O'Connor. Clearly she'd gotten involved with someone she shouldn't have. Someone, maybe, who wouldn't worry too much about being faithful, who wouldn't object if Nora made it plain that she was interested.

Someone like Patrick Dunne, who'd already been unfaithful to Hannah, maybe with more than one woman. He'd taken on Nora as his PA and they'd been working closely together for the past few months now.

She measured flour and tipped it into the stand mixer's bowl. She could be wrong—she hadn't a shred of evidence to point to Patrick. He could have changed. She shouldn't judge him on what had happened between them. And it was none of her business anyway.

As she weighed sugar, Chopin wafted from upstairs. And a few seconds later, from the sitting room next door, Kirby joined in for the very first time.

———

Geraldine had refilled the teapot twice. She hadn't had to refill the biscuit plate, because it hadn't been touched.

He started drinking after it happened, Alice had said. *I know he always liked a drink, but this was different, this was serious drinking. And it was whiskey, which he never used to drink. And lately he's taken to spending most of his time in bed—at least he's in bed whenever I'm in the house.*

She hadn't cried. She wasn't crying now. But she looked older, and more tired, than Geraldine ever remembered seeing her.

I did nothing, Alice had told them. *I saw what was happening to him, and I did nothing. I said nothing. I was too angry. I thought, if he wants to kill himself, let him. I didn't care—or I told myself I didn't care.*

Her hand had shaken when she'd lifted her cup. The tea had trembled as it moved toward her mouth.

He's agreed to go to the doctor, she'd said. *I haven't mentioned AA yet, but if he doesn't, I will. And he's going to phone you tomorrow, Stephen. He's going to ask if he can take unpaid leave, until...*

She'd faltered then, and Stephen had said quickly, *We'll sort something out Alice. Don't worry.*

He's been called to the district court, she'd told them. *On the eighteenth. The solicitor says he'll be formally charged and then we'll have to wait until the case is heard in the circuit court, another few months.*

Geraldine had pushed the plate of biscuits toward her, but she'd shaken her head. Geraldine had asked her if she'd like apple crumble, left over from dinner an hour earlier, but she'd said no.

I visited the little boy's grave, she'd told them. *I brought him flowers. I visited him often, sometimes every day.*

And then she'd gone home.

"I'm so sorry," Patrick said. "I honestly didn't think there was a chance anything could happen."

"I know," Leah said.

"If I'd had the smallest idea, of course I'd never have gone to that meeting."

"I know."

"I'd have stayed at home, not gone in to work at all. You know that, right?"

"Yes."

"You should have said if you weren't feeling well before I left."

"I know. I should have."

"But of course I shouldn't have gone off without being contactable, I can see that now. I should have left my phone on."

"Yes."

"At least your mother was here. You weren't on your own."

"No."

"And we have a beautiful son."

"Yes."

Nora had taken the day off, she'd phoned in sick. Patrick was gone to a meeting and couldn't be contacted, and Nora was off sick and not answering her phone. Leah's friend Nora, who couldn't be trusted an inch. Nora who would walk over her own grandmother's corpse to get to a man she fancied.

"Could you get me some tea?" she asked Patrick.

She wanted him gone. She didn't want to look at him.

―――――

"Listen to this," Stephen said. "'Bradshaw-Dunne, on June eleventh, to Leah Bradshaw and Patrick Dunne, a son, Reuben William.'"

"What? Show me that."

Stephen passed the paper across the table, and Geraldine scanned the notice. "Bradshaw-Dunne—that's Fiona's doing anyway; she'd be into double-barreled. And what kind of a name is Reuben?"

Stephen sliced the top off his egg. "It's biblical."

Geraldine studied the notice. "June the eleventh, and this is what?"

"The fifteenth. The eleventh was last Friday."

"So that explains Fiona missing bridge. I thought she was avoiding me." Geraldine tossed the paper aside and returned to her half grapefruit. "She'll probably be a right pain when she gets back. She'll be handing around photos, and we'll all have to ooh and aah."

Stephen smiled. "Under the circumstances I hardly think she'll be expecting much oohing and aahing from you."

"No...Not that I care about that anymore, not now that Hannah's found someone much nicer."

Stephen made no comment. Nice new man notwithstanding, he very much doubted that Geraldine had forgiven Fiona's daughter for breaking up Hannah's previous relationship.

"We're holding interviews today," he said instead, "for Tom's replacement."

"Isn't there someone replacing him already?"

"Yes, but now that he's officially taking unpaid leave, we have to interview. It's a legal thing."

Tom was due in court on Friday, and he and Alice were traveling to Dublin on the following Monday. Alice was dropping Tom at the treatment center his doctor had organized, then returning home alone. He would be gone for at least a month. Visits, particularly in the first two weeks, were not encouraged.

"She'll find it lonesome on her own," Geraldine said.

"I suppose she will." Stephen finished his egg and got to his feet. "Well, I'd better be off." He bent and kissed the top of Geraldine's head. "Don't get up," he said, as he always did, and Geraldine, who never got up, went back to the paper and read the birth notice again.

Bradshaw-Dunne. A bit of a mouthful. She'd never seen the point of double-barreled names. And Reuben sounded too like Ruby to sit comfortably on a boy.

June the eleventh. She worked backward to the middle of September, two weeks before Stephen's fifty-seventh. They'd gone out to dinner for his birthday, the four of them. Hannah and Patrick had given Stephen the boxed set of Seamus Heaney's poems. Hannah had been full of chat, Geraldine remembered, about having made the decision to look for a suitable site for her shop. Patrick had mentioned a cruise his father had just booked, sailing around the Greek islands in January. And the whole time...

Ah, who cared about all that? Ancient history now. She turned to the television listings.

————————

It was his fifth music lesson. They'd spent four hours together so far, and Vivienne remained as out of his reach as ever. Adam was becoming dispirited.

I like the name Vivienne, he'd said at the end of the second lesson. That had gotten no response. When he realized that she answered questions but generally ignored comments, he stuck to questions.

Is your brother older or younger than you? he'd asked during a pause in lesson three. *Have you any other siblings?*

What music do you like to listen to? End of lesson three.

How old is the cat? At the break in lesson four, as he tried not to taste the milk he forced himself to drink.

And at the end of lesson four, in desperation, without

thinking: *We'll have to stop meeting like this.* She'd blushed deeply at that. He'd kicked himself and retreated hastily.

He felt as if he were maintaining the most delicate kind of balance, tiptoeing toward her until he felt her drawing back, easing off until she relaxed again. Forward and back, in and out, like a pair of dancers performing some preordained routine, the distance between them never lessening.

Maybe he should just give up, admit defeat. But he couldn't.

And now they were on the fifth lesson, and he wondered how much longer it would be before she kicked him out for asking too many questions, or for not concentrating enough on the music.

This evening she wore a dark blue top and a gray skirt. The top was buttoned almost to her chin; the skirt skimmed her ankles. He wished she wore brighter colors and showed more skin. He wished, just once, that she didn't tie up her hair. He wished she wasn't still terrified of him.

"I design Web sites for a living," he told her as he unzipped his jacket. "Making music is just about as different as you can get from that, I suppose."

"Actually," Vivienne said, "it's not. Music is as logical as computing."

Adam tried not to show any reaction. This was a first: This was the closest they'd come to a real live conversation. He'd made a comment, and she'd responded.

"Really?" He was careful to keep the surprise out of his voice. Casual, keep it casual.

"Of course." She rummaged through the bundle of pages on the card table. "Music is the most logical thing there is." She pulled a sheet from the pile and brought it to where he sat. "It's even got its own symbols—I've pointed out some of them already." She indicated a flowing, curlicued sign that appeared at the start of each set of lines. "See that? Do you remember what it's called?"

"Er—"

"It's a treble clef. I told you it places G above middle C. It always does that, it never changes. And this? Remember?" Indicating a hash symbol, which Adam was pretty sure was called something different here and whose significance he couldn't for the life of him recall.

"This is a sharp sign," she said, thankfully not seeming concerned by his ignorance. "It means any note in that position is a semitone above the true pitch. It can't mean anything else, ever."

She was leaning toward him. Their shoulders were almost touching. Her nails were unpainted. He could smell her powdery scent that reminded him of babies. He could almost feel the warmth of her body.

"And look at that dot," she said. "See where it is? To the right of the note, never to the left. A dot always, always lengthens the note by one half its value. Never one quarter, or one eighth, always one half."

She wasn't blushing. There was no hint of shyness or embarrassment in her voice. On the contrary, it was filled with a confidence he'd never seen in her before.

"And look, here, the time signature, one number over another. The bottom number always represents the note value of the basic pulse of the music—so here the four represents the quarter note. The top number, in this case three, always indicates how many of these note values appear in each measure, or bar. This example announces that each measure is the equivalent length of three quarter notes. So this piece is in three-four time."

"Three-four time—that's a waltz, isn't it?"

Without even trying, he'd stumbled on a way through to her. It was as if he'd cracked a code or found a key.

"Yes," Vivienne said. "This piece is a waltz. It's Hungarian."

"I have two left feet," Adam said. "Don't ever take me dancing."

And instantly he realized his mistake as Vivienne drew back, the flush rising in her face. "Well," she said, the sheet music still clutched in her hand, "so...we'll begin."

He'd strayed into the personal, and she'd scurried away from him. But for the first time, she'd let her guard down. For a minute or so, her awkwardness had vanished and she'd been herself with him.

He winked at the cat on the piano, who stared back.

———————

Alice toasted bread, that was all. No eggs, no sausages, no pudding. She put out the box of bran flakes, but she knew that it would be untouched. She took the orange squeezer from the cupboard and put it back again. Just tea and toast.

Tom had gone to the doctor, as he'd promised. Alice had phoned to make an appointment, and the following afternoon Tom had taken a taxi to the surgery, about a mile away. She'd offered to drive him there, but he'd refused. When she got home around six—straight from work, no more lost afternoons, no more of that—he was back, sitting at the kitchen table with a cup of instant coffee in front of him.

What did he say? Alice had asked.

He gave me a prescription, he'd told her, *for sleeping pills.*

Alice hadn't known he wasn't sleeping.

And he wants me to go for . . . treatment.

Treatment? But of course she'd known what it meant.

He's going to try and get me into a place in Dublin for a few weeks. I told him I'm in court on Friday, so some time after that.

His face was so terribly bleak, his eyes empty of expression. The skin around his mouth was puckered, and deep folds ran down his cheeks. Dark shadows under his eyes. Such a gap now between his shirt collar and his neck.

Alice, I'm sorry, he'd said then, in that same hollow voice, but Alice hadn't trusted herself to give a response. She'd turned away from him and begun to get the dinner ready.

And now Friday was here, and Geraldine was doing the full day on her own in the shop. Stephen had offered to come with them to the court, but Alice had said no, they'd be fine.

She put a slice of toast on Tom's plate and filled his cup with tea. She picked at her own slice until it was time to go. Just over an hour it usually took her to drive to Galway, so they were allowing an hour and a half, because the courthouse was in the city center, and traffic might be bad, and Alice wasn't good with the one-way streets.

The day was fine, the sun shining out of an almost completely blue sky. Neither of them commented on the weather as Alice drove off, remembering the last time—was he remembering too?—they were both in a car together. The sky had been blue then, too, although it had been much colder. She remembered the whir of the heater drowning the radio. She remembered turning down the heater and hearing about a long tailback at the Red Cow Roundabout, just before—

"Put on the radio, would you?" she asked Tom. "Find something nice. Lyric, maybe."

Their solicitor was waiting for them in the lobby of the courthouse. He shook hands with them, his grip so strong that Alice's rings dug painfully into her fingers. "Soon be over," he told them. "Won't last long, just a formality."

They sat on a wooden bench outside the courtroom, waiting to be called. Alice leaned against the wall, feeling its coldness through her light gray jacket.

Soon be over. Won't last long.

———————

The bell above the door brought Hannah out from the back.

"Hey," Wally said. "Finally made it."

"Hello there." She held up her mug. "I was just having a sneaky cuppa."

"Why be sneaky?" he asked. "It's your shop, you're the boss." He looked around. "Nice little place." He spotted the rocking chair on the wall. "I suppose the high chair is for your baby customers."

She laughed. "Actually it belonged to my grandfather, whose money helped me set up this place."

He wore a green T-shirt with a cartoon apple on the front and loose canvas jeans. He was broad like Patrick, but not as tall. Chunky was how she'd describe him.

"I suppose you're here to claim your free bun," she said.

He studied the rows of cupcakes. "Well, I must confess I am. I told you I have a sweet tooth."

"You did." She indicated the display. "Take your pick."

She watched as he bent to inspect the trays under the glass counter, whistling through his teeth.

"That one," he said, pointing to a rum-raisin, "please. As long as I'm okay to drive after it."

She smiled. "I think you'll be safe enough." She took a small box from the stack. "A taxi driver who plays keyboards—you don't come across one of those every day."

"Actually, I prefer to regard myself as a musician who drives a taxi—and I'll have you know that I play guitar and flute, too."

She laughed again. "Is there no end to your talents?"

He considered, then shook his head. "None."

"Can you bake?"

"Well, no."

"Cook?"

"Er, not exactly."

"Are you sporty? Artistic? Into DIY?"

He put his hands up. "Okay, okay, I can play three instruments not too badly, and I've got a clean driving license—that's about it. Now give me that cupcake and let me out of here before you humiliate me further."

Hannah added a chocolate chunk to the box and handed it to him. "Have a nice day."

"Hey," he protested, "the deal was for one."

"You can find someone, I'm sure, to eat the second."

"Well, my little sister wouldn't say no." He tipped an imaginary hat at her. "Thanks very much—I think that officially makes us quits."

"And if you're happy, you can come back and get more," she said. "And you're definitely paying next time. I'm not made of money either."

He grinned. "It's a deal, thanks again. See you, now." As he turned away, he jerked a thumb toward the rocking chair on the wall. "Careful Grandpa doesn't take a tumble."

And then he was gone, the bell tinkling behind him.

Hannah leaned against the counter and sipped her cooling tea. She liked that dark blond hair color. She wondered when it had last seen a comb. She remembered his woolly hat and figured his appearance didn't unduly concern him. Vivienne looked older than him, but he'd called her his little sister. Imagine if she'd told him that her best friend had a crush on his little sister.

A few seconds later, the door opened again and a woman walked in.

"Nice to see someone looking happy," she said to Hannah.

———

Dave and Claire were in the courtroom.

Alice hadn't expected that. The thought of their coming had never once crossed her mind. An older woman had an arm around Claire's hunched shoulders. They sat on a wooden bench toward the front.

Alice didn't spot them right away. She walked along the central aisle behind the guard who'd ushered them in, her bag clasped tightly in both hands, her heart thudding. She'd never been in a courtroom in her life.

The guard brought Tom over to the stand, and the solicitor took Alice's arm to guide her into a bench—and as she was about to sit she saw them, two rows back. She turned abruptly and took a seat on the bench across the aisle, praying that they hadn't noticed her, that Claire wouldn't remember the woman who'd spoken to her at the bus stop.

"Are you all right?" the solicitor whispered, sliding in beside her, and Alice nodded.

The older woman had to be Claire's mother. They'd have seen her come in with Tom, so even if Claire didn't remember her, they'd know she was his wife—who else could she be? Alice's skin prickled, and she dug her nails into her palms and closed her eyes, and waited for it to be over.

And when, barely five minutes later, Tom was charged with dangerous driving causing death, Alice should have been prepared. She *had* been prepared—the solicitor had told them that this charge would be the most likely outcome—but as the judge spoke the words out loud, as he told Tom that a trial date would be set and he would be summoned again, this time to the circuit court, Alice stumbled to her feet and hurried back down the aisle and out of the room, a hand pressed to her trembling mouth, oblivious now to who might be looking at her.

In the corridor she pulled a tissue from her bag and wiped her eyes and blew her nose. She sat on the same bench as before, taking ragged breaths, trying to gather her wits before Tom appeared, knowing she had to be positive for him. When the courtroom door opened again, she looked up, forced a smile, pushed the tissue back into her bag—and there they were, the three of them, staring accusingly at her.

Her heart pounded as she looked away, as she kept her gaze fixed farther down on the opposite wall. Out of the corner of her eye, she could see Claire stepping forward. She braced herself for a blow.

"That's her. That's his wife."

Alice didn't respond. Her hands clenched her bag, her whole body tense. Her face felt ice cold.

"You stay away from us." She could feel Claire's breath on her face as the young woman leaned toward her. "You stop hanging around our house." Her voice rose in pitch, and again Alice flinched. "You stay away from Jason, you don't go *near* him. You hear me, you creep?"

Alice turned slowly to face her, her whole body beginning to tremble. Claire's face was twisted with pain. Tears glittered in her eyes, dark red patches bloomed in her cheeks. Her mother and Dave stood by silently, their eyes fixed on Alice, Dave holding Claire's hand.

"You hear me?" she shouted at Alice again.

"I hear you," Alice whispered. "I'm very sorry." Her voice shook, like the rest of her. She could feel a pulse beating in her head, the sting of incipient tears.

"Sorry?" The expression changed in Claire's face. "You're *sorry*? Your husband *destroyed* us, he destroyed our *lives*, and you're fucking *sorry*!" Her voice was shrill, her rage and her anguish terrible, the spittle flying from her mouth to land on Alice's cheeks, the tears spilling from her eyes. "I hope he's locked up for good—he's a fucking *monster*!"

"I'm sorry," Alice repeated, tears spilling onto her cheeks, her hands raised to ward off the blows she was sure were coming. "I'm so sorry."

Claire spun abruptly and stalked away, pulling her hand from Dave's, and the other two followed. They turned a corner and were gone. Alice rummaged blindly in her bag and found the balled-up tissue and pressed it again to her eyes, trying to breathe.

After what seemed like forever, the courtroom door was pushed open once more.

"Come on," she heard Tom say quietly. "Alice, come on, time to go."

But she couldn't lift her head.

Hannah read and reread the entry until she could recite it from memory.

A son. They'd had a son.

"At least you have your own room," Alice said. "That's good." Not expecting, or receiving, a reply.

Tom laid his case on the bed and walked to the window, and stood with his back to her.

"It's nice and quiet here," Alice said. "Quieter than at home. You'll be able to sleep at night. You mightn't need your tablets."

There was a tree about twenty feet from his window. It looked like some kind of a maple to Alice. They could hear the tiny rustling the leaves made in the light breeze.

"You brought books," she said, "did you?"

"Yes."

"And crosswords? Did you bring the crossword book?"

His shoulders lifted. "I didn't think of it."

"I'll post it to you," she said. "I'll get a few more."

He wore the suit he'd worn to the courthouse. He'd gotten his hair cut for the court visit. The back of his neck was heartbreaking to her.

"Well," she said briskly, before she made a fool of herself, "I suppose I'd better be off."

Tom didn't move. He gave no indication that he'd even heard her.

"I know it was an accident," Alice said suddenly, the words rushing out of her. "I understand that. And I shouldn't have made you go to work that morning."

She turned and walked quickly from the small, bare room, narrowly avoiding a collision with the doorframe. All down the corridor that smelled of cabbage, she waited to hear him calling after her.

She drove the four hours back to Clongarvin without taking a break, the journey as silent as the earlier one had been. As she walked into the house, the phone was ringing.

Alice picked it up and said, "Hello," knowing that it would be Tom. Who else would be ringing?

"Ma, how could you not tell me?" Ellen asked.

"I've packed it in," Nora said. "Couldn't hack it, too boring."

"Can't say I'm surprised," Adam answered. "I could never see you as someone's PA. Making coffee and booking hotels, not your style at all."

He didn't bring up the previous week's incident, didn't ask again how his sister had come to be standing on the side of the road on the outskirts of Clongarvin in the middle of the day. That an illicit relationship of some kind was involved, he didn't doubt—but as long as Nora was keeping the details to herself, he wasn't going to waste energy trying to pry them from her.

"So what now?" he asked. "Are you staying put in Clongarvin?"

"Wouldn't think so," she answered. "Nothing for me here, really. Don't know what I was thinking about, coming back."

He wondered suddenly if she had any girlfriends. In her e-mails to him, nobody in particular had been mentioned, no name had appeared with any regularity. And here, as far as he knew, Leah was the only one of her old friends she'd looked up, and that hadn't seemed to go anywhere.

Pity, or sympathy, stirred in him. "You know you can stay as long as you like," he said. "In the flat, I mean."

Nora smiled. "Thanks, bro," she said. "I appreciate that, but I don't think I'll be bothering you for much longer.

I might go back to the States, maybe check out the West Coast." She set her glass on the counter and slid off her barstool. "Need the john—I mean the loo."

When she'd gone, Adam directed his attention to the musicians. As usual, Vivienne didn't acknowledge the people around her. She probably had no idea that her only adult pupil had been sitting across the room from her for the past forty minutes.

Tell me about Beethoven, he'd said two nights ago, at his sixth lesson. *Did he really go deaf?*

Why is this note sharp? he'd asked. *What's the significance of that squiggle there? How do I know what key a piece is in?*

And Vivienne had answered his questions easily, and explained about sharps and flats, and had shown him how to identify the key. And then he'd said, in the same casual tone, *I like how your hair smells,* and Vivienne had retreated immediately, as she always did.

So Adam was right back to square one. Unless they spent the rest of their lives talking about music, it didn't look as if there were a hope of his having a future with her.

Hannah had told him about Wally's visiting the shop. She said he'd given the impression that Vivienne had a sweet tooth. Adam had filed the information away without a clue how to use it.

He could imagine Vivienne's reaction if he presented her with a box of cupcakes. *My friend makes them,* he could say, just to take the drama out of it, but still she'd probably faint of mortification, and her mother, followed closely by the giant cat, would in all likelihood be shooing him out the front door with a broom.

He drained his pint gloomily and nodded at the barman for another round. He wasn't even learning how to play the clarinet.

Despite his practicing—and he had to admit he'd lost some of his initial enthusiasm—he'd never make a musician, and they both knew it. Surely it was only a matter of time before Vivienne sent him packing. Maybe he should just admit defeat on all fronts and tell her he'd decided to give up the lessons.

"Hi."

He turned to see Hannah dropping her little overnight bag on the floor. She'd taken to going home with John on Saturday night and reappearing on Sunday afternoon.

"Hi yourself. Red or white?"

He was glad she'd found someone to flush Patrick out of her system. Adam had gotten on well enough with Hannah's ex, like he got on with most people, but the two men had never sought out each other's company. His and Patrick's lives had run along different tracks, leaving them content enough to interact when they came together but equally happy apart.

"I thought Nora was coming."

"She's in the loo," he told her. "She's given up the job," he added.

Hannah didn't show the surprise he'd been expecting. "Right."

"She's thinking of going back to the U.S."

Hannah's wine arrived. She swirled the glass but didn't drink.

"What's up?" he asked.

She looked at him. "They had a baby," she said bleakly. "I only discovered it today. I was looking through an old paper."

"Who had a baby?"

"Patrick and Leah. They had a boy. Patrick's a dad. I thought I wouldn't care, but..." She trailed off, her finger running around the rim of her glass. "Pathetic," she said, "isn't it?"

Adam searched for the right response. "I suppose—"

"Hey, nice top," Nora said, reappearing suddenly.

And that was the end of that.

———————

It was the last thing she wanted, to sit in a crowded wine bar with her social face on, but some instinct had forced her to stick to the plan. She'd packed her clean clothes and her toothbrush and the various other bits that traveled with her to John's house. She'd washed her hair, she'd dressed in her favorite pink top and the gray pants that she always felt good in, she'd made up her face and sprayed on perfume.

She'd told herself to stop being so stupid. She'd gone to Vintage, determined to shake off the bleakness that had descended since she'd read the news, since she'd turned a page idly in the week-old paper and seen it there in black and white: Reuben William. She'd resolved to put the whole thing out of her mind.

And in the first minute of talking with Adam, she'd blurted it out.

———————

"You're miles away," John said later. Much later, when they were lying on his bed, his arm across her stomach, the Saturday-night traffic rumbling along the street three floors below.

"Sorry," she said.

"Want to talk about it?"

"Not really..." She ran a bare foot along his calf. "I just heard something this week that... threw me a bit, that's all."

His fingers beat a soft tattoo on her abdomen. "I thought there was something up."

"Sorry," she repeated.

"No." She saw him shake his head in the dim light that filtered through the unlined curtains. "Don't apologize. And you don't have to tell me if you don't want to."

A long silence ensued. His hand moved lightly across her skin. She heard his calm breathing beside her. A siren sounded somewhere, rising and falling as it traveled through the streets. The silence afterward seemed deeper.

"A baby," she said. "My ex had a baby—or at least, his..." She couldn't finish, feeling the grief rise in her. "Sorry," she whispered, turning away from him, completely unable to stop the tears from pouring out.

———————

"It's okay," he said in the morning, when the hour hand of her watch had crawled, finally, to nine, and she could get up. "I understand," he told her, putting out cereal and bread that she knew she wasn't going to eat. "It's too soon," he said, in his boxers and T-shirt, with his unshaven chin and re-signed smile. "You need more time. You said that at the start. I should have listened."

She wished he wasn't so understanding. She wanted him to be less reasonable, needed him to get angry with her, or at least impatient, so she could feel justified in leaving him. She wanted a reason to let him go, but he gave her none.

She stopped herself from saying, *It's not you, it's me,* even though it was true. It *was* her: She was being irrational and emotional and absolutely unfair to him. They'd barely started, and here she was ending it—and for what? For the idea of a baby that would never happen now, for a might-have-been scenario that existed only in her head? Ridiculous.

He didn't offer to walk her downstairs. He made no attempt to kiss her good-bye. He lifted a hand as she walked to the door, smiled, and told her to take care.

The taxi she hailed on the street was driven by a man she didn't recognize, who didn't try to talk to her as he drove through the empty Sunday-morning streets. He charged her six euro and she gave him seven. She let herself into the house quietly, in case Adam was still asleep.

She made tea and brought the pot upstairs to her room. She undressed and brushed her teeth and got into bed, feeling the weariness of a wakeful night overtaking her. She drank half a cup of tea before lying back and closing her eyes.

Two breakups in six months. She yawned, pulling the duvet to her chin. *Here we go again.* At least this time there was no heartache, just the sad realization that she'd made a mistake, that she hadn't, after all, found the one.

July

Almost half an hour into his seventh music lesson, Adam O'Connor's patience finally ran out. He stopped attempting to play "Five Note Fun" and lowered his clarinet. Vivienne, who'd been pointing at the notes on the sheet music, turned her head toward him, her hand still raised.

"Look," Adam said, "I'm sorry. I can't do this anymore."

She frowned. "You're doing all right," she said.

"No," Adam answered, laying the clarinet across his lap. "I'm not doing all right. I'm here under false pretenses."

Vivienne lowered her hand slowly, the color rising, as always, in her face.

"I never wanted music lessons," Adam said, beginning to twist apart the pieces of his clarinet. "I just wanted to get to know you. You've probably guessed that by now."

Her face was aflame, her gaze dropping to somewhere past his left knee.

He slotted the clarinet pieces into the case. "I saw you in Vintage," he said, "and I thought you looked interesting. I didn't know anything about you, I had no idea if you were single or not, but there was just something about you...I wanted to meet you and talk to you, see what you were like.

So when I heard that you gave music lessons, I bought a clarinet. On eBay."

Vivienne's neck was pink with white blotches. He could see her throat muscles contracting as she swallowed. He refused to be put off. He hadn't rehearsed what to say, he hadn't planned any of this.

"I bought the clarinet because of you," he said. "It took me ages to put it together when it came—I almost broke it. I'd never considered learning to play any musical instrument before." He smiled briefly as he closed the clarinet case. "Believe me, I know how daft all this sounds, particularly as I'm not the slightest bit musical—which you have of course realized by now."

Vivienne's hands fluttered, a faint gesture of denial. Her mouth opened and closed again. He wondered how much longer he had before she fled from the room.

"You intrigue me," he said, nothing left to lose now. "I've never met anyone like you. You're different—and I suspect you're very sweet. I think about you a lot. I just wanted to get to know you, but you won't let me." He took his jacket from the back of the chair. "I think you're scared of me, but there's no reason to be. I'm not at all scary—ask any of my friends. I'm ordinary and flawed, just like everyone else."

He got to his feet then, holding the jacket and case. Vivienne didn't move.

"Thank you for the lessons," Adam said. "I'm sorry to have wasted your time. Don't get up. I know the way out. Oh, and—" He pulled his wallet from the pocket of his jacket, took out a twenty-euro note, and laid it on the closed piano lid next to the cat, who sniffed at it.

On impulse, Adam slid a business card from his wallet and placed it on top of the money. Something to remember him by, even if it ended up in her bin. Vivienne still didn't move, didn't look in his direction.

"Thank you," Adam said again. "I'll see myself out. Good-bye."

He opened the door and stood back to let in Mrs. O'Toole, with her tray of milk and Mikado biscuits, and her astonished expression.

"I know about Nora," Leah said to him at last. Their two-week-old son was cradled in her arms, his tiny, pink, sucking mouth fixed on her left nipple.

"Hmm?" Patrick turned a page in his book.

"I know about Nora," Leah repeated in the same calm voice, watching him over the curve of Reuben's head. *Reuben, firstborn son of Jacob and Leah,* she'd discovered completely by chance on the Internet, and it had seemed too coincidental to ignore.

Patrick looked up. "Nora? What about her?"

Leah watched his innocent face, felt the surprisingly strong tug of her son's mouth.

"What about Nora?" Patrick repeated. "What are you referring to?"

"Patrick," she said calmly, "you know what I'm referring to. I know about you and Nora."

"Leah, I have no idea what you mean." He frowned, closing his book, leaving a finger trapped inside. "I honestly don't know what you're—"

"I want you to leave," she cut in quietly, stroking her son's downy head.

"What?" His incredulous expression, all injured innocence. "What the hell do you think happ—"

"Shh," she said. "You'll upset Reuben."

Patrick laid the book on the coffee table. "Leah," he said quietly, "you've got it all wrong. Nothing happened between me and Nora, I swear—"

"Don't," she said, a new note entering her voice. "Please don't treat me as if I'm stupid."

"I'm not—"

"You slept with her," she said, "probably more than once. You were with her the day Reuben was born."

"Leah—"

"Lower your voice," she said, easing Reuben gently from her breast, lifting him to rest sleepily on her shoulder, rubbing his back in circles. "You had an affair, just like you had an affair with me."

And if, right up to this moment, there had existed within her the most infinitesimal scrap of doubt—despite Nora's abrupt departure from the *Clongarvin Voice*, despite her not having come near Leah since Reuben's birth—if some part of her still refused to accept that it was true, still longed for him to be innocent of any infidelity, she realized at last, as he stood and walked from the room, the splayed book forgotten, that it was all too true indeed.

———

The decision, when John finally made it, brought relief, and a feeling that it was the right thing to do. Despite his efforts, he'd never really settled in Ireland. The work had been slow in coming, the money never quite enough for him to feel relaxed. He missed the sea, and the familiarity of home, and, of course, Danielle—most of all Danielle.

He felt bad about letting down Wally and the band. Wally had been good to him. *I hope you understand,* he'd said, and Wally had assured him—a little too enthusiastically, maybe—that they'd find another saxophonist. *You do what you have to do,* Wally had said. *Good luck, man. Sorry it didn't work out.*

Patsy in the woodworking store had presented him with a Guinness pin and told him to be sure to keep in touch. *All the best, now,* she'd said. *We're sorry to lose you.*

He closed his Irish bank account after his last check cleared. He bought a one-way ferry ticket from Larne to Stranraer. He packed his battered van with his tools and his saxophone and his music collection and his clothes. He handed back the keys to his apartment and to the little work-shop. His deposits were returned to him.

He drove through Clongarvin for the last time. He passed a yellow-painted shop with CUPCAKES ON THE CORNER painted in curly blue lettering over the door. In the van he was too high up to see anyone inside, to make out whoever stood behind the counter.

He drove on.

"Where do you keep the cotton buds?" Fiona asked.

"Look how he puts his hand under his cheek," she murmured to Leah as they bent over Reuben's cot. "You used to sleep like that." She tucked his small bare foot under the blanket.

"His grasp is so strong," she said when her grandchild's tiny fingers closed around her thumb. "You forget that, how strong their grasp is." She smiled with real affection at him.

"Should I wash his hair?" She lowered him carefully into the warm water at bath time as Leah looked on.

"He has long fingers," she said, watching as Leah toweled

his hands dry afterward. "He'll be musical, or artistic." The talc in her hand, waiting to sprinkle it over him.

"Will I put this on him, or should he go straight into pajamas?" Holding up a yellow T-shirt for Leah's approval.

And if the phone rang: "You answer that. It's probably a customer. Give Reuben to me." Putting out her arms as Leah got to her feet.

And not once, not a single time in the week since Patrick had left, did Leah's mother say, *I told you so.*

For now, that was more than enough.

———————

"But she must have said something, she must have made some kind of response."

Adam forked beans onto his toast. "Not a word. She just sat there looking at the floor. Her mother was struck dumb, too, when she saw me leaving halfway through. I nearly collided with her on my way out. Nearly sent the milk and biscuits flying."

"I'm sorry," Hannah said, "but at least you tried. Better to have tried and lost."

"Actually," Adam said, "I think it's 'Better to have loved and lost.'"

"Is it?" She laid her fork down and mopped tomato sauce with the end of her toast. "What are we like? We're a right pair. Consoling each other over beans on toast."

"Maybe your mother was right, maybe we should get together. Doesn't look like we're going to end up with anyone else, does it?"

"Not really." Hannah considered. "Maybe that can be our last resort, when we're about sixty."

Adam groaned. "Do I have to keep looking till then?"

"I'm afraid so. What about Nora? When's she leaving?"

"End of the week. Her flight goes from Dublin on Saturday morning, so she's getting a train up on Friday."

"Will you drive her to the station?"

"I can't—I'm meeting a new client in Athlone. Nora's not bothered. She'll get a taxi."

"And what about the ad?"

"It's going into tomorrow's paper."

He was staying on in Hannah's house and getting a new housemate for his flat. They'd decided it made more sense that way.

Hannah was thirty-three, Adam almost thirty-two. Most people their age were married, or at least in some kind of committed relationship. In all his dating life, Adam had never come close to committing, and now it looked like his fixation on Vivienne was a thing of the past, too.

Hannah had just left a man who was kind and intelligent, who turned up when he said he would, and treated her right. What was wrong with them?

"I told Mam about splitting up with John," she said.

"And?"

"She was exactly as I expected her to be." She brought their plates to the sink and ran water. "She said I hadn't given him a chance, that I was much too fussy, that I wasn't getting any younger, and how many more men did I think were going to come along? The usual."

"Well, maybe she has a point. Maybe you *didn't* give him a chance."

Had she given up on John too soon? Could something have developed between them if she hadn't been so hasty? Too late now—she'd never know. "He's gone back to Scotland," she told Adam. "I heard yesterday."

She'd met Wally as she was rounding a bend in the supermarket, struggling to control the wheels of her cart.

Steady on, there, he'd said. *You're not in the fairground now.* He held a basket. She saw Rice Krispies, frozen pizza, and frozen chips.

They'd chatted briefly. She'd laughed at his choice of cereal. He'd promised not to spread the word that she was buying six bottles of wine; she'd protested it was only to get the bulk discount with a coupon she had.

And then he'd said, *I assume you know Johnny's moved back home,* and Hannah's smile had faded, and he'd said quickly, *Sorry, me and my big mouth,* and she'd said, *No, no, it's fine,* but the mood had changed, and he'd said, *Well, I'll let you get off,* and moved away, and Hannah had added toothpaste and macaroni and olives to her cart, and they hadn't come face-to-face again.

The trouble was, it *was* fine. She couldn't honestly say she missed John, now that he was gone. She regretted its not working out between them, of course—but the fact remained that she was fine without him. She missed him a little, like you'd miss the company of anyone you got on well with, but that was it.

"What'll you do with the clarinet?" she asked Adam.

"Sell it," he answered. "I'll put an ad on eBay. Easy come, easy go. Might even make a few bob." He opened the sitting-room door and whistled at Kirby. "Come on, you fat lump—time for a walk."

Left alone, Hannah dried the dishes and set out her ingredients as usual. Was this it from now on? Would she and Adam still be sitting down to dinner together in twenty years' time, with the rest of Clongarvin assuming they were living happily ever after? Would her joke about marrying each other when they were sixty turn out to be horribly prescient?

Would she meet Patrick on the street every so often, surrounded by his family, and pretend that her life was just as full?

She sighed and made her way upstairs to bed.

———

"You're not going to believe it," Geraldine said, barely in the door, her jacket still on.

Stephen lowered the volume on the *Late Late*. "What's that?"

"Patrick Dunne and Leah Bradshaw have split up." She picked up the poker. "Can you credit it, and that little baby hardly arrived?"

Stephen raised his eyebrows, genuinely surprised. "You don't say."

"And what's more, I got it from Fiona Bradshaw herself," Geraldine added, thrusting the poker into the center of the glowing briquettes, collapsing Stephen's hastily constructed pyramid, ten minutes earlier. "She told me in person, made a point of it."

I just thought I'd let you know, Fiona had said. *It didn't work out, and they've decided to separate.* And Geraldine had said, *Thank you for telling me,* because it couldn't have been easy, and they'd nodded at each other, and Fiona had drifted away again as Geraldine had reached for a slice of the shop-bought apple tart that Dolores Mulcair always tried to pass off as her own.

"That poor little baby," she said now, unbuttoning her jacket.

Stephen said nothing.

"It didn't take him long, did it?" Geraldine hung the poker back on its hook. "At least he lasted over a year with Hannah."

"Well, we shouldn't—"

"Oh, God," she said abruptly, swinging around to look at her husband in dismay, "I've just thought of something."

"What?"

"He wouldn't try and get back with Hannah, would he?" She regarded Stephen anxiously. "Maybe he already has. Maybe that's why Hannah dropped that lovely Scotsman."

"Hang on now," Stephen said. "You're letting your imagination run away with you. We've absolutely no evidence—"

"No, but it would make sense, wouldn't it? There was no reason for Hannah to finish with that nice man. They were getting on so well."

"Geraldine, we don't know that, and people break up all the—"

"Oh God," she said again, dropping onto the couch next to him. "Stephen, she wouldn't be that foolish, would she?"

"No, love," Stephen said patiently, "I really don't think she would."

"Because he'd only turn around in a few months and break her heart all over again."

"That's probably true."

Geraldine stared into the fire, frowning. "Should I ring her, do you think?"

"No," Stephen said firmly. "Definitely not. We have to let Hannah live her own life."

"Yes," she said, "I suppose you're right."

But the doubt was there all the same, the worry was there. And she knew well that Stephen was worried, too, even if he'd never admit it.

———————

"I don't know what I'll do with the pair of you," their mother said crossly. She turned to Wally. "I don't know why you bothered coming for your tea, when all you're doing is pushing it around your plate. And you"—stabbing a finger at Vivienne—"haven't had a proper meal in ages."

"I have so," Vivienne said. "I'm just not that hungry today."

"Not for ages," their mother repeated to Wally. "She's doing her best to get that anorexia."

Wally smiled. "Hardly."

He studied his sister, who did seem quieter than usual. It occurred to him that she might be pining for John Wyatt—maybe she'd had a thing for him that nobody had noticed.

"And why aren't *you* eating?" his mother demanded of Wally. "You're hardly watching your figure, are you?"

"God, no." He speared a piece of boiled potato. "Look, I am eating." But the potatoes held no more appeal for him than the poached salmon or buttered carrots—and he certainly wasn't pining for John Wyatt.

"We got a temporary replacement for the man who left the band," he said, to take his mother's mind off their poor appetites, "but we're still looking for a permanent saxophonist. It's either that or force Viv to play two instruments at once."

The ghost of a smile flitted across his sister's face. "Even I can't do that."

He wished again that he could somehow inject some confidence into her. He'd thought that being in the band might be good for her, but the experience didn't seem to have had the smallest effect. She played the pieces, but she might as well have been at home in her bedroom for all the attention she paid to her surroundings. She was as shy and withdrawn in company as she'd ever been.

In the car later, on the way to Vintage, he said, "It's a shame John left, isn't it?"

Vivienne nodded. "It'll be hard to find someone as good."

No sign of discomfiture, no indication that the loss of John mattered beyond its implications for the band. "Anything wrong, Viv?" he asked her. "Anything you want to get off your chest?"

She turned to him, and he glanced from the road to her face.

"No," she said, after the briefest of pauses. "Nothing at all."

——————

While she was moving down the columns as she always did, the name caught Alice's eye and stopped her in her tracks.

"*O'Brien, Jason,*" she read. "*Fifth-birthday remembrance. Our darling son, taken from us suddenly on 26 March. Gone but never forgotten.*"

She lay down the paper and imagined them sitting around the kitchen table of number 37. Their families there, of course, to support them. Tea cooling in cups, remembering his last birthday maybe, the four candles on the cake, the party with his little friends gathered around. None of them knowing it was to be his last.

She remembered the mother at the courthouse, the hate plain in her expression as she'd looked at Alice. *Your husband destroyed us,* she'd said, her features twisted and ugly with pain. *Don't come near us again.*

But Alice had already stopped driving to Springwood Gardens, and she'd given up visiting the cemetery. Now she stayed in the shop with Geraldine in the afternoons and went home at the usual time.

"*The house is quiet without you,*" she'd written to Tom. "*I never realized how quiet it is, living on your own. I planted out the hanging baskets. They'll be in full bloom when you get home. I'm thinking of painting the sitting room, maybe cream this time, for a change. I'm a bit tired of the white. What would you think?"*

She didn't tell him about Ellen. He didn't need to hear that now.

I can't believe it, Ellen had wept on the phone. *My father drove while he was drunk and killed a child. How could he? How could you have let him? Why didn't you tell me, Ma? Why did I have to hear about it from Avril O'Regan?*

The smallness of Ireland. Someone from Clongarvin working in the courthouse in Galway, some clerk with a sister living in the same neighborhood as Ellen. A chance remark, a few careless words, and Ellen knew.

Alice had sat quietly on the bottom stair with the phone to her ear until her daughter had run out of questions. *Listen,* she'd said then, her eyes closed, her words slow and careful. *Listen to me. I've just got back from dropping your father into a treatment center in Dublin. He's there to try to stop drinking. He'll be there for a month, maybe longer. The accident happened the morning after a night out, and neither of us realized he could still be...under the influence. I didn't tell you because, right or wrong, I thought I could spare you all this.*

She'd taken a ragged breath then, and Ellen hadn't jumped into the silence. *We have both gone through hell in the past few months,* Alice had said tightly, *so I need you not to be angry now, because I'm not sure I can take any more*—and her voice had broken then, and she'd bitten her lip and stopped talking, her eyes still squeezed shut.

Oh, Ma, Ellen had said, her voice thick with tears, too, *I'm sorry. I'm not angry, at least. I don't know what I am. It's just...*

I know, Alice had whispered. *I know what you mean.*

Ma, I'm coming home, Ellen had said then, *when Dad has to… when the case comes to court. You'll need someone with you. I can get a couple of weeks off, and Lenny will hang on to the kids. Let me know when you have a date, and I'll book my flight.*

Alice had opened her mouth to protest—and then she'd shut it again, thinking about having Ellen sitting beside her when Tom was on trial. Her daughter's hand to hold, her child's arm in hers while Jason's parents sat in the same room.

"The strawberries will be good this year," she'd written to Tom. *"I sprayed the roses—there was a bit of greenfly. I'm afraid the front lawn is full of daisies again, even after that stuff you put down last year. I've mown it, but I can't get the stripes like you can."*

She didn't mention the shop. She didn't tell him what she was planning. Time enough for that.

———

"For sale—ebony clarinet, as new. €45. Location: Ireland. Seller: Adoc2401."

He put the cursor on "submit" and pressed the mouse button, and off it went. *That's that,* he thought. *End of story.* He'd given it his best shot, and he'd failed.

"What now?" he asked Kirby, crouching to scratch the dog's rough coat. "Should I go out and get drunk and pick up a nice young one?"

Kirby grunted, tail swinging lazily.

"You're a great help," Adam told him. He shut down his computer and rummaged in the chest of drawers until he found his trunks. A swim would help. A few fast laps up and down the pool should clear his head and banish the gloom.

And if that didn't work, he might just consider a few pints later on.

———————

At the sight of him, so wholly unexpected, Hannah's stomach lurched. She pushed the tray she'd been refilling back under the counter, her heart beginning a steady, heavy thudding.

"Hi, stranger." Patrick smiled. His suit as immaculate as ever. His shirt so white it must have been brand-new. "Long time no see."

She should probably congratulate him on the baby, but the words refused to come. She could feel the warmth in her face. "Hello."

He looked around. "Hey, I like this," he said. "It's great."

She made no reply.

He moved closer, and she instinctively took a step backward. If he noticed, he made no sign.

"Han," he said, planting his hands on the counter, looking straight into her eyes, "I need to say something to you. I know this isn't the ideal place, but"—he gave a small laugh—"to be honest, I wasn't sure you'd agree to meet me anywhere else, and I can't say I'd blame you."

She said nothing. He was still full of easy charm; that hadn't changed.

He held her gaze, his expression contrite now. "You probably want to kill me after what I did to you—and you'd be dead right. I was a total bastard."

Still Hannah didn't respond. Her heart thumped, and she could feel the blood pulsing through her. She folded her arms, willing a customer, or Una, or anyone, to walk in.

Patrick rubbed a hand across his face. "Look," he said, "Han, I think this really isn't the place for what I want to say—someone could come in any minute. Can we meet up when you're finished?"

She shook her head slowly. "I don't want to meet you," she said, her voice steadier than she'd expected. "I have nothing to say to you."

"Han," he said earnestly, "I completely understand how you feel. But...I really need to talk to you. Please."

His eyes, such a deep brown you could melt into them. She'd kissed those eyes; she'd gazed into them over a candlelit table.

"Anywhere you like," he said. "Name a time."

She watched his mouth forming the words. She remembered it on her skin. She knew what it tasted like.

"No," she said. "I'd like you to leave now."

"Han, listen to me." He spoke rapidly, leaning toward her, his upper body slanting across the counter. His familiar aftershave wafting over to where she stood. "Leah and I are done, we're finished. It was a huge mistake—it should never have happened."

Hannah looked at him, her arms tight across her chest, her heart still thumping, her face too warm.

"She meant nothing to me, nothing," he said. "I was a prize idiot."

How many times had she told him she loved him? How many nights had she lain in his arms, imagining them growing old together, looking forward to all the years in between?

"She gave me the come-on," he said, "and I was stupid enough to fall for it. You must believe me—she meant nothing." He took a deep breath. "Han, it's you, it was always you. You must believe me," he repeated.

So sincere, looking at her so earnestly. Hannah uncrossed her arms. She planted her hands on the counter and gazed steadily into the deep brown eyes. Their faces were inches apart. "And what about Nora?" she asked softly. Her palms damp against the cold glass.

Patrick frowned.

"Leah threw you out, didn't she?" Hannah said. "She found out about Nora, and she threw you out." Her legs were trembling, but her voice didn't betray her.

"Han, you can't believe—"

"What? I can't believe you'd do it again?" His air of injured innocence was beginning to grate. "The thing I can't believe, Patrick, is that you honestly think I'd have you back."

He reached toward her, and she stepped away quickly. "Don't."

"Han, it's all in the past," he said. "None of them meant a thing, I swear. You were the—"

"Why don't you go?" she said loudly. "Why don't you just turn around now and leave?"

"But you haven't—"

"Patrick," she said coldly, "please leave. I have nothing more to say to you, and there is certainly nothing more you could say that I would want to hear."

He began to back away. "I've sprung it on you," he said. "I can see that. I should have waited, like I was planning to do."

Hannah said nothing.

Patrick reached the door, still looking at her. "We'll meet up," he said, "when you're ready. When you've had time to think. Give me a call, and we'll talk about it."

She watched his hand reach for the handle. She heard the tinkle of the old-fashioned bell as he pulled the door open. "I love you, Han," he said. "You're the one."

She waited until the door had closed behind him, until he'd disappeared past the window of Cupcakes on the Corner. She leaned against the back wall then, taking long, deep breaths, feeling her heartbeat gradually returning to normal.

None of them meant a thing.

She'd been right about Nora, which made two women he'd deceived. Which meant he'd slept with Nora when Leah was pregnant with his child. She wondered how many more there'd been, how many other flings he'd enjoyed when he was still with her.

How blind she had been, how trusting and blind. She remembered how she'd longed to have a baby with him, how she'd brought the subject up more than once. She thought of Leah, left now with a child to raise alone, and shuddered. How easily it could have been her.

She watched the steady flow of people past the window, the odd one glancing in. She looked around the shop—her shop—and she thought of the hours of work that had gone into achieving it, and the slog it still took to keep it afloat. She remembered the uncertainty of her first few weeks, the mistakes she'd made and learned from.

She pictured Adam draped along the red couch in the evenings, Kirby sprawled on the floor beside him. She thought of how her life was full of possibilities, and that at thirty-three she hadn't used half of them up yet.

The door opened, and the bell tinkled as Una walked in. "Well," she said, "you look pleased with yourself."

"The station," Nora said, settling into the passenger seat. "You don't mind me sitting here, do you?"

"Not at all," the driver answered, putting the car in gear and pulling in to the stream of traffic.

She'd recognized him as soon as he'd driven up. She remembered the green eyes. She decided he'd do to restore her bruised ego—not that she had any intention of letting that bastard Patrick Dunne upset her for long.

She could smell her spicy perfume thick in the air, which meant he could too.

"Going far?" he asked.

"Pretty far," she said. "California." She giggled. "But as far as you're concerned, the station will be fine."

Stretching her legs out, plenty to show in the little gray skirt. Nice and brown, too, from the spray she'd treated herself to yesterday. She caught the lightning glance he gave them. Piece of cake, this would be. Good job she'd left plenty of time to catch the train.

He stopped at a red light. "Wouldn't mind some Californian sunshine myself right now."

"Yeah, this weather's crap. I don't know how anyone sticks it." Running a hand absentmindedly along her bare thigh as she spoke. The station still a good ten minutes away. Plenty of time.

"You from around here?" he asked.

Nora yawned, stretching her arms above her head, her top rising to show golden midriff. "Born and bred, I'm afraid. But I've lived in the States for years. Just came back for a few months, and now I've had enough. You?"

"Yeah, born here, too. Grew up on Fortfield Avenue."

"You've driven me before," she said. "You wore a woolly hat—total fashion disaster."

He laughed. "Hey, gimme a break—it's chilly driving around in winter."

Nora smiled. "I have to say," she said, crossing her legs, causing her skirt to ride up further, "that you're not half bad without the hat."

"Thanks."

"I suppose you have a wife at home," she said.

He changed gears as they approached a roundabout. "Nope. No wife."

She waited for him to ask about a husband, but he didn't. "Footloose and fancy free, then, like myself."

No response—but she'd never objected to a challenge. "Hey," she said, as if she'd just thought of it, "my train isn't for another while. Fancy a coffee or...whatever?"

He glanced at her again. "Love to," he said, "but I'm up to my eyes. Sorry." He took the roundabout's second exit, the one that led to the station.

Nora turned to look out the window. "No problem," she said. "Just a thought." Who cared about a taxi driver too dumb to appreciate what was being handed to him on a plate?

He approached the station and pulled in. He unloaded Nora's luggage. She paid him what he asked for and waited while he counted out her change.

"Safe trip," she heard him call after her, but she didn't turn back.

Of course he'd been flattered by her offer. What hot-blooded male wouldn't be gratified by a come-on from an attractive woman? And he saw nothing wrong with a bit of afternoon delight, under the right circumstances.

The trouble was, Wally thought as he drove back to the taxi stand, that for some time now his mind had most definitely been elsewhere. And there wasn't a damn thing he could do about it.

———

"You still have time," Geraldine said. "To change your mind, I mean. Tom isn't home for another couple of weeks. You might have a change of heart between this and then. I won't be a bit put out, really I won't."

"I've no intention of changing my mind." Alice paused. "But maybe you're having second thoughts? Because I can always—"

"Oh, no," Geraldine said quickly. "No, no, not at all, I'm happy to take over. It's just...I'm afraid you might regret your decision and think it's too late to back out, and I'm just saying I'll understand if you do, that's all."

"Thank you." Alice took a custard cream from the plate between them and set it on the table by her cup. "I appreciate that."

When the idea had first slipped into her head, as she lay sleepless in her single bed the night after she'd brought Tom to the clinic, Alice's instinct had been to dismiss it. You didn't run away from your problems. You faced them down until you beat them.

But the problem was Jason, and he was dead, and no amount of wishing would change that. So leaving Clongarvin wouldn't be running away from anything, because wherever they went, Jason's death would be there. It would never leave them.

New surroundings might help though. Putting physical distance between them and the nightmare might somehow make it a bit more bearable, might allow them to forgive each other, and themselves. It might make no difference at all, of course, but the possibility was there; the hope was there.

And so Alice had allowed the idea to take root. They couldn't travel outside the country, not with the court case pending, but they could go to Donegal maybe, or West Cork, somewhere nobody knew them or remembered an accident that had happened in March in Clongarvin. Rent a small house somewhere, live simply. Look after each other, like they used to do.

And when she felt that the time was right, she'd bring up the subject of early retirement. She couldn't see Tom going back to work, whatever happened at the trial, and he couldn't take unpaid leave forever. What did the Americans call it? Closure, that was it. They needed closure. If he wasn't sent to jail, she'd urge him to take early retirement.

They'd have to come back here for the court case, of course. Ellen would be home, and they'd need the house so they all had somewhere to stay. So they wouldn't sell up, not yet anyway.

And naturally the outcome of the trial would have a bearing on what came next, but they'd deal with that when they had to. They'd deal with the future when they knew what it held for them.

The shop door opened, and Geraldine got to her feet. "I'll go."

Business hadn't picked up. There was no need for both of them to be there. It made perfect sense for Geraldine to run the place on her own when Alice left. It would make perfect sense for her to take over the lease completely if Alice never returned to it. Time would tell.

Alice put her untouched custard cream back on the plate. She hadn't much of an appetite lately.

Adam pressed "save" and flipped open his mobile. A number he didn't recognize was displayed.

"Hello?"

No response.

"Hello there," he said. "Can you hear me?"

"I think you should come back." All in a rush, the words running into each other. "I'd like to teach you again."

"Vivienne?"

But of course it was Vivienne. Adam watched goldfish swim across his computer screen. He wondered what it had cost her to pick up the phone and dial the number on his business card—which hadn't, it would seem, ended up in her bin after all.

"Well, the thing is," he said, "I've sold the clarinet. I sold it yesterday, in fact. On eBay."

"Oh."

Silence.

"Hello?" he said again.

"You could try the piano," she said.

"Hey, maybe I could try the piano," he said, at exactly the same time.

Another long pause. He watched the goldfish and tried to summon his thoughts, a slow smile spreading across his face.

"You know," he said then, "that's not a bad idea. I'm not sure that the clarinet was my instrument, actually. I think I'd be more suited to the piano."

Dead silence.

"Are you still there?" he asked.

"You'll need one to practice on," she said. "I could ask my brother if he'll lend you a keyboard. He has some old ones."

Adam's smile broadened. "That certainly sounds like a plan," he said.

A further long pause, and then: "All right."

"All right?"

"Yes."

"Right then," he said, watching the fish. "The piano it is. Does Thursday still suit you?"

"Yes."

"Same time?"

"Yes."

"Oh, and one more thing," he said, remembering. "Would your mother be terribly offended if I didn't have the milk at break time? Milk...gives me a headache."

Another pause. "All right."

"Right then," he repeated. "I'll see you Thursday."

She hung up without saying good-bye. Adam folded his phone slowly.

She had called him. She had dialed his number, and she had asked him to come back. Even when he'd told her about selling the clarinet, she had found another way to get him back.

She wanted him to come back.

"She wants me to come back," he said to Kirby, and the sound of his voice caused the dog's tail to sweep the floor in lazy arcs. "She misses me. Can't say I blame her, really."

Thursday was three days away. He thought about seeing her again in three days, and the delight bubbled up in him.

———

Hannah didn't recognize her at first. All she saw was another mother with a baby, struggling to maneuver the wheels of her baby buggy over the edge of the path. Two shopping bags hung from the handle.

It wasn't until she had almost reached her that Hannah realized who the mother was. She bent and lifted the front wheels of the buggy onto the path, meeting the baby's blue eyes as she did so. He regarded her calmly.

"Hello," Hannah said softly. He had Patrick's mouth, Patrick's nose.

"Thank you," the other woman said, and Hannah looked up and saw the slender, drawn face, the red dress that smocked out over the still-swollen abdomen, the hair a shade darker and longer now than when she'd sold Hannah the massage voucher. She'd changed a lot since then.

But that was a year ago. They'd both changed a lot since then.

Hannah stood up. For a second the two women looked at each other. Then Hannah turned and walked away.

"Bless us," Mrs. O'Toole said. "He's coming back?"

"Yes," Vivienne replied. "He's changing to the piano." She kept her face turned away, so her mother didn't demand to know what was so funny, and busied herself with the feather duster, pushing it between the piano keys.

"Changing to the piano?" her mother repeated. "Well, that's a . . . well, I don't know *what* that's all about."

"And he says he doesn't want milk," Vivienne added, flicking the duster at Pumpkin, causing the cat to dart at it with his paw. "He says milk gives him a headache."

"What? He gets a headache from milk?" Mrs. O'Toole snorted. "Well, I've heard it all now."

Vivienne pulled the duster back abruptly. Pumpkin, too late to stop his instinctive lunge after it, toppled from the top of the piano and landed on the floor in an undignified heap. Vivienne burst out laughing.

"Would you leave that poor cat alone," her mother said crossly. "I don't know what's got into you today, I really don't."

"Sorry," Vivienne replied, not sounding remotely apologetic. She crouched and gathered Pumpkin into her arms and pressed her face into his furry warmth. "Sorry," she murmured again, thinking about Thursday, and trying hard to keep from skipping around the room.

Bill Dunne had decidedly mixed feelings about being a grandfather. At fifty-eight he was far from ready to embrace the notion of middle age, and he worked determinedly to ensure that he kept any signs of degeneration at bay for as long as possible.

He started every other morning, whatever the weather, with a half-hour run. He drank alcohol with discretion and hadn't smoked since his twenties. He ate fairly healthily—being left a widower with two young sons had encouraged him to upgrade his cooking skills—and every fourth Friday he traveled to a hair salon in Galway for another dark brown rinse.

And the fact that he had a job that gave him access to plenty of younger, beautiful females went a considerable way toward keeping him young at heart.

Bill Dunne had been talented enough, and lucky enough, to have made a better-than-average living as a freelance fashion photographer for most of his working life. Now he was in the enviable position of being able to pick the jobs he wanted—happily, he was still very much in demand—and reject the others. He worked eight or nine months of the year, and the rest of the time he enjoyed himself, generally in the company of some of the young females he met through his work.

So the notion of suddenly becoming a grandfather, of being thrust into that pipe-and-slippers category, struck him as more than a little premature. Not that he resented the arrival of Patrick's son into the world—and Reuben looked remarkably and endearingly like Patrick had as a baby—but Bill simply wasn't ready for anyone to call him Granddad. Not now, not yet.

Of course the Dunne name's being carried on to the next generation would have been some consolation—but in this case, it seemed that wasn't going to happen.

"She wants him to be Bradshaw," Patrick had admitted the night before. "Just Bradshaw."

Bill hadn't been told—and hadn't asked—why his son's latest relationship had ended so abruptly, barely a fortnight after the baby's arrival. Given his own healthy libido, he figured it was a safe bet that another woman was involved—and he was hardly qualified to criticize. He privately regretted Patrick's betrayal of Hannah, whom he'd liked, but he figured it was none of his business, so he kept his feelings to himself.

Leah had seemed like a pleasant sort of woman, on the scant occasions they'd met—lunch in her small apartment on Bill's return from his Greek cruise, a Sunday-afternoon stroll through the nearby park, a hospital visit to view his new grandson—but now she was gone, too, and so far there was no sign of a successor.

And clearly whatever had taken place to cause her breakup from Patrick had left her bitter enough not to want their son to carry his father's name.

Would Patrick ever get to know his child in a meaningful way? Would he wander from relationship to relationship, never finding what Bill had had with Patrick's mother, albeit for a shockingly brief dozen years?

And was it really that surprising that neither of his sons was showing signs of committing to a woman, given their father's promiscuous lifestyle over the past two decades?

Bill sighed deeply as he ladled his famous chili into two warmed bowls and brought them into the sitting room, where his elder son, recently moved back home, sat watching television.

"You're back." Mrs. O'Toole regarded Adam without expression.

"I am indeed," he told her, keeping his smile firmly in place.

"And you're switching to the piano," she said accusingly, her hand planted on the doorjamb.

"Yes," Adam answered. "Vivienne thought it might be a good idea. If at first you don't succeed, and all that." He wondered if she was going to let him in.

She sniffed. "Vivienne tells me you don't want milk anymore."

"No," Adam said, letting the smile slip a little, attempting to sound contrite. "I made an effort, because I didn't want to offend you, but it really doesn't agree with me."

"The only other thing I have is dilute orange."

"That would be perfect," Adam said. "I look forward to it."

She stood aside finally and allowed him into the hall, just as Vivienne and a young boy emerged from the room along the corridor.

"Hello," Adam said, moving toward her, turning slightly to let the boy past him. "I'm back."

"Yes."

She wore a dark blue dress he hadn't seen before, which ended just above her ankles. Her hair was drawn off her face with two blue slides. It fell to past her shoulders, and it was wavy. Her cheeks were pink. She gave him a small nervous smile. Adam stood in front of her and lifted his hands. "Look," he said, "no clarinet."

"No," she answered, the smile staying put. She turned and walked ahead of him into the room. Her flowery scent wafted back to him.

The cat sat where it always had, tail twitching as it watched Adam walk in.

"Hello, Pumpkin," Adam said. "How've you been?"

"You can sit at the piano," Vivienne said, taking a sheet from the bundle on the table.

He wouldn't admire the dress. He'd pretend he hadn't noticed the new hairstyle. He'd be formal and polite and do nothing to make her feel uncomfortable.

He took off his jacket and slung it across the chair he used to sit on. He took a seat on one end of the long piano bench and waited, his eyes on the black and ivory keys in front of him.

"Would you believe I've never played a note on a piano?" he said.

"What you've learned so far will help you," Vivienne replied. She sat on the other edge of the bench, leaving a gap of about six inches between them. Adam felt the minuscule shift in atmosphere, heard the small rustle her movements caused. She cleared her throat, a single sharp cough. He smelled flowers again.

"I'm glad you came back," she said then, so quiet it was almost a whisper.

Adam kept his eyes firmly on the keys. "I'm glad you asked me," he said.

"I was bullied," she said in a rush. "At school, for years. It made me...the way I am. It's not you, it has nothing to do with you."

"Okay," he said.

He waited. The silence lengthened. He didn't look at her. Out of the corner of his eye, he saw Pumpkin's tail flick back and forth.

"See where I place my fingers," she said finally. Her nails were painted the palest of pinks. The varnish was badly applied and smudged in several places. "Now you. Don't press down, just curve your fingers and rest them lightly. Try to relax them."

She slid her hands away to allow Adam's to replace them. Their fingers made the briefest of contact as the switch was made, a feathery touch that caused her to draw away a fraction from him.

"So what now?" he asked, his fingers poised.

"Now we start with scales," she said.

He couldn't resist it. "Sounds fishy to me, but I'll give it a go."

A sound escaped Vivienne, somewhere between a giggle and a cough. "You should be serious," she said, "or you won't learn anything."

"Okay. Sorry."

It would take time. He might have to invest in a piano at some stage. It might even take a few more instruments and several series of lessons.

But they'd get there.

———————

"Now, you really and truly shouldn't have." Geraldine watched in the mirror as Hannah fastened the string of creamy oval beads around her neck. "Darling, it's gorgeous." She turned and hugged her daughter. "I dread to think what you paid."

"That's none of your business," Hannah told her. Much better to let her mother assume that the necklace had cost far more than the thirty-two euro Hannah had gotten it for on eBay. Who'd have guessed the bargains to be had on that Web site, if Adam hadn't taken it into his head one fine day to look for a clarinet?

"By the way," she said, "Adam's just started taking piano lessons."

Geraldine stared. "Piano? I thought it was the clarinet. Didn't you say he'd bought one?"

"He had, but it wasn't working out, so he sold it again. Now he's switched to the piano."

"Funny, I had no idea he was musical," Geraldine said. "He never struck me as someone who was interested in music."

Hannah smiled. "Well, he's very interested now."

"But you don't have a piano," Stephen said. "How's he going to practice?"

"He got the loan of a keyboard," Hannah explained. "His teacher's brother had an old one. So this time next year, he'll be able to play 'Happy Birthday.'"

Geraldine laughed. "I hope he'll be able to play a lot more than that after a whole year. And speaking of birthdays, I think it's high time we cut that cake before the candles set it on fire."

"Isn't Alice coming?" Hannah asked. "I thought you were going to invite her."

"I did, but to be honest, I wasn't surprised when she said no. She has a lot on her mind, with Tom coming home in a few days."

"You might as well tell her," Stephen said.

Hannah looked from one to the other. "Tell me what?"

"Alice has asked me to take over as manager in the shop when Tom gets out of the treatment center," Geraldine told her. "Just temporarily—she's planning to take him away till the case comes to court."

"Take him away? Where?"

Geraldine shook her head. "She's talking about the coast, but I don't think she cares really. She just wants the two of them to have a change of scene for a while, which isn't a bad idea."

"And what does Tom think?"

"I have no idea—in fact, I don't think she's even mentioned it to him yet. But he'll hardly object to moving out of Clongarvin for a while, after all that's happened."

"Well, no, I suppose not—but what about his job at the clinic?"

Stephen spread his hands. "Officially he's entitled to six months' unpaid leave, but however long it takes, his job will be there for him if and when he chooses to return—he knows that."

"And what about their house?"

Geraldine shrugged. "Alice was vague about that too. I suppose they might try letting it. It's all a bit up in the air right now."

Hannah studied her mother. "And how do you feel about taking over in the shop?"

"To be honest, love, it makes a lot more sense to have only one of us in there these days, it's gone so quiet. I just hope this recession doesn't last much longer, or we'll all be twiddling our thumbs." She put her sherry glass on the mantelpiece and turned to the cake. "Now, that's enough of that kind of talk—time to wish me a happy birthday."

She blew out the three candles, and they ate cake and drank her health, and then they sat by the window looking out at the endless rain as darkness fell.

Hannah told them that Nora had been in touch with Adam to say she'd found a job in a theater in L.A. "Right up her alley, I'd say." She mentioned that she was considering asking Una to do a couple of full days in the shop, instead of just mornings. "It'll give me some proper free time during the week."

She didn't add that she was thinking of approaching Una's sister, Claire, if and when the time came for her to be able to take on a second person to do one or two more days in the shop. Claire hadn't gone back to the restaurant where she'd worked before Jason's death, but maybe in another month or two she might be glad of something part-time. It might suit them all—but Hannah wouldn't mention it tonight. Time enough for that.

She told them about the mini-cupcakes she'd been asked to provide for a christening. "I'm going to introduce them into the shop, maybe three days a week, see how they sell. They're fiddly, but there's a better markup on them."

She described a new variety she was trying out in the regular size. "Pineapple-mango. I'm calling it Tropical Delight."

She made no mention of Patrick's visit to the shop. She didn't tell them that John had moved back to Scotland. She said nothing about meeting Leah and her son on the street.

Finally, around ten o'clock, she pulled her phone from her pocket. "I'd better call for a taxi. It's too wet to walk."

Geraldine closed the sitting-room curtains. "It's unbelievable, this weather. Mind you, I don't know why we always expect it to be better in the summer, because we haven't had a decent summer in God knows how long." She turned to the door. "We'll have a cuppa before you go."

They were sipping tea when it happened. The three of them turned toward the curtained window.

Hannah put her cup down. "What was that?"

"It sounded like—" Geraldine began, but Stephen was already halfway to the door. They followed him out of the house and saw the taxi leaning crookedly against the lamppost. Roof sign still lit up, engine still running, rain pelting down into the slanted beams of the shining headlights. The road silver with accumulated water. Music still playing faintly from within the taxi.

Hannah ran down the driveway. In the few seconds it took to reach the car, she was soaked. She wiped the driver's window with a trembling hand to see inside.

And there was Wally, slumped against the steering wheel, blood trickling from his temple. He opened his eyes briefly as Stephen shouted at Geraldine to phone for an ambulance, as Hannah wrenched open the door and called his name.

"Hi," he murmured, and his eyes fluttered closed again.

"It's good to be home," Tom said.

He'd lost more weight. His hair needed a cut. His shirt collar was grubby. The dark shadows were still under his eyes, the whites still bloodshot. A mesh of tiny red lines wandered across his cheeks and over his nose. He looked cold.

"I'm glad to have you back," Alice said. "It was...quiet without you."

She'd put fresh sheets on his bed the day before and opened the windows to air the room. She'd hoovered and dusted and polished. She'd filled a vase with cuttings from the shrubbery and put it on the dressing table, then on the windowsill, and then back on the dressing table.

She'd taken her nightdress from the single room and put it under the pillow on her side of the double bed. She'd placed her slippers on the rug where he'd see them when he walked in. Ten minutes later she'd gone back in and moved nightdress and slippers out again, back to Ellen's room.

"Will you have a bit of lamb casserole?" she asked. "I made it this morning. It won't take long to heat up."

"That'd be grand," he said. He stood in the middle of the kitchen, his suitcase on the floor beside him.

"Tom," she said, and then stopped. He didn't move. "I want you to know that I don't blame you."

On the last word, her voice broke, and he stepped across and put his arms around her. She dropped her head onto his shoulder.

"I'm sorry," she wept. "I was horrible to you, and you didn't deserve it." The words she'd wanted to say all afternoon spilling out now.

"Shh," he said, rocking her gently. "Don't feel bad. You don't need to feel bad, Alice, love. You were angry, I understand that."

"But you didn't mean it," she cried into his shoulder. "You didn't mean what happened."

"No, I didn't mean it," he said quietly.

"And I treated you like a murderer. I acted like you killed that child deliberately."

"Shh," he said again, holding her. "Don't cry, love, it'll be all right."

It would take time for them to heal; she couldn't expect it to happen all at once. The accident would always be with them, the death of a child forever on their consciences. But standing there in the kitchen, with his arms around her, she began to feel hope.

Tonight she'd feed him and sit by the fire with him afterward. They might switch on the telly to get the weather forecast, and she'd say something about the fact that they were calling this July the wettest on record. They'd be careful with each other, mindful of what had gone before.

He'd probably comment on the freshly painted walls. They'd look at Ellen's latest photos. She'd tell him the roses seemed to be coming along better now. She might show him the last gas bill, see if he thought they should question it.

She wouldn't ask how the past month had gone. She'd bring him up to date on what had been happening in the neighborhood, but she wouldn't mention the crash outside Stephen and Geraldine's house the other night. She wouldn't talk about early retirement, or her plans for a move away from Clongarvin. Not this evening, not yet.

And if, when they were putting up the fireguard and locking the front door, he happened to ask if she'd consider moving back into the bedroom, she'd say yes, she'd like that.

———

"Let's begin by going back over the scales," Vivienne said, "and then we'll move on to the tune."

Adam placed his right hand on the keys.

"No," she said, "your thumb on middle C."

"Middle C, got you. Here?" he asked, sliding everything one space up.

Vivienne sighed. "Did you practice?"

"Of course I did," he said. "I mean, I meant to. It's just that Wally's keyboard is a bit different, so it puts me off." He did his best to look ashamed. "Sorry. Maybe you could show me again."

Vivienne placed her fingers on the keys. "This note here is middle C. Remember, it's 'do' in the key of C." She played up the scale, moving her fingers gracefully over the keys, and back down again.

She wore a dark gray trouser suit, and a burgundy ribbon gathered her hair loosely at the nape of her neck. It was all he could do not to drop his head and kiss the pale, freckled skin there.

"Pay attention," she said softly, and he realized she could see him out of the corner of her eye. He switched his gaze back to the piano and watched her fingers as they traveled up and down the scale several more times.

She'd moved in a little from the edge of the bench this evening. Another couple of lessons and their thighs would be almost touching.

"You make it look so easy," he said.

"It is easy," she answered sternly, "if you practice."

"I will," he promised. "Honest. Swear to God. Let me try now."

She wasn't blushing as much. She smiled a little more, even if her smile was still tiny. She looked at his face when she spoke to him. She responded to comments, instead of just answering questions.

It was three weeks to his birthday. It might just be long enough.

My dear Geraldine,

Thank you for the lovely card and your very thoughtful gift before we left. It was quite unnecessary, but much appreciated by both of us.

We've found a small house to rent, just outside Clifden. We signed a three-month lease, although the owner was anxious for six, but we persuaded him to give it to us for three. We were very lucky—we only had to do two nights in a bed-and-breakfast. I thought we might be there much longer.

It's a two-bedroom bungalow, quite basically furnished but with lovely sea views. We've taken to going for long walks in the afternoons, weather permitting, and we're both feeling the better for it. Tom is even talking about taking up golf again, which I'm very happy about.

I hope all is well with you and Stephen. I was sorry to hear that Hannah's new romance was over—she deserves a bit of happiness. Let's hope someone else comes along soon.

I hope the shop isn't too much for you on your own. If it stays as quiet as it had been before I left, you'll find it easy enough, I suppose. But if it does pick up, remember you have my full permission to take someone on part-time. I'll leave it entirely up to you. It's such a relief to know it's in good hands.

Well, I'd better get the dinner on—that sea air certainly gives you an appetite! I'll post this tomorrow on our walk. We'll be going by the village anyway for mandarin oranges—Tom is addicted!

With much love,
Alice

August

I call it Saucy Salmon Pizza," the birthday boy said, bringing out the main course.

"I thought the chicken wings were all we were getting," Hannah said. "I stuffed my face."

"I couldn't help noticing that," Adam answered. "But knowing you as I do, I'm fairly confident that you'll find some space for the pizza."

Hannah turned to Vivienne. "Should I hit him now," she asked, "or wait till he's brought the dessert out?"

Vivienne smiled. "Maybe wait," she murmured.

"Bloody right," Wally said. "The dessert is what I came for."

And Hannah's smile, when she looked at him, made him want to walk around the table and grab her.

"You and your sweet tooth," she said.

"Me and my sweet tooth," he agreed, and he wondered if she was remembering, like he was, the day he'd walked into her shop to claim his free cupcake. Knowing then that he wanted her. Knowing before then, long before then.

But in the end it had taken a concussion and a broken wrist to bring them together. It had taken his taxi careening into the streetlight to get her to look at him properly, just before he lost consciousness.

"What have you done with the pizza wheel?" Adam was rummaging in a drawer. "It was always here."

Wally watched as Hannah got up and crossed the room. She wore the blue top she'd been wearing that night—he remembered the lace at her wrists when he'd come to in the ambulance. She'd been sitting across from him on some kind of bench, her hands at his eye level. He'd traveled cautiously from them to her face.

Grandpa's chair is on the wall, he'd said, and instantly she was crouched at his side, ignoring the ambulance attendant's order to stay where she was.

She'd put a palm lightly on his chest. *Are you okay?*

You have a yellow shop, he'd answered, and for some reason this made her eyes fill with tears, and he'd drifted off again as she'd raised a blue sleeve to her face.

She was gone the next time he woke, his head thumping, his wrist throbbing. He was on a trolley in a tiny cubicle, and he wondered if he'd imagined her earlier.

Was there a girl here before—I mean a woman, with dark hair? he'd asked a nurse, who was steering an empty wheelchair through the cubicle's narrow doorway.

I didn't see anyone, dear, she'd answered, pulling his sheet down none too gently.

Hey, watch it, he'd protested weakly. *I'm nearly naked here.* Someone had replaced his clothes with a blue garment that stopped long before his knees began.

The nurse hadn't batted an eyelid. *Seen it all before, dear. Come along, now. We must get that wrist of yours to X-ray and check out that head.*

They'd kept him in overnight because of the concussion, but when he woke the following day, his mother and Vivienne were standing at his bedside.

I didn't know you knew I was here, he'd said.

We were here last night, his mother had said, bewildered. *Don't you remember?*

No. How did you find out what happened?

Someone I know, Vivienne had said, her color rising. *You crashed outside his friend's parents' house. He called and drove us here. We had this exact same conversation then.*

Did we? Did you meet Hannah?

Who's Hannah? his mother had asked.

She sells buns. She has a chair on the wall in her shop. She came in the ambulance.

Silence, while they both digested this information doubtfully.

You're still a bit mixed up, his mother had said then, and Wally had felt too weary to explain.

He thought it strange that even though he had no memory of meeting them the night before, he remembered Hannah in the ambulance. He remembered the band of blue lace at her wrist, how her eyes had filled with tears as she'd looked at him.

He'd dropped in to the yellow shop two days later, pushing the door open with his good hand.

She'd gone delightfully pink when she saw him. *You're okay,* she'd said. *I rang the hospital and they'd told me you'd gone home.*

He'd thrust the bunch of violets across the counter. *This is to say thank you for looking after me.*

She'd taken the flowers, going pinker. *There was no need,* she'd said. *I did nothing, really. I just went with you in the ambulance.* She'd hesitated. *It seemed . . . a bit mean to send you off on your own.*

And you got your friend to call to my mother's house.

Well, Adam's learning piano from Vivienne, and I knew she lived with your mother, so I just thought it might be better if someone they knew called to tell them, rather than a guard or the hospital.

That was good of you.

She'd smiled. *Actually, as it turns out, I did Adam a big favor. Your mother thinks there's nobody like him now.*

Why would he want my mother to think well of him? he'd said, confused.

Because, she'd murmured, burying her face in the flowers, *he's got a soft spot for Vivienne.*

Ah. He'd said, rubbing a hand across his face. *I see. That explains a lot.*

Is your wrist broken? she'd asked.

'Fraid so—that's the end of my playing the keyboards for a while. Not to mention driving a taxi.

Oh, poor you. How'll you manage?

I'm back in my mother's house till the plaster comes off. I don't have to lift a finger, and my meals are all served up to me. He'd grinned. *It's a tough old world.*

But your car—it must be a write-off.

He'd shrugged. *Like they say, nobody died. Things'll sort themselves out. They generally do. I had good insurance.*

That's something, I suppose. She'd paused, then added, going pink again, *You didn't have to, you know.*

I didn't have to what?

Break your wrist. She'd stuck her face into the flowers again. *To get my attention.*

It was a bit extreme, wasn't it? Wally had laughed and rubbed his face again. *The least you could do, really, is go out with me now.*

Hannah had tilted her head to one side. *I suppose I owe you that much.*

She got him, that was the thing. She understood his silly jokes, she forgave his chronic unpunctuality, she teased his total ignorance of fashion and tolerated his utter uselessness with money. He was himself with her, and she got him.

She called him sweetheart. She was soft and round in his arms. Her kiss, when it finally moved from his cheek to his mouth after three dates, was delicious.

And this, Adam's birthday party, was their fifth date. And she was becoming frighteningly important to him.

With an effort he switched his attention to his sister, sitting opposite him. "All right?"

He didn't need to ask. Look at her, blooming after years of crippling unhappiness, when he'd felt powerless to help her, when she hadn't known how to help herself. Looking so different in the green dress that caught the color of her eyes.

Blushing deeply in the backseat of their taxi on the way over when Adam's name had been mentioned.

He's just a friend, she'd murmured, turning away from him to look out the window.

I know that, Wally had answered.

———

The green eye shadow had been a disaster, and when she'd scrubbed it off with a facecloth—which had taken ages—it had left the skin around her eyes all blotchy. She should have learned her lesson with the lipstick. And her hair never looked right, no matter how long she left the conditioner in or how carefully she blow-dried it. Easier to tie it up and forget about it.

Except he'd said he liked it down.

She wasn't a bit sure of the dress. The sales assistant

wouldn't leave her alone, went on about Vivienne's figure, which as far as Vivienne could see was nothing to write home about. And size eight feet, when most women took a five. So mortifying anytime she needed shoes.

And it'll be dead easy to take it up a bit, the girl had said, when it had never occurred to Vivienne to make the dress any shorter. But she'd gone ahead and bought it, and her mother had actually admired it when Vivienne showed her.

Nice and bright, she'd said. *Smartens you up.* Which was really as good as it got from her mother.

And now, halfway through her second glass of wine, the fear of dropping something or spilling something didn't seem to matter quite so much anymore. And the knot in her stomach she'd had all day had practically vanished, so she could enjoy the food instead of forcing it down.

She supposed she was a bit merry, not used to drinking wine—or any kind of alcohol, for that matter. She suspected that she might feel a little worse for wear in the morning. But who cared, with no music lessons on a Sunday?

She smiled across the table at her only adult pupil, remembering how sick she'd been at the thought of phoning him, how she'd been sure she was actually going to throw up as she'd dialed the number on his business card. How she'd forced herself to stay on the line until he answered, how she'd hardly been able to get a word out, so terrified she'd felt.

But incredibly, it had worked. He'd agreed to come back. She'd taken the initiative, and things had gone the way she wanted them to go. And now here she was, on her first-ever date at twenty-nine years of age.

Just a small little get-together, nothing fancy, he'd said. *Wally's coming.*

He'd made it as easy as he could. He'd made it impossible for her to say no. Not that she'd wanted to say no.

Not that she hadn't been terrified at the thought of it all the same, even with Wally there. But now that she'd loosened up a bit, she was beginning see why people went out on dates.

In fact, she was quite prepared to try it again sometime.

They ate the salmon pizza, and the raspberry ice cream that followed. They blew out the thirty-two candles on the giant peanut-butter cupcake that Hannah had made. They raised their glasses and wished Adam a happy birthday.

And later, when Wally and Vivienne had left in a taxi, Adam ignored Hannah's mild protest and refilled their glasses.

"Tomorrow's Sunday," he said, "and we have to toast you for being daft enough to open a shop in the middle of a recession."

She smiled wearily, easing her feet out of her shoes and leaning her elbows on the table that was still littered with plates and glasses. "Yes, that was very sensible, wasn't it?"

"And for reaching the seven-month mark, still solvent—not that I ever doubted you—and still in one piece."

"Just about."

"And for putting up with me and Kirby for the past six months."

"Yes," she said. "That was very difficult." She lifted her glass. "To us," she said, "who love each other madly and who thankfully might not have to marry each other after all."

"I'll drink to that."

They finished the wine and cut another two slices from the birthday cupcake. They made a halfhearted attempt at the washing-up and put Kirby out for the night. Hannah closed the windows, and Adam bolted the doors.

And then they went upstairs to bed.

Thanks a Million

To my agents, Faith and Lauren, for their invaluable support.

To my Irish editor, Ciara, who always mixes business with pleasure.

To my U.S. editor, Sara, for ensuring that my first book to cross the Atlantic made it in one piece.

To my family, behind me all the way since the very first novel.

To anyone who buys this book—where would I be without you?

How Not to Write a Novel

By Roisin Meaney

You know those writers who get up every morning and sit at their desks for a set number of hours each day, ignoring phones and doorbells, conscientiously committing words to paper, or to screen, until they've reached their quota? I am not one of them.

I write when I feel like it, or when the humor is on me, as we say here in Ireland. I write when an idea comes calling, or when a deadline is approaching, or when it's raining outside and I can't face the housework. I might write for half an hour, or I might spend the whole day at it. I take breaks when I want, I make tea when I feel like it, I answer the doorbell when anyone comes calling. Disciplined I most decidedly am not.

You can see, then, why it's a source of constant amazement to me that, despite my disgracefully haphazard approach to writing, I've managed to produce seven novels and meet all my deadlines along the way. I have no explanation.

Having said that, whatever the reason that gets me sitting in front of the laptop, I inevitably enjoy the experience. That's not to say I always produce something worthwhile—I've often deleted every word at the end of a writing session—but the act itself, tapping away at the keyboard, teasing out a story, shaping a scene, fashioning a conversation, all this I find immensely satisfying. Not a day goes by that I don't give thanks to whatever serendipitous circumstances finally allowed me to walk away from my teaching job and become a full-time writer at the ripe old age of forty-eight.

And when it comes to pleasurable experiences, I have to say that writing *Semi-Sweet* was up there with the best of them. From start to finish, this book is stuffed with self-indulgence. Next to writing, my favorite occupation is baking. I can't remember when it started, but for an awfully long time, I've absolutely adored tucking myself away in my kitchen and surrounding myself with cookbooks and mixing bowls and ingredients—and if the wind is howling outside and the rain is pelting against the windows (which is often the case here), so much the better. I turn on the radio and tune out the rest of the world, and beat and whisk and knead to my little heart's content.

Baking, and cooking in general, has featured to a greater or lesser extent in all my novels. I've always managed to sneak in a character who likes to bake, or who's hopeless at baking but who's just enrolled in classes, or who simply goes to a lot of dinner parties. I love writing about food—desserts and confectionery in particular. I love playing around with descriptions and trying to make everything sound as appetizing as possible, and I'm always delighted when someone says, "Your book made me so hungry." It's right up there with "Your book made me cry."

You can understand, then, why the idea of writing about someone opening a cupcake shop would appeal. For the time it took to produce *Semi-Sweet*, I was in my element, tracking down different recipes and trying them out (well, I had to make sure they were okay for Hannah to use), pondering the merits of coffee over pistachio frosting—bliss, pure bliss.

It's no coincidence that around the time I was doing all this cupcake testing, I also enrolled in a pilates class and did more walking than usual. (An added benefit of being a baker, in my opinion, is that it forces you to exercise more, so the guilt doesn't take over. Guilt is a big factor in any Irish-Catholic psyche, but it does tend to keep you pretty much on the straight and narrow.)

I was so thrilled when I heard that *Semi-Sweet* was going to the United States; the first of my books to make the long trip across the Atlantic Ocean. I've been to the States quite a few times myself—in fact I wrote my first novel, *The Daisy Picker*, in my brother's house in San Francisco—but any future trips will be sweetened with the possibility that I could walk into a bookstore and see one of my babies on the shelves.

I do hope you enjoyed *Semi-Sweet* half as much as I enjoyed writing it. I hope it made you hungry—and if it made you cry, too, my work here is done. For both conditions I would highly recommend a batch of cupcakes, preferably homemade. And when you've polished off the lot, dry your eyes and get out your walking shoes.

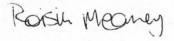

Reading Group Guide
Discussion Questions

1. At the very beginning of the novel, we learn that Hannah is about to start her own business right in the middle of a recession—a daunting challenge. Do you admire Hannah for her decision, or do you think she is taking on more than she can handle? In what ways have you challenged yourself professionally? What is the biggest risk you've ever taken in your professional life?

2. Soon after Patrick leaves Hannah for Leah, he begins to daydream about his life with Hannah. Why do you think he left Hannah? Do you think he would have left her if his circumstances had been different? Has Patrick changed in any way by the end of the novel?

3. Hannah and Patrick seem like polar opposites. Why do you think Hannah fell for him in the first place, and why does she have such a difficult time getting over him? Have you ever had your heart broken? How long did it take you to heal?

4. What is your opinion of Leah? Do you think she is ma-nipulative, or do you sympathize with her?

5. Alice has concerns about her husband's drinking, but she doesn't take any action until it is too late. Should she have done more to curb his drinking earlier on? Have you ever been close to somebody with a substance abuse problem? How did you handle it?

6. Hannah and Adam have always been best friends, yet they have never been romantically involved. Do you think their relationship is believable? Is it possible to be just friends with someone of the opposite sex?

7. Vivienne is not conventionally attractive. Why is Adam attracted to her? Why does he pursue her with such determination?

8. For much of the novel, Leah and Fiona have an uneasy relationship. Why is Fiona critical of Leah? Do you think she is too hard on her daughter, or do you understand where she is coming from? Do you think most mother-daughter relationships are similarly complicated and fraught?

9. John seems like an ideal match for Hannah. She thinks to herself: *He was perfect on paper, he was doing everything right. Her feelings would deepen, given time. She was sure of it.* Does Hannah end up falling for John? What happens between them? In your opinion, how important is chemistry in a relationship?

10. How does Alice handle Jason's death? Do you think she is too hard on Tom? Or do you think she is too easy on him? Is there a "right" way to grieve or to make sense of such a tragic event?

11. How are Nora and Patrick similar? How are they different? Do you think Nora is a bad person? Does she get what she deserves at the end of the novel?

12. *Semi-Sweet* takes place in a small Irish town where every-

one seems to know one another. In what way does setting play a role in the novel? Do you think the Clongarvin community has changed in any significant way by the end of the novel? Why or why not?

About the Author

ROISIN MEANEY was born in Listowel, County Kerry, Ireland. She has lived in the United States, Canada, Africa, and Europe. In 2002, Roisin won the Tivoli "Write a Bestseller" competition with her first novel, *The Daisy Picker*, which was subsequently followed by *Putting Out Stars*. Roisin is currently based in Limerick, Ireland. *Semi-Sweet* is her seventh book.

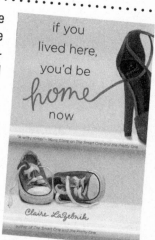